THE GIRL IN THE MIST

A Misted Pines Novel

KRISTEN ASHLEY

THE GIRL IN THE MIST

A MISTED PINES NOVEL

NEW YORK TIMES BESTSELLING AUTHOR

KRISTEN ASHLEY

The Girl in the Mist
By Kristen Ashley

Cover Art and Interior Graphics: Pixel Mischief Design

Prologue

THE LAKE HOUSE

There wasn't time to do the renovations, outside the security system (obviously), but there was a list of vetted contractors who would take care of things.

This wasn't an issue.

I could make do.

I had a plan.

Several of them.

Comprehensive.

Down to what was in my car right then.

Stuff that I myself had been carrying into the house while the movers took care of the boxes and furniture.

No, there were other issues with that lake house.

Many of them.

Starting with why I'd had to buy it.

Yes, *had to*.

Okay, not *had to*. I could have rented something, like the others did.

But still, I *had to* be there instead of home.

On expert advice, which sounded a good deal like orders, we all had to take significant precautions.

We'd had years of this kind of thing, specifically me. So many years, and so much of it, we'd all become inured to it.

But when the situation required the attention of the FBI and they had been fully apprised, they were even less happy about what was going on…

Well.

Cue me leaving LA and being…

Here.

In this house.

Which brought me to the next issue.

This house.

And no, it wasn't that the closet was a mess and needed a custom one built, because yes, I was a diva. I'd earned that distinction and was proud of it. As I was proud that I'd worked hard and put up with a lot to earn my money.

I'd come up with nothing, from nothing.

Now I had nice things.

Quite a number of them.

And I did not apologize for that.

As such, I needed a nice closet in which to put my nice things.

I digress, which happened a lot when I thought about the state of my current closet.

Back on track…

Nor was the issue with the house that the kitchen was kind of a disaster (and it was, but for the time being I could work with it).

The bathrooms weren't great either (really not great, and I'd be seeing to those…after the closet).

It was that the last owner died there.

Yes, he was old-ish, and what took him (I was told) was natural causes.

But he'd *died there.*

And I was discovering that put a stamp on the place.

Still, the view.

The quiet.

The peacefulness.

The fact that the lake was huge and there were only four houses at my end of it, and two of them were seasonal rentals.

Not only did that add to the serenity of the place, it also meant the road outside my house, which dead-ended at the rental home about half a mile from me, would hold little traffic. And the traffic it held would need for me or the residents of the house down below to buzz them in the rather daunting gate, or they'd need the gate code, or they'd need the sensor attached to their windshield (like I now had).

In other words, in the current situation, all of that that was a big bonus for the house.

There was also the wooden path down to the lake that led to an expansive dock, on which I intended to put an outdoor rug and Adirondack chairs and attractive outdoor lights on the poles.

And then there was the boathouse, which was delightfully large. As such, it was also where I was going to store a beverage fridge and (way down the list) add a small kitchenette, a wee living area, a three-quarter bath, a bedroom, all of this for guests to have privacy.

Though, it must be said, it was for ease for me when I was spending time down there, and I didn't want to walk all the way up to the house to grab a snack or a drink or use the bathroom.

Not to mention, there was the 2700 square-foot house that I'd started referring to as my Goldilocks house.

It wasn't too small, wasn't too big, but did have lots of character, great bones and was already pretty danged cool, even if it needed work.

I liked this house, this space so much, even when the situation was resolved, which would hopefully be soon—soon enough I didn't need to get into massive renovations—but I couldn't stop myself because I had this feeling, deep down, this was going to be my place.

Not like my cottage in Cornwall that I bought on a whim, because Cornwall was so gorgeous I had to have a nest there but rarely had time to get to it.

Not like my flat in Paris, which my daughters and their friends used far more than me.

Not like my cabin in the mountains of Montana that I was

certain would be the perfect sanctuary to inspire creativity, but I'd used it only once before I realized I wasn't going to get there often enough to make it worthwhile, so I'd sold it.

No, this wasn't like any of that.

I had the feeling I was going to die in this lake house, like the man who owned it before me.

And my feelings about almost anything were rarely ever wrong.

I just hoped when that happened, it would be like him in more than one way.

In other words, after I'd lived out my life and it was time to make room in this world for others.

The last issue about the lake house was a new issue.

It was the issue I discovered less than a second ago, after the movers had put together my bed. After I'd hauled up the pillows and linens and comforter and blankets I'd carefully packed in my car so I could make the bed in order for it to be ready to fall into it later.

This was, obviously, after I unpacked my suitcases that I'd also brought in my car. Suitcases that held exactly enough clothes, underwear and pajamas for five days (my estimate as per my comprehensive unpacking plans of when I'd be settled into the house, which gave me time to tackle the "closet"—in quotes because it did have some shelves and rails and you could walk into it, but it was still dire).

It was also after I put away the not-limited toiletries I felt I'd need at hand because there'd be FBI presence for the next few days, and I was, definitely, *me*.

Because I was, I had to put the face on it.

Of course, I could choose not to, but my mask was my armor, and I'd learned long ago life was a daily battle.

You didn't face it unprepared.

The cable people were coming, and the computer people too, and the contractors would be interviewed so I could decide which one from the list I wanted to work with, and all of this needed more than my oversight, the FBI would be watching.

They'd back off when I was settled (not entirely, but they had other things to do and other people to keep safe, and if anyone knew this was going on—and as a government agency, that might eventually happen—it wouldn't look good for them that some famous woman was getting that kind of attention when I could afford to make myself safe).

In the end, that was what would happen.

Ongoing, it would be me taking care of things.

Or at least paying for it.

To that end, I'd contracted with Joe Callahan (approved by the FBI), and he'd set up the security system for the house, with permission from the owners of the property down below, patching into the impressive (Callahan's estimation) system that was already there.

And for continuing security, he'd recommended an outfit led by a man named Hawk Delgado (who was *very* approved by the FBI).

I knew Callahan was the best of the best, everyone who was anyone did.

Delgado had that same reputation, albeit not as widespread, because not everyone needed his particular skillset.

I'd met him, and as it always went for me, I'd read him.

What I read was that he was beyond impressive.

Part of that was that he listened. He understood my need for privacy, how deep that went, not only as a part of my character, but also my business.

I couldn't have a bodyguard breathing down my neck.

He got that too and improvised.

In other words, on that score, I was good.

But I digress.

The new issue I'd noted was after I'd walked down the stairs from dealing with my bedroom.

I looked left, through the jumble of furniture and boxes, through the rear wall of windows and beyond, to the large deck at the back of the house.

And there she was.

Drifting through the late afternoon mist like the heroine from a David Lynch movie—dark-haired, willow-limbed, ethereal.

It was not because I had two grown daughters that my chest

tightened, and my body listed toward the back doors with an urge to rush out and gather her to me, draw her into the house, and then spend however long it took for me to feel she was safe outside my care, hissing and spitting at anyone who came near her.

I was transfixed.

She seemed caught up in the vision of the mist rolling across the lake, mist that was encompassing her.

But then she suddenly turned, her eyes coming directly to me.

My chest burned.

She lifted a hand so slowly toward her throat that the effort seemed to pain *me*.

She didn't touch her throat. Her hand kept going and turning, palm my way, at the side of her neck.

It was a peculiar wave.

I then jumped at the abrupt movement when she dropped her arm then sprung through the trees, disappearing on her way down to the house below.

The only one on the lake that was like mine now was.

Inhabited.

Awake.

And *alive*.

ONE

Considering

I stood in the upstairs room that would be my office.

It had a view to the lake.

It needed shelves.

New paint.

The desk I'd bought didn't work. I'd need to donate it. Find something else.

This was an issue.

Three days, and my careful plan was out the window.

This was not usual for me.

I planned.

I assessed the plan.

I streamlined the plan.

I carried out the plan.

I did not, under any circumstances, deviate from the plan.

The lake house had other ideas.

A kind of fog had overtaken me, like the mist that was so often on the water (and as such, one did not have to reflect too long about why the local town was called Misted Pines).

In the zone with all of the activity, I'd managed to get much of the kitchen unpacked while the movers were there, continuing to work after they were gone.

And it must be said, since it had become a marker for my week, after the girl was there…

And then she was gone.

But meetings with four contractors (none of whom I liked), hooking up my internet, sorting my computers and televisions, Hawk Delgado and two men on his team, Mo Morrison and Axl Pantera, coming personally to do another walk-through of the place and have a "sit-down" with the FBI and their local guys who would be the first responders, and my wandering mind had led me to being off schedule.

Significantly.

The kitchen was unpacked.

And yesterday's rejig of the schedule to fit my frame of mind (meaning I didn't concentrate on one area until it was complete as I had planned—instead I did a rotation of unpack two boxes, move to next area, unpack two boxes, move to next area) only found me distracted. Wandering from the projects at hand to sit with my laptop on my lap, going through websites and making lists of things I wanted for the cabin.

New lighting.

Tile.

Appliances.

Deck furniture.

Bathtubs.

Or alternately, simply staring out the back windows to where the girl had been.

The less people involved, the better. In fact, I'd been taken off site while the internet and AV people were doing their work, so they wouldn't see who lived in that house.

The contractors had signed lengthy NDAs (a wasted process, I would not be using any of them).

This wasn't the only reason I was unpacking myself even if I could afford someone else to do it.

I'd always been that person, even after Camille begged me not to be.

When they were growing up, we had a house cleaning service that came in and did the heavy lifting once every two weeks.

Other than that…it was just us.

My girls, Fenn and Camille, made their beds (as did I), and I did our grocery shopping.

And cooking.

And tidying (until the girls were old enough to do it).

It was just who I was.

I didn't want to lose touch with that person. I didn't want my daughters to be other than that person.

Unless they were very foolish, my money would mean they'd never need for anything, and they would want for very little, until the day not only they, but their children, and perhaps their children's children, died.

I set about making them not foolish.

I had two ex-husbands, or in current vernacular, two baby daddies, who thought I was mad. It was part them being fathers, part them being men, and part them being successful men, they'd wanted to spoil our girls.

However, we had one daughter who was an air force pilot and another who was finishing a master's in social work.

Therefore, as you could see, I was not mad.

But I couldn't exactly be that person.

Not anymore.

Not (entirely) by my own design, I had not been hidden, low-profile, in thirty years.

I needed to be that now.

The FBI had, as they'd told me they would, backed off. Delgado and his cameras and his team and his local contacts, "Who are tight, Ms. Larue, that's a guarantee," were on the case.

But I had been in that house, almost constantly, for four days straight. I was for all intents and purposes shut in, if not snowed in, and I could already feel a *Shining* coming on.

I needed to get on my computer and do it not looking at paint colors and lake house interior Google searches (they were all too light and carefree anyway—that vibe didn't go with the *Blue Velvet/Riverdale* one I was searching for).

And I needed not to obsess about that girl who I had seen, at the same time I wasn't sure I had.

It felt like she was a ghost.

And the fact not one mover noticed her, considering how beautiful she was, exacerbated that feeling.

But my computer could take me away.

I could escape there.

Always.

I'd done just that for twenty years.

Very successfully.

However, there it sat on a desk that was too big and too modern for that space, and I couldn't find the motivation to open a new document in Word and let it flow.

On this thought, my phone rang.

Considering it did, as all others were blocked or silenced, it meant it was one of the girls, one of the exes, or one of the others—those being someone on Hawk Delgado's team.

Or the FBI.

Obviously, I took the call.

Because it was the FBI.

"Agent Palmer," I greeted.

"Ms. Larue," she replied. "I wanted to follow up on the situation with Sheriff Dern."

Good Lord.

I'd forgotten.

The local sheriff was supposed to come by. Introduce himself. Etc.

He'd been briefed by Agent Palmer, Joe Callahan *and* Hawk Delgado.

I'd been told he wanted to assure me, personally, that I also had his department's support and protection.

I did not need to read between the lines that he wanted to meet me.

In fact, not entirely successfully hiding her smirk, which, coming from the fantastically professional special agent said quite a bit about Sheriff Dern, Agent Palmer had told me that Dern wanted to assure me I had *the entire town's* support and protection.

"We did," she noted drily, "explain in rather firm terms that the point of you being here was for *the entire town* not to notice you or know anything about your current dilemma. He promised he didn't mean it…*in that way*."

This did not give me a good feeling about Sheriff Dern.

However, he had authority and a gun, and if something triggered Callahan's sensors, or was caught on Delgado's constant surveillance, his department would be call two and that might mean he, or his deputies, could be in danger.

I had to respect that.

"Considering," Agent Palmer stated, taking me from my thoughts. "He'll need to reschedule."

Considering?

Considering what?

"I—" I didn't quite begin.

"But we're still monitoring, and Mr. Booth, Mr. Kyle and Ms. Rosellini, as well as yourself, are all getting communications as per the MO. This leads us to believe that the suspect is not aware that you've all moved to safe houses."

Well, that was good.

"As you know, but I wish to assure you, we're continuing to investigate vigorously, and we hope a break will come soon, we'll find this person, and you'll be free from his machinations. Of course, you need to live your life as usual, just please, as we discussed, take precautions," she went on.

"Of course, however—"

"Sorry to disturb you, I know you're busy. I'll leave you to it. Thank you and be safe."

And with that, Agent Palmer rang off.

For a second, I wasn't sure what to do with it.

This was because I wasn't sure I'd been hung up on since Angelo threw that fit after I told him under no circumstances was I going to pretend still to be his loving wife when he was fucking all three of his backup singers, I didn't care how many Grammys he'd been nominated for that year.

And the time before that was my agent when I flatly refused another acting gig.

I only had a second to think about all of that.

Because movement out the window caught my eye.

And when I focused there, I saw the girl was back.

TWO

No Trouble

The phone in my hand rang before I could even get to the top of the stairs.

I took the call.

"Hello, Mo."

"Ms. Larue, the girl is Celeste Bohannan. She's the daughter of your neighbor at the bottom of the lake. She's sixteen. Good grades. Good student. No trouble, except a recent suspension that we do not consider an issue. She's safe."

Good grades.

Good student.

No trouble.

But…

Recent suspension.

Wasn't that, in essence, how many wayward souls were described by those surprised acquaintances, friends and loved ones who had no idea they were psycho killers?

They were quiet. Smart. Kept to themselves. No trouble.

On the other side of that coin, wasn't that the lament of the sorrowful acquaintances and friends of beautiful young girls who met grisly ends?

What a waste. She was so young. Good grades. Quiet. No trouble.

I hit the bottom of the stairs, and Mo kept speaking.

"No idea why she's coming to visit, except she's probably bored and curious about her new neighbor."

"Thank you, Mo." My reply was a whisper.

Because Celeste Bohannan, the Girl in the Mist, was not out in my pine-needle strewn yard.

She was on my deck, at the glass doors, staring at me.

"Are you all right?" Mo asked.

We had code, and to tell Mo I was not all right, I would say, "I'm perfectly fine."

Obviously, I didn't say that, even if I did have this uncomfortable feeling, watching that girl as I walked through my new house to the back doors, that I was what that phrase meant to say.

The opposite of perfectly fine.

Something was wrong.

Very.

I might be fine, but something was not right.

Even though I felt that keenly, I said, "I'm good, Mo. Thank you."

"Take care and call if you need anything."

"Thanks again."

"'Bye."

"Good-bye."

I said this as I opened the door.

And looked, without barrier, into the eyes of Celeste Bohannan.

A wave of such melancholy struck me, I instantly longed for the uncomfortable feeling I'd just been experiencing.

My life had just changed.

The world had just changed.

With one look in the wounded, haunted, lost eyes of Celeste Bohannan.

"Hello," I greeted.

"Hi," she whispered.

Shy or affected, I did not know, but her fragile voice played its part in the overall delicacy that was so very her, it permeated the air around her.

"Can I help you with something?" I asked.

A brief pause and then, "That's why I'm here."

I didn't understand, tipped my head to indicate that, and backed it up with words. "I'm sorry?"

"To see if I can help you." Another pause before, "Move in."

When I didn't immediately allow her entry, she turned at the waist, lifted a lethargic arm and pointed to the green, corrugated metal roof down the way.

"I live there," she said, dropping her arm and turning back to me. "With my dad and brothers."

It hit me belatedly she lived there with her father and brothers.

Behind a rather daunting gate.

A gate that had, on either five-feet high column at the sides, plaques—not signs, *plaques*— that read, PRIVATE PROPERTY and TRESPASSERS WILL BE PROSECUTED.

Again, two of them, one on either side.

Along these columns was a stone fence, also five-feet high, that extended well into the woods.

I had been informed by Joe Callahan there were cameras located in random places in the woods.

Not only that, those places were changed, randomly, so anyone who would think they could clock those areas and avoid them so they could find lake access or a free campground would eventually be disabused of those notions.

Finally, she lived with her dad and two brothers on a property that was one of only four in perhaps a ten-mile radius, sitting behind a daunting gate with threatening plaques affixed (twice), a fence and cameras. All of this approved by the Federal Bureau of Investigations as a good, safe place for me to be because the garden-variety stalker myself and my former costars were experiencing had done things—done such terrible, *terrible* things, and was still doing them—and we now knew he was not-so-garden-variety at all.

And here she was, wounded, lost, for some unusual reason

suspended from school, a good kid who got good grades, on my back deck offering to help me unpack.

It was without a doubt the mother of two beautiful daughters that had me asking a question the answer to which I knew.

"What's your name?"

"Celeste."

With that, I stepped aside, saying, "Hello, Celeste. I'm Delphine. Please come in."

THREE

Foundation

Clearly, for a project to do with Celeste, we couldn't be wandering around the house, haphazardly unpacking boxes.

This wasn't about her (entirely), or the situation I was facing which brought me there.

I was accustomed to protecting my privacy.

After all these years, it had become habit.

I offered Celeste a drink, something she declined.

It was then I had to make a decision.

The kitchen was large.

To the side off the kitchen there was a dining area, complete with a truly vile, smoked glass seventies chandelier (please don't worry, I'd not only found its replacement, I'd already ordered it).

This was part of a great room that was either by design of the original house, or an indication of clairvoyance by its now-dead owner who had lived there for fifty-seven years, and thus he'd torn down walls not knowing one day the chandelier would be woefully dated, but knowing that compartmentalized living would be a thing of the past.

There was a small study and a large mudroom/laundry tucked

on the other side of a set of stairs that rose to the upper floor off to the side of the living room area.

But the remainder of the lower floor was one large room.

And an entire wall of that room was built-in bookshelves.

These, I would not be altering.

Though, I would be relieved that the glut of boxes stacked around them would be gone.

On that thought, I made a decision and I led her to the shelves.

Through my moment of contemplation, she did not survey the house.

Instead, she kept her attention solely on me.

This was unnerving due to the fact the reason for this was not because I was famous. However, it wasn't unexpected, and this was also not because I was used to it because I was famous.

The person who had lived and died in the house had been there decades before Celeste was even born. She'd probably known him since her first memories.

His space would not be a mystery.

But I was.

I came to stand in front of the bookshelves.

"Those," I indicated the smallish, square book boxes stacked six high, four across and three deep, "are my books. These," I indicated the four larger boxes on the floor behind me, "are the bits and bobs I'd like placed in among the books. The books were packed in order and the movers placed them so the first ones to be unpacked will be the ones on the end. That one there," I pointed to a box at the top of a pile, "is labeled one. If you can start there and load them on the shelf up here," I indicated the space atop the first shelf, "I'll unpack these."

"Okay," she replied, turning instantly to the box.

As she did, I wondered if I should give her a knife.

Being in my home, she'd lost the Girl in the Mist aura, and some of her vulnerability seemed to eke away.

That said, make no mistake, she did not seem normal.

She was extraordinarily stunning with the perfectly symmetrical features of a classic beauty, also tall and slender, with fine bones and thick, glossy hair.

But somewhere along the way, this sixteen-year-old had lost something of great value and great importance.

Something as integral to her as breathing.

I knew this because, whatever it was, was unhidden. It was sitting under every expression on her face, infused in every movement she made.

"There's a letter opener on the bar," I shared.

She was gazing at the boxes, but at my words, she turned only her head to me and nodded.

And with the grace carried only by one of youth holding such beauty, she floated to the bar.

I watched her, and when she was back at the box slicing it open, I moved to where I'd left the box cutter to start my own chore.

We worked in awkward silence for ten minutes, me attempting to get through the wall of gloom that clung to her so I could further my bead on her. She was more than likely intimidated and definitely introverted.

Therefore, I thought it strange it was Celeste who broke our silence.

"Mr. Nance took good care of this place."

"It seems he did," I agreed, uncovering my Emmy from bubble wrap. For the first time when handling it I wondered why I didn't donate it, and the other two, to the small museum devoted to me that had sprung up about fifteen years ago in my hometown. "The inspector was impressed."

"Yeah," she mumbled, placing books on a shelf with the care one would use to place a bust by Houdon. "Dad figured you'd be sure to look into that. But, you know, just so you know…"

She was finished with her first box, not to mention she'd apparently exhausted her only conversational gambit. She looked directly at me again, lifting the empty box.

"Do you want these broken down?"

I nodded. "Please."

"Where do you want me to put them?"

I was stacking them in the mudroom.

There wasn't much to see in the house that was unpacked, but I didn't want her wandering when I was occupied somewhere else.

It was, it's important to repeat, not about Celeste or any feeling I was getting from her that she was a problem or that I was in any danger from her.

Privacy, I'd also repeat, was important to me.

It was something else, though.

I was feeling odd because I didn't know *what* I was getting from her.

I just knew it was not good, even if I didn't know how it wasn't.

"I'm stacking them in the mud room. But just set them on the floor against the end of the bar. We'll take them to the mudroom when we have a bunch to go."

She did as told.

And as she'd pulled out of the gate, she found it in herself to share even more.

"The senior project last year was headed by this do-gooder, Malorie. She's in college now. She was kind of a pain. And everyone thought she was also kind of crazy. But the project was so good, people still use it. And at the end of last summer, before she went off to school, the town council gave her a big award."

She came back my way, and again I got those eyes.

They were, incidentally, wide, lushly lashed and a deep blue.

They were also innocence mixed with injury, a vision no person was comfortable with and no mother on the planet could endure.

I was no exception and was again fighting a deep desire to hold her in my arms.

Or build a fortress around her.

She kept speaking.

"There's this storeroom, behind the Double D. No one used it. You have to rent it, you know. And no one was renting it. So Malorie talked to the owner, because, like, a little money is better than none. Now, you go in and tell Pete at the Double D you got stuff to dump in there, he gives you the key, and you dump it. Or, if you need something, you go in and tell Pete you need it, give him a donation and go in and get what you need. He keeps the donations, gives them to the guy who owns the thing, and they pay the rent."

I did not take my attention from her as she relayed this story.

Seemingly emboldened, she kept at it.

"Like, people use it to get boxes to send Christmas presents and stuff. It's got bubble wrap and tissue paper and all sorts. Boxes are expensive, you know, especially when you need a lot of them. Like, when people move or whatever. Now, because of Malorie, they can go there and get everything they need. They'd be real happy to get all your stuff. And Jesse or Jace could take it over for you." Pause and, "Or Dad."

The pause before offering up her father was interesting.

And I couldn't read that either.

"Who's Pete?" I asked.

"He owns the Double D." Realizing I didn't know what that meant, she said, "The diner in town."

Ah.

"That *is* an excellent project, recycling and cost savings, all rolled into one," I remarked. "I'll see how it goes and let you know if I need someone to help me get all my stuff over there."

"Okay," she whispered, timidly but still visibly pleased her story was received so well.

"Okay," I repeated.

She went back to the massive stack of boxes.

I kept unpacking, uneasy about the fact that Celeste offering some banal, but unquestionably useful information, should please her like that.

The silence we then fell into was a bit more comfortable.

I had mementos scattered across surfaces, all my boxes empty and broken down, she was into box ten when I began to shift and add to the shelves, arranging the space so it would look good and speak to me.

Framed pictures of the girls.

The small piece I'd bought in the Place du Tertre in Montmartre.

The Herend giraffes Warren had given me for our wedding, which I ended up loving more than I loved him.

Case in point, I kept the giraffes.

And got rid of him.

Celeste seemed in a rhythm, and she was indeed helping, making me realize that perhaps I was procrastinating because the task at hand, especially that one, was overwhelming, even if I'd had a plan to tackle it.

Having those boxes out of the way, the shelves sorted with my books and things that had great meaning for me, would be a mental coup. A powerful visual that I was safe and home, my treasures around me, which would free headspace for me to move on.

Celeste was placing the contents of box fifteen on the shelves, working closely to me, when she said, "There are a couple of authors you like a whole lot."

I did indeed.

"Mm," I hummed.

And that was when she said, very low, "I know who you are."

I stilled, a bubble of panic rising in me, before I turned my gaze to her and realized she knew, but she didn't *know*.

I therefore replied in the same tone. "I know you do."

She pressed her lips tightly together.

I smiled wanly.

She moved away and broke down box fifteen to start on box sixteen.

I was working with her, and we were in the twenties, when I decided it was time.

"It's not my business, however, I feel as the adult in this scenario I need to at least note that you should be in class right now."

Her shoulders went up before they drooped.

She said nothing.

"Again, it's not my business," I murmured and turned a discerning eye to the shelves as it was close to time to start rearranging and adding more personal pieces.

"I said something mean to a teacher," she blurted.

My attention went back to her.

"I used the F-word." Lengthy pause. "As in *F you.*"

"Ah," I replied, not taking my eyes from her.

She shoved some books on the shelf without what had become her customary care.

"She was being mean," Celeste declared.

"Mean?" I asked.

At my question, she engaged fully with me—eyes and body.

Automatically, I braced.

"She's the chemistry teacher, and I don't get chemistry. My mind…" a head jerk, "it doesn't think like that. And I did really badly on an assignment. It wasn't the first assignment I'd screwed up. But she's not a good teacher. She just expects us to get it, not that she needs to *teach it.* And a lot of people are doing really badly in that class. A lot of them. I'm not the only one. She got mad and used me as an example."

At this point, Celeste stomped to the boxes and brandished the letter opener.

She was mumbling and slitting open a box when she went on.

"I always get picked on when stuff like that happens."

I had very little doubt.

Curvy girls thought thin girls had it so good.

Beautiful girls were passed up for dates to the prom because boys were so intimidated by their looks, they were too scared to ask.

Smart girls were destined to feel odd and wrong, because it was understood that they should be more worried about fashion than interested in code or equations.

As I'd noted, life was a daily battle.

For everybody.

Particularly if you were a girl.

She moved to shelve more books.

I moved to arrange more things.

"So she embarrassed you," I noted.

She made a noise that was frustrated but also remarkably attractive. It sounded like how Celine Dion might grunt.

"Do you need chemistry to get into college?" I asked.

"I'm going to do hair. I'm really good at hair," she decreed. "All my friends, and people who aren't my friends, always ask me to do their hair. People say I'm even better than Shelly, who's a stylist in town. The most popular one. Everyone goes to her. She's sweet, and she taught me a few things. I even do the highlights and lowlights in one of my friends' mom's hair, and I haven't gone to school to learn how or anything. Just got a few tips from Shelly."

Her shoulders went straight for the first time since I'd known her, to the point I hadn't realized they were slumped.

She then finished, "And my friend's mom says it looks like she paid two hundred dollars for it."

She was very certain about this statement for her future. Certain and proud of her talent.

It was not a make-do-because-I-live-in-a-small-town-in-the-middle-of-nowhere-and-I've-been-raised-to-understand-my-options-are-limited decision. Nor was it a people-like-my-chemistry-teacher-have-ingrained-in-me-I'm-not-good-for-anything-else decision.

She wanted it.

"Then why are you in chemistry?" I pressed.

Celeste Bohannan was not difficult to read now.

Her story was lit in neon.

In this case, her cheeks went pink.

A boy.

"She embarrassed you in front of your boyfriend?" I asked quietly.

Her gaze came to me, startled.

And she was even more beautiful.

Lord.

"How did you—?"

"I've lived a lot more life than you," I lied.

She turned her head, dipping her chin almost to the point she rubbed it against her collarbone.

With that, she returned to the boxes.

It took a few minutes before she told me, "He's not my boyfriend."

"But it's a boy you like."

"Yes," she whispered.

All of a sudden, I'd gone stone-still.

This girl's fragility had nothing to do with recently being embarrassed in front of a boy she liked.

No, it was something else.

Perhaps her teacher was aware of it. Perhaps not.

But I'd lay money, a good deal of it, on the fact that her teacher was not conventionally attractive. She might be young. She might be old.

However, she saw the beauty and promise of Celeste Bohannan, and even if there was no excuse to single any child out in class for ridicule or to be made an example of, the fact it was Celeste was maliciously conceived.

And as such, I was livid.

Consumed by it to the point I was unable to move.

"Ms.…uh, Larue?" Celeste called.

I turned to her with a jerk.

She blinked.

"I'd like you to call me Delphine," I told her.

"Okay," she said shyly.

There was a time I'd been shy.

I was that no longer.

Including right then.

"There are occasions, Celeste, in anyone's lives where we have to make decisions. Decisions about situations that it was not our choice to be in, but regardless, it's up to us to make those decisions. It seems now the decision you made to curse at your teacher was a faulty one. But I can assure you, in the future, when you realize you found the courage to stand up for yourself, you will understand that the consequences you face, which arguably you should not be facing, were entirely worth it."

Now she was staring at me.

"Of course, a school will need to have zero tolerance for that behavior," I continued. "There are many lessons you learn in high school, and they need to do their best to blanket them so the same rules apply to everyone. And sadly, for the most part, that has to be no matter the extenuating circumstances, which is totally unfair, but it's a way to teach a lesson. But this particular one, what was happening to you and how you refused to accept it, is precious because it's yours and yours alone. And I hope you will stand on that decision many times in the future. Stand on it as your foundation so that you allow no one, not one single soul, to shit on you again."

She was still staring at me, now understandably astonished.

"You're helping me immensely," I told her. "The kitchen is done, so this is the biggest job that's left." Not including my closet, of course, but she didn't have to know that. "It was blocking me psychologically. I'm glad you came up to—"

I didn't finish that.

A knock sounded on the door.

Not any knock.

A cop's knock.

And I watched with grim fascination as the color drained from Celeste's face.

FOUR

Alice

I did not know, until I discovered the ID Channel, what a cop's knock was.

Retired detective Joe Kenda explained it to me.

It was loud.

Authoritarian.

And brooked no argument.

You were to open the door.

Now.

No one should be at my door without Mo, or someone else on Hawk Delgado's team calling.

No one.

"That's Dad," Celeste said, a tremble in her voice.

Thoughts cascaded through my mind, too many of them, and none of them nice.

"Why are you afraid of your father?" I rapped out before I could stop myself.

"Because I'm suspended. I'm supposed to be home, cleaning the house and considering my actions."

Her final three words penetrated, being so normally parental, rather than scarily abusive, I found it in me to temper my reaction, which had been poor and would not be conducive to her sharing.

In my defense, she was putting me on edge, not her fault, but it was the case nevertheless.

However, I needed to pull myself together so she would confide in me.

"And since you're not, what's going to happen to you?" I asked far more gently.

She appeared confused.

"Well, he's gonna get mad." Her expression shifted to one I'd seen many times in the raising of two teenage girls. A mixture of frustrated, rebellious and guilty. "And I might be grounded for another day or something."

Grounded.

If that was her greatest fear from her father…

The knock came again.

I moved to the door and opened it.

And my world went into a tailspin.

First impression, he was taller than me.

Second, he was broad at the shoulders, lean at the hips.

Third, his hair was dark, but strands of silver threaded through it. Long hair that brushed his shoulders but was held back at the top and the sides, probably in a tail at the back of his head. His beard was full. It also was dark with silver in it.

After that, I noted he was wearing sunglasses. Completely black lenses that gave you no entry to what might be discovered behind them.

Onward, he was wearing a heavy, tan button-up shirt under a navy quilted vest, faded jeans and brown boots. He was also wearing a medallion hanging from a leather strap at his throat.

He was tanned.

He was weathered.

He was mildly unkempt.

He had features that were a mixture of sharp (his cheekbones, his nose) and broad (his full lips and deep forehead).

With this information presented to me, I made a snap, but very informed decision.

I wanted to fuck him.

I wanted to know every inch of his body, and I wanted to expose every inch of mine to his touch and taste.

I wanted him in every room in my house.

I wanted a solid week of having his cock buried inside me or his face shoved deep up my cunt, or my mouth filled with him, and my every movement, every moment dominated by him.

And then we'd be done, and he could go.

I hadn't had that feeling in a very long time.

But I couldn't have any of that.

Because he was my neighbor.

And Celeste's father.

He tipped his chin to me, and then his sunglasses moved in the direction of his girl.

He said not a word and didn't walk into my house, even after I shifted to the side as a silent indication he was welcome.

Nevertheless, Celeste spoke.

Fast.

And whiny.

"But I was *bored*, Dad."

Those sunglasses swung my way for naught but a second before he took one step over my threshold.

Another step.

Still silent.

He stopped.

I closed the door.

Celeste spoke.

"I was going crazy. I told you. *It's been a week.*"

A week?

She'd been suspended an entire week for saying, "Fuck you" to her teacher?

That seemed excessive.

"*I had to get out of there,*" Celeste continued.

"She's helped me a great deal," I put in.

The sunglasses again focused on me.

It was, by the way, a misty, gray and dreary day.

The Terminator.

Those glasses reminded me of the Terminator.

I felt it.

I tried not to feel it.

But it was there.

Swirling.

Forming.

But not coming together.

I needed to ignore it.

I wasn't going to be able to ignore it.

"I have a lot of books. She's helped me unpack at least thirty boxes," I went on.

"I mean," Celeste caught his attention, "she's nice. Delphine."

He made some movement, and Celeste quickly spoke on.

"Ms. Larue," she corrected. "She's nice."

"I told her to call me Delphine," I shared.

He turned to me.

It was back to his daughter when she said, "But I'm not up here kicked back with popcorn and a movie."

He crossed his arms on his chest.

And remained silent.

All right.

Enough.

"May I speak to you?" I requested.

The sunglasses came back to me, but he still said not a word.

There was also nothing on what I could see of his face beyond beard and glasses. Not anger or disappointment.

How Celeste was reading him was a mystery.

"In private," I pressed.

His head swung back around to his daughter.

"No," I said swiftly, "She can stay here. We'll—"

I stopped abruptly because I had his attention again and it was the first thing on him I was able to read.

I was right, I wasn't able to ignore it.

Against my will, the edges of the puzzle were slowly lining up.

Though, that was the easiest part.

But the way I had his attention now meant two of the thousands of pieces that made him came together and landed inside the frame.

This was his daughter, and some stranger did not contradict his authority.

In fact, no one did.

Perhaps in anything, not just his daughter.

I'd been wrong earlier.

I did not want to fuck him.

I wanted him to fuck me.

"Please, just five minutes of your time," I pushed.

His body language adjusted minutely, which I took as the answer, *yes*.

I glanced briefly at Celeste, who hurriedly moved back to the boxes, a ploy to show her father how much help she was being, and that she was not up here having fun with the rich and famous lady who'd moved in next door. Instead, although she chose it, it was an extension of her punishment.

I took him to the small study, a room I'd be making a reading room.

It was at the current juncture my favorite room in the house, regardless it was a shambles.

I'd selected a chair that would behoove anyone to describe it as merely a chair. It wasn't a loveseat. It wasn't a chaise. It wasn't a small couch.

It was a miracle, as it managed to be all four.

There were lamps sitting around that I had not placed, a table beside the chair, and in the boxes I had yet to unpack, a plethora of pillows, a chunky throw, candles and a tray to put on the chair so I had somewhere on the expanse of the seat to set drinks or plates or other if the table was out of reach.

I decided in that second, once the bookshelves were done, to set up this room.

I did not close the door when I turned to him.

"First, I'm Delphine Larue."

"I know who you are."

Of course he did.

And of course his voice was a deep, rough rumble.

"And you?" I asked.

From my question, I received my first expression from him.

Surprise.

He thought I knew who he was.

I didn't, even if I partially did.

Still, introductions were in order.

"Cade Bohannan."

His name was uttered in grunts, and they were not dulcet by any stretch of the imagination.

"May I ask…Celeste has been suspended for a week?"

His chin jerked up.

I had to be sure she wasn't making light of things.

Therefore, I went on, "For cursing at her teacher?"

Another chin jerk.

Lord, how he could make that movement both ludicrously attractive and faintly annoying, I had no idea.

However, I feared the annoying part would increase if he didn't start using his words.

"Just that?" I pressed on.

"Just that," he rumbled.

Good.

Words.

"Have you heard of the concept of the Five Voices of Criticism?"

He stared at me a brief moment before crossing his arms on his chest.

I took that as, *go on.*

I did just that.

"In any creative endeavor, though, I would extend it to any endeavor, if someone says something critical about your work, and that point is made by one voice, it should be ignored. Two voices, the same. Three, four, you see the pattern. The fifth voice makes the same point, that's when you start paying attention."

He made no reply or even gave any indication he was listening to me outside the sunglasses staying rooted to me. Sunglasses he was still wearing in a room that had even dimmer light than the great room.

"Obviously, depending on your reach, that five would be multiplied."

"For instance," he broke in, "your five would be fifty thousand."

That was exaggerated, but his message was clear.

"As a for instance, yes," I agreed softly.

He said nothing further.

"As another for instance, if you were a teacher, and one, or two, or four kids in your class were having trouble with that class…"

He shifted his weight.

I soldiered on.

"That's obviously to be expected. Kids are kids. A variety of factors would affect how they learn, or if they do—"

"Ms. Larue—"

"Delphine."

He grew silent again.

"I don't know how big her class is…"

I let that lie.

Cade Bohannan made no reply.

Even so, I still sensed that now, *my* message was clear.

Moving on…

"Further, there are vast resources based on even more vast research that are available globally that help us to understand a child's development, physically, mentally and emotionally. The days where it's generally understood that the moment a child can coordinate their limbs, they're sent to a factory to help the family put bread on the table are no longer accepted. At all. You would not set a pack of puppies to guiding a sled, you do not send children in to do adult's work."

He studied me silently.

"In other words, you must know this teacher's behavior is unacceptable. Indeed, even unforgiveable. She should be fired. With what she did to Celeste, she has no business teaching anyone under the age of thirty-five, and even that's up for debate. She is clearly not fit for the job."

Above his sunglasses, his dark, dense eyebrows rose but no words escaped his lips.

This meant, obviously, I carried on.

"I understand she's human. She's fallible. Perhaps she was having a bad day. However, she's in a position that she must understand that singling out a child, I don't care the age, Celeste is still a child, for that kind of scorn is reprehensible. Celeste was defending herself against an attack. Powerless in her position as a student, she perhaps took the wrong tack in her defense, but her defense was most assuredly defensible. Of course, she should have chosen her words more eloquently, but I do not agree that the lesson she needs to learn in this scenario is essentially that she needs not to protest when someone is forcing her to eat their shit."

When I stopped speaking, he didn't start.

As I had nothing further to say, I didn't say any more.

Eventually, he realized I was done, and therefore spoke.

"Are you telling me you think I should go to the high school and try to get the chemistry teacher fired?"

"No, I'm telling you it'd be lovely if Celeste could stay with me for a bit longer to help me unpack boxes."

His head listed back, his chin going into his neck and shunting a bit to the side.

And then he said, "Why didn't you just say that?"

I didn't have the opportunity to answer that question.

His shoulders rotated, his arms dropped, his neck twisted, and my breath caught.

I heard my phone ring in the other room.

My skin tightened.

Bohannan pivoted around and marched out.

Quickly, I followed him just as another cop-knock sounded at the door.

Just clearing the path to the great room that led under the stairs, Bohannan halted so quickly, I nearly ran into him.

I sidestepped him.

I saw Celeste was pale again, frail again, staring at her father with huge, terrified eyes.

She was also standing at the front door. A door she'd opened.

A man in a beige sheriff's uniform was lurking there.

His name badge read Moran.

"Alice?" Bohannan grunted.

The deputy's hard face hardened more.

"Alice," he confirmed.

FIVE

Letter to the Editor

I fought it.

I did.

Unimpressed by my virtual soliloquy, Bohannan sent his daughter home.

He left with the deputy.

I made myself finish the bookshelves, stack the spent boxes in the mudroom, and then allowed no excuse but to tackle the reading room, which took hardly any time at all. I therefore gave myself permission to kick my own behind considering I could have had that sanctuary the last few days.

Only then did I make a pot of tea and go get my laptop.

I curled into the chair that dominated that small space precisely how I'd envisioned, sipped tea, pulled up Google and typed in *Alice Misted Pines*.

I was alarmed to find, with that vague and wide-open search criteria, that I did not have to dive any deeper.

The first link was for an article in the *Tri-Lake Chronicle*.

The title for the article was "Girl Missing: Police Have No Leads."

Tasting something sour at the back of my tongue, I pulled up the article.

I read it.

And all the related ones.

And anything at all I could find that had to do with the case.

What I learned was that Alice Pulaski, the bright, red-headed, freckle-faced, eight-year-old daughter of Dale and Audrey Pulaski, had a slumber party for her birthday.

This party had occurred the evening of the first night I spent in Misted Pines.

Upon pulling up a map, I found that Dale and Audrey lived much like I and the Bohannans lived.

Goldilocks.

Not too far from town, not too close.

Not too far from their neighbors, and not too close.

In the woods, not alone, but not populated.

Alice's friends, as girls were prone to do, had decided to be naughty, and when they should have been sleeping, they snuck out of the house to go play some game in the woods in the dead of night.

When they returned to the house, they did so waking Alice's mother and father, seeing as the girls were panicked and hysterical.

Because, as they reported to Alice's parents and later to the police, once they'd noticed something amiss, they'd spent some time looking, but no matter how hard they tried, they could not find Alice.

A search by Dale and Audrey, as well as Alice's big brother, seventeen-year-old Will, who was Dale's son by his first marriage, was to no avail.

Now also panicked, they called the police.

The sheriff and his deputies had arrived promptly.

At that time, they instigated a preliminary search.

When hours went by and this proved fruitless, they brought in a K-9 unit.

This did not prove fruitless. However, Alice's trail, as followed by the dogs, abruptly and mysteriously stopped somewhere deep into the woods.

As time wore on, temperatures dipped up and down, and Alice's continued disappearance was beginning to spell out an unpleasant outcome, the sheriff's department organized a volunteer search force made up of off-duty deputies, police from other counties, fire department personnel and ordinary citizens.

All told, well over a hundred people came forward to help search.

They combed the woods.

Hide, nor hair, of Alice was found.

No ransom was requested.

No odd characters were seen about town.

An animal attack was ruled out as she might have been carried off, but the dogs would have discovered that trail and any location of attack.

Meaning no animal could make a child disappear into thin air.

But a human could.

Interviews with family, friends, teachers, neighbors, acquaintances all came up with the same thing.

Alice was a good kid. Sweet. Smart. A regular eight-year-old girl with no enemies or anyone who might wish to cause her harm. She was popular, her family was close, they were good stock, frequented church and involved with the community, and she was beloved by her parents and her big brother.

It came in a letter to the editor.

That little combination of a few of the myriad puzzle pieces that were floating in my mind fitting together before falling to the board.

A resounding censure of Sheriff Leland Dern, for his entire tenure, most recently his handling of the missing girl, Alice Pulaski.

The letter's final line?

It's time to call in Bohannan.

SIX

Nightmare

When I woke from the nightmares, I didn't do it like I suspected no one on earth did it.

Gasping in horror and sitting bolt upright in bed.

That was Hollywood's interpretation of a nightmare.

Mine was sudden consciousness and deep paralysis, caused by extortionate amounts of fear.

I didn't move a muscle.

See a shadow.

Hear even silence.

Taste a thing.

Was he there?

In that room?

Like the dream told me.

Or was he close?

Did he know where I was?

Could he get to me, without sensors blaring, his approach caught on camera, me being able to get to one of the seven panic buttons in the house, or behind the steel door that now protected my bathroom?

As the fear subsided and I was able to assess my environs and then found the courage to add sight to sense and sound, I got on an elbow, looked around the darkness of my room and saw nothing.

No one.

I was alone.

I was safe.

I rolled, threw off the covers and twisted out of bed.

It was cold. I had the habit of turning the heat down before bed. I liked to burrow, settle under the weight of more than one cover.

I moved across the room, reached for the throw across the armchair by the French doors that led out to my personal balcony and pulled it around my shoulders.

I then stood at the doors, gazing out.

The moon was behind some clouds.

The shadows ran deep.

I had not yet become accustomed to the landscape, but I saw dark outlines of pines, a muted shimmer on the water.

The very far away, diminutive triangle that was slightly lighter against the black shadows of the night.

The only bit of Cade Bohannan's roof visible to me.

It's time to call in Bohannan.

I had not only been a mother to teenage girls.

I'd been a mother to eight-year-olds.

Thus, it was also time to activate Delphine.

SEVEN

Doomed

I set aside the laptop after scanning the *Tri-Lake Chronicle*.

It was three days after I'd met Celeste and her father, she had gone, as had he.

The weekend had passed.

It was Monday, and I could only assume (and hope) that Celeste was back in school.

Try as I might, and I studied it often, that triangle of their roof that I could see told no stories.

The *Tri-Lake Chronicle* did, however, the prevailing one being that Alice Pulaski had not been found.

This was a curious mixture of horrifying and comforting.

It was horrifying, obviously, because Alice had not yet been found.

It was now more than clear that she had not wandered off, got lost, became scared and holed up in a cave where some intrepid deputy would run across her, dirty, hungry and dehydrated, but alive. News I'd been hoping I would wake up and read in a relieved article accompanied by a joyous photo of parents and child reunited.

It was comforting because this was still the top story in the local newspaper, splashed underneath the online masthead.

A community like this did not have girls missing, or, as I'd become accustomed to in spending so much time with the *Chronicle*, hardly any news at all…but good news. Bingo nights and bridge tournaments, boys and girls basketball league signups at the rec center and a local woman who still lived by herself and stitched stunning embroidery reaching the age of 105.

And whoever ran the newspaper did not feel that their readers would get Alice Pulaski fatigue.

This was not a sensational piece of news offered up for information and digestion in a digital landscape where people experienced sorrow or outrage but had no interest in follow-through. Their only craving being getting their hit of sorrow and outrage. Their only thought being, what was next to devour?

Alice Pulaski was important, and the community cared.

A video had been posted on Saturday—one I could only stand to watch for forty-five seconds before I had to shut it off.

Audrey Pulaski begging whoever took her daughter to bring her home.

Dale Pulaski stood beside her looking ravaged.

Sheriff Dern stood behind her, appearing solemn.

I didn't even have to be in his presence to sense his puzzle.

Whereas Cade Bohannan's covered a twelve-seater dining room table, and it was made of thousands of pieces that held subtle shading that only the most patient of players could fix together, Leland Dern's could be assembled by a five-year-old.

This did not bode well.

I'd made the decision, and upon watching that forty-five seconds, I carried it through.

I called Hawk Delgado.

It was no surprise this situation in Misted Pines was known to him. He was tasked with keeping me safe, and although this had nothing to do with me, it had to do with Misted Pines, and that was where I was. It was also not a surprise that he currently did not have any resources to devote to assisting with it.

However, he gave me two names.

Nightingale Investigations, an outfit located where Delgado was, in Denver, Colorado.

And Tanner Layne, a private investigator who worked out of a shop in Brownsburg, Indiana, which was, to my astonishment, where Joe Callahan was based.

Neither were close.

But Nightingale was closer.

Though for reasons I didn't understand (they probably had to do with Callahan), I called Layne first, left a message as it was the weekend and waited.

It was not long before he returned my call.

He had a full caseload, but said he'd look into it and get back to me.

I then reached out to Denver, leaving another message.

Not much time passed before a woman named Shirleen Jackson got in touch, saying she'd assessed it and presented it to her boss, the man behind the name, Lee Nightingale. She would follow up with me as soon as he'd made his decision.

Within hours, I had two replies.

Layne: "We're ready to roll when we receive word from the investigator on site that he welcomes assistance. We have a message to him. But if he doesn't give us the greenlight, I'm afraid at this time we can't get involved. I hope you understand. I would feel the same if someone I didn't know pushed into one of my investigations, especially at this early juncture. Trust me when I say that it's never helpful."

I didn't know who "we" was, I also didn't ask, but I suspected he'd consulted with Callahan.

I also didn't think this was "early." At that point, she'd been missing nearly a week.

Which begged the question, what parents had a slumber party for their eight-year-old on a Monday evening?

I didn't ask Layne that either.

Jackson: "We understand your concern, but Lee looked into things and the investigator contracted to assist the local authorities is second to none. In this kind of situation, although it seems contradictory, more hands on deck can make a mess."

That was two nos of the same ilk.

I decided to focus on the "second to none" comment, knowing they were referring to the fact it was clear the locals had called Cade Bohannan in. She was not talking about Dern.

This seemed to be quite a bit of esteem for Bohannan, but knowing it, no puzzle pieces fell.

Even so, I was undeterred.

Which was why, upon indication that Alice had yet to be found, I left my laptop where it lay, and did what I hadn't done in the entire week since I'd been there (save one epic trip to the grocery store, this trip accompanied by Agent Palmer).

I walked into the kitchen, grabbed my purse and keys, then made my way through the mudroom and to the garage, where I got into my Volvo XC60, pulled out and drove into town.

I'd memorized the directions, and in less than fifteen minutes, I was there.

I checked all mirrors and rechecked the pocket of my purse, where the GPS emitting panic fob Delgado had given me was ensconced.

Only then did I get out of my SUV.

I walked into the sheriff's department to find it buzzing.

This came as no surprise.

It was also no surprise when the deputy, who was walking swiftly across the unstaffed front counter, did a double take and stutter step when he turned his head and caught sight of me.

He stopped.

I approached the counter.

He opened his mouth, closed it, blushed.

I put him out of his misery with a quick scan to his name tag.

"Hello, Deputy Dickerson, I'm Delphine Larue."

I reached out my hand.

He stared at it, and his Adam's apple bobbed.

It took a moment, and then he clasped it, letting it go quickly, like his lowly touch might infect my famous person and turn me to ash.

"I know this is likely an imposition at this time," I continued. "But I was wondering if I could have a word with Sheriff Dern."

"I'll get Polly," he announced, and then he took off in a way I was surprised a blossom of dust didn't bloom from his heels.

I stood there, outside the polished wood counter that ran the whole front of the station and separated the reception area from the inner workings of the department.

There were people behind the counter, quite a number of them, and I now had much more attention than when I'd first walked in.

Except from the men who were all in a glass-walled conference room at the back, discussing something with what seemed great intensity, while staring at a board that had its back turned to the window wall.

Sheriff Dern was not among those men.

Nor was Cade Bohannan.

A further note, there was not a woman in that conference room, or in uniform outside of it.

Ditto that for a person of color.

But the rest of the area looked like a mashup set design directly inspired by *Veronica Mars*, several dozen *Supernatural* episodes and *Twin Peaks*.

"Oh my goodness, oh my gosh, oh my goodness," a woman sing-songed.

I turned right.

And I had to reach out a hand to the bench and curve my fingers around as a plump, diminutive, red-cheeked, helmet-haired woman, wearing an ill-advised pleated skirt and a twinset with requisite string of pearls, appeared.

She looked fresh from wardrobe.

Honestly.

What was happening?

"Oh my goodness." She lifted the section of counter that swung up and over (because of course it did) as she exited the back to approach me, her hand already raised. "I'm Polly Pickler."

She was not.

No one was named Polly Pickler.

Unless she was named by Dashiell Hammett.

"And I know you get this a lot," she went on, taking my hand, clasping it in both her own, and hers were so small, both of them didn't even cover one of mine, "but I'm your biggest fan."

I opened my mouth to speak but was unsuccessful.

Still holding tight to my hand, she bounced it with her words.

"I really, really, *really* loved *Those Years*. I didn't miss *that first episode* when it was airing. I even taped it *while* I watched it, just in case. I have them all on DVD now. Boxed sets. All ten seasons. Even so, I watch them on Hulu." She released me only to snap in the air. "I just pick an episode, any episode from any season, and I'm transported back to happy times for at least a half an hour. But I tell you, most of the time, I'll just settle in and watch four, five, even more episodes all back-to-back."

I again opened my mouth.

And was again foiled.

She leaned into me, and I unconsciously bent down from my five-eight height (well, more like five-eleven in my booties) to her four-eight as she carried on.

"But *We Pluck the Cord* is the *best book of all time*. I will argue it with anyone. And *I have*. Yes, *To Kill a Mockingbird* is fabulous. Of course. A classic. But don't hand me any of that *1984* or *Lord of the Flies* or *The Sun Also Rises* nonsense."

I stared aghast at her.

"And yes, *The Handmaid's Tale* was exceptional. But just because the author also starred in one of the funniest, and I'll say most poignant and often very touching and real sitcoms in television history does not mean she hasn't written *the* modern classic that will be on par with Woolf, Fitzgerald and Salinger."

She wagged a finger in my face.

I'll repeat, *she wagged a finger in my face*.

"Mark my words," she concluded.

I didn't know what to say.

Obviously, considering *We Pluck the Cord* won every literary award going, made a fortune in royalties (and still does), was added to high school literature reading lists across the globe, and had more than nine dozen credit hours devoted to the dissection of it at universities in seven different countries, and I wrote it, I was not going to debate her opinion.

However…

"We teach it in school, here, in Misted Pines," she proclaimed proudly. "And that was *before* you moved to town."

"I—"

"I've called Sheriff Dern and told him to get his keister here right away."

She did not use the word "keister."

"No lip from him," she blathered on. "No excuses. He was supposed to get out to the lake and see you, I know. I *told* him he needed to go."

"Oh no, that's not why—"

"And now look what he's done." She blew an irritated puff of breath out of her mouth that was so strong, I felt it go through my sweater and touch skin. "You had to come all the way into town."

"It isn't that far," I said swiftly.

"You're right. Still. I mean," she leaned in again, "you… are…*safe*. No one would harm a hair on your head. Including keeping mum about you being here with us. We love you in Misted Pines. *Everyone* loves you."

That was part of the problem.

There was one man out there who loved me way too much.

"Though," her mind seemed to drift, "it prolly would have been good when you came in that you brought Jace."

Jace?

She waved a hand far up over her head like she intended to pat her crown but missed. "Now it's no never mind. You're here and you're as safe as you could be, right here where—"

"Woman!" a male's voice boomed from behind me. "This better be damned good to call me—"

I turned.

Sheriff Dern was blustering in, shaking his oilskin coat at his shoulders like he was voiding it of drops of rain, though it wasn't raining.

He was wearing a brown sheriff's campaign hat with a star on the front and gold cord wrapped around, the tassels resting jauntily on the front of the brim.

He caught sight of me.

Shut up.

Stood still.

And stared.

I did too, my heart sinking, my stomach twisting.

Because upon sight of him, as I suspected, all his puzzle pieces fell right into place.

And I hoped Bohannan was as good as everyone thought.

Because her fate in this man's hands, Alice Pulaski was doomed.

EIGHT

The Toy Aisles at Target

The first thing I noticed in Sheriff Dern's office was the large, gleaming, intricate and impressive, custom glass-fronted gun cabinet.

It's interior, however, did not boast a collection of antique firearms, such as pearl-handled pistols or Revolutionary War muskets.

It displayed a frightening set of automatic weaponry, the scope of which even Rambo would turn his head to the sheriff and grumble disapprovingly, "*Dude.*"

"Impressive, don't you think?" the sheriff asked.

I did not.

There were pieces of the puzzle when it came to the male gender that I tried very hard never to read. But in the face of this cabinet, I had no choice but to understand this lawman had a very small penis.

"Take a seat, take a seat," Mr. Magnanimous said, not noticing I did not reply, nor, I knew, caring that I didn't.

He was sweeping off his hat and putting it on a very populated coat tree that clearly had been where he deposited things for a very long time and forgot most of them. Shunting his oilskin came next, and it was hooked on the tree. Both of these were accomplished with natural movements that were nevertheless exaggerated.

The man was in the room, you mustn't miss it, he's here, he's in charge, pay attention.

Onward to the desk with his shoulders swaying like they were broader than they actually were, and he needed to use them to conduct his weight forward.

He rounded the desk, not looking at me.

Though, when he did, and he noticed I'd come to stand in between the chairs at the front of his desk, he threw his arm out at the same time he aimed his "keister" to the old-fashioned, wooden rolling chair that he'd stolen from the set of the *Andy Griffith Show*, indicating I should claim a seat.

However, this action threw off his coordination, or perhaps even his office furniture knew he needed to be expelled from it, and it did the best it could, being inanimate, because that keister glanced off the edge of the chair and he nearly landed on the floor.

He grabbed the desk and caught himself in a squat, shifting back, his cheekbones sharpening as a flush of anger at his embarrassment rushed across them.

I looked away and took my time arranging myself in a seat opposite him, tucking my purse in my lap.

When I looked back, he declared, "Polly will never let me hear the end of this, making you come—"

He didn't finish that, appeared alarmingly befuddled for a moment, his gaze drifting to the door.

It snapped back to me. "Where's Jace?"

Who was this Jace?

"I'm sorry. Jace?"

"You came here without Jace?"

"As I don't know who Jace is, I did indeed."

"You don't know who Jace is?"

I decided to stop talking.

"One of the twins," Dern told me.

This seemed important to him, it made no sense to me.

"Jace, Jason. Of Jason and Jesse," he continued. Then he shared that he'd buried the lead. "Bohannan. Cade's boys."

I'd forgotten.

Celeste had mentioned them, Jace and Jesse, though I didn't know they were twins, even if I assumed they were related to her.

Considering Celeste was sixteen, I also didn't know they were old enough to provide physical protection to a millionaire who was paying a great deal of money for said protection.

In fact, I was so wound up in Celeste, I didn't think of Jesse or Jace at all.

"I haven't yet met…the twins," I told him.

"What are you doing, wandering around town without a bodyguard?" he demanded.

I opened my mouth to reply.

Whereas Polly, in her excitement at meeting me, and just because she was nice, I had no issue being interrupted or not allowed to speak.

My reaction was instant when Dern did it.

I found it infuriating.

"It's my understanding you have some sicko sending you pictures of women he's torturing, making them play out episodes of your TV show in between raping them."

I flinched.

He again didn't notice that, or care.

"And you're wandering around on your own?" he asked incredulously, like you'd scold a child for leaving your cart and zooming to the toy aisles in Target.

"I have—"

"I know. That Cuban told me you're covered with all that tech crap, but also, he's got the Bohannans looking after you. You've still got no business going out on your own."

I felt a tingling at my lower back. It was urging me to do things I might regret, like stand and tell the local sheriff to go fuck himself before I walked out.

I did not know Hawk Delgado's ethnicity.

I did know he had *a name.*

That was one.

Two, I was an adult who, in the course of my life, had no small amount of attention from people who had, in some cases, rather severe issues with their perceptions of me. Thus, they acted on them.

I was also an adult who participated fully not only with the FBI, but my hand-selected security team, deciding what was best with the utmost goal being to keep me safe.

But also, there were no guarantees this person who was currently making two women's lives a living hell would be caught anytime soon. And even though those women's lives had been horrifically derailed, I was fortunate enough to have mine, in large part, free to live.

As such, I had worked with my team to make certain I could live it, even if I did so under the cloud of unsuccessfully attempting to bend my brain into taking no responsibility for the horrors a man I'd never met was perpetrating on two women who would, even if rescued, never recover.

Delgado told me he would, on regular occasions, either come himself or send members of his team to make certain the plans that were made and carried out were still effective.

In the interim, I had locals he trusted looking out for me, but he didn't want me to know who they were.

There was sound reasoning for this.

That being, if something got through their net, and someone was watching me, he didn't want them to see I had someone at my back. And even knowing I shouldn't do a thing to let this information be known, unconsciously, I could communicate it. That would put me in danger, because it would give my stalker a target to take down my shield before he took me.

Unless I didn't know who was watching me.

Now, I knew who was watching me.

The Bohannans.

"I'm calling Jace," Dern announced, reaching for the phone.

"Please don't do that."

He ignored me.

"I said, don't do that."

The receiver of his desk phone was in his hand, but he did not mean he'd call Jace.

After punching a button, he barked into it, "Polly, get Jace on the line."

The man couldn't even make his own phone call.

"Jace is probably outside right now," I informed him after he put down the receiver.

"What?" he snapped.

"I was not meant to know who my local detail was. Was that not communicated to you?"

He stared at me, befuddled again.

I sought patience, and as I had practice doing this in my life, what with the two men I chose to marry, and a lot of other men besides, I found it.

"I know you have quite a bit on your plate, Sheriff Dern, but my understanding from Mr. Delgado was that he'd explained all this to you. Personally."

He threw his chest out. "I do got a lot on my plate."

Right now, he did.

But this was explained to him before Alice got carried away in the woods.

If I was not wrong, prior to Alice, his department's main objective was to make certain the senior citizens didn't get too rowdy during bingo at the rec center.

An old-fashioned intercom sitting on his desk chirped with Polly's voice.

"Leland, Hawk Delgado's on the line for you."

It was good to know *Jace* knew what he was doing.

I was relatively certain I did not smirk, but I looked at my lap anyway, just in case.

I heard the receiver snatched up and the click of a button being pushed and then, "Yeah?" Pause then, "I know. I know."

He did not know.

A longer pause and then, "Listen, don't you—" A pregnant pause and a clipped, "Understood."

The receiver crashed in the cradle.

It had been a long time, but I *was* an award-winning actress, therefore I had the appropriate expression on my face when I lifted my head again.

"I got things to do, Ms. Larue, and it seems like you got yourself covered, so can you tell me what you're doin' here?" he commanded.

I could and I did.

"I would like…*anonymously*…to offer a ten-thousand-dollar reward to anyone who provides information that leads your department, or anyone working with your department, to find Alice Pulaski. And if that information leads you directly to her, that reward will be one hundred thousand dollars."

His face went slack.

"I understand when you announce something like this, everyone will be calling. You probably have limited resources. So, if this is deemed necessary, I will be happy to pay for a phone bank to be set up to take those calls." It was difficult to say this next, but since it was also smart, and I hoped in the end, helpful, I said it, "It's probably better if trained personnel take these calls, rather than volunteers, which could mean a task force is needed and likely, overtime for your staff. So, I'll make a further one-hundred-thousand-dollar donation to your department to cover that."

Sheriff Dern had nothing to say.

"Again, for obvious reasons, but also for personal reasons, this needs to be anonymous. Although you undoubtedly need to discuss this with the Pulaskis, but even with them I'll ask you not to mention me. And overall, I would really appreciate your assurance that I will be kept completely out of it."

He found it in him to speak.

"No one will know."

I nodded.

His gaze fell to the purse in my lap then came back to my face.

"You got your checkbook with you?"
Lord.
I couldn't fight it.
Though he was who he was, so I didn't much try.
I hated this man.

NINE

Terrifying

I was not born yesterday.

I also did not carry my checkbook with me.

But those weren't the only reasons I declined to proffer my offer before Dern had even discussed that line of strategy with the family whose daughter had been taken, not to mention his team, or the man he'd called in to help handle this.

Nevertheless, I was surprised, that in the three days since I'd left the sheriff's department, I hadn't heard anything from him.

I had heard from Polly, who called the very next day and told me her nephew was, "real good around the house, he knows how to do everything."

Indication that those lengthy NDAs did nothing to keep the local contractors from talking.

I made a mental note to share this with Hawk as I listened when Polly spoke on.

When she did, she told me her nephew also had a newly pregnant wife and needed some handyman work because, "we'll take care of them, we do good baby showers in Misted Pines," but, "diapers don't come cheap, and you only get one shower, but you got a kid for a lifetime."

I explained I'd have to look into her nephew, but I would, as, at the very least, the new light fixture had been delivered and I could get that unsightly smoked-glass contraption out of my great room.

I did not ask how a woman who seemed pretty together (pleated skirt at a fashion-disaster length for someone of her stature notwithstanding) worked with that pompous, incompetent piece of garbage.

But apropos of that, nothing, except perhaps in working with him, her innate understanding that anyone who met with him for any reason would experience some form of disaster, her voice dropped when she told me anyway.

"Someone's gotta be around to see to things, you know?"

In history, there were innumerable unsung heroes like Polly who "saw to things" when some asshole conned his way into a position he had no business occupying.

Thus, my answer was, "I know."

There had been silence since the call.

Hawk had shared that Polly's nephew was all good to meet. He also shared the fact that he'd communicated to all four contractors that I already had the money to relocate should my current situation become unsafe. However, they still would be paying for that effort after I took their businesses, homes and children's college funds if one of them breathed another fucking word about Delphine Larue being in Misted Pines.

He assured me that this message had been received.

And when Delgado assured you of something, you were assured.

As the days went by, though, I began to understand why Sheriff Dern hadn't jumped on my offer.

This was because he was being eviscerated by the *Tri-Lake Chronicle*, as well as the very local paper that came out once a week, the *Misted Pines Herald*.

Letters to the editor had gone from cranky to outraged, and no one had anything to say about anything else but Sheriff Dern, and that wasn't only because of Alice Pulaski.

But bottom line, people wanted Alice found.

Of course, this would lead *me* straight to a press conference where I offered substantial rewards for information.

But what did I know about finding missing girls?

I had my own situation happening, this being my eldest, Fenn, who was also getting impatient.

I knew this when she'd called that morning, and upon my greeting of, "Hello, love of my life," I received, "What the fuck, Mom?"

Allow me a moment to offer a lesson in why you shouldn't stereotype:

My eldest, who had dreamed of flying, my guess, since she tore down her teddy bear mobile and the very next day stole a plane toy from a friend in her toddler group and refused to give it up, no matter how much he bawled or how much I tried to tug it out of her strong baby hands, entered college on an ROTC scholarship she did not need. Four years later, she did not wash out of UPT (Undergraduate Pilot Training). She was currently stationed in Korea, and she would wear false eyelashes behind the visor of her helmet in her cockpit, if she could.

I had nursed honesty and openness between us since they were little girls.

So I also knew she was enjoying the smorgasbord of male delicacies offered to her, because, "You gotta find the right dick to commit to, and it's good to get a look at a lot of them so you know you got it right. You hear what I'm saying?"

I heard, and understood, as getting it right was a lesson I'd inadvertently taught her by getting it so very wrong in marrying her father…and then her stepfather.

On the other hand, my youngest, Camille was just as outwardly girlie as Fenn (when Fenn was allowed to be).

And she was still with her high school girlfriend, who was even *more* girlie, Joan.

There was one box we all fit in to.

We were humans.

Any other box was just plain bullshit.

"I mean, this is the *FBI*," Fenn ranted on. "They've got nothing on those poor women and you're in Bumfuck?"

"The FBI is not keeping me informed of the intricacies of their investigation, but I feel sure they're diligently investigating."

"The intricacies are, when that dime-a-dozen, crazy piece of shit didn't get what he wanted from you, your hand in marriage after he asked you every week for three years, he kidnapped two women, roped Michael, Russ and Alicia in on his bullshit, and now you all are living under the control of one serious sick fuck."

I gave it a moment, and then said, "I love how much you love me."

My daughter gave it a moment and replied, "Obviously the United States Air Force doesn't care much you're dealing with this, not because they're assholes, just because our remit is a whole lot broader. But I told my squadron commander that shit is real at home, and if some miracle occurs, even if it's a random TDY that brought me closer to you for a while, I want it."

"Don't tell your sister, but you've always been my perfect daughter."

"You say that shit to her too, don't you?"

"I don't recall," I lied. "But in my old age, my memory is slipping."

"You're using that way too soon."

"Hmm…"

"I met someone," she announced, and I perked up. "His name is James. He flies F-16s. He's a total ass. And I think I'm falling in love with him."

For reasons I was not about to reflect on, visions of taciturn Cade Bohannan standing in my reading room, arms crossed on his chest filled my head.

Particularly around the "total ass" part.

But the last part too.

I mean, it had not been mentioned…

But there was Cade. And Celeste. And Jace and Jesse.

But no word of Mom or Mrs. Bohannan had been breathed.

"It does tend to go that way," I said to my daughter.

"If I don't kill him in the meantime, maybe we can arrange leave at the same time and he can come meet you."

Oh.

Well then.

This was not a perkiness false alarm.

"I'd like that," I replied.

"Whatever, I'm probably going to break his heart."

"Why would you say that?"

"I'm Warren Packard's daughter, am I not?"

Warren hadn't only done me in, he'd had two other wives, both of whom had divested him of a lot of money, so he got smart, and from then on, only had girlfriends.

And he had *a lot* of those.

I did my best not to affect how my girls saw their fathers, one way or the other.

I also had to admit I might have failed in this.

But relations were strained between Fenn and Warren, and Camille and Angelo because Warren was Warren, and Angelo was Angelo, and my girls were smart and strong. So for the most part, their fathers dug their own graves.

"You're also my daughter, and I didn't repeat the sins of my mother, did I?"

I could hear the smile in her voice over thousands of miles when she decreed, "You rock the pep talk, Mom."

"Thank you, lovely. Now stop worrying about me and stop worrying about falling in love. It's a good thing, regardless of how terrifying it is. Go off and keep our country safe."

"Okay, that 'terrifying' thing might have taken some of the shine off your pep talk."

I laughed in a way I was sure she heard it and that it was genuine.

We talked longer, not much, but her call was the pep talk I needed.

And things were looking up. Since the call, I got an email from Delgado's office manager, Elvira, and they'd arranged a meet with Polly's nephew, so maybe my new lighting could go in.

This news had set me to hitting go on a variety of other things, which would be additions to the things I'd pressed go on over the last few days (namely a new office desk and furniture and accoutrement for the deck and the pier).

I'd also found this nifty software that you could enter a room's measurements, it gave you a mockup and a bunch of digital tools so you could *design your own closet.*

I spent at least an hour (okay, maybe two) on that and was still enthralled by it when instinctively, my head came up.

Celeste was at the back door.

Her hand was pressed against the glass.

Her eyes were aimed to me.

Her expression said it all.

The sour taste was back in my mouth as I got up, walked to the doors, opened one and said to her, "Go to them, I'll be right down. Is there a direct path or do I need to use the road?"

"There's a path. It's—"

"I'll find it, lovely. Go."

She went.

I ran upstairs to put on some shoes.

TEN

Pistachio Green

The path was direct from a spot between two trees at the edge of the clearing of my yard (as it was, there was no grass, just dirt, pine needles and cones), to a spot in the clearing at the back of the Bohannan compound.

And a compound it was.

There was the green metal-roofed house that was much larger than mine (it had at least a thousand extra square feet, maybe two). There was an even bigger pole barn. Another, smaller house was tucked up into the woods on the hill beyond the main house.

They had a pier as well, and again it was bigger than mine and extended so far out into the lake, it was a trick of nature, their swell of the water going inward, that I couldn't see it from my place. And a boathouse that housed an actual boat. A sleek speed one.

Around the space there were vehicles parked haphazardly everywhere. A new blue Shelby Mustang, two Ram trucks—they seemed matching, though one was black, and one was silver— both of those parked up by the smaller house. There was also a black GMC Yukon. And there were two muddy ATVs sitting outside the pole barn. Last, but not least in this vehicular collection, a restored, old-model, light-blue, soft top Ford Bronco.

I took all of this in at a glance, jogging across their pine needles to their back deck (also bigger than mine) to their back door.

I stood at it nary a second before it slid open.

Gratitude shone almost as brightly as the dismay and worry on Celeste's face.

I stepped in.

They had a great room too. Though instead of the doors leading to the living room area closer to the lake, which fed into the kitchen and dining that was closer to the front door, it was all spread out so no matter where you were doing the things you did in the natural course of your day, you had a view to the lake. The living room was to the left, kitchen to the right.

However, this was not the house of three men and a teenage girl.

This was a veritable showplace.

Large chef's kitchen.

Shag rug with such a rich, deep pile, it looked like fur and had to be a bitch to vacuum.

This sat over the gleaming wood floors and under the pistachio green velvet couch with steel nail details.

High-backed leather armchairs.

Enormous brushed-steel circular coffee table.

It looked like someone had told a designer, "Make it pretty, but not so the men will be uncomfortable."

I could not wrap my head around the idea of Cade Bohannan resting his faded jeans-clad ass on pistachio velvet.

Nor could I imagine his sons doing it, but there they were, identical to each other, and the image of him, one watching me intently, one scowling at me magnificently.

Bohannan himself was in the kitchen, leaned into both hands splayed wide on his bar, his sunglasses gone.

He had close-set, hooded eyes, and they were not the deep blue of his sons' and daughter's.

They were clear gray.

He was also staring at me.

"Who the fuck is this?"

I turned my head back to the couch and the belligerent twin was clearly the one who spoke.

Okay, since I'd done what my mother's intuition had told me to do, without thinking, and I was here—*now* what did I do?

But I knew.

I did what any mother would do in an uncertain, but intense situation.

I waded in…

And winged it.

"I'm Delphine," I told who I knew was Jesse. "Your new neighbor. And you're coming to dinner." I turned to Bohannan. "Six o'clock. Sharp."

He didn't hesitate a beat.

He said, "We'll be there."

ELEVEN

Whadaya Know?

I had a dilemma.

Because, by the time I'd raced back up to my house, dashed off a grocery list for dinner and got ready to roll out, I had to stop.

Because I had been to the grocery store in Misted Pine (once), so I knew where that was.

But I also had an FBI agent looking out for me when I did.

And I was supposed to have locals taking my back when I did it again.

But they were currently busy.

I called Delgado's team.

Elvira answered.

"I need to go to the grocery store," I told her.

"I bet you do," she murmured.

Her reply made one thing crystal clear: nothing got by that team.

Further indication, not that I needed it, that I'd chosen well.

"Give us ten," she said. "We'll call Moran."

Then she hung up.

But I made note there was someone I could trust within the local police, and that was hard-faced Moran.

I got a text in less than ten minutes that it was all clear to roll out.

So I did.

And when I did, it was 3:45.

This was not conducive to wowing anybody with my culinary artistry, of which I had a lot, by 6:00.

But I'd have to figure it out.

I did.

Sear-roasted pork tenderloin. Cheesy polenta. Asparagus. Fresh-baked bakery rolls. And for dessert, brownie bites with a Rolo shoved in the middle.

So the brownies were made from a box.

I had a feeling the Bohannans wouldn't complain.

I was pleased when the doorbell rang at 6:07.

Goldilocks.

Not too early.

Not too late.

Also, they didn't tramp up to the back door.

I went to the front, looked out my peephole (you couldn't be too careful, and I definitely couldn't be).

And froze.

I couldn't say I'd noticed the state of their grooming a few hours ago.

But now, all three of the men had hair still partially wet from showers. They were wearing button downs and clean jeans. And Celeste had changed into a dress.

I felt the need to start sobbing. Not crying. Not weeping. *Sobbing.*

I beat this need and opened the door.

"Welcome," I said, stepping back immediately to allow entry.

I'd had time to do the most important thing of the evening.

I'd figured it out.

I knew exactly how I was going to play it.

"Dinner's almost ready," I shared as they marched in, doing this in a manner that it wasn't the first time they had all shown as a family to my house when I was in said house. "We'll get some drinks and then I'll fill your stomachs."

I had thought about something else in the time since then and now, and it came to mind again as I watched them filter into my house.

Jason, Jesse and Celeste looked like brothers and sister, very much so, even if the boys' looks swung much closer to their father. And Bohannan had dominant features, so even though he didn't have them, somewhere in his genes, those blue eyes could come from him.

But Jason and Jesse were much older. I'd be shocked if they were under twenty-five. My guess would place them at twenty-eight or nine.

Celeste was either a late baby or there were two former Mrs. Bohannans floating around.

Or, I hated to think it and hoped it was not true (though, it might explain a few things), one former and one no longer of this world.

I did not comment on this.

I said to Jason, "I know you don't know me, even if you do. What there is to know now is that my home is a home, to everyone I know who has meaning to me. In that vein, would you get your dad and brother a drink, yourself and your sister too? I've got mine. There are some finishing touches I need to make on dinner."

"Sure," he agreed equably.

I nodded to him. "There's beer and all sorts in the fridge. If something harder is required, the liquor chest is over there, there's mixers and such in the cabinet."

I pointed into the living room.

He nodded.

I turned to Celeste. "And, honey, that pitcher of ice water on the counter, could you fill the water glasses on the table? Then refill the pitcher and set it on the table."

"On it," she decreed, practically jumping to do something that didn't have anything to do with carrying the heavy load she'd been carrying.

I moved to the French oven on the stove and the butter and parmesan beside it, saying, "Cade, I have a question for you."

The guard in his tone was almost entirely concealed, a herculean feat considering the circumstances, when he offered, "Shoot."

I glanced sideways at him standing on the other side of my bar and simply said, "David Ashbrook."

He dipped his chin and replied with equal simplicity, "Solid."

Okay then.

Good.

If he seemed to know what he was doing, I could hire Polly's nephew to help me with the house.

"As a rock," Jesse bit out with such acidity, my movements were wooden when I twisted to regard him standing next to his father opposite me at the bar. "His dad's a dick," he continued.

"Jess," Bohannan murmured.

"She should know. And she should hire him," he said to his father. Then to me, "He got Robyn pregnant in high school."

"Oh, well, I—" I didn't quite start.

"His dad told him to tell her to get rid of it. He told his dad it's her body, he wasn't gonna tell her to do shit."

When it came, it was quiet, but as this story unfolded, Bohannan sighed.

Jesse was undeterred.

"She was gonna get an abortion anyway, but ole Don wasn't gonna be *talked to like that* by *his son*, so he kicked him out. Robyn was sixteen. David wasn't yet eighteen. He lived with us for, I don't know, eight, nine months. By the way, she lost the baby."

I turned fully to Jesse.

He kept talking.

"He worked for some outfits, not ever long because his dad kept dicking with him, and his bosses couldn't be dealing with that shit. But he learned a lot because he's sharp. Robyn graduated and got an associate degree. She's a court reporter now, which is some serious cool. They got married a couple of years ago and whadaya know? They want a baby right away, because they're that couple. They just didn't want it when they weren't ready, as, you know, it's their freakin' *right*."

I had a sorry feeling I understood why Jesse was in such a bad mood, and it didn't have much to do with the dastardly fathering of Don Ashbrook.

Even with his mood, I still knew I liked Jesse very much.

And because of his mood, I remained quiet and listened.

"But she didn't lose the baby ten years ago because she was stressed or anything. She lost it because there's something up with her womb. Not my business," he shared, while sharing all David and Robyn Ashbrook's business. "But they been having troubles getting pregnant. They're over the freakin' moon the latest whatever-they-did worked. She's in her second trimester. She's taking a break from work because court reporting can be serious stress. Until the baby comes and after, she's being super careful. So they need money and David will break his back to do you right."

"I'm talking to him tomorrow," I said in a conciliatory tone.

"All right," he spat.

I looked him right in the eyes as I said, "You found her."

"Yes," he hissed.

"I'm sorry," I whispered.

He took such a strong sniff into his nostrils, they rested against his columella.

And his tone was much changed when he muttered, "Thanks."

My attention slid to Bohannan.

He was studying his son.

He felt my gaze, and his came to mine.

His shake of the head was barely a movement.

I still caught it.

Therefore, I announced, "Right! Dinner! Everyone sit. Cade, at the head, please. I'm at the foot. You boys and Celeste, you get your pick."

Bohannan and his sons took their beers, Celeste worked at my side to finish then dish up food and take it to the table, and we all settled.

We passed around platters and bowls.

I caught some looks being exchanged and declared, "I have a rule. You eat what you like in my house. If you don't like it, and you're still hungry when the meal is done, I'll make something else."

I nearly burst out laughing when, upon those words, Jesse scraped the asparagus off his plate back to the platter it had been presented on.

"Bro, you gotta consume green things," Jason admonished.

"I do, shamrock shakes when it's St. Patrick's Day," Jesse retorted.

I couldn't bite back that laugh.

"I like asparagus, Ms. Larue," Celeste piped in.

I glanced at Bohannan.

Another sigh, this one louder.

I looked back at Celeste. "Honey, please, I'm Delphine."

She glanced at her dad.

He inclined his head.

She smiled at me.

"Delphine."

That wasn't Celeste. Jason was calling me.

I turned to him and lifted my brows.

He was pointing at the polenta on his plate with his fork.

"What's this?"

I was about to answer when Jesse, mouth full of polenta, answered for me.

"It's boss, man."

"Polenta," I said quickly in order to get it in.

"Cool," Jason muttered, and bent to his food.

I looked at Bohannan, who was watching me.

My clitoris contracted.

My mouth opened.

"So, I've had a think on things, and I like it here. I'll probably be staying. And when I do, I'm running for the school board. I have a feeling my campaign will be successful. Anyone have any ideas about how our education system in Misted Pines can be improved?"

There was complete silence at the table.

And then Celeste, Jason, and even Jesse exploded with laughter.

Bohannan's beard twitched before he looked down to his plate and started eating.

TWELVE

The First

I was in my reading nook when I saw his shadow cross the window.

I wasn't surprised.

In fact, I was ready.

I set my book aside, got up, and in my thick socks and warm, knitted loungewear, I padded to the back doors in the living room.

I opened one.

Bohannan slid in.

There was a lamp on the kitchen counter lit, a small one. The glow was golden but didn't extend very far.

Without a word, Bohannan went to my armchair and sat on the arm.

I closed the door and stood at it.

His shoulders were slouched, his neck partly bent, but he turned his head to me.

"We got things to talk about."

To communicate I agreed, I moved to the arm of the couch, which was caddy-corner to him, and sat.

"Beer? Bourbon? Whisky? Vodka? Other?" I offered.

"I only drink beer. My dad was an alcoholic."

Boy.

That was forthcoming.

"So do you want a beer?"

"I don't drink it when I need it. I drink it whenever."

"Right."

He straightened, both his hands coming up, and he swiped them over the sleekness of his pulled-back hair.

He dropped them to his thighs.

"She was a man's woman," he declared.

We had a lot to talk about, I figured.

Though what he was saying, I did not understand, I was simply glad he was finally conversing (we could just say that Jason and I carried the dinner conversation, with some interjections from Celeste—Jesse had again started to brood, and more pieces had fallen, declaring that Bohannan, naturally, was just not a talker).

"I'm not following."

"Grace, my ex. Their mom."

Interesting place to start.

"Okay," I said encouragingly.

"She was good when she had three boys to spoil her. She was not so good when we accidentally got pregnant eleven years down the line, and it was a girl."

I sat straighter.

He didn't miss it.

"Yeah," he agreed.

"I…does that…I don't know, um…does that mean—?"

He put me out of my current misery by adding to it.

"That, when me and Jess and Jace fell in love with Celeste and acted like it, she lost her shit and eventually said it was either her or my daughter, and I picked my daughter, and that's why she's not around? Yeah. That's what it means."

"She…gave you an ultimatum…about your daughter?"

"It wasn't laid out like that. It was laid out like we spoil her. Or something. When, okay, maybe there was some of that, but it wasn't a lot. It wasn't unhealthy. Though, we'd done it unhealthy, what we gave to Grace. She was spoiled rotten. In the end, putrid with it. I thought she'd have her tantrum and get her shit together. She didn't. She left. Seein' as I'm good at finding things, I found her. When I did, she communicated that, unless things changed to her specifications, this being we sent Celeste away to attend school, she would decline to return. I declined to pack my daughter off to school because her mother is a bitch. That was five years ago. Celeste was eleven. The boys were twenty-two. Grace hasn't been back since. No calls. No cards. She could always hold a mean grudge, but this shit is something else."

It truly was.

Something else.

"And Celeste was young, but not so young she didn't sense why her mother was gone," I remarked, carefully concealing (I hoped) the revulsion I felt for his ex in my tone.

"No love there. Not Celeste. She's all about love. I mean Grace. She was never that kind of mom where she got into mom things. I didn't think that was weird. Not every mom is gonna be supermom from start to finish. She got in her groove though. She adored the boys."

At least there was that.

"She didn't want to be pregnant, not the first time, and the fact we made twins didn't help. Absolutely she didn't want it the second. But she was sure it would be a boy, so she thought, after we got through the bottles and diapers and potty training, and we got him to school, she'd have her life back. Like she did with the boys. Not that she did bottles or diapers or any of that shit. It made me sad for her. She missed out."

She missed out.

My heart squeezed.

"She'd also have someone else to kiss her ass, like we all did. Even with the ultrasound telling us it was a girl, Grace refused to believe it. Said it was an error. Said we'd see when he was here. I thought she was scared of havin' a kid she didn't know how to raise, since we were through a lot of it with the boys. Celeste came out, shit went south immediately."

I kind of wanted him to stop talking again.

Though, the pistachio velvet couch was explained.

"Although I appreciate you sharing this, Bohannan, I'm not certain why you are."

He didn't hesitate in giving it to me.

"She needs you and she needs that bad. So, I'm sharing this with you because my girl has been hurtin' for some kind of good woman to be in her life and show her the way. And she's been hurtin' for that since birth. And what happened today means she's decided it's you. She was gone for maybe five minutes before she was back. Five minutes more, you're at our door. We don't know you from boo. But you're at our goddamned door because my daughter needed you. Now, if you mean to stay and be that woman, I'm down with that. If you don't. If your situation resolves itself and you're out of here. You leave my daughter out of it."

And him being unimpressed with my diatribe the day we met, disallowing Celeste to stay with me and help unpack, was explained.

"I have two girls."

"I know you do."

"I would never harm Celeste."

"I don't think you get it."

"I think I do."

"You've been around her what? Three times?"

"I knew the instant I saw her because she's me. My mom wasn't into mom things either. She wanted an abortion, and I know that because she told me, I lost track of how many times. My dad did the right thing and married her, then he did the usual thing and left. He came back, around the time I hit the cover of *People* magazine. They both love me and are oh-so-proud of me, when neither of them has any clue if I like asparagus or have even tried it in all my fifty-three years."

Bohannan retreated to silence.

"I did not lie. I like it here. I liked it here before I met Celeste. My life is my own. I can't say I don't have commitments. I have two daughters. I have things I do. But when I say I won't harm Celeste, even if that means I won't be here every second of every day until I die, that means *I will move mountains not to harm Celeste.*"

Bohannan made no reply.

"So I got this," I asserted, and I had to admit, those words were firm and they held some affronted heat.

"Okay, babe," he whispered.

Angelo called me "babe."

I hated it, from the first time, and deep down, the thousands of times in between.

There was something connective about it with Bohannan.

Maybe it was because he used it while sharing that he trusted me with his daughter.

Yes.

That would be it.

Time to change subjects.

"Can you talk about it?" I asked.

"You don't want me to talk about it," he answered.

Oh God.

"Bohannan," I warned.

"I shouldn't have taken him," he muttered.

"Tell me."

"You don't wanna know."

"That bad?"

"Worse."

Oh God.

"Your boys work with you," I surmised.

"Yes. Jace is…his heart is more open. Shit digs in. Jesse's the rock. It isn't that he doesn't care or have empathy. It's just that, if Jason saw what Jesse saw, he'd be burning the woods down in the slim chance the fire would find this fuckin' guy. Jess can keep a lock on shit."

"Until now," I noted.

"Until now," he confirmed.

"You found her, not the guy?"

"We found her body. Not the guy."

Poisoned darts pierced my skin.

Everywhere.

"How are her parents?"

"Medicated."

"That's probably a good call," I mumbled.

"Chemistry boy?" he asked.

"Yes."

"Will Pulaski."

Ah hell.

Celeste's crush.

She was haunted by her mother leaving, and that was constant.

She was also haunted by her crush's sister having disappeared.

Though, one thing that shared, Celeste confided girl things in her father or one of her brothers, and they all stayed informed about Celeste's world.

Beautiful.

Button downs and dresses.

Bohannan.

Unable to contain it, I stood and demanded to know, "Why didn't they bring you in earlier?"

"Jace told me what happened when you went to the station, Delphine. So you get that Leland's got his head in his ass half the time, it's buried in other people's asses the rest of it. He's stupid. He's crooked. He's from an era that's like a goddamn cockroach. Men like him just never seem to die."

That was the sad truth.

"Me and the boys volunteered for the search party," he continued. "Dern sent us home."

Christ.

He continued, "I am not that man. I don't know. I don't get it. Competition? He doesn't wanna look bad? His last two elections, there were folks pressing me to run. Got no interest in that, didn't do it. Could be that. But if I had to give my take, I'd say it was just incompetence. Doesn't matter. I was already nosing around. Dale reached out almost immediately. It was just that shit wasn't official. Until it was."

I jerked around and stormed to the liquor cabinet.

He could abstain.

I needed a goddamn amaretto.

I got out the bottle and a snifter.

I poured.

A lot.

And sipped.

Then sipped again.

"After we find this one, Jesse wants to go after your guy," Bohannan announced.

I turned to him and finally asked what had been pressing on my mind since I met his sunglasses.

"Who are you?" I asked.

"Former Green Beret. Former FBI field agent. Former profiler. Current contractor."

"How did you find her?"

"I think like you."

That caught me short.

"What?" I whispered.

"But you don't take it further."

"*What?*" I said it as a demand that time.

"You saw the sunglasses, Delphine. You didn't take it further to wonder why I didn't take them off."

Holy cow.

He knew I could read him.

So he limited what I could read.

And now.

The lights were not on.

I could see him.

But barely.

Wow.

Taking this further, it was not a coincidence I was in this lake house.

The FBI took me on, I took on Joe Callahan and Hawk Delgado, and this house was suggested to me.

Not because it was remote and out of the way, and I was a nature girl, the former I needed, the latter I was.

Because it was close to Bohannan.

"I take it further. I always wonder why," he finished.

"Alice wasn't the only one." My voice was a horrified breath.

He shook his head and stood. "It's all not in. Responses to my queries. Fucked up how they don't talk to each other, keep a central database for this shit and requirements to feed things in. But at least the FBI has no reports and nothing local. Tri-Lakes. Adjacent counties. I got asks out farther afield. The state and entire northwest. But from what we know, she's the only one."

I let out my horrified breath.

But he wasn't done.

"And if she is, she's also the first."

Fuck.

I turned my head.

Then lifted my snifter and took another sip.

THIRTEEN

Viking

I'd paid for expedited shipping, so the rug, Adirondack chairs and tables I bought for the pier arrived quickly.

The deck furniture was from a more exclusive store. They said six to ten weeks.

I made a call to someone who made a call, and it would be there in two weeks.

One of the ways I was lucky to be me.

It was cold. Fall wasn't putting up much of a battle with winter.

But I also had a scrunchy new outdoor throw that was wrapped around me.

And I was out on the pier, you see, because I couldn't see the Bohannan compound, but it was reflected in the lake.

Therefore, when the Yukon showed, I was out of my chair and trotting up the wooden path that was part path and part stairs to the house.

I went in the back door.

My team in all their incarnations was right, David Ashbrook was solid.

And I was right, that big, wicker-domed light was phenomenal over the dining room table.

It transformed the space.

David took my closet design and said, "You don't need to order this. I can do it custom."

He was starting on the closet Monday.

I was beside myself with glee (about that).

But now?

Now, I put on some oven mitts and got the casserole out of the oven.

I walked it to the car.

The rest of the stuff was already in it.

So I got in myself, pulled out, drove down and parked beside the Yukon.

I grabbed the hot casserole first.

Celeste was sliding open the door before I got there.

She was still wearing a nice black sweater over a slim-fitting, black wool skirt and high boots.

"Set the oven to two hundred, lovely," I murmured as I squeezed by her. "We'll keep this warm."

She dashed to the Viking stove.

I followed her and saw her father enter the room from somewhere else (I had yet to get a tour of the house, though that was not my second time there).

Dark gray turtleneck, black trousers, hair not pulled back in a tail, but he had some product in it that kept it away from his face.

His son came in behind him.

Black sweater, blue button down under it, midnight blue trousers.

Jace.

"You gonna feed us 'til all's well in the world?" he teased.

"Maybe," I replied.

"Good, 'cause you cook the bomb."

Needless to say, I'd discovered my in.

For the past five days, I'd been feeding the Bohannans.

"More in the car?" Bohannan grunted.

I placed the casserole in the oven and straightened, turning to him and nodding.

Celeste made a move.

"Not you. You," he ordered Jace.

He didn't need to say that. Jason was already on his way to empty my car.

"On a scale of one to one thousand, how awful was it?" I asked Bohannan.

He leaned his ass against his marble countertop and crossed his arms on his chest.

"Ten thousand."

Considering we were talking about Alice's funeral, from which they'd just returned, that was better than I expected.

His gray gaze slid to his daughter. "You got homework to do?"

"Dad," she complained.

Important to note, Celeste liked to be involved.

In everything.

It was about the fact she clearly worshipped her brothers and had practically deified her father (when he wasn't punishing her for telling off a teacher or asking her to skedaddle because the adults needed to talk).

But fallout from a mother leaving when you're eleven and your house being filled with men— you became the woman of it.

She'd become the woman of it.

I supposed that wasn't a terrible thing. She'd need to take care of her own place one day, with roommates, and by herself, and eventually sharing that task with a partner.

It still filled me with rage.

But suffice it to say, she didn't like being left out.

And she hated to be treated like a kid.

"Fifteen minutes," he said.

She gave him a look. Shot me a look. Then she stomped off in that way only teenage girls could do, which was loud, but feminine, and annoying, but cute.

Bohannan took several beats while he listened with Dad Ears.

The door opened and Jace came in with the rest of the stuff.

I knew Celeste was out of ear shot, and Jason (as ever) was not out of the loop, when Bohannan asked, "You offer a reward for info on Alice?"

I stood silent and still.

I then stomped off, as only middle-aged women could do, not loud, not feminine, not cute, but determined.

I stood on their back deck.

I stared at the lake.

I clenched my teeth very hard.

When I understood I wouldn't scream in frustrated fury, I turned back and re-entered the house and kitchen.

"Feel better?" Jace asked.

"No," I answered.

"Yeah, Dern has a lasting effect on everyone," he muttered, lifting up a container I'd bought online yesterday, had overnighted, and filled not two hours before. "What are these?"

"What do they look like?"

"They look like cupcakes."

"Well deduced, Sherlock."

"Will you marry me?"

"I'm way too old for you."

"You have daughters."

"One's a lesbian and one's flying sorties in Korea and falling in love with a fighter pilot named James."

"First you give a guy cupcakes, then you destroy him."

"I'm sorry, that's the way life goes."

"Are you two done?" Bohannan broke in.

Another important note, Jason and I were bonding.

He was hysterically funny, and I liked people who were hysterically funny.

It was a win-win.

I turned back to his father.

"You seem to have a very diverse and accomplished skillset. Do you know how to commit the perfect murder?" I asked him.

"Yes," he answered.

That was it.

Further important note, in our late evening conversation five days ago, Cade Bohannan had used up his share of words for the next, I wasn't sure, but I was guessing probably two to three months.

As you could see, he had a reserve. But he was conserving them.

Jason grinned at me as he walked toward the doors to the deck.

With the cupcakes.

And now an aside, Jason and Jesse were roommates. They lived together in the house up the hill. A house Bohannan had built for them when they were twenty-two and both had shared that they intended to be his apprentices (my take, they didn't want to be far from their dad and sister after their mom flew the coop, but also, they wanted to follow in their father's footsteps), and therefore they weren't leaving home.

Bohannan felt kids needed to get out of the house.

Building one for them next door became the compromise.

David Ashbrook, incidentally, helped them build that house.

"That's all the cupcakes," I said to his back.

"I know, thanks," he returned, and disappeared out the door.

I turned again to his father.

"I half wish Fenn wasn't falling in love. Jason deserves her particular art of being a pain in the ass. And she deserves his."

"Babe, the entire fuckin' town knows about the reward."

I thought when Bohannan told me about it five minutes ago, that meant Dern had mentioned it to him.

Not everybody.

"Wait, *what?*" I demanded.

He jerked away from the counter when I made to stomp out again.

"Don't," he ordered tersely, holding up a hand. "It's Dern. You had to know that was not a good call."

"No, I had to do something."

"No, you didn't."

"Yes, I did."

"Larue."

"Bohannan."

He glowered at me.

Another aside, I'd started it, he'd jumped on board, and now we'd fallen into the habit of calling each other by our last names.

I'd always loved my first name. It was the only good thing my mother and father gave me. I used it to concoct extravagant fantasies when I was a little girl about living in Paris and wearing fabulous clothes and eating croissants and dating artists who wore berets. These fantasies took me away from the neglect and loneliness that limned my childhood.

But the way his growly voice wrapped around Larue, I hoped he never again called me Delphine.

He leaned back against the counter, resumed his crossed-arm pose and shared, "I had to inform the FBI. They were about as happy you did that as I am."

"I—"

"You are very, very safe here."

With this new tone to his voice—low and purring and dangerous and exciting—I was transfixed.

"You might not be as safe somewhere else," he went on. "Cut the crap, and for Christ's sake, lay low."

"I was speaking to the sheriff, and I told him that was an anonymous gesture. He promised me he would keep it to himself."

"You were talking to Dern. He's in deep shit because he's got a predator on his patch who mutilated a little girl, so he's gonna use everything he can to make that shit stink less, and he threw you right under that bus. Just you living in town is enough to turn people's minds. The fact you stepped up like that gives it warmth he's not getting. Me and Jace and Jess and David did what we could to get the word spread that you're here because you wanted a private retreat, away from people who treat you like a celebrity. Most folks in this town are gonna be good with that. They'll go to the mat to keep quiet and make things normal for you. But most folks are not *all* of them, and some of that rest would sell their grandmother's used underwear if they thought it'd get them a few bucks."

I made a face. "Gross."

"You, of all people, know I'm right."

I did.

My eyeballs studied the ceiling.

"It's a little freaky how much you remind me of Celeste."

I focused on him. "What a nice thing to say."

"I meant it in the way you act like a teenager."

"I'm deciding to take that as you find me girlish, which I've further decided to take as a compliment."

"Of course you have."

"If you're grouchy because your son stole all the cupcakes, don't take it out on me. You know where he lives."

He tipped his head back and I liked the way he studied the ceiling a lot better than how I did it.

One last important note, Cade Bohannan looked absurdly incredible in a turtleneck.

"Speaking of your sons, where's your other one?"

He righted his head and stated baldly, "Searching for a girl to bury his troubles in."

My mouth tightened.

"We had a convo. He told me to fuck off."

"Your daughter said much the same thing, and she was suspended for a week and grounded for two," I pointed out.

(Yes, I'd learned quite a bit about the Bohannans, that happened when you fed people—the patriarch might not be a font of information, but food loosened his kids' lips, or at least it did Jason's.)

"She's not an adult."

"Mm-hmm," I hummed, lacing the noise with how unconvinced I was by his lame defense.

Bohannan returned to unresponsive.

"I know it's none of my business," I began.

Bohannan re-entered the conversation. "You don't know that. You know it became your business when I agreed to bring my family to dinner."

I was taken aback.

But this needed to be confirmed, so I set about confirming it.

"Are you really giving me permission to meddle in your lives?"

He glanced pointedly at the Viking before looking back at me. "Are you really pretending you need permission?"

"Fair point," I mumbled.

"So what's none of your business?" he pushed.

This was serious, so I got serious.

"Jesse needs professional help."

He nodded. "I got someone I talk to. In my line of business, shit can get dark. This is some of the darkest shit I've ever seen. So yeah, he needs some tools to deal. I've trained both my boys, this was not edited from their training. He's just that fucked up by it."

"I usually hate to point out the obvious, but this is a problem."

Bohannan held my gaze.

And agreed, "Yeah, babe. This is a problem."

FOURTEEN

Silent Treatment

I stood on my back deck and punched my phone with my finger. I put it to my ear.

"What?" Bohannan greeted.

"I need to get out of here, or I'm going to kill somebody."

"David says that's the most complicated closet he's ever seen. David says even the Kardashians wouldn't dream up that closet. David says he's installed a dozen custom closets, and they've all taken one to four days. And David says yours might not be done until his kid graduates from college."

"I prefer you not talking."

"You can't ask a guy to build you a closet and then get hassled because it's noisy."

"And my clothes and shoes and handbags are strewn all over hell's half acre."

"I feel your pain."

He did?

"Do you like clothes?"

"No, I had a wife who liked them, and she'd lose her shit if I put the clothes away, and I hung something pink in the wrong shade of pink section."

"Not to defend a woman who walked out on you and your family, but that *is* a high crime in closet organization."

"I was happy to be guilty. My punishment was that I didn't have to put the clothes away."

"I sense a scam."

"Stop with the evasive maneuvers. You're under house arrest."

Why had I not worn sunglasses during our every interaction so he hadn't been allowed to read me?

And what was the equivalent of sunglasses when you were talking on the phone?

"Bohannan."

"The funeral was only a few days ago. Let Dern's shit die down before you start showing up around town."

"Bohannan, I can't avoid town *forever*."

"Give me three weeks."

God, I hoped they found my stalker in less than three weeks. It had already been way more than that.

And those women…

"I can't cook another meal," I informed him. "I can't believe I'm going to say this about the mastery I create in the kitchen, but I'm sick of my own food. I need to get out and not just to escape this closet. I haven't been out since I visited Dern, and that was no fun. Wait, no, the grocery store, but that doesn't count, because that was no fun either."

"Baby, I'm tryin' to find a kid killer."

I shut up because one, that was way more important than me escaping the noise and dust and piles of clothes, and two, he'd called me baby.

"Babe" was common. You called your girlfriends that. You could call the grocery store clerk that.

"Baby" was something else.

He had not once given any indication he was into me.

He ate my food. He watched me banter with his son. He allowed me to take some of the onus off his daughter.

That was it.

In large part, I'd left the public life.

Every year, my agent and I selected—from the hundreds of requests we received—a half a dozen high schools and universities for me to visit to talk about *We Pluck the Cord*.

Other than that, nothing.

Yearly, and sometimes more often, I got requests to do reunions or make a movie or star in the first episode of a reboot of *Those Years*, and I always turned it down.

Incidentally, this was to my costar, Michael's, extreme displeasure.

Constantly, I had offers to do other things. TV shows. Movies. Advertisements.

I turned those down too.

I was not a recluse, but I was private.

It was the enduring love for that show and the reach of the book that kept me rather forefront in the public conscious.

That, and the fact I'd married a still box-office-topping action star (Warren) and a rock 'n' roll legend (Angelo), and whenever they did something—and they were always doing something—my name got dragged into it.

Which made it all the more important to keep the work I currently did strictly secret.

I shared all of this because I was no longer an actress. For all anyone knew, I wasn't anything (even though I was).

What I was, was vain.

I blamed my mother because it was all her fault.

She was vain.

She was about being slim and in shape and perfectly put together *at all times*. She was about the right shoes and purse combo. She was about perfecting the art of the Just Nipping Out Look so you never left the house without your face on, even if it wasn't the normal effort you put into making up your face. She was about moisturizing your skin from an early age to combat future lines and drinking enough water to do the same thing and shouting at me when I didn't let her sleep because I had to, say, get to school or something (and sleep helped you combat lines).

I wasn't certain while growing up if she very much cared if I lived or died.

But she took the time and effort to drill all of that into me.

I might not be as slim as I was when I was younger, but I'd taken pains to keep hold on what I could for as long as I could.

What I was not, was a striking classic beauty, like Celeste.

And although Bohannan was tall, built and attractive, he was not classically handsome or conventionally so either.

Celeste got that from somewhere.

Which meant she got it from Grace.

I was also trouble for a man, even when I didn't have a psychotic stalker out there holding two women hostage until I agreed to marry him (though, I was sure it didn't say, "I love you," to send a bomb in the post to my dear friend and ex costar, Alicia's house; poison my other dear friend and ex costar, Russ's dog (don't despair, Russ noticed Bookworm acting weird and got him to the vet just in time); or send disturbing pictures of men with their members cut off to Michael, who had been my love interest and eventual husband on the show).

But it had to be said, that was a lot.

Though it was more.

I was independently wealthy.

I was highly successful.

It was widely considered that I was very talented in two high-profile fields.

And many men didn't like it like that.

So I could have the greatest ass in the world (and I kind of did) and perky tits until I died (and I had those too, now, only because of a reconstructive boob job I got a couple of years after I had Camille), these two things being valued very highly by the opposite sex, and I'd still be toxic.

"Okay, fuck, fine," he said, cutting into my reverie.

"Fine?"

"Don't cook. We'll go to the Double D tonight."

"Am I…getting my way?" I asked tentatively.

"Are we going out tonight?"

Were we?

"I'll tell the kids to prepare. The Double D is a three-course meal for Jace and a four-course one for Jesse," he shared. "They'll be pissed they eat something and fill up before we go."

So *we* weren't, but we were.

And why, when it was far from normal, did I like it so much that his family was so close, to the point he thought of going out to dinner and his grown sons were invited.

"Let me get this straight," I started. "I gave you the silent treatment for I don't know, what? Maybe ten seconds? And you caved?"

He said nothing.

"You do know I've filed that away in the special vault only females have that's hermetically sealed and preserves things for eternity, right?"

"We'll swing around and pick you up at seven thirty," was his reply. "Don't kill David in the meantime, and if you need a break, I got a TV. Come down. I'll get Jace to come home and let you in."

And then he hung up.

I heard a drill coming from inside my house.

Which meant I texted, *I'll be waiting outside your door in ten minutes.*

Bohannan didn't respond to the text.

But Jason was there to let me in ten minutes later.

FIFTEEN

Double D

"As you know, I'll start with a vanilla malt."

We hadn't even made it to a table when Jesse called this out toward the horseshoe-shaped, Roseanne's Lunch Box counter in the middle of the Double D Diner.

"You got it, bub," a tall, curvy woman with platinum blond hair, a dab hand with a teasing comb and an artist's touch with eyeliner called back.

I thought this place was great, I wanted a vanilla malt, I was so excited not to be at my house (or theirs), I could spit, so I was surprised when I heard Jace mutter, "Oh shit."

"Just ignore her," Bohannan muttered back.

"That never works," Jace replied.

Jesse was leading us inescapably toward a corner booth covered in red vinyl with baby-blue edging that was almost a circle, and with the easy manner they all migrated to it, it was obviously their regular haunt.

I was *taking it further*, seeing that my seven thirty pickup time was about the fact it was now almost eight, and this meant not only would we all be hungry, the diner would be mostly cleared out. There were only a couple of patrons there.

Fewer people to see Delphine Larue out and about.

More control of the situation for Bohannan.

And then, before I could ask what Jace and Bohannan were talking about, something happened.

Jesse held back, Jace stood to the side, and in a way I wasn't sure I experienced what I'd just experienced, Bohannan scooted us into the large booth so Celeste and I were crunched together at the back. Bohannan was practically glued to my right side, and Jesse and Jason sat sentry, nearly falling off the ends of the bench seat.

And yet *more* control of the situation for Bohannan.

Further, an explanation of why his grown sons were invited to dinner (maybe).

However, this seemed overkill.

So I stage-whispered to Bohannan, "Are you packing?"

Celeste giggled.

"*Cade Bohannan!*"

I jumped.

Okay, maybe not overkill?

"Told you it was gonna be bad," Jason muttered.

"Kimmy! What's shakin'?" Jesse asked as a woman wearing a Christmas cardigan (and it was October) and jingle-bell earrings (again, it was October), with a green and red foil-wrapping-bow headband in her hair stopped at the end of our table.

I tensed.

She didn't spare me a glance.

Or Jesse, who'd spoken to her, for that matter.

She only had eyes for Bohannan.

"Are you finally interested in hearing what I have to tell you?" she asked him.

"Kimmy, we've had this conversation," Bohannan replied with studied patience, which, *taking that further*, meant they'd had it many times.

"But you never *listen*."

Then Bohannan said, "They're all dead."

The woman leaned forward.

I pressed into him and grabbed his thigh.

"There's no statute of limitation for *murder*," she snapped.

My fingers dug in.

"The FBI *needs to know*." She was getting shrill.

"Kimmy, why don't you tell me," Jesse offered.

She turned to him, openly offended. "You don't even know who John F. Kennedy was."

"Yes, I do. He was the thirty-fifth president of these United States, assassinated on November twenty-second, 1963, in Dallas, Texas. He was a member of the Democratic Party. The Bay of Pigs was not his best call. But his handling of the Cuban Missile Crisis rocked. Oh…and his wife was hot."

Christmas lady appeared vaguely impressed.

"Do you know who killed him?" she sniffed.

"I know you know," Jess returned.

"I *do* know," she declared.

Jesse slid out of the booth, deftly taking the vanilla malt out of the hands of the approaching waitress as he led Christmas lady to the bar, saying, "If we're gonna do anything about it, then I need to know too."

The platinum-haired waitress waited until they hit the bar before she told Bohannan. "She's gonna be real pissed when Fidel Castro's ghost doesn't stand trial on Court TV."

Bohannan covered my hand with his, gave it a squeeze, and I decided maybe I should let go.

I did.

And he did.

Which was disappointing.

The waitress pointed the eraser of a pencil to Jace. "You. Fried mushrooms. Reuben with waffle fries. And apple pie, two scoops of cinnamon-vanilla à la mode."

"Nailed it," Jason replied.

"You." She aimed the eraser at Celeste. "I think you're feeling northwest burger tonight."

"You always know what I want, Heidi," Celeste replied.

"Are we waffle fries or curly fries?" she asked Celeste.

"Curly."

"Gotcha. You." It was Bohannan's turn. "Chicken fried steak, extra potatoes and gravy."

Bohannan just grunted his affirmative.

Her attention came to me. "You're new, and if you order salad, I'm gonna warn you, I got lettuce, but I don't remember the last time we switched it out."

Wasn't it a mortal sin to go to a diner and order a salad?

"I want to start with a vanilla malt as I peruse the menu," I told her. "But please, don't hold everyone else's food. I can catch up. Also, please tell me you do a patty melt."

She did not answer me.

She gazed around the diner.

Which was her answer.

No diner worth its salt didn't serve a patty melt.

She then turned to Bohannan. "I approve. Now, will you please tell Kimmy the mob killed Kennedy?"

Bohannan's beard semi-smiled.

"Tra-la," she said and moseyed away.

"I love it here," I declared, reaching for one of the ginormous trifold laminated menus stuck between the napkin holder and the ketchup and mustard squirty things.

"Their patty melt is really good," Celeste told me.

"What's the northwest burger?" I asked.

"Just a regular burger with cheddar cheese that's made at a local farm."

"Yum."

"I'm not a very adventurous eater," she admitted.

"Is that a prerequisite to get into hair styling school?" I asked.

She giggled again. "I don't think so."

"Then don't worry about it."

"I bet you've eaten in a lot of fancy places."

"I once spent four thousand dollars to sit for four hours and watch a chef cook all thirty-three teeny-tiny courses I ate, ending in him fanning a river of chocolate over dry ice in front of us and carving each of us a personalized, very pretty chocolate bar."

"Wow."

"And I think the best thing I've ever eaten is a fried pork tenderloin sandwich I got in a greasy spoon in Dubuque."

"Really?" she asked.

"I'm not lying," I answered.

"That must have been a great sandwich."

"If I try real hard, I can still taste it."

She rested some of her weight against me before she pulled away.

Bohannan lifted his arm over my head and draped it on the back of the booth.

Jesse returned.

After resuming his sentry position, he declared, "I think I have to take a break from hunting this psycho to go down to Cuba."

"I'll be waiting for your call, Jesse Bohannan!" Kimmy yelled across the diner from her place at the door.

"I'm on it, Kimmy!" Jesse lied.

She glared at him then pushed out using more strength on the door than she needed.

The bell over it rang, and I could swear I heard the tinkle of her jingle bell earrings too.

It was official.

I was never leaving Misted Pines.

SIXTEEN

Elephant

I woke, petrified.

The dark pressed on me.

Celeste's weight was a ghost resting against my side.

He was out there.

He was out there.

Not here, but *out there.*

I turned, reached for my phone, lifted it from its charger and engaged it.

I ignored the light from the screen assaulting my eyes and found the number.

She was in my time zone.

A glance at my clock said it was 2:37 in the morning.

I did not care.

She was trained. Her phone rang only twice before she answered, sounding fully alert.

"Ms. Larue."

"I need to be moved," I announced.

Agent Palmer said nothing.

"The town knows about me," I noted.

"Yes, they do. And your team has assessed this, and we feel, as that has stayed under wraps, that you continue to be safe right now."

"Those women," I whispered.

"Ms. Larue."

"What's being done?" I demanded.

"You've done so well so far," she muttered.

"What is being *done*, Agent Palmer?"

"What he's doing is not your responsibility," she said firmly.

"You do get you can say that. Freud could come alive, knock on my door, lay me on my couch and say that. Birds can start speaking English and say that. And I will still feel responsibility for *what he's doing to those women*."

"Your service reported those letters by the time you received your third one. We were aware of his tenacity. He gave no indication this would escalate as it did. And you'll remember, Ms. Larue, that one day, it was your usual marriage proposal, same stationary, same exact words, almost like it was a tick, a habit he'd gotten into that was something he compulsively needed to do to live out his week, and then he was sending bombs and poisoning dogs and kidnapping women. We were all caught unaware."

"You haven't answered about what's being done."

"She shouldn't have come visit you," she mumbled.

I knew exactly what she meant by that.

"This isn't on Celeste," I snapped.

"She's safer than you are, and you're extremely safe."

I felt my heart settle because that was the truth.

But it didn't settle enough.

"Listen, it's not protocol to share this," Agent Palmer continued. "But when Bohannan was brought on board, he looked at your case, he did it thoroughly and he worked up a profile. This opened new avenues to the investigation, and we are…we feel we're…" A long pause during which the specter of Celeste's weight leaning against my side began to feel as heavy as an elephant. "We feel we might be close."

"I think I need to leave the country."

"Please, try to get some sleep, Ms. Larue. And if you're still feeling that way tomorrow, the next day, we'll talk again."

I said nothing.

"This isn't protocol to say either, but you have the best in the business at your back, Ms. Larue. And I'm not blowing sunshine."

I sensed that.

It didn't help.

"I'm sorry I woke you," I said shortly.

"Try to get some rest," she replied.

We hung up.

I put the phone back on the charge and stared into the dark.

My phone rang.

The screen told me Agent Palmer had a big mouth.

I picked it up and engaged it.

"I'm fine."

"I'm coming over," Bohannan growled.

I opened my mouth to speak but there was no one there to listen.

He'd hung up.

I turned on the bedside light, got up, slipped on my slippers, went to the armchair, pulled on my cardigan and left the room.

I went downstairs, turned on the little lamp on the kitchen bar, both ones on the table behind the couch, and went to hit the outside lights at the back.

I then stood by the security panel, and when I saw him coming, I disarmed it, walked to the door and opened it so he didn't have to break stride as he stalked across the deck and into my house.

This I accomplished.

I closed the door and turned to him to see he was turned on me.

"What's the matter?" he demanded.

"She shouldn't have called you," I replied.

"I'm the lead on your local detail. You're making noises about switching your location. This means you're getting agitated. Agitated is not a good state for anybody, and not something any security detail will take lightly. She'd be reprimanded if she didn't call me."

Huh.

"What's the matter?" he repeated. "What's happened?"

"I lied about being that person for Celeste. Not a *lie* lie, but a lie. I'm going to have to go, and after he's caught, come back."

"From now on, Jace, Jess or me are sleeping on your couch."

"*No!*" I cried.

He didn't speak.

"That leaves her even less protected."

"No one is going to harm my daughter."

At this new tone—flinty and terrifying—about one hundred and fifty pieces flew together and landed in his puzzle.

I shouldn't have turned on the lights. I did it to read him.

But I knew he was reading me when he ordered, "Come here."

"He's hurting them," I whispered.

"Larue, come here."

"You saw the pictures. Agent Palmer told me you'd looked at my file."

"I'm going to touch you in a second."

I didn't move.

He came to me and wrapped his arms around me.

His body was like his thigh, warm and hard.

I dissolved.

He held me up.

"They need to find him," I sobbed into his chest.

"They'll find him," he murmured, one of his hands gliding up, going under my hair, curling around the back of my neck, his other arm sliding further along my back, pulling me deeper into him.

"I have nightmares."

"Okay."

"If it wasn't for me—"

"He'd fixate on someone else. C'mon, Larue. You know this. It's his damage. If it wasn't those women, it'd be other ones for some other reason he became obsessed. He was cracked, set to break. He broke, and it had nothing to do with you."

I took a ragged breath.

"Is Celeste by herself right now?"

"Jess and Jace were gearing up in front of the Xbox when I was walking out the door."

I relaxed.

"You profiled him?"

His fingers and arm squeezed. "We're not talkin' about that."

I closed my mouth.

I opened it to say, "But you did?"

"Yeah."

"Is he going to kill them?"

"Larue."

"Tell me."

A sigh so deep, my body moved several inches as he did it.

And then, "With you inaccessible, the others disappeared, his frustration will be mounting, and if they don't find him in say, the next week…yes."

I shoved my face in his chest.

"And he'll get new ones," I mumbled.

"Yes."

I tipped my head back, his beard came down, and I got that clear gray.

"Are they gonna find him?"

His gaze didn't leave mine.

And he said, "Yes."

SEVENTEEN

Dark

"I never thought in my entire life I would say this, but I want one of these."

Jesse and I were standing in my glorious, brand-spanking-new closet.

David was in my office, painting.

My new desk would arrive in two days.

Which was good, because if I could sort my head out, it was time to get to work.

"I don't know. I'm thinking maybe I should have torn down a wall," I replied.

"The only wall you could tear down leads to a bedroom."

I looked at him. "Yes."

Jesse was very sharp, like his father, like his brother, but it took him a second to process the fact I was lamenting that I didn't make my closet, which was already the size of a room, into a closet that was bigger than the master bedroom.

But when he processed it, he started to laugh.

It was time.

"It takes the sneak out of the attack to warn you, but I'm about to perpetuate a sneak attack."

He stopped laughing.

I put it out there.

"It takes one to know one, and you're an excellent actor."

"Delphine," he muttered.

Right there.

Sharp.

"Your sister is worried, and your father needs you. You can't be messing around with this, Jesse. People are depending on you now, and more will in the future. You have to take care of yourself."

He looked angry, very, and like his father (and I suspected his brother), he was not the guy to let that loose on me.

Therefore, he turned to leave.

"Don't walk away from me," I commanded in Mom Voice.

He got the voice and pivoted to me.

"You aren't my mother, and newsflash, you aren't Celeste's either. I don't give a fuck how many dinners you make us. We barely know you."

Okay, maybe I was wrong about him not letting loose on me.

But I could take it.

"No, I'm not. I'm your neighbor. I'm your friend. I've grown to care about all of you. A good deal. And I can tell you, living in the purgatory I'm currently occupying, and that purgatory revolves around two females I've never met and likely, for their mental health, never will, I get something you don't. So I can say with some authority, considering it was their daughter, regardless of the outcome, it is so much better for the Pulaskis to know where Alice is than if she was never found. For you, the job is undone. Them as well. They want justice even more than you do. But for them, you've given something precious. It is not a treasured gift, but it's a gift nonetheless. Now, you have to keep yourself together to finish the job."

Jesse nor Jason had beards, just the scruff of two men who weren't fond of shaving.

So the muscle racing up his cheek was unhidden.

"You do know how much it says about you that what you found has affected you so," I said in a gentler tone.

"You'd have to be that fuckin' guy for that shit not to twist you up," he bit off.

"Do you want to tell me about it?"

He looked appalled. "And give it to you?"

"Yes."

His body listed.

It started with a dip of the shoulder and ended with his chin lazily drifting to the side.

Through this, he stared at me.

Because through this, puzzle pieces were landing.

For Jesse.

About me.

"I'll talk to somebody," he said quietly.

I released a breath.

"I don't know…" he began but didn't finish.

"Yes?"

"I don't know…"

I waited patiently.

Shame filtered through as he admitted, "I don't know if I can finish this job."

"Your father will understand."

"We find him, I'll kill him."

"Your father will understand."

"The things he did to her."

My stomach hurt.

"Your father, Jesse, honey, will understand."

"He shouldn't have to do this alone."

"He knows how to deal."

"Does he, Delphine?"

I nearly gagged, my mouth filled with saliva so fast at the same time my throat closed.

"He's got years of seeing shit like that and hunting the monsters who do it," Jesse continued.

"Do you sense that he—?"

"What is dark on dark?"

"Dark."

"How much dark can someone absorb before they're consumed by it?"

"Jesse, do you sense your father is having issues dealing with this case or his work?" I demanded.

"He's human."

"And I offer this with great care, but you might be projecting."

"You didn't see her, Delphine. He did."

I didn't say anything or move.

Jesse didn't say anything or move.

That bad?

Worse.

He turned to gaze out the window.

I did the same.

That window was a bonus to the closet. It even had a window seat. David knew a talented seamstress in town, I'd ordered some material online, and she was making a fitted pad and some toss pillows for it.

Considering the age of the house, I couldn't imagine this closet was fit for purpose. That room was meant to be a nursery, a studio, a reading nook.

Why the old guy who lived there before me, considering a wife or partner was never mentioned, made it into a closet, I didn't know.

I didn't care.

It had room for an island, which David had also crafted. He'd found a beautiful antique bureau, gleamed it up, and in a clever way that made it seem like that was how it had always been, he'd added onto it at the sides and back. Now it had boxes for shoes or scarves, and shelves at the back for sweaters and folded jeans. He'd also located an offcut of marble to put on the top.

It was divine.

When I'd first seen the island, which had come only after David had looked at my closet design and said, "Trust me," and then I found out he had a hobby/side business of repurposing old furniture, I marveled at all the varied signs that pointed me to Misted Pines.

I knew without a doubt that piece would be worth thousands of dollars in LA.

And yet there it was, crafted in David's garage in his free evening hours, just for me, and it wasn't cheap, but it wasn't what he'd get in the big city.

"Celeste is worried about him too, you know," Jesse informed me.

That cinched it.

"I'll talk to him," I said.

I then jumped.

Because Jesse moved, coming to me, giving me a brief, tight hug, letting me go, and then he walked away.

EIGHTEEN

A Fan

My conversation with Jesse was two days after my conversations with Agent Palmer and Bohannan.

And now, it was two days after that.

I was on edge, because this meant the week that Bohannan had given it before my stalker killed his hostages was coming to an end.

I was on edge because I figured this two-day thing was a good pattern, and it was now a good time to assess where Bohannan was at mentally in dealing with the murder of Alice Pulaski.

As yet, I'd heard no word that Jesse had extricated himself from the investigation, which, considering the boys never shared anything about the investigation with me, wasn't a surprise.

I had also not heard if Jesse had sought someone to talk to, but as he'd told me he'd do this, I had every faith he had, and from now on, that was none of my business.

I was also on edge because Bohannan was over to my place for dinner, and although he had brooked no further argument, and either Jason or Jesse slept on my couch since he said they were going to (and I had a feeling he stayed home so I wouldn't freak about Celeste not being under his personal watch), now was the first time he was over for dinner alone.

And last, I was on edge because Bohannan played his cards close to his chest. I was getting a better bead on him, but I wasn't even close to focused, and still…he wasn't hiding that *he* was on edge.

So, of course, I stood across from him where he was seated at my bar, in each of my hands I held a plate covered in salmon and lemon couscous, and I threatened, "I'm throwing these in your face if you don't tell me what's going on."

"Celeste is out on a date."

Instantly distraught, I let both hands drop so the backs of them were lying on the counter, the plates on top.

Bohannan reached out, took one and put it on the placemat beside him, then the other, and put it before him.

"Bohannan," I warned.

"Don't worry, Jess is trailing her."

I glared.

"And Jace is trailing him."

I relaxed.

Then I tensed again.

"Is it Will?"

He nodded.

Now, I was hurt.

"When did this happen?" I asked, wounded that Celeste hadn't told me.

She was a communicator of the Cade Bohannan variety, not like Jace and Jess, who both knew how to express themselves somewhat openly.

But she still shared, mostly through texts, things like, *Do we really need algebra in real life?* (to which, obviously, I replied, *No*), and *Do you think I'd look good in red lipstick?* (to which, obviously, I replied, *Everyone looks good in red lipstick*), and *When are we starting dinner tonight?* (which, obviously, meant she'd started cooking with me).

News of this import, I thought she'd give to me.

"It's okay, baby," Bohannan said gently. "It came as a surprise to her too. I guess he upped and asked her in chemistry today. She said yes, obviously. They got a malt after school at the Double D, went to a movie, and they're having dinner after."

Well then.

That meant she might not have had time to tell me.

"That's a marathon date."

"Figure the kid needs not to be home."

I'd lay money on that being right.

But…

I studied him.

Wait.

Oh boy.

"What?" I asked.

"Are you gonna sit down beside me so we can eat?"

I rounded the counter and sat down beside him.

I even picked up my fork.

Then I turned to him and repeated, "What?"

His eyes moved over my face.

I waited impatiently.

As such, I lost my patience.

"Bohannan, *what*?"

"Kid's solid. Dale's a decent guy. The wife though," he murmured.

I twisted to him. "Alice's mother?"

"Dale cheated."

The plot thickens.

"Go on."

"They worked together. Audrey got pregnant. Dale divorced Will's mom, married Audrey. Didn't hide it so much that he did it because he thought it was the right thing for his unborn daughter. They had Alice."

This put into question the *Tri-Lake Chronicle's* depiction of them being as a church-going, close-knit family.

They could go to church and probably did.

The close-knit part though?

"Well…shit," I whispered.

"Uh-huh," he agreed.

"Does he love her?"

Bohannan shoved salmon in his mouth and gave me a side eye.

He didn't love her.

Close-knit was out the window.

"Where's the first wife?"

"In town."

"Bitter? Vengeful?"

"Hurt. Reclusive. Wondering what she did wrong."

"Still? After eight years?"

"Still," Bohannan confirmed. "After eight years."

That was losing-the-love-of-your-life kind of grieving.

I sat up. "Right. Now I'm getting pissed."

"Sarah wouldn't harm a fly. Literally. I've seen her shoo them out of the house."

"Not about that."

Bohannan turned to me. "I'm not gonna defend a guy who stepped out on his wife. I will say, he got his punishment."

"Audrey isn't cool?"

"Audrey's known wide as a woman who gets what she wants."

"Pregnancy a trap?"

"Generally accepted it was."

"Was he unaware he wasn't shooting blanks?" I asked sarcastically.

"I'm not exonerating him, Larue. He loved his first wife. He told me that a couple of nights ago, drunk and fucked up pretty much beyond recognition, and the fucked-up part wasn't about the drink. Why he dipped his wick elsewhere, I don't know. He says *he* doesn't know. Though, that's now, after nine years with his current wife and without the one he loved in his life. Bet if I asked nine years ago, he'd have a reason. And it wouldn't be about Sarah, even though he'd tell himself it was. It'd be about him being weak."

Considering my own history, and the fact that Bohannan had a dick (I assumed—alas, I hadn't seen it), I asked a question I'd been longing to ask a man for thirty years.

"Why do you guys do that?"

I nearly reared back at the look on his face.

"What guys?"

"Okay, I'll rephrase. Why do *some* guys do that?"

He turned to his plate, muttered, "Better," and shoved salmon in his mouth.

Damn it all to hell.

I could fall in love with this man.

Crap.

"So?" I pushed.

He chewed, swallowed and turned back to me. "How do I know? I loved my wife. I fucked my wife. Didn't stop attractive women being in my life, but I didn't fuck them. Didn't occur to me. So I can't begin to answer that."

Seriously?

"Are you for real?"

"Yes."

"Okay, take a stab," I pressed.

"I already did."

"What?"

"Weak."

"Oh. Yeah. You did say that," I mumbled, finally turning to my food.

"Commit is the root of the word commitment," he stated as I shoved in some salmon and couscous. "Some people find that hard. Just the word seems like it's supposed to be work. You commit to a workout regime. You commit to a diet. You commit to earning a degree. You commit to a career. The way I see it, when you're talking about a relationship, you don't do it unless you feel it. If that means half the population of the planet didn't commit to a partner, world would be better for it. Hearts gone unbroken."

More pieces falling: Bohannan was a sage.

He kept giving me that.

"I hate the word commitment used about a relationship. It's inaccurate. You're with someone because you want to be with someone. A relationship is not a diet or a contract with an employer or a goal to be attained. It's based, or it should be based, solely on feeling, intuition, attraction. It might be my inability to identify with someone who doesn't think the same way I do, but unless you feel it, *really feel it*, you've got no business making a promise to another human being. The 'work' it's supposed to be to keep a relationship strong will fail if you don't have the foundation to be in that relationship in the first place, be it the strength of your feeling for them, or the strength of character to do right by them."

I sat silent and enthralled.

"I spent twenty-five years of my life with Grace. She wasn't perfect. I'm not perfect. Our issues were severe as we closed in on the end, and I not once thought we couldn't clear them. When she left and refused to come home, a piece of me went with her that I'll never get back."

"Honey," I whispered.

It was like I said nothing.

He kept going.

"Went to a seminar given by a psychiatrist. He said as animals, monogamy is not in our genes. He said in the beginning, when that concept was formed, you were lucky to live to the age of forty, so it wasn't as hard as it is now. But mostly, he said, the idea was created so men would know the children they sired on a woman were theirs. Also, so men could use the idea of exclusivity against women for a variety of reasons, when for the most part they ignored the concept was supposed to adhere to them as well."

Bohannan took a break from bestowing his wisdom on me to down some of his drink, and then he carried on.

"From the things this doc said, it's easy to follow the path of centuries of men getting away with it, and society condoning that in deed if not word, but something more was expected from women, as in they were not allowed to get away with it. A 'good woman' was expected to be pure and chaste and faithful. Relics of all of this still exist in the societal ideologies today. This being the answer to your question."

I decided not to say anything and simply let my eyes scream, *See!*

Bohannan read my eyes, his beard twitched, then he used the lips buried in it to go on and declare, "But bottom line, this doc said monogamy isn't natural in our species. And to that, I call bullshit. I don't give a fuck about history or philosophy or the male of a species needing to know about his offspring. If you love somebody, if you pledged your life to them, you don't fuck around on them. The end."

My eyes were no longer screaming, but my heart felt loud due to the fact it was beating incredibly hard.

"I don't think you're normal, Bohannan."

He turned fully to me. "I'm a fan, you know."

I was confused. "Sorry?"

"Watched your show. All ten years. You have great hair. A better ass. And a cute smile. Grace liked the show too. She watched for you. She liked your clothes and thought you were funny. I watched for you too."

I didn't know what to say, but if I did, my heart still pounding in my chest taking all my attention, I wouldn't have been able to say it.

"She got your book because she was a fan. But she wasn't a reader. I don't think she read it. I did. It changed my life."

Wow.

"Bohannan," I breathed.

"I should have known you'd be this person. Only someone who understands the human condition as the prism it is could write that book. It made me go to my bureau chief. It made me ask to be transferred. It eventually made me a profiler. I wanted to understand the human condition like you do."

A tear slid down my cheek.

His arm came out, he cupped that cheek in his palm, his thumb sliding the wet away.

"It made me move back here, home, to Misted Pines, after I left the Bureau. It led me on an exhaustive search to find the right corner of this country, until I learned that returning to my hometown would be where my daughter's first date with her big crush is started with a malt at the local diner and a movie. In part, you gave me my career, and until Alice, you guided my way to giving sanctuary to my family."

Another tear fell.

His thumb swept it away.

And his voice was low when he perpetrated his own sneak attack.

But he was far better at it.

"Right now, a team is going in to capture a man named Bob Welsh and to rescue his two hostages. I'm how I am right now because my daughter is on a date with a boy whose sister was murdered, and I'm waiting for a call from the FBI to tell me your situation is over."

Now, I was panting.

He slid the pad of his thumb under my eye again and leaned slightly toward me.

"Now, Larue, I need you to eat your dinner and drink your wine and keep your shit. Celeste will come home messed up, because she likes this boy and she's too good of a person, she takes on hurt and it doesn't do her favors. So she's gonna need us. And you being free is going to tweak her, because she's terrified you're gonna leave."

"I'm not going anywhere."

"I know."

"They're sure it's the guy?"

"Yes."

"Your profile," I deduced.

"Partly."

"Don't be modest."

"Shit like this is always a team. That's why Dern is such a fuckup. Or one of the reasons."

"Right."

"Your husbands?"

I just stared at him.

He gave it to me.

"They were weak. They were stupid. And I can guarantee they've spent the years in between putting a lot of effort into ignoring that voice in their heads that's telling them the truth. They made the biggest mistake in their lives, losing you."

"What's happening here?" I whispered.

"You're feelin' me out because you don't wanna get hurt again. I'm feeling you out because I don't wanna get hurt again, and I can't have my kids dragged through shit like that."

"You're into me?"

His heavy brows knitted.

"You're into me," I mumbled.

"There's also the sitch that I'm getting paid to look out for you, which is why my sons are taking turns on your couch, because if I had a turn, I wouldn't be on your couch. Distractions like that lead to mistakes that I'd never be okay making. With you, absolutely not gonna happen."

Oh my.

"This guy is getting caught tonight, Larue."

He said that like a warning, his hand sliding away from my face.

I took it another way entirely.

That was the reason why I smiled.

NINETEEN

Nervous

Later that night, we were on Bohannan's pier for two reasons.

One, his daughter's curfew was soon.

Two, he had a loveseat Adirondack chair on his deck.

Just around the hook of the trees, I could see the lights of my house reflected on the mist that had formed on the lake, precisely like I could see the lights of his when I was on my pier in the evenings.

Any further sign of humanity was much farther away.

"I know it's fall, and cold, but it's weird that those two rentals haven't been booked the entire time I've been here," I remarked.

"It isn't, considering I own them, and I cancelled the bookings when you came to town."

I was sitting beside him, not nestled into him as I would've liked to be after his spectacular speeches during dinner, but he had his arm around my shoulders and there was closeness.

I didn't want to mess with that, so I twisted only my neck to look at him.

"What?"

"I own everything at this end of the lake. As the road goes, five miles from end to end. Except your house."

"Holy crap."

"Came home to MP because it was a good place to raise my family. But the idea of it cleared through the block I had about it when my dad drank himself to death and left me all of this."

I had no idea.

I communicated that by saying, "Whoa."

"Yeah. Long time ago, he got drunk, did it while playing poker, was on a losing streak, bet your place to Fred Nance. They didn't like each other when they started the game. They liked each other a lot less when it was over. Dad tried unsuccessfully for over fifty years to get that land and house back. Fred wasn't gonna have it. To the point he had it in his will that after he died and that lot was sold, since he had no wife and no kids and wasn't a big fan of the rest of his family, it'd go to the state of Washington before he'd let me buy it."

"That's one mighty grudge," I noted.

"Dad had been dead over a decade, and I did nothing to the man to deserve being cut out like that, so…yeah."

"Did your dad do…other things like that?"

"This land was his dad's land. And his dad's before. And his father before that. The people who owned it before didn't own it, according to white man ways, since they were Native Americans. That's how far back it goes. Dad didn't quit drinking. But he did learn his lesson about poker."

"Well, at least that's good."

And it was.

What he said next was bad.

"Beat the shit outta me, which was okay, seein' as once he started doing that, he quit beatin' the shit outta Mom. Problem with that was, she could take it, but she wasn't a huge fan of him dishin' it out on me. So she hid baseball bats and knives around the house. Meant when he'd get in the mood, a weapon wouldn't be too far off, and apparently, a woman sober as a judge and determined to make it so you don't lay your hands on her boy makes even a drunk stand down. I cannot tell you how many times I came home from school and his shit was out on the deck. She loved him, though, and took him back. Then she loved him and didn't take him back. He lived in a shack that way for years until she died."

He pointed to the left of us.

And kept talking.

"No running water. No heat. Electricity from a generator. He bathed in the lake. What he couldn't cook on an old Weber outside, he ate at the Double D. First thing I did when I came home was tear that shack down."

This didn't surprise me.

"How did your mom die?"

"Breast cancer."

"I'm sorry. She sounded like something."

He nodded. "She was beautiful. She was ballsy. She met a guy who loved her more than himself and moved him into her ex-husband's house that she did not own, but Dad never turned her out, and they lived it up. Until he stood at her side through the shit of cancer. He lives in an RV now, on the road, chasing the end, lost without her. Just like Dad. When she was done with him, he was lost without her. Problem with him was, he was lost when he was with her too."

"I'm getting the whole 'beer whenever' thing now," I murmured.

"Yeah," he grunted.

"Did you like your stepfather?"

"Learned how to love from him, what I didn't learn from Mom."

"I'll take that as a yes."

"You'd be correct."

I studied his profile. "You're messing up my puzzle."

His body shifted in surprise against mine. "What?"

"The Cade Bohannan I met after his daughter came 'round to alleviate her boredom and curiosity, defying your punishment. Mr. The Fewer Words Spoken is not this Mr. Let It All Hang Out."

He roared with laughter.

Since he had never done that around me, I was both struck and captivated.

The moon was diffused by clouds.

His outside lights were on, they dispelled some darkness, but they didn't fully reach us.

I could see him, yet he was in shadow.

And he was beautiful.

However.

"What's funny?"

"Fuck, I wanna kiss you," he muttered to the lake, his beard still forming a grin.

I turned in the curve of his arm.

"Why did you say that?"

I asked this instead of, *why don't you do it?*

He looked down at me.

"Larue, you're you."

"That's indisputable."

"You're pretty as hell. Famous as fuck. Talented like crazy. And I'd been a fan of yours for thirty years. I was pissed at my girl. Worried about her. And I had to show at your place to get her, try not to embarrass her. And try not to embarrass myself."

"You were…nervous?" I asked in shock.

He turned more to me. "Babe, you're pretty as hell. Famous as fuck. Talented like crazy. I watched you on TV for over seven thousand minutes, and your show was funny, but like I said, I tuned in *for you*. I read your book three times. You open the door and you're prettier in person and your ass is better than when you were twenty-four. So, fuck yeah, I was nervous."

"So you weren't talkative at first because you were nervous?"

"Nope," he answered. "Got over that real quick when I realized you wanted to jump me."

I sat back into the chair and glowered at the lake. "I *so* should have put on sunglasses."

He chuckled and squeezed my shoulders with his arm.

"Then you wouldn't shut up so I couldn't get a word in edgewise," he went on.

"You can *really* stop talking now," I invited.

He didn't accept my invitation.

"Though, that Five Voices of Criticism was some deep shit,

baby."

I was rethinking my desire to jump him, or vice versa (though, not really).

"And in *my* hermetically sealed box, I filed away that you're one serious hardass. A small-minded chemistry teacher, who will mean dick to my beautiful daughter in the glorious life she's gonna lead, under your chopping block? I'd advise against the school board. There aren't enough teachers in the country to pass your tests."

"You keep speaking, but I might never do it again," I warned.

He gave me another squeeze.

"I don't talk a lot because you can't observe when you're flapping your mouth," he explained.

A point to ponder.

"Right."

"But we can't get to know each other if I don't tell you about me."

"Right again."

"You pissed?"

He sounded surprised.

As he would be, since I wasn't pissed seeing as there was nothing to be pissed about, even the teasing, which was sweet.

I was disappointed.

"No. I'm upset because I wanted to jump you so much, I didn't realize you were nervous and that was probably cute. But instead, all I saw was hot."

"I'm not broken up about that," he muttered.

I rolled my eyes at the mist on the lake.

It lightened because headlights hit it.

We both turned, nearly bumping heads as we watched the Mustang pull in, followed closely by silver Ram (Jess) and black Ram (Jace).

The Mustang skidded to an angry halt and Bohannan murmured, "Oh fuck."

"I'm thinking she wasn't a fan of chaperones."

We both stood.

Wearing nice burgundy cords and a cute pink sweater, a tan,

cropped jean jacket fashionably accompanying these, Celeste tramped down to the pier.

Jess got out and headed our way.

Jace got out and did the same.

Her father and I waited.

She unleashed.

"*Daaaaaaaaaaaaaaaaaaaaaaaaaaaaaaaaaaaaaaduh!*"

I heard air release from Bohannan's nostrils, which meant he was trying not to laugh.

Other than that, nothing from him.

I guess this was on me.

"Honey, you know why I'm here, yes?"

"Delphine, *Jace and Jess sat behind us at the movie!*"

I looked beyond her to where her brothers stood.

"You couldn't be more stealth?" I asked.

"Dude's gotta know that dude's gotta be cool," Jace declared.

"I think he got the message," Jess added.

I returned my attention to her. "I know this is lame, but one day, you'll understand how awesome it was to have two protective brothers."

"That day is not *now*," she pointed out.

"I understand," I said soothingly.

"Will took us to The Lodge for dinner. They sat at the bar and stared at us the whole time. He didn't even try to hold my hand."

"That was an unexpected score," Jace mumbled to Jess.

They bumped fists.

I gave them a laser-focused *You're Not Helping* glare that was so strong, it had to penetrate through the shadows.

"Perhaps your father will give them a tutorial on boundaries," I suggested to Celeste, at the same time I was suggesting it to her father.

"I'm probably never gonna get another date again," she lamented.

"Another unexpected score," Jess noted.

There it was.

My glare didn't penetrate through the shadows.

She whirled on them. "God! I *hate you*!"

Bohannan's phone rang.

I went still.

Jace and Jess's attention whipped straight to their dad.

Celeste's body jolted.

Bohannan took the call, stepping away from me.

"What's happening?" Celeste's voice was trembling.

I didn't have it in me to reply, my laser focus was now on her father.

"Yup. Yup." Pause and, "Good."

Good.

I twisted my tush around and melted to the loveseat, primarily because my legs could no longer support me.

"Yeah. Good. Yup. Right. Okay. Tomorrow. Later."

Bohannan hung up and now *his* laser focus was on me.

"Welsh is in custody. The hostages are at the hospital. Their families have been informed, transported and are with them. They're still sorting through shit, but they got enough to pin the bomb on him, and the pictures sent to Booth. Caught with the women, and with the rest, he's never gonna feel freedom again."

For reasons unknown to me, people expressed that they wanted to be "strong" and hold their shit together in times like these.

I didn't know how it communicated strength to pretend you didn't feel such extreme relief and release that something tragic and terrible that was happening to you, and worse was happening to others, was over, you might be temporarily insane with it.

Which was what I was.

I folded double, and with face in my hands, I wept uncontrollably.

I did not feel Bohannan gather me in his arms.

I didn't feel him lift me in them to carry me to the house.

I didn't feel my ass hitting pistachio velvet, and his hold remaining tight on me.

I didn't feel anything.

I didn't think anything.

Except *Their families…are with them.*

TWENTY

Fugly

Celeste and I were at the grocery store.

I was free.

Free.

Free.

Free.

And as a celebration, I was carving jack-o'-lanterns.

And my sixteen-year-old, twenty-seven-year-olds and fifty-five-year-old (Celeste told me Bohannan's age) were carving with me.

Celeste was all in.

The other three didn't know about it yet, but we'd spring it on them after we filled their bellies and got them compliant.

It was the afternoon after it all went down.

I'd woken up, still half-catatonic from my crying catharsis, to immediately experience near panic because I didn't know where I was.

Fortunately, it didn't take long before it hit me.

I remembered the phone call. Bohannan holding me. Being on his couch. Sensing the kids loitering close. Eventually getting it together enough to perpetuate my first breach of their domain that didn't include the kitchen, living room and powder room, this being

Bohannan guiding me upstairs to a bathroom. He handed me an electronic toothbrush, a new head and a tube of paste.

I remember hearing Jess murmur, "She likes it low." And Bohannan's reply of "Set it at sixty."

I remember Celeste walking in with some cleanser and moisturizer.

I remember that I didn't care Bohannan was there when he led me to a big bed, and I took off my boots and socks and jeans and sweater, to stand there in my panties and a thin thermal while he threw out a blanket over his comforter.

I remember he pulled the covers back.

I remember he tucked me in.

Kissed my temple.

And I was out when he turned out the lights.

I sat up to see he did not put me in a guest bedroom.

Instead, I was in his bedroom because no guestroom would have that view of the lake, which was uninterrupted at window level across and around a corner, and it was expansive, because the room was huge, and last, it was *insane* as in, *insanely amazing*.

I assessed the bed to see he hadn't slept in it with me, which was good. I wouldn't want to miss that.

I also noticed the room was a study of shades of sand and lake blues and forest greens, the perfect mixture of masculine and feminine.

One could say Grace Bohannan had failed as a wife, a mother, and arguably (and I'd argue the pro side of this) a human being.

But the woman was talented with interior design.

I also saw a note on the nightstand closest to me. It was held down with my phone and a plain keyring with three keys on it, one with a red band around the bow, one with blue and one with white.

I picked up the note, and upon scanning the bottom and assessing the thing scrawled there *might* be Bohannan, I took a number of memories of him further to see if he might have exhibited signs he was a serial killer, because his writing sure made him seem like one.

Once I'd decoded enough letters to decipher the note, I read it.

Babe, (Incidentally, I'd never tell him this, but I thought that was a nice start.)

We've all hit it. Text me when you wake up. Your choice for dinner tonight, whatever you want, it's yours. (What I wanted was a jack-o'-lantern carving ritual, but I'd utilize this offer to get my way if that was needed.)

FBI wants a debrief. Call them when you're ready. Old habits, text me when you leave my house. Text me when you make it to yours. That'll fade. It hasn't now. But you always keep your doors locked and the security set when you're home, forever. (Very sweet.)

Keys are blue, the big house. Red, the twins' house. White, the barn. (I had no idea why I'd need a key to the boys' house or the barn, but points to the man for being so thorough so shortly after officially declaring his interest in me.)

Lock up when you leave.

At the end, there was what might be an *x* to indicate the first kiss he'd ever given me (not including the temple one, which I'd decided officially not to count), or it might be part of the rather elaborate, but even so, mostly illegible *B* in *Bohannan*.

And that was it.

I texted him before I got out of bed.

He texted me right back, in the middle of me making said bed.

You doing okay?

My reply, *I'm free*. And I added an effect, that being fireworks exploding when the text opened.

I'd made the bed and was dressing when he sent, *Yeah, baby*.

I sent three dozen hearts-surrounding-face emojis, two dozen flamenco dancers and a hang ten.

He didn't send emojis, but he thumbs-upped my text.

I finished dressing, texted him I was leaving, left his house, locked up, practically skipped to my house, got another thumbs-up on my text and texted him again when I got inside my place.

His reply, *Good. See you tonight.*

I made coffee. Took a cup upstairs. Took the longest shower in my personal history, symbolically washing Bob Welsh away. Dressed in a lounge outfit, and called my daughters, leaving messages for both to call me back when they had a minute, but telling them I had very good news.

I then called Agent Palmer who gave me some specifics about what had gone down and what was going down.

It included the fact that once they'd pinpointed him, and were pretty sure it was him, they started investigating other things, and they did this double time while strategizing a takedown to get the women free from where they were relatively sure he was holding them, as soon as safe and possible.

They had not so far, at his house, or at the other house where he was keeping the women, found much (outside the women, oh…and a great deal of evidence of the extent of his obsession with me).

However, they had visited a variety of stores and internet cafés in his area. The stores were where they had witness accounts and store receipts of purchases of bomb-making paraphernalia. The cafés were where they found cached (even though deleted, they were restored) internet search histories of unhinged web searches he'd done on computers he had logged into.

They might have a line on how he got his hands on the poison that fortunately did not take out Bookworm.

But regardless, he'd already confessed, as he would, to a number of charges around kidnapping, assault, sexual assault and other.

He had a lawyer, but right now, what they were haggling about was not how long he'd be in prison, but which prison he'd be in and how comfortable he'd be behind bars until he died.

I did not care.

I cared about the women.

"We're giving them assistance. It'll be a long row, but we'll keep our eye on them," Agent Palmer assured.

I told her if they needed anything financially, I should be her first call. Or if they needed anything at all, please contact me.

She made note of that.

And we were done.

But I wasn't done.

I called Hawk Delgado and got Elvira, who told me they'd wrap up, send me a report, handle the devolvement of what they were doing to keep an eye on Camille and Joan, and their final invoice would come with the report.

I called Alicia, who already knew, and was beside herself with glee, for her, for Russ and Michael, and for me.

I called Russ, who also already knew and was relieved and happy, but a little worried about me.

I called Michael, who further already knew, and said, "Maybe now we can stop living under your shit."

Fun facts: Russ had gone on to star in two long-ish running sitcoms and a two-season, one-hour dramatic comedy that didn't have a long life but was rife with critical acclaim and still had fans demanding its return.

Alicia had moved to film and had done a slew of successful romantic comedies and was still doing them, perhaps not to the same box office, but it wasn't anything to sneeze at.

Michael had two failed sitcoms, did so many pilots that weren't picked up we'd lost count, and a short guest-starring stint on a political drama that earned him a Golden Globe and led him to believe he could be a dramatic actor, to unimpressive results.

I put Michael out of my mind, nothing was going to mess with my good mood that day.

I then talked to my two jubilant girls, ignored the calls and texts of my relieved exes, briefed a couple of friends who I knew would be worried, and texted Celeste with *You up for an adventure after school?*

To which I received, *YES!!!!!*

Which brought us to now.

Standing wearing cute sweaters and corduroy pants, scarves wrapped around our necks, both of us with fabulous knit caps over our hair, looking autumnal fabulous as we perused what was on offer in the huge crates outside the grocery store.

In other words, we were selecting pumpkins.

She held up a fugly, messed up one. "This is *so* Jace."

She was *so* right.

"Toss it in."

She put it in our cart.

I located a massive one. "Your dad?"

"Totes."

I put it in the cart.

She found an even fuglier, messed up one for Jess, and we picked out ones for each other (she found one that was sheer pumpkin perfection for me, I found one that was even more perfect for her, and we both giggled about this).

Celeste had commandeered the cart and we were going to roll through the store to get what we needed for dinner, when I heard, "Ms. Larue?"

I turned.

And looked right into the face of Audrey Pulaski.

TWENTY-ONE

Aromacobana

"I…sorry, I thought it was you," Audrey said.

Celeste came up so close to my side, her arm was pressed to mine.

"Hello," I said gently to Audrey.

She took a step toward us, glanced at Celeste and said, "Hi, honey."

"Hi, Mrs. Pulaski."

At her reply, I almost looked down at Celeste because her tone wasn't her usual shy or warm and quiet, it was kind of cold and definitely remote.

Interesting.

"You and Will have fun last night?" she asked, her tone fake cheery and painful to hear.

"A little," Celeste allowed.

"Good," Audrey muttered. "I wanted to…" She looked in our cart and paled.

My heart stuttered as there were probably no jack-o'-lanterns at the Pulaski residence this year.

She pulled herself together and returned her attention to me.

"I wanted to thank you. For what you did. Offering those rewards. That was very kind."

"Don't." I was still going gently. "Really." I couldn't say it was my pleasure. So I said, "Anyone with my resources would do the same."

"I'm not sure they would," she replied.

I had no answer to that, so I gave her a careful smile.

Another small step toward us, and her head tipped a little, but the movement was strange, like a bird's.

"Do you...well, do you have any idea why Leland didn't announce your offer?"

Goddamned Dern.

"No, I'm sorry. I don't," I told her.

She turned to Celeste.

I shifted my arm so it was around her.

Audrey did not miss this, and she winced.

God, this was torture.

It was plain to see her puzzle was broken and dark, re-forming even as she stood there, and it was one of those three-dimensional ones.

Dimension one: before Alice, and how Audrey was now plagued with thoughts, wondering if she should have done what she (allegedly) did to trap Dale by making Alice.

Dimension two: those now hazy, and getting terrifyingly hazier, days of the time with Alice and having everything she thought she wanted, though, even as she denied it, she knew there was a pall over that. A pall she'd lived with. A pall that might now bite her spectacularly in the ass. Last, a pall that had hung over her daughter her whole life.

Dimension three: the now, knowing she birthed a child who ended in a way so unimaginable, it shook a cocky, sharp, strong, intelligent young man to the point he was questioning his ability to control his actions, and in a very real way he feared he might commit murder himself as retribution. But it was Audrey's actions (in Audrey's mind, this was not the actual case) that led Alice on a collision course from birth to devastating death at the age of eight at the hands of a madman.

I was no psychologist. I could not tell her those hazy days would come back into focus. She'd never forget the beauty of her girl.

In fact, I could do nothing.

Her puzzle would have to re-form on its own, even she had little control over the process.

"Do you know, sweetie, if your dad told the sheriff not to?" she asked Celeste.

"No. He didn't," she announced. "Dad didn't even know about it until..." I squeezed her, because that "until" was the day of her daughter's funeral. "Later," she finished.

Apparently, Bohannan's Dad Ears were faulty, and Celeste hadn't been out of hearing distance when we'd had our discussion, or one of the boys or someone at school told her.

Audrey's gaze wafted—and I mean it—it *wafted* to mine.

"Don't you find that strange?"

"I don't really know much about these types of things," I said.

"I wish I didn't," she told some point over my shoulder.

"Do you want to go somewhere?" I offered, and Celeste put her arm around me and poked me in my side.

What was that about?

I ignored it in the face of Audrey's disorientation and pain.

"Sit down?" I went on. "Get a coffee. Talk?"

She semi-focused on me. "You were the nice one in that show. So very sweet. And they all said that was the way you are in real life. Like, you were playing yourself."

I wasn't.

I didn't tell her that.

"I guess they were right," she concluded.

I looked down at Celeste. "Is there a fun coffee shop in town?"

"Yeah. Aromacobana," she answered.

Excellent coffee shop name.

"No, no." Pause as we looked at her. "No. You're in the middle of something."

"I'm sure we can set these aside and come back for them later."

"No, really, I have to…get…" a very long pause, "home."

I asked a pertinent question. "Are you okay to drive?"

She looked surprised at the inference, squared her shoulders and said briskly. "Yes. Of course. Yes. I'm fine. It was nice to meet you and thank you again."

"Please, don't mention it."

"Celeste, honey," she whispered, her voice husky.

She then turned and scurried away.

I watched her but Celeste didn't.

She disengaged from me, grabbed the cart and asked, "Ready?"

We went in. I left it while we picked up some things, but I went for it in the chip aisle.

"You were a little distant with her. No shade, just wondering."

"Will hates her."

I stopped at the Doritos.

She piled some in.

"That was, like, the first thing he said to me. He ordered a chocolate malt, turned to me and said, 'I fucking hate Audrey. She's such a bitch.' And I know I'm cursing, but that's what he said. Word for word."

"The first thing he said?" I asked as she took us down the aisle and stopped at the Ruffles.

She opted for cheddar and sour cream.

I approved of her choice but only in my head.

She was talking.

"I wasn't surprised. Everyone knows about her."

"What does everyone know?"

She was now at the Pringles and considering her options.

I wasn't sure who she was feeding, but my guess was she had a mental list, and if this was what fueled the Bohannans when I wasn't around, I wasn't going to stop her.

"That she broke up Mr. and Mrs. Pulaski." She looked at me. "And by that, I mean the *real* Mrs. Pulaski."

"This is known? In high school?"

"Will is popular," she mumbled, adding more sour cream to the collection, this one with onion, and spicing things up with BBQ.

We rounded the end cap, and she kept talking.

"Anyway, she did it before."

"Hold up," I said.

She stopped.

"Before?" I asked.

"Yeah. To some other guy. He was smart enough not to get her pregnant, though. But when he wouldn't leave his wife for her, she told his wife all about them hooking up. They almost got divorced. But they went to counseling and sorted themselves out. I bet she didn't see that coming."

I bet she didn't.

Celeste continued, "So she set her sights on Mr. Pulaski."

"I don't want to talk trash about Mr. Pulaski, and when I say that, I really don't. The man is in hell, and I have no idea about any of this. But I do think it's important to note that, in things like this, it always but *always* takes two to tango."

"Oh yeah. Will isn't, like, clearing his dad. But, you know, he's *his dad.* And they both, like, *totally loved* Alice. Like, you know how Dad and Jess and Jace are with me?"

"Yes."

"That kind of love, except she's still little." She let that sit only a moment before, wistful, she said, "Or she was."

"Does Will say that Audrey isn't cut up about losing her daughter?"

If he did, he was talking through hurt.

The woman we just saw was destroyed.

"Oh no, she loved her too. Just that, you know, Will hates her. Audrey. Mrs. Pulaski. And, like, you're new to town and you're, like, able to go around and meet people and get to know stuff now. So you should know, no one in town likes her either. Not with what she did to that other couple. Not with her breaking up Mr. and Mrs. Pulaski. Not with her being...*her.*"

Before I could ask what that meant, Celeste started moving down the aisle again.

But she did it still talking.

"It's actually a weird kind of gross because we all have to

pretend to like her when none of us do. I mean, we feel sorry for her, but we don't like her."

"That's a pretty strong collective we."

She stopped. "What?"

"We, as in *you*?"

Her nose scrunched. "You know, when a mom and dad are together, they should be able to stay together. It's already hard enough. They don't need some…some…I don't know what she is…making it tougher."

All righty then.

"Agreed," I said quietly.

She moved onward. "And anyway, Will feels like he has to be nice to her and feel sorry for her, and he can barely stand to look at her."

Apparently, their first date was Celeste acting as sounding board to a justifiably angry, hurting young man.

"That has to be confusing," I noted.

"Uh…yeah."

We were in the cookie aisle.

And the Bohannans liked mega-stuff, both chocolate and golden.

How did these people keep fit?

"Does your dad know all this? I mean, about the earlier affair."

"Everyone knows."

I reached for an actual ingredient we needed for dinner, remarking, "I have to admit, I think it's odd that this is talked about in high school."

"Will's a really good hockey player. We like our hockey in Misted Pines. You know, like other people like football. People just pay attention to things around guys like that. And he's not quiet about it, or he wasn't before. And the town isn't that big. So it just…gets around."

"Hmm…"

She stopped abruptly, and her gaze skittered to me.

"I'm not being mean," she declared.

"You're allowed to have an opinion, Celeste," I replied.

"Obviously, it's awful, what happened to Alice."

"We're not talking about Alice. We're talking about something else."

"I don't want you to think—"

"Listen," I said firmly. "I want you to share anything you want with me, how you want, unadulterated."

"Un-ah-what?"

"Unadulterated. Honest. Straight." I flapped a hand between us. "This is a no judgment zone."

"Cool," she whispered.

I gave her a wink. "Cool."

We pushed forward but didn't get far, when a lady in a home-knit, chunky wool sweater and beat up Dickies pants stopped at us.

"Won't take up too much time in your day," she said, voice low and chin in her throat like she was about to "ho, ho, ho" like Santa Claus. "Just wanted to say it was real kind, you doin' that for little Alice."

"I actually didn't end up doing anything," I replied.

"That's 'cause Dern is a horse's ass. But you met him, so s'pose you know that by now."

I didn't reply.

She squinted at me and said, "Yep. You know." She squinted at Celeste. "Heya, gurl."

"Heya, Frances."

And true to her word of not taking up time, she moseyed on, saying, "Later."

"Later," Celeste called.

It took an aisle or two before Celeste said, "It was, you know."

"What?"

"Really kind of you to do that for Alice."

I shot her a grin, wrapped my arm around her shoulders, gave her a squeeze, she did that sweet teenager thing where she scrunched her shoulders forward while I did, but she didn't pull away.

I let her go and we finished shopping.

TWENTY-TWO

Jack-o'-Lanterns

"We're doing what now?"

Jace.

"No offense. But this is stupid."

Jesse.

"Men."

Bohannan, in what could only be described as a leashed bark.

Both boys looked to their dad.

Jace then turned to me.

"Right yeah. Totally into this, Delphine," he outright lied.

Translation: *We saw you sitting in the loveseat on the pier under the moon with Dad, but even before, we knew what was happening and no way are we gonna cockblock. So we're up to pretend we're good with carving jack-o'-lanterns when we so totally are not.*

"It's not just carving pumpkins," I told them. "It's a ritual."

Both boys stared at me, trying very hard to exude interest when they just wanted to stab some pumpkins a few times to make me happy, which would make their father not pissed at them, and their sister happy too, then go out to a bar, drink a few beers and maybe pick up a girl.

Bohannan watched me with Bohannan's normal level of interest, that being he didn't give much away, but he didn't take his eyes off me.

Celeste was practically dancing because I'd told her this part already, and she was all excited to do "witchy" stuff because "witchy stuff is *so cool* right now…a few weekends ago I bought my first tarot deck and *everything*."

"Okay, I do this every year in October, and when my girls were old enough, we did it together. Camille and Fenn would be over at my house doing it now, if Fenn wasn't an ocean away, and I wasn't two states from Camille."

This spoke to Jason and Jesse, because doing something dorky and for children to appease their dad's new girlfriend (maybe) was one thing.

Participating in a family tradition was another.

"The thing is…" I touched my pumpkin where it lay in front of me on newspapers that were spread over their dining room table (we all stood in front of our own pumpkins). "You carve off the top, like normal. But when you scoop out the seeds, you think…to yourself, you don't have to share…about all the things you want in your life in the coming year. All the good things. Things you have you want to keep. Things you don't have you want to find. It can be anything. It's yours to decide."

I picked up the knife I was going to use.

And I carried on.

"Then, when you start carving, you think of all the things this year that you weren't a big fan of. Things you want to cut out of your life. Things that happened or things you felt or things about yourself you want to change. Each piece of pumpkin flesh carved out represents those things."

When I took a moment to assess their interest, I saw even Bohannan was now paying a lot closer attention.

"Then," I continued, "we clean up the seeds, spread them on a tray, salt them, roast them and consume all the good things we want for ourselves for the next year. While the seeds are roasting, we take the pieces to the yard, dig a hole and put the bad things in the ground. Bury them. We do this to literally bury them, but we also do it to turn them positive. Change them. Because that happens when you return something of the earth to the earth. It nourishes it."

I looked among them.

"Does that make sense?" I asked. "Are you okay to do that?"

"I'm in," Jason said gamely.

Jess looked down at his pumpkin, and it was quiet when he said, "I'm in too."

"Totes!" Celeste chirped.

Bohannan's answer was picking up his knife.

I grinned to myself.

We stabbed and cut and carved and scooped. There were times of quiet. There were more times of conversation and ribbing. Jess had some chops with carving. Jace's attempt was terrifying. Bohannan's pumpkin looked exactly like a winking emoji…with eyebrows. Celeste's had bow lips and eyelashes carved into the flesh. Mine was traditional with three teeth.

When we were ready to rumble, Bohannan ordered, "You girls get those seeds ready. We'll go get the shovels and figure out where to dig."

Clearly, this fixed gender allocation of roles should be addressed.

Except I didn't know where the shovels were, it wasn't my property we were digging on, and bonus to having men around during this ritual, I didn't have to dig any holes like had been my job in the past because neither of my girls liked digging either, though I will admit, digging a hole wasn't hard.

We'll just say I selected acting and writing as my career trajectory for many reasons.

Therefore, I didn't argue.

Before the men took off, though, Bohannan slid his arm around my shoulders, pulled me into him and gave me unofficial first kiss number two (which, as you can tell from my use of the word "unofficial," I also wasn't counting), he pressed his lips to the side of my head.

He then whispered in my ear, "Don't put them in the oven yet."

He pulled away just enough to catch my eyes and my confused but affirming nod, since dumping the stuff in the ground didn't take that long at all.

Celeste and I cleaned the seeds, spread them on the tray, salted them and set the oven to preheat.

We then gathered the pieces of pumpkin at each station in newspaper, keeping track of whose was whose.

We went out and found the men leaning into shovels about twenty yards away from the pier, still in the clearing, but just. You could reach out and touch the first tree.

An excellent spot.

It wasn't as much as normal, but mist was on the water again, even if the moon was bright, the sky was cloudless, and the weather was for once warm-ish.

Celeste and I handed out the parcels.

"Any words of wisdom?" Bohannan prompted.

"Just do you," I said. "You want to say a few words, out loud or in your head, go for it. As for me…"

I stepped forward and dumped my bundle in the rather deep hole (another bonus to men around, I'd never put the effort into digging that deep of a hole, and what I had to bury this year needed to go down deep).

And there went Bob Fucking Welsh.

I knew, of course, he wasn't gone. What he did wasn't gone.

But I'd learned over the years there was strength and power in rituals like these, and this wasn't the only one I participated in (it was just the only one I did with others).

And somehow, in my head, doing this lessened his hold on me.

Celeste went next, and she also dumped.

Bohannan went next, the same.

Jace dumped his, saying "*Sayonara*, bullshit."

It was then, we turned to Jesse.

And it was then that I knew what Bohannan knew before we even walked out there.

I hadn't taken it further.

He always did.

Jesse was frozen, staring into the hole.

"Son," Bohannan murmured, starting to move to his boy.

He stopped when Jess took a step back but only to freeze again and continue to stare at the hole.

Everyone was silent.

Jesse broke it.

"I don't want Alice in that hole."

Celeste made a move, but I caught her hand. When I did, she stilled but held on so tight, my fingers hurt.

Jesse looked to his dad.

"I can't bury her in with all that."

"We'll take her to the pier," Bohannan said quietly. "We'll give her to the fishes."

"I don't wanna let her go."

Celeste made a moaning noise.

Jace was done and went to his brother, crowding him but not touching him.

Bohannan reached to his back pocket, pulled out his wallet, flipped it open and tugged something out I couldn't see.

He showed it to Jesse.

"Movie stub. Her name was Laura. She was fifteen. I swiped it from her bedroom. I've carried it in my wallet every day for fourteen years."

Oh my God.

Jesse stared at his father.

"Dad," he said.

No one moved, except Bohannan, who was swiftly tucking the movie stub back into his wallet.

He'd just returned it to his pocket when Jess spoke again.

"Dad."

That cracked in the middle.

That was when Bohannan caught Jesse on both sides of his neck and pulled him almost violently into his body.

Jesse's frame heaved.

Bohannan wrapped his arms around him, and Jason moved to

stand behind him. He then rested his forehead on Jesse's back.

Jesse made an animalistic noise that punched right through me.

Okay, there was something that night that *was* official.

I'd fallen in love with this family.

"Let's go," I whispered to Celeste, starting to tug her around toward the house, thinking that Jess might not want her or me to see his emotion.

"No," she replied, holding fast to my hand and not moving.

It might be good she was there, but I wasn't sure I should be there.

The instant I had that thought, Bohannan turned his head and pinned me with his gaze.

Well, that answered that, though I didn't know if it was a *You're one of us now* or a *You got us into this mess, you're seeing it through.*

I also didn't know which one of those was scarier, considering I hadn't even had an official kiss from the patriarch of this crew.

"Weak," Jesse grunted.

"Strong," Bohannan contradicted.

"I'm never gonna let her go."

"She's counting on that."

Jesse's head came up.

Jason stepped away, but not too far.

"What?" Jess asked his dad.

"You know," Bohannan answered.

Bohannan's back was to me, but I could see father and son did not lose eye contact for several, very long beats.

Jesse nodded and moved out of his father's embrace.

Bohannan turned to Celeste and me.

Jace came to his brother's side.

Jesse looked at me.

"Who needs therapy when they can go out and buy a pumpkin?"

Oh no!

Disaster!

"No, I didn't mean—"

"Chill, Delly," Jesse said softly. "I'll tell her about this my next go. She needs to incorporate this shit into her regime."

"Her" must be his therapist.

My smile was tentative.

So was his.

"Are the seeds burning?" Jace asked, and not for the first time I wondered if he was a medical miracle, and his brain could be found in his stomach.

"We didn't put them in yet," Celeste told him.

That made me look at Bohannan.

Jesse came and claimed his sister, and by that, I mean *claimed.* Her scream was fake and shrill when, even though he had his bundle of pumpkin bits tucked under one arm like a football, he tossed her over his other shoulder.

Because, obviously, after crying in his dad's arms, he had to do something manly.

I'd give him that play.

Celeste gave it too.

They headed up to the house, sister hanging down brother's back.

Bohannan came and claimed me with an arm around my shoulders and aimed us to the house.

"So, we gonna have a conversation as a family, you know, like pumpkin-carving extreme therapy, where you two announce you're an item and what that means to all us kids?" Jason ribbed as he sauntered at our sides. "You know, Dad, like, how you still love us and we're very important, but you might not be around as much because you're getting it on with a super famous TV star."

I thought for certain Bohannan would shut this down with a tonally significant grunt.

He didn't.

He said, "Something like that."

Jason barked out a laugh.

I stared at Bohannan's profile and spied suspicious movement around his beard.

But I definitely didn't miss his arm tightening around my shoulders.

"Though, I don't think the family meeting is necessary," Bohannan finished.

I moved my stare to Jace.

He was watching me.

And his expression was so far from teasing, my breath caught.

"Nope," he agreed. "Don't suppose we do."

TWENTY-THREE

Bigfoot

I sat at my desk, staring at the empty Word document on my computer, not thinking about the fact my deadline had been put in limbo while Bob Welsh put me in limbo, but now that Bob Welsh was in his own limbo, my deadline would contractually be taken out of its.

I also wasn't thinking about how fabulous my office now was.

The desk was perfect with the lamps I'd bought, the rug I'd bought, and the Eames leather lounge chair tucked into the corner with its ottoman and gold, swooped-arm, globe-shaded standing lamp hanging over it.

And the paint color I'd chosen to cover the walls above the wood wainscotting was inspired.

My desk was set between the windows so my desktop monitor didn't obstruct the view on either side of it, and I could look out at the lake.

The décor of the room was a mix of mid-century modern, old-school tradition, girlie, with unusual pops of color (for instance, a distressed turquoise table in a corner, which had no purpose but to hold a beautiful vase of dried flowers).

I loved it.

It was no Cade Bohannan Bedroom (and there was a reason the Bohannan clan picked that stretch of land to build that particular house, because my view was tranquil and stunning, albeit narrow and restricted in parts by pines, so it kind of felt, especially upstairs, like it was in a treehouse—but the expansiveness of their view was dazzling).

No, I wasn't thinking of that either.

I was thinking that Bohannan had not thrown himself with gusto into finding Alice's killer because he was keeping me safe.

Now that he wasn't keeping me safe, he was throwing himself with gusto into finding Alice's killer.

I knew this because, for the last four days, we'd texted, and once, he'd swung through his house to give his daughter's forehead a kiss, mine as well (and I wasn't counting that one either) while she and I were camped out on the sectional in their TV room in their basement (that had, Celeste shared, at one time been the boys' domain, as their bedrooms had also been down there, but now it had been reclaimed). And then he'd swung right back out.

She and I were watching Russ's comedy drama (I'd forgotten how good it was).

Bohannan had seemed distracted in the twenty seconds he was with us.

And then he was vapor.

So I guessed that warning he'd laid on me during his back-to-back "Relationships Are Feelings" and "I'm A Fan" speeches, which I took as an indication he was going to jump me when he no longer had to look after me, was a false alarm.

I knew that finding the man who did what he did to Alice was a priority level so high, there was no word yet created to describe it.

I still yearned to connect with Cade.

The thing was, I was celibate, and I had been since my second not-so-fun, not-very-long-lasting relationship after Angelo.

I did not hate men (as some claimed).

I very much enjoyed them in many senses. Their company. Their attention. Their penises (if they knew how to use them).

I'd just learned that I didn't need them.

This was a thing that had been one of the controversies of *We Pluck the Cord*.

My heroine didn't need men either.

Women were aghast (mostly conservatives), because…*values*. This idea could obviously not be borne because it might lead to breakdowns in traditions they held sacred. Namely marriage, and the insidious subtext therein of what they thought was a woman's place in society.

Men were aghast (mostly all of them), because…well, honestly, it was rare I ever met a man who hadn't had ingrained in him how crucial he was to just about everything, especially women, from practically birth.

I'll repeat, I did not hate men. They couldn't help the role they were cast in in the drama of life, and a large number of them understood that was bullshit.

Of course, in the end, my heroine finding love—with a man—but on unusual terms set by (Lord God, no) *her*, was ignored.

The fact she loved him but understood she could live without him, now that, somehow, was sacrilege.

Though, I will say the uproar was awesome for sales.

You write what you know, or at least you should, a reader won't believe it if you don't.

I wrote what I knew.

But as with my heroine, I always knew, even if I didn't need a man, that didn't mean I didn't want one.

It didn't mean I didn't want company, I didn't want attention, I didn't want someone to share my time and life with.

It didn't mean I didn't want someone to love.

I loved loving people, and as far as I was concerned, the more people to love (who were worthy of my love), the better.

I just didn't want to put up with the bullshit of a not-the-right-one.

I hadn't known him that long.

But I sensed that Bohannan was the right one.

It didn't matter if I wasn't yet sure, though.

Because I wanted to find out.

I had a lot of strong evidence to many facets of his character with how he was with his kids, his job, me.

Not to be crass or anything, and not simply because it had been a very long time.

But I felt the time was nigh.

I wanted to know if he knew how to use his dick.

His hands.

At the very least his lips and tongue.

I did not have that.

Any of it.

Even after he walked me home after pumpkin carving, he kissed me on the forehead then shoved me in my house, closed the door for me, pointed toward the security panel, then waited outside until I locked said door and signaled off (my arrival) and on (secure windows and doors) to the alarm.

I knew, obviously, it'd be all kinds of bratty to demand he pause his hunt for a kid killer to come over and fuck me senseless (if that was in his sexual repertoire).

But that didn't mean I wasn't tempted to do it.

I stared at the blank Word document, willing myself to bring up the outline I'd written months ago so I could get the juices flowing, hearing David working in the kitchen—he was scraping off the backsplash (the cabinets would remain, but we'd ordered new countertops, new tile was going up, a new sink would be there in a week, the new faucet was in the garage, and new appliances would be placed as and when in the project).

We both felt this was a good way to go considering the next big projects, the bathrooms, were going to be complete overhauls and that would take time.

Needless to say, David was breathing easy (at least in one part of his life). His wife was due in five months. We both figured he'd finish his last project for me (all-over-the-house floor refurbishing, or perhaps the boathouse) a couple of months after that.

And David was delightful. I was not only glad I was getting this house as I wanted it, I was glad I was giving him some peace of mind.

On this thought, my phone rang.

I looked to it, hoping for one name, dreading the idea that it might be two others (I had eventually touched base with Warren and Angelo just to let them know I was okay, but was now avoiding them because this event had disastrously triggered some base protective instinct in both and they were driving me batty), and getting the name I expected.

Camille.

She'd called every day since Welsh was caught.

I knew her ploy.

Before he was caught, she'd mostly left me alone, a subtle communication that all was well, I was safe and alive and should live my life with normal sporadic, but relatively frequent, communication with my grown daughter.

Now that the situation was resolved, the threat behind bars, but the women entering a new period of hell—that being the journey they'd be taking to find themselves, whoever that self ended up being after he'd shifted their life's trajectory so drastically—Camille knew I'd obsess about that and was all over me like a rash.

I should have worn sunglasses a lot more with her too, that's all I'm saying.

"Hello, lovely," I greeted.

"Hey, what's happening?" she replied.

"It's raining. And…surprise! There's fog on the lake. Last, my kitchen tile is being chipped away."

"Okay, this is good, right here, an immediate segue because I've been wanting to talk to you about that."

"About my kitchen tile?"

"About the fact that Fenn and Joan and I all think it's weird you didn't do what Alicia and Russ did. Get out of town, rent someplace safe and far away, so after this was done, you could come home. Instead, you dug through all that stuff you kept in storage from the Montana house, stuff you should have sold, so we kinda already knew, and bought and furnished an all-new house." Pause, then loaded and heavy she went on, "Mom, we all feel you should understand that you have a real estate addiction."

I burst out laughing.

"I'm not being funny," she said through my laughter, my serious, caring, I'll-find-a-problem-to-fix-even-if-there-isn't-one girl. "How many properties do you own?"

"Honey, I'm rich," I reminded her. "And I don't remember you complaining the five times you hung out in Paris for the whole summer. Or that winter you used the Cornwall cottage to write your dissertation."

"Well, the Paris place doesn't count. That's like a family retreat. And, I mean, the Cornwall place is the same, obviously."

Of course both didn't count.

I was still laughing, just not as loudly, when I reminded her, "Outside the house in the Hollywood Hills, that's all the property I own."

"Except some random place about five miles south of the Canadian border."

"It's beautiful here."

"I know, you sent pictures. It's still totally rando."

"Camille, I've met somebody."

Utter silence.

"It's very young, but he's very...*him.*"

That got her talking.

"What's *him* mean?"

"He's intelligent and he's a loving and involved father, and he's not conventionally handsome, but he's exceptionally attractive."

She broke in.

"Please tell me he's tall. I know. I know. It's stupid. I can't even mention it to Joan. It ticks her off. But it's an aesthetics thing. And we can just say I'm super glad she's model-tall-taller than me." Another pause, then, "And obviously, I'm super glad she's model-model gorgeous. But don't tell Joan I said that either. She threatened to burn herself with acid once to break me from my societal brainwashing of beauty norms. She wouldn't do it but...yikes."

I was again laughing when I told her, "He's tall."

"What's his name?"

"I'm not telling you."

"Why not?"

"You'll Google him."

"I won't Google him."

"I know you're lying."

"Okay, I won't deep-dive Google him," she allowed. "I'll make you a deal, I get to check his Facebook page, Twitter and Insta feeds and, say, click on the top five search backs that pertain to him, if he has them."

The concept of Bohannan having any social media was so hilarious, my laughter was so deep, it was silent.

"Mom!" she snapped.

"Honey, he's an ex-FBI profiler. He doesn't have social media." That was a guess, but probably a good one. "And no, let me have this. Let me have him for a while. If it looks like it is what it feels like it is, *something*, then I'll tell you all about it."

"Oh my God. You're so annoying and manipulative. Because, how can I say no to that?"

"Please, have children so I can teach you my ways."

"Yeah, right. Joan is all up in my shit about societal brainwashing, and she refuses to carry our baby, and I know it's so she won't put on weight, because her mom is constantly *in her head*."

It must be said, Joan's mom was a bit of a pill.

"And why do you refuse to do it?" I asked.

"I'm not going to be pregnant and earning a doctorate."

This was news.

"You're going for your doctorate?"

She answered.

I didn't hear her.

Because I pulled a real-life Hollywood.

I bolted upright in my chair.

This was due to the fact I was gazing out the window, concentrating on my conversation with my daughter, but I didn't miss the movement.

And when I focused…

The man.

Behind my boathouse, walking through the fog, into the pines toward the Bohannan house.

A pulse exploded at the base of my spine, radiating needles digging all over the skin of my back, shoulders, up over my scalp.

I stood, voice shaking, and said, "I have to go, honey."

She was immediately alert. "Is everything okay?"

"David needs me for something. I'll call back a bit later. Love you."

"Mo—"

I hung up, and since the man had disappeared into the pines, I bent my head to my phone and pulled up a group text: Jason, Jesse and Bohannan.

Are any of you home? I asked.

I stared back at the place he disappeared.

Come to my door.

Come up to my door.

He was dark-headed.

It was far away.

Murky.

He could be one of them, noticing something through the rain as they came over to see me, and checking on it.

It was not that far away.

It was not one of them.

I knew it.

No, Jesse.

Nope, Jason.

My phone rang.

Bohannan.

"Hey," I greeted, staring at the pines, seeing if any of them moved, like someone was jostling them as they walked through them.

They were too sturdy, too tall, that was impossible, unless he was Bigfoot.

He was not Bigfoot.

I still checked.

"Why did you text that?" Bohannan demanded.

"I saw a man—"

"Do not leave the house. Make sure all the doors and windows are secured. Make sure the alarm is set. Get close to David."

My skin crawled.

"Bo—"

He was gone.

TWENTY-FOUR

As I Think We'll Be

I was loitering at the back door.

David was loitering with me.

So we both caught it when Jess and Jace came into view, approaching then hopping up on my pier down below, just as Bohannan showed on my deck up above.

David didn't leave my side (he'd gotten a text from Jess) even as I moved to the back door to unlock it.

Bohannan gave David a nod, and I looked to the brawny, ginger-haired man who was about two inches shorter than me who stood at my side. He nodded back to Bohannan, to me, then walked to the kitchen.

Yes.

I really liked David.

Bohannan took my hand and led me to the reading room.

He closed the door.

Well, hell.

"You're scaring me," I told him.

He led with, "Hawk didn't come and get his equipment yet."

This wasn't scaring me any less.

"We agreed, just for a while, he keeps you on their radar," he continued. "Not constant surveillance, but they've got cameras and they're taping. I called. They pulled it up and did a rollback. He was in the frame of a camera they have down at the boathouse. They didn't get a clear shot of him, and he moved out of frame quickly."

"Who is he?"

"I don't know. But I do know there isn't anyone local who steps foot on this property. Not after my dad shot at trespassers for sixty years. My granddad did it before him. My great granddad did the same. And my great-great granddad just shot them. Also, we got sensors, a lot of them. I guess you can imagine how I'm not a fan of surprises."

I could imagine that.

But I deflated.

"Shit, so this is about me?"

"You need ongoing surveillance, baby. The boys and me, we just don't have time right now to set that up for you and monitor it."

I *never* wanted them to do that.

I was Delphine to them. Delly.

Larue.

I wasn't a client.

(At least, anymore.)

I grimaced at him then stormed away three dramatic steps in order that I could glare sullenly out the window.

"The boys are checking things," he continued.

"I just don't get this preoccupation with famous people," I grumbled. "Okay, fine. Come to my table while I'm eating dinner at a restaurant. I'm out and about, and it's not like I don't live a really great life because you watched my TV show or read my books. So I can say hello and dash my name on a piece of paper for you. I'm happy to do that. But lurking on my property?"

"Hang on," he said.

I turned and watched him take a call.

"Yeah, I wanted to talk to you. Pains were taken, Leland. Now, Delphine has some asshole wandering around her place. You'd have to have forensic skills and about three months to uncover she owns this property. What the fuck?"

Pause and…

"Why am I asking you? Because you and your deputies are the only people in town who know where she lives."

Another pause and…

"Do not go there. It wasn't one of my kids and it wasn't David."

Pause and, beginning to get irate (or more irate)…

"How do I know? Are you fucking with me?"

Another pause and…

"Yeah, my full weight, asshole. And you dick with him until that time, you'll regret it."

He then rang off.

"You think Sheriff Dern told someone where I live?" I asked.

His answer was wry.

"How'd you guess?"

There were situations where wry was a good call.

I didn't feel this was one of them.

I shot him a look that communicated that.

"You know I kind of like you," he bit off.

I thought so.

However, the absence of a kiss was another story.

I didn't share that in his current mood.

"And I kinda want you to be happy, and settled, and enjoying the great northwest, getting to know my daughter, shoveling shit at my sons when I have certain things off my mind and the time I need to dedicate myself to all the things I'm gonna do to you."

Oh.

Well then.

I silently lauded the invention of padded bras as I carefully watched him.

"So, fans crawling all over your place, flipping your shit, taking me and my boys off target is not conducive to any of that," he concluded.

"I see."

"And it's pissing me off."

"I understand that now."

"I shouldn't take that out on you, I know. But Dern's behind this and that pisses me off even more."

"I understand that too."

He jerked up his chin.

"What are you throwing your full weight behind?" I asked.

"Harry Moran is running for sheriff against Dern next year. He's already filed and got more than enough signatures. His campaign officially kicked off about two weeks before you moved here."

I felt my eyes grow big. "Um…"

"Yeah," he grunted.

"Were you public with your support for him?"

"Everyone's public with their support for him. But yeah, I don't have a sign out by the gate, but if asked, I don't hold back."

"Prior to Alice."

Not even a beat passed before he confirmed, "Prior to Alice."

I was horrified.

And furious.

"Dern wanted to bag that," I whispered, the words trembling with negative emotion.

"He had Harry checking parking meters. We have five parking meters in this entire county. And Harry's the best investigator they got."

"Oh my God!"

Yes, I shouted it.

"He didn't want Harry, or me, shining even a little when it came to Alice."

"She was a little girl," I hissed, my torso spiking toward him like a snake striking.

"And now you get why I was an ass to you, because Leland is pissing me off."

"Is he interfering with your investigation now?"

"He isn't helping it, but he also isn't outright hindering it. He's too busy with damage control."

"But, say, I sit with you and your kids at the Double D. I'm grocery shopping with Celeste. Maybe he lets slip where I live, which lets slip your focus on Alice's killer, because he knows where we are with each other."

"You're taking things further, baby," he said low, with hints of pride.

I definitely felt the pride, my shoulders going back with it, and I decided to focus on that, rather than Dern, because there was nothing I could do about Dern.

But Bohannan could, and I knew he would.

"Maybe you can hire me," I suggested.

"Not gonna happen."

My eyes squinted.

"We need to discuss societal stamps and how pigeon-holing genders, races and cultures has likely led to us not having a cure for cancer yet," I informed him.

"I'm not pigeon-holing you. If you worked for me, when would you have time to write Priscilla Lange romance novels and Jack Mullally thrillers?"

I stood very, very still.

"I'm a big Mullally fan, Larue."

My lips didn't move even as the words came out.

"How did you know?"

"It'd be cool I could tell you I noticed patterns and cadence between your pen name work and *We Pluck the Cord*. But that isn't my expertise. It's because you have every single one of their books on your bookshelves in your living room, Lange then Mullally, chronological, before you get into the other books you keep, which are kept alphabetically by author. And those are mostly literary, with a good deal of mystery and very little romance or thrillers, because, I figure, you keep those in your office. And, the obvious clue, they're both very successful and very famous for the fact the true name of their author remains entirely anonymous."

He was right.

I kept those genres of books in my office.

And he was right.

No one knew who Priscilla and Jack were.

Because they were me.

"But I wasn't sure," he kept going, "until you just said, 'read my books,' plural."

Damn.

I'd slipped.

"It's been fifteen years and not a single person has figured that out," I informed him.

"My guess is, not many people who don't know have been in your living room."

His guess was correct.

All of his guesses were.

I turned my head to the wall that led to the living room as my mind changed my afternoon's course to rearranging my bookshelves.

"I haven't told the kids. I won't." I looked back at him as he spoke. "That's yours. And I'm down with giving you a second job if you want one. But how 'bout I get in your pants first? If we can survive stalkers, murderers, teenagers, bro boys, and we're as great together in bed as I think we'll be, we can add working together to that catalog and see if it's a fit."

Okay, now that I had him…

"Can I ask why you won't even kiss me?" I whispered.

"Think about it," he whispered back.

If…we're as great together in bed as I think we'll be.

Cade Bohannan was full of surprises.

I smiled.

His gaze homed in on my smile and darkened.

Yes.

He definitely should not kiss me.

"Heads up," he said to my mouth. "I'm a good kisser and I bet you taste great."

"You're also cocky."

He tore his attention from my lips and looked into my eyes. "No, I'm not. I know because I was voted best kisser in high school."

I clicked my tongue and studied the ceiling, but I was still smiling.

When I looked back to him, I saw his beard was too.

A knock came at the door.

"Yo," Bohannan called.

Jace swung in, just his upper body, hand on the knob, eyes glued to his father.

Studiously.

That needle bomb exploded at my back again.

Because he looked spooked.

"Dad, can we talk?" he asked.

Jace still didn't look at me as his father walked to him and they disappeared from the door.

TWENTY-FIVE

Somethin' for Nothin'

On the brick wall at the side of Aromacobana, there was an extraordinary mural painted around the words NORTHERN EXPOSURE, which included the image of a bear with a rifle shooting a hunter, a plethora of distinctively green straws floating down an otherwise crystal-clear river, the sun obliterated by the smoke of a logging mill smokestack. This was all complemented with a dozen tie-dyed peace signs scattered about just in case anyone missed the overall bent behind the message.

The inside of the café was a carefully curated cornucopia of antique, vintage and repurposed furniture, including the pastry case, espresso bar, cash counter and everything behind it that contained the guts of the business: shelves, industrial mixers, ovens and espresso machine.

I was waiting for Celeste. We were having an after-school coffee before we went home to start dinner for ourselves and men who would, sometime along the line, and that time would be when I was in my own bed, be eating leftovers.

I was also distracting myself from the fact that, when Bohannan and Jace disappeared, so did Jess, and they *disappeared.*

Including the fact that for the first time, Bohannan didn't reply to my text within fifteen minutes.

He didn't reply at all.

And the text read, *Is everything okay?*

So the fact he didn't reply to that made it even worse.

I was sucking an iced latte out of a paper cup that had a straw made from avocado pits, sitting in a thick-armed, low-backed, wine-colored upholstered chair that had to have been built in the fifties, watching the door for Celeste and trying to pretend I wasn't famous.

This didn't work, as it never did.

People were staring at me, and eventually, as it goes, one got up the gumption to approach.

She was very pretty. She was also young, perhaps three or four years older than Celeste. She had an exceptionally well-crafted balayage. Her anti-contouring contouring was inspired. Both of which seemed somewhat at odds, and somewhat not, with her T-shirt that proclaimed MAKE LOVE THEN MAKE MORE LOVE.

"Heya!" she greeted.

"Hi there," I replied on my patented Delphine Larue Welcoming but Not Too Welcoming Smile.

The welcoming part welcomed.

She got closer on a hop slide: one foot the hop, the other foot she left behind then dragged over, toes never leaving the floor, this reminiscent of the dance stylings of Gene Kelly, and her face was set to GRIN!

"Ohmigod. We were all like…*waiting* for you to…*show*…and here you…*are*."

If the Gene Kelly move didn't herald it, added with the balayage and makeup chops, the way she spoke did.

This was a former cheerleader.

And there was something so charming about her, even in my current troubled mood, I felt a little cheered.

"Yes," I agreed, because there I was.

She leaned slightly closer to me setting her face to SAD! like it was necessary for an entirety of crowded bleachers to read it.

I didn't know what she did for a living, but her emotive projection was spot on. She'd excel onstage.

"It was so, so nice that you tried to help with Alice."

"I'm sure the town would have pulled together a collection eventually," I remarked.

She swayed back and her face said SURPRISED!

"I didn't even think about that!"

"'Scuse, please," someone said, and Ms. Kelly was swept aside. "You. Yeah you." Kimmy of the Christmas attire was standing there, confirming she was talking to me when she was staring down at me, I was staring up at her, and so she couldn't be talking to anyone else.

Incidentally, she was again in Christmas attire, a T-shirt that was Santa's coat with black belt and gold buckle and some thick white fuzz around the neck, down the front and ringing the hem. This was under a cardigan that had a line of tree ornaments stitched into the pattern of the knit across the chest, upper sleeves, and although I couldn't see it, I was assuming all the way around the back.

Oh, and a reindeer antler headband.

I had to admit, that tee kind of rocked.

Nevertheless, I instantly went into damage control mode.

"I'm so sorry. The boys have been really busy. They haven't had time to gather any evidence about Castro."

"Of course they haven't," she returned. "They're hunting that nutjob who killed that little girl."

Well, one could say she was direct.

I nodded soberly. "They are, indeed."

"What I wanna know is…"

Oh boy.

"When are you gonna write another book?"

That was what I feared was coming, because it often came after, "What I wanna know is…?"

"'Cause, you see," she carried on, "I liked that other one. That girl had gumption. She was like…" She turned to have a fake conversation with the air at her side. "'You know what? I'm just gonna be me. And you know what else? I got a vulva, and you might not think I can be me, but guess what?" She leaned in to drive her point home to her imaginary audience. "*I can be.*" Back to me. "I think every girl on the planet should be required to read that book."

"That's a very kind compliment."

"I mean the boys?" she continued. "They think they got Holden Caulfield. But what's that boy teaching them? I do not know. But we girls? We girls got Delilah Spinnaker. And I'll take me some Delilah over Holden a million times."

I wasn't sure that was the compare/contrast to go for, but the reason I wrote the book was to let a reader do their own thinking.

So all I had was, "Thank you."

"So, when are you gonna write another?" she pushed.

And then what I expected to come next, came.

Even so, what came wasn't what I would have expected.

"Because I think in the next one, she should become a commando, and her boyfriend can be her sidekick."

I'd had a lot of people share what they thought my heroine in *We Pluck the Cord* should do next.

Commando, though, was a first.

I tried to let her down easy by saying what I'd said around fifty thousand times.

"I really feel like her story has been told."

Kimmy settled her weight in like a coach did in the locker room prior to giving a pep talk to the team.

"I was afraid you'd say that. 'Cause, see…*it hasn't.*"

"Ohmigod! Hi, Shelly!" Celeste exclaimed, rushing in front of Kimmy to give Ms. Kelly, or apparently Shelly, a big hug.

Shelly hugged her back and Celeste turned on Kimmy.

"Hey there, Kimmy. I need those antlers."

"They're at my shop, gurl."

"I'm gonna stop by." She looked down at me. "You wanna stop by Kimmy's shop after coffees, Delly?"

I loved the "Delly" thing was catching on.

"Let me guess, it's a Christmas shop," I drawled.

Celeste and Shelly burst into giggles, but Kimmy stared at me like I had a screw loose.

"Yeah, I got Christmas all year 'round, 'cause, duh...*Christmas*," she explained. "But obviously, right now it's Halloween."

"Wait!" Celeste grabbed her arm. "Do you a have those vampire teeth that are actually wax that you can chew? Like, the anti-gum, gum...but in vampire teeth."

Did they still make those?

"Yep." Kimmy popped the "p" of her yep.

They still made them.

"Okay, we're gonna get those too," Celeste declared, and I had to say, I liked how she seemed to be...carefree.

This was not the girl I first met.

This was something else.

In other words, I made a decision the likes I'd made a lot over the years.

A mom decision.

And this one was not to let Celeste know my fans (or paparazzi or whatever he was) were causing problems.

She looked again at me, precisely, my drink.

"You've got yours. Do you want a cookie? Or a brownie? They make great brownies. I'm gonna go grab a drink," she said.

"Let me—" I made a move to get up, and, let's face it, escape Kimmy and Shelly (no matter how cheerful or entertaining they were—from experience I knew these things were apt to turn, and I'd learned it was best for all concerned to make your exit before that happened).

Celeste thwarted this endeavor.

"No, I have money." She turned to Shelly. "You good?"

"For sure," Shelly replied.

She turned to Kimmy. "Good?"

Kimmy didn't answer except to lift her paper cup and avocado straw an inch away from Celeste's face.

Not that she could, but still, Celeste didn't miss the communication.

"I'll be right back." She began to take off.

"Wait! I'll come with. I need a brownie for Ray," Shelly called after her, then whirled on me. "So nice to meet you, Ms. Larue."

"Delphine," I corrected.

She hopped, clapped, and instead of shouting, "Rah, rah, sis kum bah!" she cried, "Ohmigod! I...*love you*."

Then she took off.

I winced, because Kimmy had latched onto a heavy wrought iron, French bistro-inspired chair with a wooden seat and was scraping it across the cement floor.

Everybody else in the shop winced too.

She set it beside my chair and plopped down in it, before sucking back some coffee, pounding her chest, and focusing on me.

"So, what the boys got on this psycho?" she asked.

"I don't really...they don't talk about the case."

She bent forward, elbow to knee, in order to commit fully to conspiracy mode.

"I reckon you heard your fill about Audrey," she said low.

"Ummmmm..."

"Yeah, well, I mean, even karma isn't that big of a bitch."

I could agree with that.

So I hummed, "Mm."

"Now, guess who stumbled out of Sarah Pulaski's back door in the wee hours of the morning yesterday."

I tried to stop her. "Kimmy—"

I failed to stop her.

"You guessed it. *Dale*."

"I really don't—"

"Now, obviously, this isn't the best timing. And as a modern woman, I would not advocate Sarah taking him back. But, I mean, if you're gonna stick it to the woman who destroyed your life..."

She let that hang, and she was right to do so, because indeed, that was some intense vengeance.

"I feel like we should—"

"And you know who's, like, cackling over her brew?"

Something about that question made me pause and listen.

"*Lana*," she said, like *gotcha*.

"I haven't been in town that long, I don't know—"

"Right." She scooched her chair closer, it made another, thankfully much shorter shriek, then she launched in. "Lana of Lana and Bobby. Audrey's *first* target, 'cause, see, Bobby's got more money than God, which is what Audrey was after, and why Lana didn't kick him to the curb when he stepped out on her."

This must be other couple that Celeste was talking about at the grocery store.

"She had to go *way* down the line, you get me, 'cause then there was Annie and Jay, and after that Wendy and Dwayne. And she ended with Dale, who does all right, but he's no Bobby, Jay or Dwayne. To be honest, I think the only one she didn't put the screws to, and that pun was intended, or tried to and got shot down, was your Cade when he was with Grace."

Okay, maybe the high school kids weren't very well informed, because that was a much longer pattern.

Kimmy patted my hand.

I didn't take my eyes off her.

"He's a good one, that one. Be a waste of her time. Cade Bohannan is a one-woman man, like his daddy was, and *his* and so on."

I was beginning not to regret this gossip sesh.

She wagged a finger at me. "So you best let it be known that's your property, gurl."

"I don't mean to cause offense, but humans can't be property, Kimmy."

"I was younger, prettier and less weird, I'd stamp that boy *all over*."

I couldn't stop my giggle.

She turned her head slightly, keeping her gaze on me, and slowly nodded.

Even though I didn't offer my one-cent piece, in for a penny…

"Do you have an idea of who might have hurt Alice?"

Kimmy sat back, sipped her drink, and considered this somberly.

Her straw left her lip, and she told some point in the air above us. "Well, there's that old whackjob, Paddy Tremayne. But I reckon everyone thought of him first, except Leland, who probably had a brain freeze for the first seventy-two hours she was missing, thinkin' only about how he'd stop himself from shittin' his pants."

She looked to me.

And declared, "He failed at that. Figuratively."

I sucked in my lips.

She sucked back more of her drink.

And concluded, "But other than that, I can't say. Been thinkin' on it. But nothin's comin' to me."

"That's a shame," I murmured.

"If I get any bright ideas, I'll look for you or one of your boys."

One of your boys.

This time, I couldn't stop my smile.

She studied me.

Then she said, "You know, didn't think there was a woman alive who was good enough for that man. Guess I was wrong. Wasn't thinkin' big enough. Still, you do him wrong, you best leave MP behind. Because not a soul in this town will be okay with that, I don't care how great that book is you wrote. And I'll tell you somethin' for nothin', I don't know what went down with them, but the minute she left, you better believe Grace Bohannan knew that too. And I'd bet you a thousand dollars, that's why that woman never came back."

She glanced toward the counter, saw Celeste still was waiting for her drink, and out of earshot, which was a little too late, but thankfully Celeste wasn't close, then she came back to me.

"Come on by to the shop. I don't give discounts to rich people, but I'll give you an early look at the Thanksgiving stuff."

She slapped my knee so hard, it didn't hurt badly, but it hurt.

She then got up and walked away.

TWENTY-SIX

Just Starting Out

I finally got my return text.

At 11:47 at night.

It read, *You up?*

Yes, I replied.

On my way over.

You will note that wasn't a question of whether I wanted company at nearly ten to midnight.

I wasn't in a good mood, and not because it took so long for Bohannan to reply to my text.

It was because I felt obliged to pull the curtain on my wall of windows, which normally gave an incredible view of a tranquil, mist-shrouded, moonlight-gilded lake, which was one of the reasons why I bought this place.

It also meant that I didn't see Bohannan coming up.

But I heard his knock.

I headed to the security panel and disarmed it before I went to the door, pulled back the curtains and let him in.

He gazed approvingly at the curtains.

I shut the door.

"Beer or an Aromacobana brownie?" I offered.

"Just ate," he replied.

"At nearly midnight?" Those three words were filled with wifely disapproval that wasn't mine to have because he was a grown man, he could eat when he wanted, but also, I wasn't his wife.

He made no reply, but he was watching me closely.

In other words, this time with his quiet, he read my mood and was proceeding with caution.

I moved to the couch. "Do you want to sit?"

I felt him behind me.

I also was in a titch less of a bad mood when I sat down, turning his way and lifting my bent leg to the seat, and he sat close, so his thigh was against my shin, and then he one-upped that by curling his long fingers around the back of my knee.

"What's up?" I asked.

"Why you up?" he asked.

"Because I consumed a massive latte at around three o'clock, and I really can't have caffeine after, maybe, ten, or it keeps me up late at night."

"Right," he muttered.

"I answered yours…" I prompted.

He didn't cushion it.

"Hawk is sending a guy. His name is Billy. He's gonna be living at the rental property up your lane. Hawk will also be monitoring the feeds from your cameras again, twenty-four, seven."

Now it was me with no reply.

"Jess and Jace, they caught a trail. They followed it," he said.

"Okay," I whispered.

"We got sensors, even a few cameras. They send alerts to our phones, me and the boys. We have a lot of them. We move them around from time to time. But it isn't like every inch of the woods is lousy with them."

"Okay," I repeated.

"Though, it's just the woods we keep track of. I own the land. No one owns the lake."

"Right."

"Trail they tracked says whoever it was, they knew to avoid the wood. They came lakeside. On foot. Practically in the water. But not in the water, like they wanted the trail found. And not through the woods."

Suddenly, I felt very cold.

"Beyond your boathouse, maybe six, ten feet, that trail disappears. Just stops."

I started trembling.

Because I'd heard that before.

When they followed the trail of who took Alice.

It led into the woods.

And then it just stopped.

Bohannan pulled my knee fully up on his thigh, which scooted me across the seat closer to him.

"Hawk checked that footage again and again. But did you see the guy walk back the way he came?"

I shook my head.

"He did not retrace his steps?"

I kept shaking my head.

"You see a boat at all?"

Again, I shook my head.

"Did you keep watching?"

I nodded, but said, "It wasn't like I watched for hours. I texted you and talked to you and then started checking windows. But except for the texting, and until after we spoke, I didn't take my eyes from the windows."

Bohannan nodded.

Once.

"There are blind spots to Hawk's coverage, but on one feed or another, he'd see that guy. He didn't see the guy. Even if he came around the front of your house. And when I say retrace his steps, what I mean is, to make no trail, he'd have to be walking backwards, placing his feet exactly where his feet were on the way in and *retracing his steps*. And I figure anyone would notice that."

"So, um…what does that mean?"

"It means I know we're just starting out…"

Oh boy.

"But I want you to move in with me."

Well.

Damn.

TWENTY-SEVEN

They Got More Signatures

The next afternoon, I was standing outside Aromacobana, studying the mural, impressed by the tie-dye effects in the peace signs, and the choice to make the bear and hunter look like a real bear and hunter, not cartoons, when I felt someone come up to my side.

"It's obscene."

I turned my head to see a blonde woman of around my age wearing a lovely sweater, well-cut trousers and stylish, low-heeled booties.

She was glaring at the mural.

"I started a petition," she told the mural. "Gathered *quite* a number of signatures. Took it to the town council." She turned to me. "But the hippies had their own petition, and they had more signatures than me. And by that, I mean they had only *seven* more signatures than me. So that monstrosity remains."

She tossed a manicured hand toward Aromacobana.

I allowed myself a moment to ponder this small-town reflection of the state of our country.

Since she seemed to require a response from me, I noted, "It's a little on the nose."

"It's in*DE*cent."

I felt it made a strong statement, but I didn't feel it was obscene or indecent.

Therefore, I chose not to reply.

"I've not read your book," she announced.

I could have guessed.

"I hear it's very good," she went on. "It's just that I don't read those types of books. I don't read to think. I read to escape."

"What types of books do you read?" I asked.

She turned back to the mural, and like so many of our kind, she sounded abashed when she admitted, "I like romance."

"Do you read Priscilla Lange?"

She turned to me, her face now animated. "You?"

Naturally I did, since I wrote them.

I smiled.

She leaned in conspirative, now that we were HEA sisters.

"They're racy," she told me. "Racier than my norm, but it's not trashy."

I hated the word "trashy" in all its uses, particularly when it was used to describe romance novels. I had equal acrimony for the word "smut."

I didn't share that and decided to accept the compliment she didn't know she was giving.

"Agreed."

"I never miss one of her books."

"I don't either."

"I wish she published more than one a year."

I said nothing.

Her tone grew warm and serious. "It was a beautiful gesture, what you tried to do for Alice."

I dipped my chin.

Her gaze wandered off, I would know, with what she said next, in the direction of the sheriff's department.

"Sheriff Dern is a disaster," she decreed.

I again made no reply.

Her attention came back to me. "I mean, considering…" an

appropriate pause, "what I heard happened to her. It probably wouldn't have helped. The reward. But we'll never know. And everyone is talking about it. Why he didn't announce it. I mean, it doesn't help to share that at the little girl's *funeral* for God's sakes."

"Yes," I said.

"And of course you know about the dogs."

The dogs?

"Sorry?" I asked.

"He should have called in the dogs. Like, right away. We don't have this kind of thing happening here. So we don't have a K-9 unit. The next county over has them. I heard that, before they even left the station to go to Dale and Audrey's, Harry said call for the dogs. For no good reason but to point out he's in charge, to put Harry in his place, Leland didn't call for the damn dogs. And then it was hours before they called for those dogs."

I felt my mouth tighten.

She didn't miss it and hissed out, "Yes." Then carried on, "And you're very aware Cade should have been called in even *before* the dogs. I mean, the man himself found Percy Gibson and led the cops in Wichita to the Rooftop Gunman."

That made my entire body tighten.

Holy hell.

It seemed like sometime in the midst of all my obsessive keeping track of what happened to Alice, or in all the time since, I should have Googled Bohannan myself.

I had no idea.

Though I knew about both.

Percy Gibson was known as Ted Bundy Lite (because, you know, the media is so cruel and clever with those kinds of things). In the end, he'd been convicted of killing seven college women from three different colleges in two different states. But it was considered by the authorities there might be more, they just couldn't find them, and he wasn't talking.

The Rooftop Gunman in Wichita had had a Son of Sam-type spree, though thankfully much shorter. He'd taken aim from random roofs in the city eight times in three and a half weeks before he was caught. In the end, he killed three people and wounded seven.

He'd committed suicide by cop.

He'd been a veteran army sniper.

The government had swiftly and boisterously lauded how quickly he was caught with the local and federal authorities working together, making so much noise about that, it hid the fact that they did not take this as further evidence they needed to do more to take care of our veterans.

He was not Percy Gibson, Ted Bundy or David Berkowitz.

He was a man who served our country who deserved better well before whatever demons he'd acquired had the chance to accomplish their takeover.

"I mean, you have that kind of local resource, a girl vanishes into nothing, you call on it, don't you think?" she asked me.

"Yes, I think," I replied firmly.

She turned fully to me. "You know, we're all happy you're with him. A good man needs a good woman just as much as that works the other way around."

Yes, even though I wholeheartedly agreed, she probably shouldn't read *We Pluck the Cord*.

And yes, this was a small town and news traveled very fast.

"And Grace was not a good woman," she continued. "I knew that even before she left. Everyone noticed how she treated Celeste."

Now she had my attention.

"And how was that?" I asked quietly.

"Like she was a nuisance," she told me frankly.

As my heart squeezed, I looked at Aromacobana.

Which was where Celeste was right then, on a coffee date with Will Pulaski.

"Grace was liked only a little bit more than Audrey," the woman shared. "I know Cade loved her." I looked to her. "She treated him and her boys like gold. Dedicated to them. So I, for one, am glad she took off. Because if she hadn't, Cade would have eventually had to make the decision to cut her loose so he could get Celeste safe. And that would have killed him."

"Yes," I whispered. "That would have killed him."

"I'm Megan," she introduced, holding out her hand.

I took it. "Delphine."

She gave me a squeeze, we let go, and she invited, "We have a book club. We meet once a month. Romance only. I get that we're just townies, but no one will be weird with you, and we'd love to have you."

"That's really nice. I think I'd like that."

Her expression shifted, her regard of me did too.

She then dug in her purse, came out with a little, monogrammed, leather covered notepad, slid the small pen out of the attached holder and flipped it open.

She tore off what she wrote and handed it to me.

I took it.

"I'll leave it up to you to call me."

"Thanks," I said.

"It's not my place but I'm going to say it anyway, I know you're worried." She jerked her head to the coffee shop. "Will's a good boy. But he's a *boy*. And now he's a boy who's hurting. He has no business dating right now."

I held her gaze steady.

I wasn't sure what she meant by "he's a *boy*," but I was sure she knew why I was fretfully standing outside Aromacobana, staring at a mural.

"Also, you should know, this Alice thing?" She shook her head. "Anomaly. It's safe here. I've lived here my whole life. I promise you. It's safe here. If you need a place to disappear, be around real people, you found your spot. And we'll protect that for you. You know how people are wherever Harrison Ford lives in Wyoming? That'll be how we are for you. No one will breathe a word you're here."

"Thanks again."

The things she was saying were making me feel good in all that seemed to be going bad.

Until she carried on.

"Except Leland. He's running scared and you're high-profile.

Bigger media gets wind of Alice, and his bungling of that, no telling what he'll do. Be careful."

"I appreciate the warning."

She nodded, glanced to the paper in my hand and back to me.

"I hope you call."

I nodded this time and promised, "I will."

She started to walk away but turned back.

"I don't have to like it, and I don't like it. But they got more signatures. Do you know what I mean?"

At that, I gave her my full smile.

"I know exactly what you mean, Megan."

She gave me a full smile back, and she was very pretty.

"See you at book club," she said.

"See you there," I replied.

TWENTY-EIGHT

Warm and Fuzzy

As a mother, semi-stalking your children was a highly sensitive operation.

As the new-semi-woman-in-a-kid's-life, it was almost impossible.

However, after Megan left me, I did my best to saunter casually, and very slowly, in front of the windows of Aromacobana, glancing in to find Celeste and Will.

I did.

They didn't notice me.

But I got a good look at him.

And…

Well.

Shit.

LET ME TAKE YOU BACK...

Last night, Bohannan got into my bedroom.

That would be to stand, leaning against the jamb of the door of my closet while I packed light to move to his house, doing it light because it was late. I was going to come back in the morning to pack heavier.

He did this after he whistled low when he saw the closet.

He'd been pensive and careful with his expressions since he'd shown up that night, but his eyes were twinkling when he said, "My closet is better."

Even though I knew it was because he gave it to Grace, I still felt that sexually.

I had a feeling on the drive to his place, which was in my car, which meant I drove, Bohannan suffered a hit to his manhood that he wasn't behind the wheel, but he let his brooding fill the cab of the car without making it verbal.

He also told me on the short ride to his place, "I want you in my bed because I want you in my bed, I also want you close. But you're going to stay in our guestroom. Celeste knows we're a thing. She's nearly grown up. But it's too soon. And we both got tension to release, and I'm far from high school, but you that close, I'm not feeling testing my control."

How he managed the marvel of being a good father, a protective boyfriend-ish-type person and sexually charging one short speech, I did not know.

But he did it.

Regardless of the fact I was freaked out that I was moving in with my boyfriend-ish-type person I hadn't even kissed yet, and mostly *why* I was, a mixture of euphoria and excitement and a deep-down warmth that couldn't be denied filled me when I added my Volvo to their collection of vehicles.

Celeste, he also shared as we walked into the house, had been briefed.

As an aside, he'd commandeered my bag, which held a pair of pajamas, face cleanser, moisturizer, deodorant, a clean pair of panties, jeans and a sweater, so it probably weighed less than ten pounds. But he strong armed his way to it so I suspected his manhood got revived at least a little bit.

When we arrived, Celeste was in bed, so after Bohannan got me sorted, he hung out in my bedroom with me.

This being, we cuddled in the armchair across from the bed.

But I got to be in his lap.

He had a very comfortable lap and a long arm reach, so I also got to use him as a kind of cocoon.

It was lovely.

He shared I had not read it wrong.

For whatever reason, they were thinking Alice's killer was prowling Bohannan land.

Which led to a more in-depth questioning for me.

What he looked like. Age. Height. Weight. Race.

(Dark hair. I couldn't tell age or height, but at a guess, between twenty and forty, and average. He didn't appear overweight, or under it. Last, white.)

What was he wearing?

(It looked like a light blue sweatshirt that was wet. No hat. No umbrella. No slicker. In the rain.)

Did he appear interested in my house?

(No, he didn't even look up at my house, but I had him in my sights mere seconds.)

Did I get a look at his face?

(No, alas, I did not.)

It also led to more questioning for Bohannan.

He seemed hesitant, but in the end, he gave it to me.

"It isn't unusual for someone like him to want to play with someone like me."

This just kept getting worse.

He continued speaking.

"That said, it wasn't yesterday we found Alice. With this kind of thing, there's no telling what his actions might be. Some like him could take years to start playing games with investigators. Leaving a definitive trail the way he did says something, though he chose a day it was raining, and if you hadn't seen him, that trail could have been gone before we saw it. And you said he didn't look to your place to see if you saw him. But he could just know there's activity at your house, and hope he was seen. That seems thin. So my read on that might be wrong. I would think there would be something. Something concrete. A sign. Him leaving a present. Something to announce he's going to dick with me. So maybe I'm being hypersensitive." He gave me a squeeze. "But we're not taking any chances."

"I'm guessing that with where I am," I noted.

Another squeeze and, "We'll be giving you some Taser lessons. Once we do, I'd like you to carry one with you. Hawk's got your GPS fob still tracking. He's sending one for Celeste with Billy. Billy is going to help us keep an eye on the property, you and Celeste. David has been briefed, and he's going to go about his business at your place but keep an eye out. I also told Moran, but not Dern. He knows who the good deputies are, and who they aren't, and he's already formed a loose, unofficial team who are working this themselves, but we're coordinating. He told me he'll do what he can. As for you and Celeste, you live your lives. You do your thing. You do it knowing you're covered, one way or another, though do that smart and watchful. But when we take downtime, I don't want our resources scattered."

"Circling the wagons," I murmured.

"Precisely."

"Can you tell me about the case?" I asked.

"I could, if I had anything to tell you."

"But…" I started carefully. "You found her."

"He wanted us to."

"That easy?" I asked.

"For Dern? No. Even for Harry. Maybe not. For me. Yes, that easy."

"And?"

This was when he finally allowed his frustration to come out.

Which meant I pressed closer.

"And, I'm running through every playbook I got, Larue. And there's just not enough there to get a good read on him. I actually *want* whoever you saw to be him. I need more from him if I'm gonna catch him. What I don't want is for that more to come in the form of bodies."

. . .

I HAD AGREED WITH HIM, and I would have liked to end the night with a make-out session, but I didn't think that would help things for Bohannan.

So I got another squeeze and a forehead kiss before he went to his bed and I went to mine.

But that was why I was free to wander town, semi-stalking Celeste on her date, even though Jess, Jace, or the unknown Billy were out there somewhere watching her (and me), because before Megan gave me her warning, I was thinking the same thing.

I wasn't fond of how Celeste described their first date as her being the dumping ground for Will Pulaski's anger.

Of course, he needed someone to talk to.

Celeste simply wasn't that person.

Sure, if she'd been his girlfriend prior to that, and they'd had time together, establishing history, a connection, where she knew all the players from more than just high school gossip, naturally, she'd be one of those resources for him.

But she hadn't been his girlfriend, and she wasn't mature enough to have the tools to deal with his emotion, or the ones it might stir in her.

So I wandered town—the residential part of which snaked into the hills and valleys, but for the business district, it was a pretty much one street that ran five blocks—taking in what I had sensed, but hadn't yet been able to take in completely.

This place was strange.

It simply wasn't normal.

Bear-shooting-hunter mural aside, as an example, they had a movie theater.

But the latest big release wasn't playing.

Halloween was a few days away, and although it was apropos, I could not imagine with this small population it would be financially responsible to be showing a double feature of *Carrie* and *Christine*.

I also wasn't sure, in the current climate, that a double feature with two horror films with female names was the way to roll.

But there it was.

There was also the fact that the Aromacobana was the only—

and I mean *the only*—sign that anything beyond the new millennium had touched Misted Pines.

Example, they had a Five and Dime, capitalized because it was called Hoot's Five and Dime. Glancing inside, I saw it had a pegboard wall filled with stuff hanging on miniature rods, a table at the front advertising a sale on skeins of yarn, and a soda fountain at the side. Therefore, I was mildly shocked it didn't have girls in petticoats and saddle shoes sitting on the stools sipping cherry cokes while their ponytails swayed.

Honestly, as I walked the sidewalks, in looks and mood, it felt like I was traversing the outdoor location of *Stranger Things*.

And that was the *earliest* I'd date stamp this place.

The Double D being the perfect set piece for a new rendition of "Beauty School Dropout" was not an incongruity.

Truth told, there was something very wholesome about it.

Like, you wouldn't blink if Marty McFly raced down the sidewalk on his skateboard.

That said, there was something…*off* about it.

Like, in seeing the tall, broad-shouldered, russet-haired young man talking earnestly to Celeste in the coffee house and looking exactly like the handsome, charming love interest who ends up date raping the innocent, sweet, open-hearted heroine…

Well….

Suffice it to say.

That didn't make me feel warm and fuzzy.

TWENTY-NINE

Maybe Fourteen

I got a text early that evening saying the men would be home for dinner.

I didn't have a lot of experience with a house that was boy-heavy, but I was learning fast.

That meant I pulled out their huge family Foreman grill and had it heated up and ready to rumble by the time the parade of Yukon and Rams hit the Bohannan compound clearing.

I would learn in short order that something had changed.

I learned this as they all trooped in, Celeste and I were in the kitchen, me perhaps hopelessly crafting a salad, Celeste definitely more fittingly air frying some tater tots.

Regardless that food was openly being prepared, Jace and Jess went directly to the pantry and tore into the stash of chips that Celeste had curated for them.

Bohannan, however, came direct to me.

As I stood, head tipped back, staring at him in titillated shock, he slipped an arm around my waist, pulled me to his body, dropped his head and took my mouth.

Okay now.

This one *was* official.

There was no tongue, but his lips were firm, his beard was exquisitely tickly, the pressure perfect, and up close he smelled like mist and man, so those high school kids in his senior class knew what they were talking about.

He lifted his head. "Hey."

"Hey," I forced out.

His beard was stingy with smiles, but still, I was forming a catalog of them.

The one my breathy "hey" earned was a new variety and it made my vaginal walls contract.

He let me go, and as I came back into the room, I realized there was something about him doing that the first time in front of the kids.

Something nice.

What was not nice was Jess scarfing down Cool Ranch Doritos like he was attempting to win a contest.

"You do know we're eating five minutes after I slap the burgers on the grill," I informed him.

"You do know the men are here, so that grill is for sissies. Real men cook meat outdoors," Jess replied.

Taking the Pringles cannister with him, Jace proved his brother's point by saying, "I'll fire up the grill."

Jason went outside.

Mutely, I turned to Bohannan.

"Pick your battles," he advised.

He then moved to his daughter and kissed the side of her head.

I watched this knowing there was already a battle I'd selected.

But I needed reinforcements.

SINCE I WAS NOW LIVING THERE, that morning, before I drove up to pack and properly (if temporarily) move in, I'd helped myself to the Bohannan house.

I'd found there was nook nor cranny that had not felt the touch of Grace Bohannan.

Translation: Bohannan did everything in his power to make

every inch of her environment something that made her happy, something that made it hers, so that she would settle into that home with her family and give as good as she got.

I had a life where I'd cruised on luxury yachts and stayed in castles as a guest of people who owned castles.

This was not that.

Bohannan was not a billionaire.

But everything was high-quality, if not luxury, and as mentioned, Grace had great taste. She put her stamp on things, but she did it with an eye to keeping her boys comfortable.

Her bedroom was a somewhat different story.

I'd been so jubilant after Welsh was caught, I hadn't poked around.

But that day, I discovered not only was Bohannan's bedroom pretty danged rad, his closet *was* sweet (though, no windows or window seat). His bathroom was a dream.

And the private sitting room off to the side, which had floor to ceiling windows that fully opened to the elements, had a direct view to the lake and a modern Juliet balcony, was pure sanctuary.

This was where we found ourselves after dinner, again not making out, but perfecting the art of cuddling, luxuriating in that with the windows open, the fresh air coming in, blanket tucked around us providing insulation, and body heat doing the rest.

"What's with the mist?" I asked.

He chuckled. "Took you long enough."

"Sorry?"

"Usually, if it's fall and winter, people ask that right off the bat."

"I had other things on my mind." I reminded him.

"Hydrothermal springs."

I took my head off his shoulder to look at his face.

"Seriously?"

A nod.

I stated the obvious. "It's huge."

Another nod. "Yup. There's a band of them along the bottom. All year long, no matter how cold it is outside, there are spots in the lake that feel like summer. Sayin' that, there are spots where it's colder. It's just that, there are enough of the hot ones, it heats the whole lake, so when the outside temperature drops, and the air hits the water, mist forms. It doesn't go away from October to March, sometimes September, if we get cold early like this year, and April, if we stay cold late. And if it's very cold, it's just straight up fog throughout this whole valley."

"And thus the name, Misted Pines."

"Yeah, and that's what the Okanagan called it, translated to English."

"Okanagan?"

"The Methow and Okanagan tribes lived on this land. Now they live southeast on the Colville Reservation."

"Right," I muttered.

"Also, that's the name of the really big lake, east of here."

"I'm afraid my Washington state geography isn't all it should be."

"We'll get you there."

"Mm."

"The indigenous tribes thought this was a spiritual place. Used it in healing. After it was taken from them, stories turned. Early settlers thought it was haunted. Or cursed. Tales told of people boating into the mist, never returning."

"I'll note at this juncture, neither the real estate person nor the FBI shared these stories with me."

He smiled and cuddled me closer. "Then there's the story of Cornelius Ruck."

Of course there was.

"His name was not Cornelius."

Another smile. "It was. Wealthy fur trader and local big man. Cornelius would meet his mistress at a cabin he built at the side of the lake. He did this until his wife followed him, carrying a pistol. Allegedly."

"Allegedly?"

"Allegedly. The cabin burned down. Nobody inside. Mrs. Ruck was seen rowing into the mist, where she disappeared. She was not seen rowing out of it. But the day after the fire, she was doing her normal business in town. Folks found it interesting she didn't report her husband missing until days later."

"And Cornelius, and his, I'll note unnamed, mistress?"

Now a grin and he gestured to the windows. "Never seen again, but they're out there, haunting the lake."

"Something to know about me."

"Yeah?"

"I'm not good with ghost stories."

"Then you picked the wrong town, baby."

That sounded ominous.

"I don't want Celeste dating Will," I blurted.

That had not been the way I'd rehearsed it.

His brows flew up.

"I intended to preface this by saying, you and I are bonding. She and I are bonding. The boys and I are bonding. But I understand my place here. I'm new. We've officially kissed once."

"Officially?"

"All the forehead kisses, etcetera, don't count."

His beard twitched.

I pulled a bit away from him (but not too far).

"However, as an authority on this, seeing as I successfully raised two stunning, perfect, wonderful, strong, capable girls, and upon some sleuthing today, which others might erroneously refer to as—" I did air quotation marks, "—*stalking*, I got a look at Will. And I don't like him."

"You got a look at him."

"Through the window at Aromacobana."

"You got a look at him through the window of a coffee shop."

"Yes," I confirmed.

"And you're raising your banner on this."

"Yes."

"Can I ask what has your intuition sparking?"

"I don't like the look of him."

"Explain."

"He's tall and handsome."

Bohannan stared at me.

"I know both of those *sound* good. You just have to trust me."

"Reading between these lines, you're telling me this so I'll tell my daughter she can't date the guy she's been crushing on since sixth grade. The guy who finally noticed her and asked her out. The guy whose sister was just murdered, and she has a soft heart, and she would want to be there for him, and now she gets to be there for him. You want me to tell *that* daughter she can't date this guy and find some way to do it without laying you out that I'm telling her that because you don't like the look of him."

"Obviously, this sounds impossible, so we have to form a plan."

"Babe, you do know that doing that, no matter how awesome a plan we form, is gonna lay *me* out with my girl."

"Okay, how about just say, until you sort out Alice's killer, she has to stay at home unless she's at school."

Another eyebrow raise.

"You think that'll go over better?"

"Bohannan—"

He turned to me and pulled me into his arms.

"Larue, listen to me, Celeste isn't my first rodeo. I learned with two boys, who, growing up, and sometimes still, have more testosterone than brains, what a heavy hand in parenting means to a kid. You gotta let them make their own mistakes."

"Cade, honey, listen to me," I said softly, lifting my hands to curl them around either side of his neck. "When it comes to dating, the consequences of mistakes a boy could make, and a girl could make, can be two very different, very life-altering things."

His head ticked.

And his voice was growly when he asked, "You got that vibe off the kid?"

"I do not like stereotyping. I avoid it. It's not just. It's not right. But that doesn't mean some aren't earned. To mix metaphors, he's the cock on the walk with a bird on a string. He has the perfect pressure point to push to get what he wants. Maybe I'm wrong and all he wants is a beautiful girl to spend time with and to listen to him after something heinous happened to him and his family. Or he could be a piece of shit in a high school hunk disguise. At the very least, she needs someone to explain the intricacies of consent versus cajoling, and make it very clear only she gets to decide."

"And that's supposed to be me?"

I winced and noted, "You *are* her father."

He let me go, turned to the windows, sat back, and for the first time since I'd known him, he looked flummoxed.

He was a great guy.

I was living with him and cooking for him (and his kids) and anxiously awaiting having sex with him, so he was, for all intents and purposes, my guy.

Damn it all to hell.

"I'll talk to her," I mumbled.

He turned instantly to me, eyes sexy and happy and victorious, and gathered me in his arms.

"You owe me," I warned as his face disappeared in my neck.

"You got it. Once we tear the lid off, first month, every go, you get three orgasms to my one."

His beard was tickly and his lips were firm on my neck too.

Lord.

"Can you do that?" I asked.

That was a mistake.

Because he pulled his face out of my neck and I liked it there.

Though, with the look on his face, I wasn't complaining.

Wow.

He could do that.

"I'm celibate," I announced. "I haven't had sex in thirteen years."

He blinked.

"Maybe fourteen," I went on.

Bohannan didn't move.

"So, no pressure," I finished.

He growled.

I grinned.

And the mist clung to the lake.

THIRTY

The Second Shoe

I stood at the sink, cradling a cup of coffee in my hands, staring at the lake…

Fretting.

Allow me to catch you up.

From our time cuddling in his sitting room to now, I'd been living with Bohannan for three weeks and three days.

It was nearing Thanksgiving.

Fenn had wrangled a miracle, and she and James were coming home on leave for the holiday.

That home being…*here*.

Even before Fenn and James made these plans, Camille and Joan had planned to come up. Though I suggested I go down, Camille would hear none of it. Joan would hear none of it.

They wanted to meet these Celeste, Jesse and Jason people I kept talking about.

And, of course, Cade.

And yes, you could take that for what it was.

My dastardly daughters—plotting.

Incidentally, I had not shared with my girls that there recently was the very dramatic death that I was marginally embroiled in of a pretty eight-year-old child.

I told myself they'd worried enough about Welsh; they didn't need me to add to that with Alice.

And although that was true, I had concerns that neither of my girls was going to be very accepting of that truth.

Onward from that forthcoming debacle…

We were hitting critical mass with how desperately I needed to have sex with Cade Hunter Bohannan (yes, I'd learned his middle name, I'd learned a lot about Bohannan, except how good he was in bed).

Living with a man you were preposterously attracted to but sleeping in a different room from him, with some hard kisses, your neck having been made fair game along the way and lots of cuddling the only things you got, was—believe me—*torture*.

So there was also that.

Celeste and I still had GPS panic buttons we carried with us and had been given several Taser sessions, which were equal doses of scary and fun. But I felt (somewhat) like I could handle myself with one.

As a Bohannan, Celeste was a natural.

She didn't carry one to school, as that would not be cool, but she carried one everywhere else.

So did I.

The boys had put more cameras up and sensors out.

Hawk's man, Billy, had flown back to Denver.

Nothing had led to anything regarding Alice's killer, to the point Bohannan had sent both boys out on two different jobs—Jace gone for three days first, Jess for four days after—because someone had to make money.

(Don't ask me what these "jobs" were, none of them would tell me, so I let it lie.)

Bohannan himself spent a lot of time in his office (the only room in the house that Grace had decorated with a thoroughly masculine hand—think *leather* and *wood* but fortunately no antlers—then again, I'd learned Bohannan and both his boys weren't only non-hunters, they were anti-hunting, regardless of their lustfully meat-eating ways, "Because in a civilized world, I see no reason why I, or anyone, personally needs to kill a living thing."—Bohannan's firm words on that subject).

He was in that office going over files he was sent, which he was consulting on, from not only police departments across the United States, but also ones from different countries, including ones that had to be translated.

So…yeah.

He was that big of a deal.

I had not moved home, because David decided to take this time I was away to renovate my master bath, and that was noisy, messy, dusty work that not only put me out of my bedroom, but made it impossible for me to work there.

My kitchen was done (and it proved a little updating—like a new herringbone backsplash and quartz countertops—could work wonders for a space).

My bath would be finished in another week, just in time to have the house together for my girls to be there.

Though, I was also not back home, sleeping in one of the two other bedrooms, because Bohannan wanted me to stay.

I was writing again, and on the weekends would go to my place for several hours to work in my office. But when David was working, I set up in the sitting room in Bohannan's bedroom (or the living room, or in the local library doing research, or wherever, as laptops do travel).

This was the only interesting twist of the last three and a half weeks, seeing as I was writing a Mullally, and Bohannan had asked to read it as I wrote it.

I let Alicia read my writing as I wrote, and that was it.

But I found when he asked, I had zero qualms with saying yes.

So I let him.

And it was my favorite part of the day when Bohannan would surface from his iPad, look at me and say, "You're crushing it."

Life had formed into a rhythm, and as with these things, the horror of Alice's loss diminished with time—for us and in town.

Make no mistake, the gloom had not lifted. Alice and her loss would be remembered for decades to come, but people were getting on with their lives.

Bohannan and the boys had not forgotten about it, but you can't investigate a case with zero leads.

Fortunately, everyone was blaming Leland Dern for this, exulting Harry Moran for his patience and continued tenacity (because he wasn't giving up) and exonerating Bohannan for stepping back.

He had been doing it free of charge, for one, and everyone understood people had to get paid.

And you couldn't make up psychological factors to build a profile, and the murderer was giving them nothing.

So all was good in my world even if all was not good.

I was nervous the girls were coming. I was beginning to wonder why Bohannan was delaying our consummation, because his excuse didn't seem like an excuse anymore. I felt like the second shoe was imminently about to drop.

And considering, until recently, Celeste had had constant company in one form or another during their dates, and Will had not taken things out of the public domain, say, taking her to his house for a study date or something, I had not had much to worry about on that front.

However, that night, Celeste and Will were going to some party in the woods.

First, I had not had my conversation with her about Will, which was foolish procrastination on my part, but lest we forget, I was a relatively new entity in her life. So, although I was already madly in love and enjoyed spending time with her, feeling God had granted me this beautiful boon of being in the life of another young woman (though this one I didn't have to push out and potty train) I was still, as noted, new to her life. And with a teenage girl, bonding was always tentative at best.

I had to be careful about rocking that boat.

And second, things happened in the woods. Case in point, Alice being carried off. And pretty much every TV show or movie that had any kids in any numbers—from a few, to a few hundred—depicted all the pitfalls of partying in the woods.

In fact, I was surprised Will wanted to go to this party.

Apparently, however, it was an MPHS tradition. Post-Halloween, pre-Thanksgiving, after-football-season, let it all hang out before fall semester finals and Christmas break, where many kids could scatter to the winds.

Celeste had gone to the party last year.

The boys had gone every year for four years running when they were still in school.

And I was assured it was high school only. Jace had told me he and Jess wouldn't be caught dead there after they'd graduated.

"It's taboo. Total loser move. I don't know anyone who showed who wasn't in high school. Even back in Dad's days."

And yes, I quizzed Bohannan on this. And yes, this party happened back in "his days." And yes, if you showed and you weren't in high school, not before, not after, you earned an immediate loser label.

So, at least there was that.

Taking everything about this into consideration:

The good news was, Celeste did share, what I felt was rather garrulously, about her burgeoning relationship with Will. And she was blooming under his attention—dreamy and happy, not moody and secretive. In her sharing, she hadn't again mentioned Will talking trash about his stepmother or dumping his shit on Celeste.

The bad news was, Will did not ask her for a study date at his, or to come for a study date at hers. And at this juncture in a high school relationship—where most nights, she was driving back into town to have dinner with him or to study at Aromacobana after he was done with hockey practice, and they always did something at least one day on the weekends—this was like three months (at least) in Adult Relationship World.

In other words, in my view, it was past the time to meet the parents.

It seemed like he was avoiding that.

It could be he was protecting her from whatever was going on at his house. It was clear he avoided being there as much as he could (when he wasn't with Celeste on the weekends, it was because he was out with his bros).

And this was a real possibility, for obvious reasons.

Though, I had deeper insight into this.

I'd called Megan and had coffee with her (my first book club meeting was Monday, and thankfully, we weren't discussing a Priscilla Lange). During our coffee date (at Aromacobana, she either held no ill-will, or it was to her what it just was, the best place to get coffee in town), she'd filled me in on all the goss, which was that Dale wasn't letting grass grow. The glue that held their marriage together had been murdered. He was now courting his first wife right under his grieving wife's nose.

(Which begged the question of how Bohannan thought this guy was a "decent guy," and being me, I asked it. His reply was, "He hadn't pulled this shit when I said that. Now that he's pulling it, I retract it." Further evidence that *my* guy was a decent guy.)

On the other hand, it could be that we hadn't yet met Will because he was a little pissant, he knew Bohannan would read it, and he was giving Celeste's dad a wide birth.

I couldn't know unless I met the guy, face-to-face.

And as you could see, I hadn't.

However, between now and when Will came around to pick Celeste up that night at seven, I had to figure out how to talk her into not drinking at all, but if she did, not accepting a drink from anyone else. Not partaking of any other substances. Sticking with the crowds. And communicating no matter how cute and earnest Will might be, everything was always her choice. And if he ever made it seem like it wasn't, got pushy, whiny or physical, and she got uncomfortable, she was to get away from him, get with a group of girls and call her father or me immediately.

We'd come get her, no questions asked (I'd have to alert Bohannan about that no-questions-asked part, but he'd saddled me with this, he had to give me something).

Therefore, I was sipping my coffee and wondering when my fucking orgasms were going to begin because it was hard enough to do this stuff with my two girls, I thought it was over, and there I was again.

This was what I was thinking when a beard found its way into my neck, a warm, long, hard body pressed to my back and an arm wrapped around my stomach.

I would like to say I had the strength to withstand this unscathed, but we must remember, *it had been thirteen (or fourteen) years.*

I was about to verbally remind someone else of this when that beard tickled my ear and a gruff, deep voice said, "Kids are all gone tonight."

Oh my.

In all my mental meanderings, I hadn't noticed that Jess and/or Jace often hung at their dad's (I'd not been to their place yet, and Celeste never went there either, so my suspicions were that it was wall-to-wall Bro Town and likely smelled like a used sock, so, being boys, they didn't clean it, they just escaped it) and Celeste's curfew was ten, but she was usually home around eight thirty or nine.

But tonight, all the kids had dates.

Which meant tonight was the first night we'd be home alone.

I'd been so deep in my pout about not getting laid, I hadn't noticed.

"First, in my bed." Bohannan nipped my earlobe as I shivered. "After David gets done, we can start spending nights at yours."

"I—"

I didn't finish telling him I was all in with this plan.

Something bobbing in the water down by the pier caught my eye through the weak morning pre-dawn light and the ever-present mist.

"What's that?" I asked.

His mouth left my ear, and I felt the whisper of his whiskers against my cheek as he looked out the window.

And I knew it was bad even before I knew it was bad, when the reaction exploding from him buffeted my back so hard, I felt my spine bow and my hips press into the counter.

"Stay in here. Do not leave this house. Do not let Celeste leave this house," he growled.

"Bo—"

He was off, but he twisted to me at the door and jabbed his finger my way, "And do not watch."

Do not watch?

Oh my God.

Him saying not to watch meant I couldn't *not* watch.

So I did.

He had his phone to his ear as he jogged to the pier.

"Hey, Delly?" Celeste called from behind me.

I whirled and my coffee sloshed, but fortunately, I'd consumed more than half of it.

"You know that cream sweater you have?" she asked.

"Yes," I pushed out.

"Can I wear it?"

"Yes," I repeated.

She smiled. "Is it up in your room?"

I nodded. "Unh-hunh. Middle drawer of the dresser."

"Thanks, you're the best."

She was still in her robe, but her hair and makeup were done.

It was almost time to go to school.

I started to turn again to the window.

"And…"

I shot back into place, faking a smile while choking back coffee hopefully appearing to do it casually as Celeste returned.

"Do you think I can use that purse you use when you wear it? You know. The Chloe one," she asked.

"Of course, lovely," I replied. "Do you know where it is?"

"Closet."

"Yes."

"You really should just move in with Dad. He's got tons more closet space," she said.

This was momentous, her saying this.

I didn't glory in the momentum.

"I'll take that up with him."

She gave me a saucy grin and took off.

I waited, listened, waited more, listened more, waited.

Then I turned back to the window.

Jess and Jace were now there.

Jace was bent, hands to knees, staring in the water over the far side of the pier.

Jess was in a squat at the pier's edge, doing the same.

Bohannan was also doing the same, standing with his phone to his ear.

They weren't close enough for me to read their expressions.

But their body language said it all.

I turned and raced up the stairs to help Celeste.

And to get dressed.

Because I had a feeling I needed to be ready.

THIRTY-ONE

Black Hole Sun

The boys and I performed a minor miracle in getting Celeste off to school without letting on Black Hole Sun was upon us again.

After she was gone, I had just enough time to get a fresh pot of coffee brewing before the first sheriff cruiser pulled up.

They kept coming, and I handed out coffee and made two tubes of cinnamon rolls that Celeste had thrown into the cart the last time we were at the grocery store.

I then began a steady process of intermittently pouring mugs of coffee and scooping rolls onto paper plates, in between watching outside, noting how the game was being played, even desperately evaluating it, so I wouldn't have to pay attention to why they were playing it.

There was hard-faced, yet handsome, Harry Moran and his deputies, who seemed to be in a détente with officious Leland Dern and his deputies.

They were playing nice.

And I suspected they were, because after some people did some things at the end of the pier and a lot of pictures were taken, a body wrapped in clear tarp was fished out of the water and put on the pier.

As it was, cold coated my skin like I, too, was wrapped in plastic tarp, just fished out of a lake.

I felt something and shifted my gaze to see Bohannan's head turned, his eyes on me.

I wanted to go out and hug him.

I wanted to scream.

I wanted to vomit.

There was a very big difference from seeing this kind of thing on dozens of television shows, and seeing it happen at the foot of the pier on which you'd spent a romantic night sitting beside the man you were falling in love with just a month before.

I didn't know who was in that tarp.

I just knew whoever had been put in there had been put there for Bohannan.

Things seemed to be going okay between the different sides, and I'd stepped back so Bohannan couldn't see me watching, but I could still watch.

Things stopped going okay when Polly Pickler showed up in a silver Toyota Camry.

In fact, she'd barely been out of her car and talking with Bohannan and Moran for a minute, before things devolved spectacularly to the point I had to race out of the house, seeing as a brawl was forming, Moran's men against Dern's men.

And if I'd read things right, Jess and Moran were the ones who started it.

By the time I got out there, Bohannan and Dickerson, the deputy I'd met at the station (he was on Moran's team) were holding back Moran, with some difficulty, and Jace and a couple of other deputies were holding back Jess, with even more difficulty.

Dern was blustering while his guys formed a shield around him.

Polly looked like I felt, except a hundred times worse. Like she didn't know whether to cry, shout or throw up.

Though, there was shouting going on, back and forth between the two camps.

I didn't get close, but I got close enough to say, "Jesse."

Like magic, instantly he stopped fighting to get to Dern.

Moran wasn't ready to let it go.

But Bohannan pushed him off, he flew back five feet, set his body to charge again, and Bohannan barked, "*This won't help.*"

Moran wasn't thrilled about having to pull himself together, but he started doing it.

So at least whatever that was, was sorted.

Except I was wrong.

In the melee, I hadn't noticed how pissed Bohannan was.

And he…

Was…

Pissed.

He turned, flicked two irate fingers at Dern and declared, "You're done. Get off my land."

"This is a crime scene," Dern snapped. "And I'm the sheriff."

"If you don't go back to your office and resign, I'm making a phone call. In an hour, there'll be an emergency session of the county commissioners, and you'll be facing recall, but in the meantime, they'll suspend you from duty."

Dern assumed an arrogant expression. "The commission would never do that."

He had friends there.

Bohannan's other arm came out, and he pointed at the pier.

"You don't think so?"

Dern tried to stare him down, but there was a flicker of uncertainty.

"She's on you," Bohannan said low.

"Fuck you, Cade," Dern bit.

Bohannan gave up on him and addressed the crowd. "We need everything we can get from this. Every…*fucking*…thing. Or one of your daughters might wash up next. *Get your fucking shit tight.* This isn't about politics. This is about *girls.*"

This was about girls.

Oh God.

Some on Dern's side looked chastened, others continued to look combative.

But Bohannan was done with them.

He walked to Polly.

"You give him that, you're not only fired, I'll bring you up on charges for theft and obstruction," Dern threatened.

"Arrest me," she snapped. "See how that'll play at the polls."

And she handed a brown folder to Bohannan.

"We got a girl lying on that goddamned dock whose parents don't know where she is and don't know yet she's not coming home," Moran declared in an imposing, but pleasantly deep voice. "Let's get this shit done and her out of here."

Men moved.

Bohannan flicked his eyes at me, to Polly and back to me.

I went to Polly.

"Come up for a cup of coffee and a cinnamon roll," I urged.

She was staring at the pier.

"That's Malorie," she whispered.

I turned to the pier to see the tarp had been pulled away from her face.

She'd had blonde hair.

My jaw set with a tingling ache, a precursor to getting sick.

Except in a casket, I'd never seen a dead body before.

I looked away, casting my mind anywhere other than to what I just saw, and it set to thinking, *Where had I heard the name Malorie?*

"Get up to the house, baby," Bohannan ordered, it was brusque and still pissed, but edged with gentle.

All that was going on, and he was worried about me.

I took Polly's hand. "Let's go."

I got her up to the house. I got her a cup of coffee and a cinnamon roll.

She ignored both, sat at the bar and stared at the counter.

I busied myself with coffee mugs and making another pot just in case, wiping down counters and cleaning out a tin I'd made the rolls in that had been emptied.

I did not look outside.

It took time, the deputies and other folks who had come weren't done, and an ambulance had arrived, when Bohannan, Jace and Jess came in.

Bohannan immediately put the folder down on the bar, opened it and started sifting through it.

But with great care.

His tone was soft when he asked Polly, "This chronological?"

"I don't know. He hid it from me," she said, sounding almost robotic.

"There aren't any envelopes in here, Polly."

She lifted her gaze from the counter to him.

"I looked everywhere. The first one came in, I open his mail, I saw it. It was addressed to the station, but attention to you. I'd opened it and read it before I saw that on the outside. I took it to him, asked him if he wanted me to call you. He said no. He said it was some crackpot, giving us the run around. But that was when he demanded the mail be brought directly to him. I should have known then, Cade."

He absolved her. "A lot's been going on, Polly."

She rejected his absolution. "Still should have told you. I know better. And I got a real bad feeling when I saw that folder." She indicated it with her head. "He was looking at it when I came in one day. When he saw me coming, he shoved it in the drawer he always keeps locked so I can't see what's in it. I know it sounds like I'm defending myself, but the truth is, he's always hiding stuff from me. I learned a long time ago to focus on the boys, not his dysfunction. The boys want to do good, he's got his own agenda. If I focus on the boys, they can do a little good."

"I understand," Bohannan said.

She nodded, but she didn't look convinced of the movement.

"After we got the call today, I went in and jimmied that drawer. That's what I found. Went through everything in his office so I could be sure to get it to you if it was pertinent. But that's all I found."

"That's okay, Polly. We've got this and this is good. But you saw that first envelope?"

"Yes."

"Attention me?"

"Yes."

"Postmark?"

"Misted Pines, Cade. I checked that after I saw what was inside."

Bohannan nodded.

"I read them. He's messed up in the head, Cade, real bad."

"Yeah, he is, sweetheart."

"And he's out there…"

"Where's Pete?"

"He's at the diner."

"We'll call him, and he can come get you."

"I'm okay, hon."

"We'll call him."

Bohannan jerked his chin to Jace.

Jace peeled off, pulling out his phone.

Bohannan closed the folder.

And for now, that was that.

It took more time for everything to be wrapped up outside. Pete, who was obviously Polly's husband, came to get her (yes, Pete and Polly Pickler, he was maybe two inches taller than her, and when he arrived, he only had eyes for her—they were adorable, I already knew I loved them).

And when it was just the four of us, that being approximately point-oh-two seconds after Pete's car started pulling away, Bohannan again opened that file.

He scanned the first piece of paper, set it aside.

The next, set it aside.

Then he picked up a coffee mug that was sitting on the counter, turned and side-arm threw it with great might across the kitchen.

It crunched through the wood of a cabinet, and I heard some plates breaking.

"Dad," Jace said quietly. Both he and Jesse were positioning for lockdown.

Bohannan turned back to the file and said to it, "Dead girl at my pier, he left her for me. Told me he was gonna do it right…" he stabbed a piece of paper with his finger, "fucking…" he stabbed it again, "*here*."

Oh my God.

I closed my eyes.

I saw her.

Malorie.

They'd closed her eyes.

So I opened mine.

THIRTY-TWO

Invisible

Humans are animals.

As such, we adapt.

We're also individuals.

As such, how we do that is unique to every one of us.

I'd learned how to read people, to quickly but carefully observe every nuance I could gather in order to construct the full visual of their puzzle, and then behave accordingly, because I grew up in a house without love.

My mother didn't have a good relationship with her parents, so they were in my life, but not deeply. My father left before I formed memories of him, and his parents hated my mother and weren't thrilled she had me, so I had no memories of them either.

She did not beat me, though there were time's I wished she did.

I wished she did because I could understand that as a crucial flaw in her character. Everyone knew it wasn't right to physically abuse a child.

She fed me. She clothed me. She didn't leave me alone to fend for myself. When she wasn't around to watch over me, I had keepers.

She was also an ambitious woman. She worked to get ahead. We were not wealthy, but by the time I hit double digits, we lived in a relatively decent condo in a neighborhood that wasn't great, but it also wasn't as terrible as the ones we'd been in before. A condo that, even if it wasn't much, it was decorated to impress.

As for me, I was "normal."

I had friends. I was always pretty, so I was relatively popular. I liked school, I liked to learn, and I did well there. I dated. I lost my virginity at the age of seventeen to a boy I liked very much and had been seeing for some time. It was the worst sex of my life, and there was a bit of pain, but it was my choice, and it didn't mark me or turn me off future interludes.

But I lived in the world, so I knew that a mother was supposed to love you. Care, not only for you, but about you.

And I did not have that.

So I found ways to adapt.

One of those ways was to watch TV, which was why I became an actress. A decision I would later realize was a mistake, not only because it wasn't my true calling.

Another way was to read, a lot. This didn't only take me away. I was naturally a dreamer. I would understand about myself years later that I was born to be a writer not only with the way I consumed books nearly all my life, but also with the way my mind sought stories.

This was one of the few things I had from my mother. She often bought me books, and I was grateful she did, even if I grew to understand she did it because she knew she wouldn't have to put up with me if I was in a book.

She also never refused me permission to go to the library, which I frequented and in which I spent a good deal of time.

Indeed, the only semi-motherly woman in my life was a librarian named Donna, who not only shared my love of books, but who read in me why they were so important.

It was not her job to look after me and give me the love I didn't have.

But she did her best, and it was she who was sitting beside me in the audience when I won my Emmys. And it was her name in the front of *We Pluck the Cord*, because it was dedicated to her.

It was also she who was buried with a first edition, the first one I signed, of that book folded in her hands and my National Book Award medallion resting on her chest.

As I grew up, my mother complained about me in a way that was both constant and consistent, but it too was negligent. An aside. A nuisance.

She did not like me dragging on her time. She did not like me dragging on her resources.

I remember with an alarming clarity the day she came home with her first pair of Manolo Blahnik shoes, a pair she'd found at a consignment store.

I remember how she put them on, traipsed around the house admiring them, and as if talking to herself, not even glancing at me, which was how she always did it, she said, "I can't wait until you're gone. I'll have the money to buy more of these. Next, I'm getting Chanel."

I also remember those times I was meant to disappear.

Not literally, but as close as I could get.

"I'm probably going to be bringing someone home tonight, Delphine, and you do not exist. You hear me?"

I'd learned what she meant when, in the beginning, I'd had no idea what she meant and inadvertently existed when I wasn't supposed to, and her negligent abuse became much more focused.

What she meant was that I was not to do that first thing to be a discoverable presence in our home when she brought a man there to fuck him. She was an attractive, single, unencumbered professional, and I was not to belie that.

Eventually, she'd learned, if there was one she might want to keep, this wasn't the way to play it. Men, understandably, were not fond of finding out at the third hour that the woman they were banging, a woman they were thinking they might want to spend more time with, had a kid—and she'd hidden that.

In this time, I would find there was an irregularity in my mother's behavior.

She'd had three men in her life who she also introduced into mine. The irregularity was that they were all good men, and I knew that because I still had relationships with all three. All of them reaching out to me when I found fame and fortune, doing it in a genuine, proud, not-quite-fatherly but definitely affectionate way.

I still had them when she did not have any of them.

But as an animal, I'd learned to adapt to my circumstances.

TV.

Books.

Fantasies.

Dreams of escape.

Making plans for a better life.

Puzzling out the pieces of everyone who came into my orbit.

And total shut down.

I did not like to hear my mother, who was loud during sex, having said sex.

Mostly, I did not like having a mother who not only wished I was not alive, not only told me at times to pretend I wasn't alive, but was oblivious to the fact I was so very good at it.

I didn't even get a pat on the head for doing what she asked.

I left home at eighteen with five hundred dollars in my pocket, but long before that I'd been living a separate life to my mother.

Those Years debuted when I was twenty-two.

Once it did, it was impossible for me to disappear.

But there were still times when I'd done it.

For instance, when my friend Isabella came over. She was starring in a movie with Warren. And she told me she'd walked in on him fucking his PA in his trailer. Everything about her screamed she hated saying it, but as a friend she couldn't not, so I believed it.

Then he'd come home, and I'd confronted him, and he'd denied it, then admitted it, then denied it had happened before while he was married to me, and everything about him screamed he was lying.

I'd shut down then. Warren said later he thought he'd have to call a doctor to admit me to a hospital. I was completely non-responsive, walking around like an automaton.

And then it happened again, when an irate female percussionist in Angelo's band was fired because he was done screwing her, and she wasn't happy about that, and she reached out and told me he was fucking his way through his latest tour. She also shared that I should know he did that his last tour, during which he'd been married to me.

I'd had time in with Angelo (unlike Warren). I'd been older and wiser when I married him (I thought), and it wasn't that I didn't love Warren, it was just that I realized I'd been too young to make that kind of commitment with him.

With Angelo, it was different.

I'd loved him sensibly. I'd loved him sincerely.

But I'd also loved him deeply.

Therefore, in a fit of self-preservation, I'd first confronted the tour manager, who'd predictably and complicitly lied.

Then I'd taken it to Angelo, who had done the same, but it was half-hearted. The jig was up. He knew with my history with my mother that I'd adapted by fitting puzzle pieces together so I'd never read a situation unclearly and put myself in positions that were worse than I was accustomed to.

That was, I did this except with the two men in my life, both having been able to successfully hold important pieces from me until I was in too deep to protect myself from the pain (enter a decade and a half of celibacy).

I'd shut down with Angelo too, but I'd told Angelo how I used to do that and why.

Therefore, he'd led me to our bed and held me until he could get me to snap out of it.

That was the last time we laid together. The last time he held me.

He'd eventually claimed sex addition.

I'd filed for divorce.

And the last I'd shut down was the last I'd been in her presence.

It was Christmas four years ago.

My mother had nagged an invitation for her and her husband to share the holiday with us. The girls were not keen. Although they'd formed an uneasy relationship with their grandfather, they had zero tolerance for my mom.

She was retired. Going on cruises. There was some tour of Scandinavia they were considering. During a trip to New York City, she'd seen Carolina Herrera at Sotheby's.

She'd married a year or so after I left.

I had not been invited to the wedding.

Her husband sat in my living room by the Christmas tree, staring off into space, and that flipped some switch in me.

Because she was so pathologically self-involved, he'd now been conditioned to live a life as I'd learned to be.

Invisible.

And she was being self-involved then. Talking to us about things we didn't care about because we didn't care about her, not letting anyone else speak.

Being there at all when she'd done not one thing in her life to be welcome there.

It was Camille who shook me out of it. As usual, I hadn't known I was doing it.

It wasn't as if I slipped into catatonia. I did not speak, but I went through the motions.

When I came back, I saw how alarmed my daughter was, which alarmed me.

After my mother was gone, Fenn had declared, "That bitch is never coming back."

Fenn hadn't missed it either.

That bitch never came back.

I could do my daughterly duty.

But I was not again going to force that on my girls.

I explain all of this, because it happened that day after Malorie Graham's body was found.

I've no idea what triggered it.

It could be any of a number of things.

The fact that, after Bohannan had his fit of anger, Jace and Jess walked out of the house without a word but clearly on a mission, knowing their role and setting about doing it.

Or the fact that Bohannan came to me, hooked me under the chin with the side of his crooked finger, touched his mouth to mine, and said, "I gotta dive into this, baby, you gonna be all right?" and I'd nodded mutely before he disappeared in his office with the file, his door closed.

Or the fact that the killer was sending letters to the sheriff, addressed to Bohannan, which was scary in itself, but it led to a new body that was floating at the end of Bohannan's pier.

Or the fact that it came to me, where I'd heard the name Malorie, and that was when Celeste mentioned her as the senior who'd started the shipping materials recycling locker in town. A senior last year, so if it was her, that put her dead at nineteen.

More than likely, it was the fact that I had no role to play in this, a feeling I had felt often growing up, that I had no place in the life I was living with my mother.

And more, the fact *I* was a mother. I'd lived through my two beautiful girls making it beyond age nineteen, and I had in my life another who I got to love and guide and share time with. But this one, this unknown girl, I could not help in any way. She was beyond help. And she'd more than likely died, alone, scared and wanting her mother.

But all of this was exacerbated by the fact that right then, I was living a life. A beautiful one. But a life where, one second that morning, the man I cared about was holding me and whispering promises in my ear, and the next we'd learned a girl would not live to stand in the arms of someone who loved her, listening to them whispering promises in her ear.

For whatever reason it was, it happened.

I had absolutely no idea what I did in the few hours after it went quiet that morning.

I just knew I shut down.

And I was glad I could do it when no one was watching.

Because it would come to pass that I had no choice but to start up again.

THIRTY-THREE

Bedlam

It started with a door slam and Celeste crying, "*Delly!*"

I was sitting in one of the high-backed, leather armchairs that were pointed toward the kitchen.

The pistachio couch had a view to the lake.

I remembered I'd selected that seat because I didn't want to look at the lake.

Then I didn't remember anything else.

Until then.

I came to, my body jolting, my head turning to her.

"I've been *calling and calling*," she said, racing to me.

I stood just in time for her to hit me.

I held her in my arms, and she squeezed tight with her own, exclaiming, "Oh my God! Everyone is *freaking*."

I looked over her shoulder to the kitchen, trying to read the time on the microwave, but it was too far.

Celeste answered my unasked question by pulling away, now holding on to my wrists, and saying, "No one could concentrate. They let us leave school early."

"Celeste—"

"Oh right, maybe you don't know. They found another girl dead, Delly. *Malorie*."

Well…

Hell.

She'd heard the news.

She just hadn't heard where they'd found Malorie.

And she'd been in such a state, she hadn't seen the crime scene tape that now cordoned off the pier.

I really liked the guy, and he had it rough right now, and I'd take the hit of talking to her about boys.

But this was all Bohannan's.

It was like I'd conjured him, because the second I had that thought, he prowled down the hall into the great room, gaze moving between Celeste and me, face set to neutral with a smidge of pissed (maybe) or impatient (better possibility).

He said, "Hey, honey," to Celeste, then instantly turned to walk under the exposed landing of the upper floor, which meant walking to the front door.

He opened it but it didn't seem like he opened it. It seemed like it exploded.

It seemed this way because he was forced back when a balding, burly man of somewhat below average height surged in, shouting, "*I'm gonna fucking kill him! I'm gonna fucking rip his fucking head off and shove it up his fucking ass! I'm gonna fucking piss on his dead body and take a shit every day on his FUCKING GRAVE!*"

As the man had made it to the great room, Bohannan had moved in, and with him came a tall, attractive woman who had at one point that day been exceptionally well put together.

Now she was not.

"Bobby," Bohannan murmured.

Bobby's arm raised, his hand slanting to jab with his finger downward, probably because Bohannan was taller than him, and like an angry bear, he was making himself be as big as he could get.

"*This is on fucking HIM! Before I shove his fucking head up there, I'm gonna bend him over his fucking sheriff desk and RAPE HIS FUCKING ASS!*"

"I appreciate you're feeling a lot right now, Bobby, but my women are here and so is yours. That means you either get a goddamned lock on it or I'm tossing you out of my house."

Bobby swung around to look at me and Celeste.

Mostly Celeste.

And when he did, it was all over.

"Cade," I said swiftly.

But it was too late.

Bobby's face went red in an instant. It crumpled, and he did too.

Right to his ass on the floor.

He curled, chest into his thighs, covered his head with both arms, started rocking and moaning, "My girl. My girl. My girl."

The woman who came with him whimpered, but she did not go to him.

Bohannan did.

He approached, crouched and patted him on the back, muttering, "Let that shit out. We got work to do, man. You gotta let that shit out."

Bobby made a very loud snuffling noise that ended with him releasing a breath that sounded like it came from a mouth that was closed, so it made *shee, shee, shee, shee* noises as it broke four times.

He was crying, and it wasn't that he didn't want to cry and was fighting it, it was just the power of it was overwhelming to the point he could barely breathe.

Unmistakably, Malorie's dad.

"Honey, why don't you go upstairs," Bohannan said to Celeste.

"Okay, Dad," she replied.

She gave a careful, tender look to the woman, whose lips curled up in a tremulous smile before she turned away.

I took her hand, squeezed it, Celeste glanced at me while I did, then I let her go—and alive and full of youth and grace—she dashed out.

I watched her do it.

And I memorized every step.

The woman watched her do it too and didn't quit watching even after Celeste disappeared from sight.

"Would you like to come in and sit down?" I invited, bringing her attention to me. "I can make some coffee." I had no idea what time it was, but still, I offered, "Or open a bottle of wine."

"No."

That was all she said.

She wasn't being rude.

She was Malorie's mom and probably only had that syllable in her to give.

"Okay," I said quietly.

Bobby was reaching out to the couch, face now nearly purple and wet, nose running, without much coordination trying to pull himself up off the floor.

I moved swiftly to the kitchen where there was a box of tissues.

"He's fucking this up, Cade," I heard the man say as I was on the move. "He's relieved Harry of his duties. He fired him."

Great.

Bobby carried on.

"He's fired Polly. We went to the station after we went to the fucking morgue. It's bedlam there. Half the men are packing up their desks. Leland took us into his office and told us he has it all in hand. Like we didn't see what we saw out in the bullpen. Then Pete storms in, and he's shouting, because some deputies came over and demanded permission to search his house. Saying some shit about how they're building a case against Polly for obstruction." His voice was rising. "What the fuck is going on, Cade?"

There was no table close to set it on, so I approached, arm extended, to offer tissues.

Bobby turned to me like he forgot I was there, startled and jumpy.

Bohannan took the tissues, murmuring, "Thanks, babe."

He then offered them to Bobby, and Bobby snapped out half a dozen, using the lot to run them over his face then blowing his nose in that wet wad.

Bohannan ignored the information dump and instead remarked with studied nonchalance, "I thought Malorie was at Berkeley."

"I thought so too," Bobby bit off.

"She wasn't home for a visit?"

It looked like things were going to get emotional again as Bobby groaned, "I wish she was. I wish she'd been home. We haven't seen her since parents' weekend in September, except her face on a fucking phone doing FaceTime. She was heading home soon. Soon." His voice dipped with his anguish. "We were excited to have her back for Thanksgiving."

Bohannan handed Bobby the box of tissues and reached into his back pocket.

He pulled out his phone, engaged it and extended it to me.

"Find Polly in my contacts, Larue. Phone her and reiterate what she knows. They need a warrant to search her house. They also need a warrant to arrest her. No judge has had time to sign off on either yet, and no judge in this county would do it anyway. She hunkers down. And if they try to do something stupid, she does not waive her right to an attorney."

I took his phone and nodded, stepping back and bending to it to find Polly in his contacts.

So I didn't miss it when he addressed Bobby.

"Now this seems to be the thing, Bobby," he began. "If she was at Berkeley, then it might be, he went there to get her. Which means he took her over state lines. Which means this is no longer Dern's case. This is now under the jurisdiction of the FBI."

The woman made another noise, a kind I'd never heard, was unlikely to hear again and wished I hadn't heard it at all.

Extreme relief and immeasurable sorrow.

For Bobby, his breath burst out of him like a bullet.

I found Polly's contact, retreated to the kitchen and hit go.

THIRTY-FOUR

A Wife

Once I'd surfaced from my call to Polly—who had gone from misguidedly taking responsibility, to being livid, which of course meant she indulged in a mini-rant with me, and this made me feel better, at least for her, because she held no responsibility, and she should be angry—I had a decision to make.

Bohannan was in the foyer, murmuring on the phone.

Bobby was on the couch, bent with head in hands, elbows to his knees.

And the woman had stepped outside on the deck.

She was smoking a cigarette and staring fixedly at the pier decorated in yellow police tape.

So, I guessed not a choice because what I had to do next was obvious.

I went out on the deck.

The day was cold.

The mist was thick.

And she had her forearm crossed at her ribs, her elbow resting on her hand, the cigarette held up into the air.

A defensive posture.

And a rebellious one.

I stopped at her side.

"Why don't you come back inside?" I suggested gently.

"He'd do it, you know," she said, bent her wrist, took a drag, lifted her hand and exhaled a precise plume of smoke from pursed lips, not taking her gaze from the pier.

"Who would do what?" I asked hesitantly.

"Fuck Dern up the ass. It'd be an intriguing twist for him. He likes it up the ass. That's what Audrey gave him that I didn't."

Oh boy.

I'd heard the name Bobby before.

He was Bobby of Bobby and Lana, the first couple Audrey tried to break up.

Therefore, this must be Lana.

"To get him back, I learned how to do that." Another plume. "I even learned that I like it." She looked at me and everything about her was a dare. "I don't have to bother with him anymore. I haven't let him touch me in years. So I do it to my new guy. The minute I suggested it, he rolled over. Men love it. I don't even have to touch his dick. Hold him down, fuck his ass, he comes into the sheets."

She was lashing out.

And she was a sister.

So although I didn't want to hear this (at all).

I stood there for her.

"We have a club." She told me. "Me and Annie and Wendy and Sarah. Audrey did it all. She was a full-service whore. Jay, she dressed up as his secretary and he spanked her, or she dressed up as his teacher, and she spanked him. Dwayne, he likes pain." Her lips peeled back from her teeth in a vicious grin. "Dale is like Bobby. He's all about ass. He comes over now, and he's Pavlov's dog. He walks in Sarah's back door, undoes his pants and drops to his hands and knees. He lets her shove whatever she wants up there. I've given her toys the size of which you wouldn't believe. She knows he's punishing himself. He cries half the time, even as he begs for more and covers her floor in spunk. But she's there for it." Another plume. "She's totally there for it."

She turned her gaze to the pier.

And kept talking.

"That's all we have. And I know how spiteful it sounds. It sounds sick. Like *we're* the ones who are sick. When what did we do but fall in love? Fall in love and get married and make babies and think life would happen the way it was supposed to. There'd be bumpy times, and hard times, but we had him. We made a family. We'd be okay. He'd be there. But we were so wrong. We didn't realize we're the untouchables."

She huffed out a husky laugh, swung her cigarette in, another plume of smoke, she swung it out and kept going.

"Like, how hard is it to say, 'Hey, let's do something different. Let's play.' That's not hard. I said it to Dean, my current fuck, and he was all in. We both get off on it. We love it. But *no*. We're *the wife*. You never stop being *the right type of girl*. The marrying type. The wifely type. The motherly type. The other type stretches over your thighs with her ass bare or uses some apparatus that hangs off your balls. Not *your wife*. Incidentally, I love it when Dean spanks me. I fuck him until he comes into the sheets, he spanks me, and I come in his lap."

Suddenly, her lazy drawl turned snide.

"Christ God, I'm so *sick of it*. So fucking *sick of it*. I'm not a wife or a mother. I'm a fucking *woman*."

Another plume and she turned to me.

"You know what's hilarious? He's not gay. He actually isn't," she shared. "But after I quit fucking him, he found some other bitch so he could get his pussy, but he found some guy to take him up the ass. That's funny. *Hysterical*. Because he's so goddamned weak, he can't ask her to do it. But he got a taste of it, and now he needs it. So there you go."

I did my very best to find a delicate way to get us off this subject, but onto a different, more delicate one.

"Do you think that maybe this person who did this to—?"

"She's not mine," she declared, and I tensed, because the anger was leaking, the snide was evaporating, and another emotion was coming. "His wife before me died in a car wreck. We got together when Mal was three. I raised her." She turned to the pier, and whispered, "I raised her."

Suddenly, she dropped her head, the cigarette held up still burning in her fingers.

"I'm not sure you should be out here," I remarked.

She whipped her attention to me.

"You think?" she asked. "His girl…our girl…*my girl's* found dead out there," she pointed with her cigarette at the pier and the ash dropped to the deck, "and I say, 'Bobby, do not drive me to that fucking place.' But does he fucking listen? No? Because I am not a woman. I am not a person. I am *a wife*."

"Please come inside with me."

She ignored me.

"You'll note, he's listening to Cade. He's ranting and raving in the car on the way over here. Ranting when he gets in your house. Cade says to shut the fuck up, he shuts the fuck up. I beg him in the car to calm down because he's driving, it's like I'm not *even there*."

She needed to get this out.

So I stood there and let her get it out.

"We have other babies. Two boys. One's a freshman. One's in seventh grade. They won't be next. You know why?"

I shook my head. "No. Why?"

"Because they're not girls. Those sick fucks, all of them, *all of them*," she twisted at the waist and stabbed a finger toward the house, indicating her husband, "they punish *the girls*."

With that, she lost it, broke down, and I moved in and gathered her in my arms.

Her body heaved, her tears wet my neck.

This went on for some time.

She was much more adept and elegant at getting herself together, pulling away, and she had her own tissues in her purse.

"Sorry," she said to the slats of the deck as she wiped her nose. "I'm being awful."

"No judgment here."

Her gaze came to me, timid now, embarrassed.

"To answer your question, yes. The club, me and Wendy and Sarah and Annie, the day after they took Alice, we got together, and we wondered if it had something to do with Audrey. When they came around…when they…when…" She took a second, then carried on, "When they came to the house today, and Bobby was calling on my phone, and I knew, a part of me wasn't surprised. And it figures, don't you think? It isn't Bobby in the lake. It isn't Dale in the ground. It's Alice."

She swallowed, sniffed, took a shuddering breath and turned to the pier, and her voice was guttural when she finished.

"And my Malorie."

THIRTY-FIVE

Sweet and Cute and Wonderful

We weren't quite done with the drama of Bobby and Lana.

Though the finale was brilliantly crafted by Lana.

Because, while I was on the deck with her, she took out her phone and sent a text, received one, and we stood in unsettling silence for a spell before she said, "No offense. You're being really kind. But can I be alone for a little while?"

I didn't like it, with the way she kept looking at the pier, but I nodded and left her as she was lighting another cigarette.

When I stepped inside, Bohannan's warm gaze came to me.

Bohannan was still on the phone.

I didn't want to, because I wasn't his biggest fan, because he'd broken his wife's heart, and I knew what that felt like, but I asked Bobby if he wanted a drink.

"No. Thanks. I…"

He gave me the once over, it wasn't creepy, or inappropriate, even as it was both.

Mostly, it was habit.

So, yes.

Confirmed.

I did not like Bobby.

"They're all saying you're really nice. I guess they're right," he concluded, like only his own eyes and experiences could confirm this.

In other words, it was likely women who told him that.

I made myself smile and retreated to a stool at the kitchen bar where I could keep an eye on what was happening in the house, and out on the deck, and mentally explored my options.

Option one was going upstairs and telling Celeste what had happened that morning at the pier or finding a Celeste who had been talking to friends and had discovered it on her own.

This was what I should do.

Option two was staying there, because Lana was in a mood, entirely justifiably, and I wasn't sure how that would go when she returned inside.

Which was what I decided to do.

Because Celeste had had an earful of it from Bobby, and that was not okay.

And I'd learned she *really* didn't need to hear what Lana might have to say.

I fretted I'd made the wrong decision.

I found out it was right when Lana came in, and gently, even lovingly, but stupidly, Bobby said, "Sweetheart, you shouldn't smoke."

She didn't even look at him.

She looked at Bohannan.

"Cade, someone is coming to get me. When he gets here, will you let him in the gate?"

That mystery was solved, even if I hadn't yet thought about it. Bohannan went straight to the door because he'd gotten a call from Bobby to open the gate, so he knew he was coming.

"You don't need a ride, honey. We're going home," Bobby told her.

She looked at him. "I'm not going home."

He stood, starting, "Honey—"

"Mom has already got the boys," she shared. "Dean's coming over to get me."

Oh dear.

I got off my stool and my gaze skidded to Bohannan.

Bohannan was watching Lana carefully.

"Dean?" Bobby asked, appearing genuinely perplexed.

"My boyfriend." She shook her head. "At my age, that sounds idiotic, so…my lover. The guy I fuck who fucks me. The guy who, before we fuck, he makes me dinner a couple of times a week, when you think I'm having my hair done or getting a facial or playing tennis, or whatever you don't really care I'm doing. He listens to me bitch about you and talk about my day, and he actually cares. I'm moving in with him. When we find a big enough place, the boys are moving in with us too. And I'm divorcing you."

Bobby stood there, his chin in his neck, his mouth open.

"I got smart this time," she continued. "My own job. My own money. Don't get complacent," she warned. "I'm going to take my share of yours. But I'm done with this bullshit game."

"My daughter just died," he reminded her.

"*Our* daughter was just *murdered*," she corrected him. "And I'm going to need someone to help me navigate the grief, and if there's one thing I've learned, that someone will never be you."

She turned her attention to Bohannan, then to me.

"I'm sorry this is happening here, and you have to witness it. But I can't wait. I hope you understand."

I opened my mouth.

And Bobby blustered, "Are you *serious right now*?"

I could tell by his face he was going to blow.

Bohannan could tell by something else because he was looking at the back of his head.

So he ordered, "Bobby, calm down."

He whirled on Bohannan. "Now, are *you* serious?"

"You're going to stay calm, and when Lana's friend shows, you're going to keep calm and she's—"

Bobby blew. "*You can't be serious right now!*"

"I warned you once," Bohannan clipped out. "This is the worst day of your life, that gets you two warnings. But I won't warn you again. You're in my home. I'm not putting up with any more of that shit."

Bobby's face started getting red, for a different reason this time, but he said nothing.

Lana turned to me in a non-verbal, *See?*

I gave her an understanding look.

"Now, before this person gets here," Bohannan went on. "I had thoughts about what we spoke about earlier, and I called the FBI to put them on alert after the scene had been cleared. I just called to tell them, they're up. They've already got agents heading out. I don't know what shape the sheriff's department is in, but these agents are trained to set up a field post anywhere, so it doesn't matter. They'll be in touch, and they'll keep you both informed of what they can share."

"That bitch is not Malorie's mother," Bobby bit out.

Bohannan let his gaze rest on Bobby a beat and then he turned it to Lana.

"They'll keep you both apprised," he told her.

"Thank you," she said quietly.

"Fuck this shit," Bobby decreed, and stormed to the front door.

Bohannan didn't stop him.

He slammed the door behind him.

Bohannan sighed.

"How long will it take for Dean to get here? Are you sure you don't want a glass of wine?" I offered Lana.

She was staring at the door, but she looked to me.

And she said, "He told me he'd hurry."

He hadn't lied. It wasn't five minutes later when Bohannan's phone chimed, and not long after that, we were waving her and her lover off.

Dean, incidentally, had burnished blond hair and a magnificent physique and was a couple inches taller than even Bohannan, and a good ten years younger than Lana.

He was also solicitous, his face haggard, angling out of his truck and jogging to where she was making her way to him, sliding an arm around her waist and holding her to his side as he escorted her to the passenger seat of his truck.

In other words, his puzzle came together quickly. Nice truck, he made money. Nice body, he took care of himself. Younger than his lover, he was confident in what he liked, who he was, and smart enough to find a woman who was also smart, but further mature enough to know the same. Ravaged expression when he'd probably never even met Malorie, but he knew Lana loved her like she was her own mother. All of that meant he was head over heels for this woman.

Which, so far, watching that was the only bright spot in my day.

We barely got back inside when Bohannan demanded, "I want to know everything she told you."

"I think you need to talk to your daughter first."

His eyes went to the ceiling, he nodded, then moved to the stairs.

I was making us sandwiches for lunch when he got back.

By the way, the police had left at about 10:30.

It was now 2:46.

"She heard," Bohannan said, strolling in, face his normal neutral but this time subtly laced with equal doses of annoyed and troubled.

The annoyed part was partially explained when he slid Celeste's phone on the counter by the bread.

"Oh boy," I said, eyeing it.

"Her phone was blowing up. Everyone wants to know if she saw anything and what we're doing." He leaned the side of his hip into the counter. "She also informed me she's going to the party tonight, which is still on. That isn't a surprise. It's the perfect opportunity to spread gossip and rumors. That, and teenagers are drawn to anything that tests their immortality."

Wasn't that the truth?

"She wasn't thrilled when I told her she was not going. We had words. She didn't like my words. I didn't like hers, and I'm the boss.

So now she's grounded until Monday. Since it's Friday, that didn't go over too good. I've been briefed that's *torture*, and don't I know Will is especially going to need her now. I said if Will needs her, he can come to the house, and I'll pour him a Coke. At that juncture, she shared Will is 'anti-parent,' and I have to respect that…considering. I told her I could get that, but I'm not his parent, I'm hers, and she's not going to that party or seeing Will unless he comes to the house. She said something I didn't like a whole lot more than all the other shit she was saying." He tapped her phone. "And now she's grounded from her phone too. She 'pretty much' hates me and ordered me from her room until she can stand to look at me again. I obliged."

That "anti-parent" part was interesting.

"I'll give her some time to cool down and then go talk to her," I mumbled.

"We need to do this because you and I are doing this," he announced.

I was kind of following, but I let him speak on before I commented.

"In this house, you don't get off easy from a hissy fit. And don't give me shit. When the boys had them, I called them hissy fits for them too. They hated that."

I bet they did.

I smirked.

One side of Bohannan's beard twitched before he kept going.

"What I'm saying is, there is no good cop, bad cop sitch when it comes to that. I've heard some of the greatest minds speak about a full spectrum of facets of psychology. I get hormones. I get peer pressure. I get developing psyches. I get kids are sponges soaking up everything around them, the vastness of which it's a wonder their heads don't explode, and they haven't developed the mechanisms to filter out what they don't need, especially the shit that's harmful. I get that high school is a microcosmic cesspool of all that, and I swear to Christ, with some of the things I've seen and read, I sometimes wonder why we make our children endure it. But she doesn't disrespect her dad. It's not that I feed her, clothe her, put a roof over her head, and I'm older than her. It's because I love her. I don't do a fucking thing except out of love for her. And if she can't respect that, then she's going to learn."

"You could have just said, 'there is no good cop, bad cop sitch, if she's acting up, we're both bad cops,' and I would have got the message," I joked.

He stared down at me.

"But you even manage to turn bitching about your daughter being mean to you into something badass," I concluded.

"All her life, from when she was a little girl, but especially recently, when I was alone with it and she needed her mother most of all, I had no one to unload this shit on or talk it through with."

That sure shut me up.

He slid a hand around the back of my neck and pulled me closer to him as he dipped his head down to mine.

"I'm not saying don't tease me," he continued. "What I'm saying is, it sure as fuck felt good to come and unload that on you."

Well…

Just fuck it.

I pressed into him, wrapped my arms around his neck and kissed him.

His tongue slid between my lips, and I truly tasted him for the first time.

Part of me felt, with all the buildup, this might be a letdown.

It wasn't.

He tasted better than I expected, and he used his tongue like he used his brain, his body—assured and talented, creative and unexpected.

He'd been right, we shouldn't do this until we could *do it*.

I liked it so much, I automatically arched into him, holding on, letting him explore, feeling—

"Oh, I see. Come up and be a jerk to me, come down like that was nothing and make out with Delly," Celeste snapped.

We stopped kissing, but Bohannan didn't let me go, which was good, because my knees were weak, and I needed a second (or thirty of them) to catch my breath.

He just turned his head to his daughter.

"You know, it's stupid, you two in different rooms," she went on. "It's like, I mean, what do you think I am? Wait, it's not stupid. It's *insulting*."

"Good you think that, because Delphine is moving to my room tonight."

That was news.

Excellent news.

I fought smiling.

"Good," she sniped. "Fine," she kept at it when he made no reply. "I mean, *somebody I know* was *floating dead* out by *our pier* this morning, off I went to school, *and nobody told me*."

"Yes, sweetheart, and that's upsetting for all of us, but you don't see me, Larue, Jace or Jess throwing tantrums and acting like a five-year-old."

I sucked my lips between my teeth because that was *so* not the thing to say.

Celeste confirmed my thought by skewering her father with a look, shouting, "I guess I'll just starve!" and running from the room.

"Please tell me that's normal," Bohannan said to the place she'd just been.

"It's totally normal." He looked down at me. "In fact, it was beginning to seem a little weird, how sweet and cute and wonderful she was. I feel a whole lot better now."

He smiled at me.

The smile faded when he said, "Now, tell me everything Lana said."

"Maybe after you eat," I suggested.

"Why?"

"Because I write romance novels and I have a vivid imagination and a firm philosophy that you should do whatever makes you feel good, so I don't hold judgment. But you might have a different take."

His gaze drifted to the sandwiches, and since he'd just used a bevy of them, apparently, he'd run out of words for the time being, because he made no reply.

I let him go and urged, "C'mon. Let's eat. Then let's get your Lana brief over with."

Bohannan turned fully to the sandwiches.

Which meant he agreed.

THIRTY-SIX

Pleasantville

After turkey and Swiss, and cheddar and sour cream Ruffles, we went to Bohannan's office, where I sat in a club chair by the window and he rolled his desk chair to it, up close, so one of his knees was touching one of mine.

And if that wasn't enough, even as I sat back, comfortable in the chair, he leaned into his elbows on his knees to listen to me.

There, I laid out the tale of Bobby, Lana, Jay, Annie, Wendy, Dwayne, Sarah, Dale and Audrey.

I was pleased he didn't sneer or make some comment or do anything but watch me and listen attentively.

Then again, he'd probably seen it all, and his G-man, "Just the facts, ma'am," persona was always in place when he listened to stuff like that in order that he didn't give anything away.

And even if I was no-judge about most everything, including people's sexual appetites, still, there had been hurt and harm, and I might have only had one side of the story, which my own history meant I'd be sensitive to and prone to support.

However.

"This place is like a warped Pleasantville," I decreed. "It's all hunky dory in black and white when everyone's playing their roles and no one's asking too many questions, but inject a little real life in there, and the colorful characters stand out, but instead of bright and beautiful, they're squalid and tawdry."

"Yeah," he muttered, like he wasn't really listening to me.

"What?" I asked.

He focused on me.

"I don't get how Lana moves from what happened to Alice to what happened to Malorie, and she made mention she's not surprised by it."

I thought maybe he took that part the wrong way.

"I don't think that's a thing, Bohannan. I think she was just letting off steam. I think she's devastated about Malorie, but she isn't behaving how people expect women to behave in a time like this. She's cynical and bitter and there are reasons why she's those things. I didn't get a bead on her that she was faking any of that, especially when she was crying. Seeing how he was with her, I also think her boyfriend cares a lot about her, and he's been waiting for her to make this move. But she's not making it because she's seizing an opportunity, she's making it because she genuinely needs to be with someone who gives a shit about her because she's wrecked at the loss of Malorie."

His reply was, "There is no time in my life when I've ever been able to say Bobby Graham was a decent guy."

There you go.

"He's an unqualified ass," he went on.

"Right," I murmured.

"What I meant was, there are people who do things to kids. There are people who do things to teenagers. There are people who do things to women. There are people who do things to boys or men. Although not unheard of, a suspect jumping from an eight-year-old to a nineteen-year-old doesn't fit neatly into a profile. Dahmer was convicted of killing seventeen men and boys. Of them, ten were in their twenties, three were nineteen, two were in their thirties, and two were fourteen. The ages ranged from fourteen to thirty-six, which is a large gap. But even though you and I think of fourteen-year-olds as boys, they weren't eight."

"I see what you're saying."

"He's earned that blame, but she blames Bobby for a lot. And if she formed this club you explained with the other women whose men Audrey targeted, she and they have been feeding their resentment for a long time. Not only not letting it die but nourishing it so it grows."

It really couldn't be argued they'd done that.

Bohannan kept speaking.

"Jace, Jess, Harry and me have turned over every stone. Including all the shit that swirled around Audrey. Lana and Bobby stayed together, until now. Wendy and Dwayne too. Annie and Jay broke up. Word is, Wendy busts Dwayne's balls, and Dwayne kisses Wendy's ass, and I'm not talking in a way that Dwayne evidently has a proclivity for that to be. That wasn't the way they were before Audrey. She's making him pay for the long haul. What Lana said to you, she's been waiting to get her ducks in a row. When Bobby was having an affair with Audrey, Lana was a stay-at-home mom. She didn't have any power, in terms of the fact she didn't have an easy way to strike out on her own. I'm pretty stunned about Sarah. Revenge fucking doesn't seem like her thing. But if she's egged on by her posse, that's a different story."

"You can't blame them," I defended.

He shook his head. "What I'm saying is, that's their damage. And they've been embroiled in that damage for a really long time. All of them, hanging on to it. So it stands to reason with what happened to Alice, that would be Lana's go to. We've looked at everyone who has anything to do with Dale, Audrey, Will, Alice or Sarah, which sent us looking at everyone who had anything to do with those players. Unless I'm losing my touch, there's no one in that mix who would drive all the way to Berkeley to snatch a college freshman and drag her back to Washington to kill her, roll her in plastic and leave her in a lake."

"Okay," I said slowly, knowing he saw Alice, knowing how deeply he investigated that, knowing he saw Malorie, knowing he just listened to all I said about Lana and that lot, and last, knowing he'd spent hours with those letters, I asked, "So what do you think?"

"I don't wanna say what I think."

"Say it anyway."

"Right, then, you don't wanna hear what I think."

I leaned to him and grabbed his hand.

"Bohannan, I'm not just here for my sage wisdom on how to valiantly and highly successfully raise teenage girls."

His lips tipped up, but his head dropped down, and he watched himself as he turned my hand in his.

What he didn't do was tell me.

I was about to prompt him when, abruptly, his head came up.

"When you saw that guy out your window, and you texted us, what was your first thought?"

I sensed this was a very important question, but I felt the answer was obvious.

"That he shouldn't be there."

"You were surprised when we thought it was about you. A fan or some photographer," he noted.

That needle bomb exploded again, piercing my skin everywhere from the small of my back to up over my scalp.

"You'd seen him seconds, who did you think he was?" Bohannan pressed.

"Alice's killer," I whispered.

"Why?"

"Needle bomb."

"What?"

"It just happened again. Just now. It starts at my lower back, but it feels like, in a wave, thousands of needles are being jabbed in, from my back all the way up over my head."

"Have you ever felt that before?"

I shook my head, but then clenched his hand.

"Mom had a man friend I didn't like. I was there, in the house, when she told him about me, when before, she'd kept the fact she had a kid from him, and he lost it. Shouting at her. I came out of my room and looked at him, he looked at me, and it wasn't as intense, but it happened then. I was probably, I don't know, eleven."

"You see him again?"

I shook my head.

Bohannan didn't say anything.

Now I was clutching his hand. "Do you still think this is about me?"

"No, baby," he said quietly.

He then took in a big breath.

And he held my eyes when he said, "I think it's about me."

THIRTY-SEVEN

You Pay Attention

"Explain," I demanded.

"You like me."

"Yes."

"A lot."

I gave him a look.

He smiled, but he didn't mean it. He was trying to inject levity.

I wasn't feeling like being leavened.

"You're not tight with your mom."

I shook my head. "No."

"But she's your mom."

"Yes, Cade, just tell me," I snapped, impatient.

"She's your mom, and you were eleven and you needed her, you probably felt something for her, if only because she was what you had. And this guy shouting at her was a threat to her."

Now I was following.

And my skin started prickling.

Bohannan explained it anyway.

"You saw that guy out your window, heading to my home, you like me, you sensed a threat...*to me*. And you pay attention. You can read people. And we aren't sure, but we think you were right."

"Oh my God."

"So, baby," he scooted closer, and held my hand tight, "what I think is, this isn't about Audrey or Alice or Malorie or Lana, or Bobby and Dale being cheating assholes who didn't know how to talk to their wives about things they wanted in bed. It's about me. He's calling me out. He's testing me. And that means…"

Oh God.

Oh dear God.

"There's not going to be a pattern. There's not a profile. Malorie being vaguely connected to Alice is a red herring. It's to lead me off track when there isn't a track. The next person could be anybody. Because this is him versus me."

THIRTY-EIGHT

Catastrophic

If you have an abundance of it, as a parent, you strategize the real estate of your house very carefully.

Even before Bohannan *really* kissed me, I understood why Grace and he put the boys in the basement, and Celeste's room was all the way down the hall, to the front of the house, whereas Bohannan's was at the opposite corner in the back.

Warren and I had not lasted long after Fenn was born.

Angelo and I were married for almost eleven years, and we had Camille right away, because I wanted my kids to be born close together and have every opportunity to build that brand of sibling camaraderie (fortunately, in this, I succeeded, though truthfully, they did it).

Me not having sex did not mean I wasn't sexual. I gave myself orgasms regularly and had what I would estimate was an above-average, very healthy sex drive.

Angelo was a self-professed sex addict, and perhaps this was a thing (and I'd done research on it not only because of how it affected my life, but possibly using it in books, and I still thought it was a cop-out, but I say that with the caveat that I have a block to it, because it might exist as a bona fide psychological condition, but Angelo had used it in an attempt to keep me).

In other words, Angelo and I had sex all the time.

So we made very good use of baby monitors and our real estate.

This was on my mind as I was standing in my jammies, brushing my teeth in Bohannan's bathroom.

It wasn't the only thing on my mind, which was understandably cluttered.

After the bombshell Bohannan dropped in his office, as I fought hyperventilating, he explained that this was not outside the norm. In fact, it had been one of the factors that led to him searching for someplace out of the way and safe for him and his family.

He'd been fulfilled by his work with the FBI, and as such, wanted to keep his name out of the high-profile cases. But the media tipped it, and investigative journalists-cum-authors pushed it, and he was outed.

And when you get that kind of reputation, it can detrimentally affect your work.

An example of which, it could trigger disturbed people to play cat and mouse with you.

"When I quit the Bureau, and we moved here, I installed the fence and gate. And I don't have cameras and sensors around the property just because I want privacy for my family," he explained.

I had not put this two and two together, but Bohannan went on to share that law enforcement types did not herald where they lived. From something as minor as keeping their names off their mailboxes, to taking pains to minimize their digital footprint, to Bohannan's fortress-type setup.

So, although this bombshell wasn't great, he was not surprised by it.

And he assured, "Baby, just because you might not be able to build an accurate profile because your subject is actively working to make sure you don't, doesn't mean you can't investigate murders. Criminals leave clues. He's leaving clues. We just have to find them and follow them."

He seemed so collected about this, so unaffected by and aloof from that particular mindfuck, I felt a modicum of comfort.

But only a modicum.

I'd wanted to ask if I could read the letters.

But Jason and Jesse came back at that moment, and our brief reprieve to take a second to have lunch, a breath and think things through was obliterated.

The following hours were a jumble of happenings.

These included Bohannan not even blinking before he asked his sons to brief him in front of me.

They shared all about what they'd been doing. And in the intervening hours from them heading out and then, they'd tracked down someone who saw, on the other side of the lake, someone boating into the mist last night.

This was not unusual. Apparently, it was a thing in Misted Pines and its surrounding areas. It proved your mettle, like flying over the Bermuda Triangle just to say you did.

Though last night might be a different story.

Too far away, the person who saw this couldn't see much of anything, except there was only one person in the boat, and it looked like a white fishing boat with a thick, dark stripe.

Not much to go on, but a clue.

It was around this time that all three of their phones started blowing up, and in a less dramatic fashion, mine did too.

It was actually a surprise it took that long.

First, there was Malorie's death on the heels of Alice's.

Second, there was Sheriff Dern's shenanigans, and Bohannan's threat had not been empty. He'd called members of the Board of Commissioners, and with increasing pressure from other citizens of Misted Pines, they were convening an emergency session.

Third, parents were freaking out, and they wanted the annual MPHS woods party shut down.

The problem was, the people who would do this were the sheriff's department, and they were in disarray, with more than half of their deputies on walkout, and the ones left were under the command of an authoritarian who didn't have his right-hand woman to even out his nonsense.

In other words, they were useless.

There were murmurs of setting up a crew of concerned citizens to go into the woods and break up the party.

Teenage rebellion was thick on its heels with pinging texts and underground high school social media posts moving the location around to undermine these efforts to put a stop to their fun.

In the meantime, Harry Moran had shown at the house with some of his brethren, and they were going rogue.

They might have been stripped of their badges, but they intended to find the killer.

This meant a closed-door session in Bohannan's office that I wasn't invited to.

It also meant, about half an hour later, he and the boys took off with Harry and his guys. But not before he took my phone, downloaded an app on it and gave me a quick tutorial.

This tutorial included how to activate the view on a camera that had been motion triggered (which would result in a specific ping and an accompanying notification on my phone). Or what to do if a sensor had been tripped (which also would result in a notification on my phone).

I was to keep the window coverings closed, the doors locked, my Taser and phone at hand, and I already had the app to open the gate…but I was not to open it, *to anybody*.

"The only people who should be going through can get through on their own," he'd said. "And remember, me, Jace and Jess get those notifications too, so if we see something or suspect something, we'll be on our way home."

He'd said something else too.

"Move your shit to my room."

This caused a probably inappropriate, but definitely strong clitoris tingle.

Then he and the boys were gone.

To the lament of my curiosity, they took the brown folder with them.

Before dealing with phone calls from Megan and Kimmy, the latter who I had, along the way, maybe rashly, given my number, or moving my shit to Bohannan's room, I decided to go see how Celeste was.

Although she was not in full-on brat mode with me like she'd been with her father, when she ascertained I was not going to be on her side, she moaned, "I'm sure you *think* you understand. But none of your boyfriends' sisters were *murdered*."

Really, she had me there.

I decided to let her nurse her hurt. Maybe while doing that she'd realize how much pressure her father was under, how much he loved her and wanted her safe, how it would affect him in deep and ugly ways to fish a girl only a few years older than his daughter out of the lake at the end of his pier and cut him some slack (but I was not hanging a lot of hope on that).

I then had a long gab with Megan (she totally thought all this was about Audrey) and a short, one-sided gab with Kimmy, who clearly watched more true crime documentaries and was closer to what might be happening when she proclaimed, "Malorie isn't a kid, this puts a whole different spin on it."

I made dinner, knocked on Celeste's door, was told, "I'm not hungry!" and ate my solitary meal with the lake closed off from me, not turning on music or the TV because, if something went bump in the night, I wanted to hear it.

I then moved my shit into Bohannan's room.

Which semi-kinda brought me to now.

Because the boys had come home a half an hour ago.

They'd scarfed down the meals I'd kept warm for them, Jess and Jace rinsed their dishes and put them in the washer and headed to their place.

Bohannan and I went upstairs.

I SPIT, rinsed and lathered my face, wondering if tonight was orgasm night.

When I emerged from under the soap, Bohannan could be seen in the mirror, walking to the sink beside mine.

He was in pajama pants and nothing else.

The tail was gone in his hair, and it was flopping in his eyes.

I'd never seen his hair like that.

It was *delicious.*

His pectorals were life affirming.

He had chest hair that covered a good area, but it wasn't too much.

He didn't have a full six-pack, but under that fur, I counted four.

The veins running along his bulging biceps instantly became my new religion.

And since moving in with him, I'd used my vibrator, which was quiet, and I'd used it quite a bit…for obvious reasons.

But in that second, I vowed, tonight, I was using it again, even if he was lying beside me. He'd have to listen if he didn't do something about it.

"If you keep looking at me like that, I'm gonna fuck you in the bathroom."

My eyes moved from his chest in the mirror to his face.

I said nothing.

He went still.

I remained silent.

He didn't move.

I didn't either.

We stared at each other in the mirror for three years.

Then my upper arm was seized in a firm grip.

I was hauled across the space and my pajama pants were at my ankles.

My panties joined them.

My ass hit the counter between the sinks.

Bohannan hit his knees.

I guessed I'd had one kind of kiss that day and Bohannan was intent to run the gamut, because with no further ado, he spread my thighs and buried his face between my legs.

I was never allowing him to shave off his beard.

Never.

I lifted a bent arm over my shoulder, palm on the mirror, my other hand I clenched in his hair.

I came for him within seconds.

It was *catastrophic.*

I was not even remotely recovered before I was on my feet, whirled, one of his arms around my belly, holding me up.

He kicked my feet apart with one of his, wrapped his other arm around my chest, and I watched dazedly in the mirror as he drove up inside me.

I also watched as he buried his face in my neck as he fucked me.

The familiar intimacy of his whiskers at my neck and the newfound joy of his big cock thrusting inside collided in a way so profound, I shattered.

I wasn't Delphine.

I wasn't Larue.

I wasn't a writer.

A mother.

An ex.

A woman.

I was a body.

A cunt born to be fucked.

By that cock.

His face came out of my neck, his eyes locked to mine in the mirror, his hand slid down my belly to curl between my legs, and he worked my clit as he fucked me.

His face in sex was an aphrodisiac. Brutish and barbarous.

We stared at each other as we stumbled back millennia. We didn't know language. We didn't know culture. We didn't know manners. There were no rules.

There was instinct.

This wasn't sex.

It was a rut, natural, evolutionary.

We were born to connect like this.

His finger wouldn't be denied, his dick couldn't be, my head flew back, colliding with his shoulder, and his hand at my chest covered my mouth, lightly, to muffle any noise, but there was something delectably villainous about it.

So when I came again, and it was going to be huge, I came, and it was colossal.

There was a cry, but what was happening between my legs was too much for it to be loud.

Mostly it was a gasp. A need. A need to pull in oxygen as everything that made me isolated between my legs, and I temporarily forgot how to breathe.

I clutched him with my pussy, he grunted, then, face back in my neck, cock buried to the root, he growled into my flesh.

Another three years passed as I clung to what we just shared, emotionally and physically.

"Shit," he muttered against my skin. His lips slid up to my ear. "I hurt you?"

"Not even close."

His mouth still at my ear, his head tipped slightly so he could look from under his brow into my eyes in the mirror.

God, he was pure fucking *sex*.

How did I survive without having this with him for two months?

He curled his fingers around my throat.

"That wasn't what I wanted for us," he told me.

"I'm not complaining." A beat of concern, nerves, then, "Are you?"

"Baby, that was the hottest fuck I've ever had," he said. I lost his eyes, and he licked the shell of my ear before he whispered in it. "And I like to fuck. It's been a while. But for the record, my bed is a playground." Pause then, "Anything goes. You want it. You ask for it. And I'll give it to you."

That was quite a promise.

I shivered.

From the other room, his phone rang.

He lifted his head and said to me in the mirror, "Goddamn fuck."

I seconded that emotion.

He then slid out, fixed his pajama bottoms, knelt to help me step into my panties, which he pulled up, then my pajamas, and he stood.

"Be back," he muttered, touched his mouth to mine and stalked out of the room.

I watched.

Full report?

He had an insanely beautiful back.

I allowed myself a second (okay, it took ten, but it could have taken a year) to reflect on how wholly beautiful what we'd just shared was.

Then I went to the little toilet room to do some clean up.

I came back out, he wasn't there, so I washed my hands and wandered into the bedroom.

I was still in a daze, part of me happy we waited, thinking that might have built the need, which was what made what we shared so elemental, part of me ecstatic because I knew that wasn't true.

That was us, and it might not be that intense every single time.

But it was going to be great.

Coupled with the rest?

Suffice it to say, I'd waited fifty-three years.

But in Cade Hunter Bohannan, I'd hit the motherlode.

On this thought, it struck me he wasn't in the bedroom.

And on *that* thought, he prowled in from the hall.

"What were you—?" I began to ask.

"Checking on Celeste. Fortunately, she didn't do anything stupid," he bit off, walking directly to his closet.

Hesitantly, I followed him.

He was dressing.

"Bohannan, what's going on?"

"Scared parents, an incompetent sheriff and defiant kids aren't a good mix," he muttered.

Ah hell.

As he did up his jeans, he looked at me.

"I gotta get to the woods."

THIRTY-NINE

Abundance of Caution

There were many bonuses to living in Misted Pines and being with Cade Bohannan.

One was, after he got home from dealing with the clusterfuck that happened in the woods, he worked off his frustration by fucking you so hard facedown into the bed, if you could think (and trust me, you couldn't, but you also didn't want to, you just wanted to *feel*), you'd worry that he'd have to buy a new mattress because there would be an indelible female-shaped dent in the springs.

And two, when you showed at the hustling, droning, riled, crowded meeting in the town council chambers the next evening, even though it was standing room only, five people would exit their chairs so Bohannan and his family could be seated.

This begged a question I had not thought to ask.

Why was Bohannan such a force in that town?

It couldn't be denied him being ex-Green Beret, ex-FBI and an expert, and even famous, profiler was cool. And I would suspect, in a small, and what seemed until recently had been a sleepy town, this would lead to him being a favorite son.

From this, I could see the local townspeople wanting a man of his experience to replace an ineffective sheriff. I could also see them wanting him to be involved in a highly charged, highly emotional set of murders.

But people scrambling to give up their seats for him and his family took that to a new level.

He accepted two men's seats and planted Celeste's and my asses in them.

He indicated in a way no one would deny him that the women who got up should sit their asses back down, so they did.

Then he, Jess and Jace found a spot on the wall closer to the front and claimed it, assuming identical arms-on-chests, shoulders-to-wall, scowls-on-faces positions.

Yeah, the woods thing last night was not a clusterfuck.

It was a *clusterfuck*.

A shots-fired, thank-God-no-one-was-hurt, deputy-on-administrative-leave *clusterfuck*.

And that was only the worst part about it, it wasn't the only *bad* part about it.

The long, curved desk up front was crowded, not only with all the town council members, but with seats added so the county commissioners could sit with them.

And there was a line down the center aisle of people waiting to take the lectern because they had something to say.

A gavel was struck, and the guy sitting in the middle, who was eighty-five if he was a day, didn't have to request in his microphone that he wanted everyone's attention.

Upon the gavel strike, quiet swept the room.

That didn't last long.

"We sense it's going to be a long night," he began.

"Yeah it is!" someone shouted.

"Ya think?" someone else shouted.

"Remove Dern!" another shout.

This started up a chant of those two words that consumed the company with somewhat frightening ease.

Dern, who was at the very end of the curve, opposite to where Bohannan was standing, sat there, face set to a fundamental fury borne of a man who'd lived his entire life seated in the lap of privilege, and his adult life wielding power that should be handled with regard solely to protection and service, but he'd considered it elsewise. Therefore, he was utterly incapable of grasping the concept he couldn't do whatever he pleased.

That room was filled with people who wanted him out, and they were all wrong.

He was right.

A man with black hair cut and carefully arranged into a style that should have died in the eighties, sitting next to the octogenarian, shoved forward with torso and hand, moving the microphone his way.

"Order! Order!" he yelled, commandeering the gavel after a brief tussle the older gent had no hope of winning since his bone density left the building at least a decade ago. "*Order!*" he bellowed.

Deputies moved forward, for what reason I didn't know, and of course jostling began.

I reached for Celeste's hand to be prepared to make a break for it if needed, my gaze darting to Bohannan.

It did this just in time to catch him thunder, "*Cut it!*"

There were still titters and a few hints of elbowing, but the majority calmed down.

Yes, he was a force in this town.

"He can be a jerk, but mostly, Dad's super cool," Celeste muttered under her breath proudly, yet sulkily.

Even though the woods party ended in pandemonium, she wasn't over it.

I beat back a smile.

"Thank you, Cade," Mr. Greed Is Good said into the microphone. "Now, we know you have a lot to say. But I'll start with the preamble that it's our job to weigh the welfare of our citizens and make difficult decisions—"

There were groans and a loud, "You have *got* to be *kidding*!"

Another gavel strike and, "I said I'll have *order!* We called this meeting. We can just as easily adjourn it!"

Shuffling, muttering and unease as he waited for everyone to bow to his power trip, and I watched this with a sinking heart.

It sunk further when he stated, "This is a precarious time. In a time such as this, regardless of what you might think, because riot thought isn't rational…"

"Way to escalate proceedings, bozo," I mumbled, because so far, there'd been no riots. Just some unruly kids, terrified parents and trigger-happy cops.

The woman sitting in front of me turned around and grinned.

I returned it.

"…an abundance of caution and a steady leadership is the only way forward," the gent up front carried on. "Now—"

His attention was taken.

Which meant everyone's attention was taken.

And what it was taken by was Megan making a show of making her way to the front.

The line to speak had to be at least twenty-five people deep.

But the guy up front didn't hesitate to step aside, and the room could hear her demure, "Thank you, Tony," before she took her position at the lectern and squared her shoulders.

I was impressed.

I was also settled in for her to make mincemeat out of him.

And this she did.

She just didn't start it the way I might have expected.

She did it by ordering, "Gary, stop being a horse's ass."

The crowd erupted in cheers.

But Megan was opening her handbag.

She whipped out a slew of papers and brandished it in the air.

Once she thumped it on the lectern she announced, "*That* is two thousand, one hundred and twenty-seven names on a petition to relieve Sheriff Dern of his duties awaiting his recall."

And *that* was a lot of signatures in a very short period of time.

Though I suspected she'd been on this case for a lot longer, however, she hadn't mentioned it to me.

So, the people of Misted Pines couldn't come together about a mural.

But when the safety and welfare of their children were threatened, they were a tribe.

Yes.

Murders aside, I'd picked the right place.

"Megan, honestly," Gary said, his tone somewhat diffident at the same time attempting to retain control, and I sensed she was one of his campaign donors.

But Megan wasn't listening to him.

She was reaching into her handbag and pulling out another slew of papers.

She thumped it on top of the others and said into the microphone, "And *that* is a petition with one thousand, three hundred and fifty-four signatures to have *you* recalled. Both of these I'm hand delivering to the governor's office tomorrow, Gary, if you do not relieve Dern and reinstate Moran *this evening*."

Another roar from the crowd.

Well then, *that* was definitely a lot of signatures in a short period of time, because that was a power play that could only have been conceived of yesterday.

"It is not the Commission's position to bow to public pressure —" Gary shouted over the cheer.

"It isn't?" she asked. "If you don't listen to the public you serve, then what's your purpose?"

That had him stumped.

"Megan, and all of you," he addressed the crowd. "Please know, we appreciate your concern. But mob rule never—"

He stopped talking and looked to his right.

Which meant I looked to my left.

Bohannan was walking down the side aisle, Jace and Jess following him.

He stopped at the row Celeste and I were in and held out his arm.

We got up and "excuse me'ed" our way past the people in front of us.

Celeste got to him first, and he took her hand and gently moved her to his back, between him and her brothers.

When I got to him, he just took my hand and held it as he led, and we moved with some effort in the limited space afforded by the end of the seating and the wall lined with bodies toward the exit.

"Cade!" Gary called.

We kept moving.

"*Cade!*" Gary shouted.

Bohannan didn't even hesitate.

"You're a civic leader whether you like it or not," Gary, his voice now a shout, so I knew he wasn't using the microphone, and he was standing. "And you leaving these proceedings in a snit does nothing to assist your community!"

A snit?

That was even worse than a hissy fit.

And thus, that stopped Bohannan and he turned.

He did not look at Gary.

He spoke to the crowd.

"I'm working with the FBI to find out who's hurting our girls. This is their case, and Dern has no authority over their investigation. The two agents assigned are good men who give a shit. Harry is helping too. He hasn't abandoned you. I haven't either. I can't make any promises except to say Malorie and Alice are in good hands, the hands of investigators who want to find who hurt them and will do everything they can to make sure no one else gets hurt."

He shifted his attention to the front of the room.

"Meg, take your petitions to Olympia. If you need a ride, Jace'll take you."

Only then did he look at Gary.

"You'll be dead, so it won't matter to you that in your footnote in history, your tenure will be recorded at best, corrupt, and at worst, disastrous and life threatening."

With that, he tugged my hand and we all walked out.

FORTY

Romance Novelist's Heart

A mixed bag of what it meant to be living with Cade Bohannan in Misted Pines during a crisis that involved the FBI, was that a good place for the FBI to set up their field office when they encountered a hostile local law enforcement agency was the house up the way that Bohannan kept as a rental but was empty.

Until now.

It was a good thing that more trained professionals were close, and anyone in their right minds would have added reason to steer clear.

The thing was, the person they were hunting was not in his right mind.

Nevertheless, it meant, when Bohannan was done for the night, he didn't have far to drive to get home.

I was in his bed with Elizabeth Little's *Pretty as a Picture*, hoping with my romance novelist's heart that Marissa would get together with Isaiah, but with my thriller writer's mind knowing that was unlikely, when Bohannan strolled in.

One look at him and I understood Dale Pulaski's response to getting what you needed in troubled times (or any time).

If Bohannan tossed out dollar bills and ordered me to crawl to him on my hands and knees picking them up along the way *à la* Mickey Rourke and Kim Basinger in *9½ Weeks*, I wouldn't have hesitated.

I didn't hide this thought, which was probably why Bohannan's gaze darkened, he changed course and entered the bed beside me, stretching out at a diagonal, up on an elbow at my hip, and his hand came out so he could trail his fingers up the back of my calf starting at my ankle.

It was the most sensual touch I'd ever sustained.

"Fallin' down," he murmured. "Made a promise, fucked you twice, three orgasms when you were owed six."

"You're forgiven that debt," I told him. "Seeing as it's about quality, not quantity."

His beard grinned.

I put the book aside.

He wrapped his arm around my hips and pulled me under him.

I yanked the tail out of his hair, and it fell forward.

I ran my fingers through it, pulling it back.

"Is sucking cock like riding a bicycle?" he asked.

I trembled.

"I don't know."

His gaze dropped to my mouth. "If not, I'll be there to coach you."

Yes, he would.

But in the end, to my delight (and something else for him), he didn't need to.

FORTY-ONE

Hubris

Outside her shop on Main Street, I sat sandwiched between Kimmy and a life-size stuffed Santa, on a green painted bench abounding with gold fretwork and upholstered in bright red velvet button back.

She was in a voluminous Christmas sweater, I was in a thin wool heathered-gray crewneck with a slimline, dusky lilac puffy vest over it, and we both had fresh Aromacobana brews in our hands (mine decaffeinated, Kimmy's with a triple shot) and our eyes to the passersby.

"What're we lookin' for?" she asked, then took a sip.

"I don't know," I answered.

"What're you freakin' out about?" she asked.

"My daughters arrive tomorrow, one with her girlfriend who's like another daughter to me, one with an unknown fighter pilot who's stealing her jaded heart," I answered, then took a sip.

"Not good timing," she muttered, then took a sip.

"I had to call them both yesterday and share that there's a good possibility there's a serial killer hunting my new boyfriend's patch, I'm not actually living in the house they're going to stay in because he didn't think it was safe for me to be there alone, and our neighbors are FBI agents running a command post out of a rental. Fenn called from the airport having just landed for the layover, one-night mini-vacation she and her fighter jock are taking in Hawaii, and thus getting the message I ill-advisedly left on her voicemail. She was so loud, I feared TSA would take her down. Camille started and stopped fifteen sentences before she gave up, hung up on me and Joan called back sharing that 'she's just worried.'"

"Got three, two girls and a boy. Got no clue when I stopped bein' the mom and they thought of me as their kid. But it happened. According to them, I can barely brush my own teeth in the morning." She took a sip. "It'd crawl right up my ass if it wasn't about love."

Damn it.

I hated it when people had good responses to stuff that was annoying me.

"Want some good news?" she asked.

"Yes," I stated the obvious.

"Full Metal Meg marched her uptight ass right to the governor's office yesterday. Heard tell the man wasn't ignorant of our situation. Not sure how they do all that with their red tape muckin' things up. But I suspect Harry's going to be acting sheriff pretty soon, and we're gonna have a full ballot come election time. Because rumor is, Megan has very recently decided to aim for Gary's seat."

I turned to her. "That *is* good news."

She turned to me. "You do know that whackjobs don't have, 'I murder girls', tattooed on their foreheads, Manson notwithstanding."

"I can read people."

"So can I. So can Bohannan. If he thought this nutcase would stroll down the avenue, he'd be sitting where we are."

I turned to our quiet compatriot then back to her. "Santa settles the soul."

She looked to the street, brought up her paper cup, and muttered to it, "Ain't that the truth."

And she took a sip.

IT WAS on the ride home from hanging with Kimmy that my car rang.

I accidentally hit the wrong button on my steering wheel, and instead of declining the call, I got Angelo's voice filling the cab.

"What the fuck, Delphine?" he blistered.

It was Monday. I'd sat too long with Kimmy, assessing the citizenry of MP in hopes I'd zero in on a killer, therefore Celeste would be home before me.

There'd been a drama in the kitchen yesterday that resulted in her weekend grounding extending for a week.

I needed to be home for moral support for Celeste and to make sure Celeste came home.

Megan had canceled book club that night, which was a bummer. I could have used talking about a happily ever after, if just for the distraction of it.

Though I understood this play. A curfew hadn't been called, but come sundown, Misted Pines moved behind locked doors and kept vigilant.

My need for sisterhood and love-of-romance-books solidarity grew as Angelo's famously gravelly voice came at me again.

"Hello? I asked, what the fuck?"

"Camille called you."

"So you go from one psycho to another?"

"I'm not sure it's politically correct to call them psychos."

"Do I give a shit? They're psychos. I'll be culturally sensitive to people who don't rape and kill other people."

He had a point.

"And you're seeing someone?" he demanded.

Ah.

"Angie—" I started.

"You think maybe you'd give me a heads up about that so Cam doesn't blindside me with it?"

Blindside him?

"Angie, we've been divorced for fifteen years."

"You dated that record exec, who was an asshole. I knew you were doing that just to get laid and maybe piss me off."

For goodness sakes.

"Then you shacked up for a while with that sculptor, but that was more about the fact he lived on that farm in the middle of nowhere and you needed a break than about wanting to be with that guy. In other words, you weren't serious about either of them. But you were married to me for eleven years and then you didn't replace me."

It had been so long since I dealt with a man in any day-to-day meaningful way (and I didn't mean a man like Bohannan, because I think we all can agree he's a unicorn), I forgot how much hubris they could have.

So much it was stunning.

Thus, I was stunned.

"Are you saying you think I've been pining for you for fifteen years?"

"Del," he chuffed, like, *duh*.

"I haven't been pining for you for fifteen years."

"Babe, you and me, we need some time. We'll go to my place. Down on the island."

We needed some time?

A decade and a half later?

"That place you had orgies?" I asked.

"That right there," he crowed. "You wouldn't care if you didn't care."

"I'm simply pointing out how insensitive you're being, which is only one of the reasons why we ended, and that was *the end*."

"It's a spiritual place now, babe. I've had it cleansed. I meditate there. I swim. I read. You'd love it."

I didn't have time for this.

Strike that.

I just didn't want to do this.

"Okay, Angie, the truth of the matter is, I loved you once. I did it in a way that parts of that love will never die. And those parts aren't solely wrapped up in the fact we created Camille and you were an incredibly wonderful stepdad to Fenn. But the other parts, the important parts, the parts around trust and safety and security and unconditional love, the parts I needed because I grew up starved of them, are gone. Never to return. We had this conversation before you even put a ring on my finger, and still, you did what you did. Now, I cannot say that it doesn't make me feel good to know that you still care about me in that way. But you have to get, I don't return those feelings."

There was a beat before, "Right, then go down to the island to get away from a fuckin' serial killer."

"Bohannan is part of the team that's trying to find that serial killer, and I'm falling in love with him, and he likes me around, so that's not going to happen."

Several beats of silence before, "Are you safe?"

"Am I ever really safe?" I asked quietly.

"I don't like this, and the girls don't either."

"Well, they're not girls and neither am I. It's sweet, this concern, but I'm not only where I want to be, I'm where I need to be."

Many, many beats of silence, so many, the gate to home was coming into view before, "Love you, Del. Always. Yeah?"

That was very sweet.

And it was very sad.

And it was very unlike me not to notice that not only had I not replaced him.

He had never replaced me.

But…

Thank God this was done.

"Love you too, Angie. Thanks for caring."

"Take care of yourself."

"I will."

I heard him accidentally start saying a tortured, "*Fu—*, before he'd successfully hung up, and my heart hurt hearing that.

But not enough.

And not for long.

Because I cleared the gate and the trees surrounding the front of the house.

But I didn't even make the clearing behind it before I saw Celeste standing outside her Mustang, beautiful face pale and haunted, watching a violently gesticulating Will Pulaski shouting at her.

FORTY-TWO

Shine out of the Dark

The Volvo rolled five feet with my door open and me half out of it before I realized I hadn't put the bitch in park and turned it off.

I did that in record time, shot out of the car and sprinted to Celeste.

I pulled her back and got between her and Will, who could take us both and looked like he was going to, but I wasn't going to go down without a fight.

"You need to calm down," I informed him.

"Delly—" Celeste said softly.

"*You don't get it!*" Will shouted.

"Take a breath, stand back and calm down," I ordered.

He got in my face, nose to nose, and I flinched when he roared, "*You don't get it!*"

We were surrounded by tires-skidding-over-wet-pine-needles noises as a Ram and a Yukon raced to a halt, and it was indisputable Jace and Bohannan were way more badass than I was in angling out of their vehicles.

Will was already retreating as, unhurriedly but with a mission, Bohannan advanced on him.

Jace stopped at us, which was good, since the look on his face said he wanted to tear Will's head off.

"Mr. Bohannan—" Will began.

"You don't talk," Bohannan warned. "*I* talk."

He stopped several feet away.

Will tried not to cower while cowering.

I wanted to watch, but the sleeve of my sweater was being tugged.

I looked down at it, then to Celeste who was doing it.

Wordlessly, she showed me her phone.

A video was playing on it. I wasn't interested, but at the glance I caught, I did a double take and took it from her.

What I was watching, I didn't want to watch.

But I couldn't turn away.

At its end, when the visual stopped on a still that was no less shocking than the rest of it, my eyes drifted up to her.

"His parents. It's everywhere," she whispered. "Like, *the whole school has seen it.*"

Dear Lord.

I knew one of the two people in it was Dale Pulaski. I'd seen him in another video, the one where he was standing by his wife while she was entreating their daughter's kidnapper to bring her home.

This one, though, had a different woman in it.

And apparently, that woman was Sarah.

I kept hold of her phone and called, "Bohannan."

"—listening to me?" he was asking Will.

I approached him, repeating, "Bohannan."

I shot a sympathetic look to Will as I stopped at Bohannan's side.

Will watched me lift Celeste's phone then he turned his face away.

I hit play and whispered, "It's made the rounds."

Bohannan's head cocked down, and he watched the video of Sarah Pulaski fucking Dale Pulaski, her fingers in his hair, pulling back his head so there was no mistaking him, or missing a thing as he took it on his elbows and knees. The angle on the action and focus was exceptional. The intent of the video crystal clear.

But Bohannan didn't wait for the money shot at the end.

He reached out and touched the screen to stop it and looked back to Will.

Before he could say anything, Will said, "I wasn't shouting at her. I was just shouting."

"Take a second and take a breath," Bohannan demanded.

"I'd never hurt her. I'm just so *sick* of their *shit*," Will said.

I did not blame him.

Not about shouting at Celeste, but if there were extenuating circumstances for anyone, no matter the age, there were here.

But he was only seventeen.

So there was that.

"That's my *mom* and *dad*, Mr. Bohannan," he spat. "I mean, that's *sick*."

Before Bohannan could reply, Will's phone rang, he pulled it out of his front pocket, his face twisted, he took the call and said into it, "Like I said, *fuck you*! Fuck you now and fuck you *forever*. I'm *never* coming home. *I never wanna look at you again*."

He then ended the call, jabbed his screen with his finger repeatedly, and at a guess, blocked his mom and/or dad.

"Your dad?" Bohannan asked.

"Mom," Will clipped. "I already blocked my sickfuck of a dad." He looked up from his phone. "Who would have thought the only non-fucked-up one would be fucking *Audrey*?"

Hmm.

"Right, Jace is going to take you to his place, and you're gonna get yourself together," Bohannan said. "You can stay there tonight. I'm gonna have a conversation with your parents."

"I'm not going back to them, Mr. Bohannan. Neither of them," Will declared.

"Let's just get through tonight," Bohannan returned. "You can have dinner with us, but I don't want you alone with my daughter when you're in this state."

"She's the only person that gives a shit about me," Will replied.

"That isn't true, even though I figure you think it is. But if it was, I'd kick you off my land."

Will's body jerked as that hadn't occurred to him until Bohannan pointed it out.

Which made it clear that, probably since Alice was taken, and maybe even before that, the adults in his life had been so enmeshed in all their chaos, they hadn't had a thought about him.

And frankly, the fact they hadn't broke my heart.

Not only for Will.

But also for Alice.

Bohannan took a breath and a step toward Will, but he didn't push it.

"I get it," he said. "You're learning too many lessons about how shit life can be. I hate that for you, but bottom line, Will, life can be shit. Now, you can either boss up and deal, or you can lose yourself in it. You got some time to figure that out, here with us, where you got space to think. But I'll warn you, I'll only accept that first choice when it comes to who spends time with my daughter."

Will looked to Celeste, back to Bohannan and then to me.

"I'm sorry I got in your face, Ms. Larue."

I didn't exonerate him verbally, but I nodded.

"I'm sorry, babe," he said, quieter to Celeste.

"It's okay, Will," Celeste said sweetly.

"Jace, show him his space for tonight," Bohannan ordered then looked to me. "What time's dinner, baby?"

I had no idea. We ate when I was done cooking.

I preferred to eat later, and since I was doing all the cooking, that was when we ate, whether it was just Celeste and me, or all of us.

But I figured Celeste and Will wouldn't be able to wait that long, so I said, "Five thirty."

Bohannan's beard moved in an upward motion because he knew my gambit, but he turned to Will.

"Come on over at five and you can help Larue if she needs anything."

Will nodded.

He and Jace walked off.

"Thanks, Daddy," Celeste said.

I'd never heard her call him that, but it was cute.

"He's gonna need you, honey, so get in there and do your homework so you can have your head clear when he comes over," Bohannan advised.

She made to take off, but he stopped her by calling her name.

She turned back.

"You okay with…what you saw?" he asked.

What was this I was seeing?

Bohannan…*uncomfortable*?

"I'm grossed out because…gross," she answered.

Bohannan's attention slid to me.

It shot back to his girl when she went on, "But I'm more worried about Will."

"Okay, you got any questions about that kind of thing…uh… you know…"

Oh my God.

I was *loving* this.

"I won't, Dad," she replied very, *very* promptly.

"Right," he muttered.

I bit my lip.

"Go on," he urged.

She sent a curious look my way before she dashed off, her bookbag bouncing. So desirous of fleeing, she left her phone with me.

I turned to Bohannan.

"You're ridiculously cute."

"I wanna kill myself."

I started laughing and got close to him.

He slid an arm around my waist.

"Have you talked to her about the birds and the bees?"

He nodded, paling, actually *paling*, under his tan at the memory.

"And her periods. And STDs. And condoms and birth control. So also pregnancy and the consequences of an unwanted one. It was not my finest hour. We both hated it. But we also both thought it was over."

"*Hell hath no fury*," I quoted.

"You got no idea," he said, pulled out his phone, let it read his face, then he held it up so we both could see.

And I learned that a man, who could only be Dwayne, didn't like pain.

He liked *pain*.

Bohannan thumbed the screen.

And I saw that Bobby didn't like dick up his ass.

He liked big dick, and he didn't want just any ole delivery system. The guy he picked wasn't only hung, he was built and gorgeous.

Another thumb swipe and there it had to be Jay, his ass very red, his dick very swollen, his teacher with her glasses perched on the tip of her nose very determined to punish her naughty boy.

"Yikes," I said.

"I hadn't seen Dale and Sarah's. I didn't think. With Alice…"

He didn't finish that.

He said something else.

"Those videos were texted wide throughout the day. This kicks that vengeance club up a few solid notches," he said. "Wendy left Dwayne this weekend. Word on the street is that Lana's the ring-leader. Apparently, her defecting from Bobby meant the gloves could finally come off."

"Seems so."

"It's shit. It's childish. And it's piss poor timing," he bitched.

"You're right about all that," I replied.

He drew breath into his nose, re-engaged his phone, and didn't let me go as he made a call.

He put it to his ear.

"Yeah, Sarah, lis—" Pause then, "What did you think was gonna happen?" Pause then, "Yeah, I'd hope you didn't want your son to see it." Another pause and, "Are you telling me I gotta explain the concept of copy and paste to you?"

There was a longer pause, but it wasn't that long before Bohannan spoke again.

"I gotta interrupt you, 'cause I need you to listen to me. Will's here. We got him. We're taking care of him tonight. But he's not staying here because he's my daughter's boyfriend and I'm not okay with that. You need to find somewhere safe for him to be with someone who has a mind to him and doesn't have their heads up their ass."

That was saying it straight.

"No, see, because I got a visual on one of my cameras of your boy shouting at my girl, lookin' like he's gonna beat the shit outta her, so I had to haul ass from what I was doing, which, Sarah, you know is kinda fuckin' important, to shut that shit down. I show, and he's got his face in my woman's, and I mean that literally. He's messed up."

He took a big breath.

And kept at her.

"Now I know Dale done you wrong. And I know Bobby, Dwayne and Jay are assholes. And I know you women got a beef. And I'm a guy, so you gotta know I don't take it lightly when I say there are some men who deserve to feel emasculated. Where I draw the line with that is not when there's someone killing girls in our town. But I'll take this opportunity to remind you that Alice Pulaski might not have been your daughter, but she was *his* sister."

I bit back cheering him on.

"Where I draw the line with it is parents causing damage to kids they might never recover from. You fucked your boy up today, and I know how a lot of messed-up minds work, and the vast majority of that happens when parents don't think about what their actions might do to their kids. You didn't think about what you'd do to your son, and I got no idea how you're gonna fix that. And that is not on Dale. That is on *you.*"

And that was straighter.

"Now figure it out and text me where your kid is gonna go tomorrow after school, and pack him a couple good bags. Because he's blocked you and Dale, and you got no choice but to give him some time. Time I suggest you take to remember what's important in this world. So you text me because I'm not gonna talk to you until I've lost the shit taste in my mouth I got from having to deal with you."

And with that, he was finished.

"Christ," he muttered, shoving his phone in his back pocket.

"Well said," I praised.

"I got into this business because bad shit happens to good people, and I wanted to play a part in making it stop or making it right, or just doing something. But I'm running out of good people."

I turned and pressed into him.

"I'm not."

He looked down at me and his expression gentled.

"I think Will really likes her and he's just caught in a shitty situation he doesn't know what to do with," I deduced.

"Yeah."

"I still think Celeste and I need to have a conversation, and today I added a few things."

"I would be grateful, baby, but today she also got something else."

"I know." I wrinkled my nose. "We'll talk about exploring sexually and how it isn't wrong, even if today it wasn't right."

"That's not what she got."

"What did she get?"

"She thinks you're the shit because you're pretty and you're famous and you're rich, and you got great clothes she can borrow, and you put on mascara every day and shovel shit back at Jess and Jace and you make me happy."

I made him happy.

I was holding my breath.

"But today, she got a woman who'd stand between her and an angry young man who's six-one and two hundred pounds and can check the fuck outta someone against the boards. He's up in that woman's shit, and for Celeste, she doesn't stand down. You could leave me tomorrow, and I'd hate it like fuck, but you'd leave having given her a taste of that, so I'd be able to live with it."

"I might cry," I whispered.

"There's a reason your girls are perfect."

I shoved my face in his chest.

He wrapped a hand around the back of my head.

And into the hair on top of it, he said, "I got sordid and tawdry all around me, but these days, all I gotta do is think of you and know a cycle can be broken and light can shine out of dark."

My shoulders heaved.

Bohannan wrapped his arm around them.

And as we stood there, we didn't notice the temperature had fallen.

And the mist swallowed the police tape on the pier.

FORTY-THREE

Perfect

"I, honest to God, don't know whether to spew or go out and buy an apron."

"Oh my God, please, don't go out and buy an apron."

"I'm buying one…for *you*. I know it's my mom, but this June Cleaver deal is hot."

"I will never forgive you for this."

"Don't get any ideas. I burn water when I'm boiling it."

In succession:

Fenn, to me.

Joan, to Fenn.

Camille, to Joan.

Joan, to me.

Fenn, to James.

Important note: if James felt the need, the need for speed, he didn't let on. He was quiet and very laid back. I liked him within seconds of meeting him. It wasn't that his puzzle was simple or uncomplicated. It was just that he was perfect for Fenn.

Though, it was clear, even if so far I'd only seen him in jeans and a Henley, he'd be very fun to watch playing beach volleyball.

I was making dinner for my brood and Bohannan's brood in Bohannan's kitchen.

Will was staying with his maternal grandmother who, as of yesterday, stopped talking to her daughter, except to tell her to get her grandson to her house.

However, he was over now because Celeste was becoming his touchstone, and, according to Annette, his grandmother, "I don't think any of us can argue that boy needs the example of some decent men in his life."

And truly, no one could argue that.

This next concerned me, however, I felt they could use the mental break; but rather than being on the hunt, Bohannan, Jason and Jesse were home with us.

My kids were settled in at my house, which all of them, including James, gave a stamp of approval, and Camille had even stood staring out the back windows, muttering a disgruntled, "Okay. I get it."

And at that time, she hadn't seen Bohannan's view.

Or met Bohannan.

Or his brood.

Now, the gang was all together.

And I was slipping.

Because I hadn't even noticed I'd fallen into the role of the little woman.

Or realized how much I was enjoying it.

Jace approached me (eating a cookie…and yes, he was eating said cookie while I was cooking, and yes again, I had baked that cookie) and he slung an arm around my shoulders.

"Why is everything about you suddenly explained?" he asked.

"Takes a wiseass to make a wiseass," Jess stated sagely, his face in the fridge.

"We're going to eat in ten minutes, Jess," I admonished (you will note, I didn't say a word to Jace, I'd already given up on this kind of thing with him).

Jess came out of the refrigerator chewing on a stick of string cheese. "Yeah, it smells awesome."

"I have wanted a brother all my life," Fenn declared, gazing between them approvingly. "And look, now there are two."

"Hey, gee, thanks," Camille said.

Fenn looked at Camille. "When I was seven, you asked Mom to give me a penis."

That did happen, Camille so badly wanted a big brother.

"I was four, I probably didn't know what a penis was," Camille shot back.

"She still doesn't know," Joan whispered to James.

James grinned.

"Can you not embarrass me?" I requested of my girls.

"How are we embarrassing you?" Fenn asked, seeming genuinely perplexed.

"I don't know, maybe carrying on a conversation about penises is a topic for discussion pre-seventh or eighth dinner we share with my new man and his family," I suggested. "I know!" I suddenly exclaimed. "Let's save it for Thanksgiving."

"No, please go on," Jess said, leaning into one elbow on the counter of the bar, his other hand held another stick of string cheese. He bit some off and said through chewing, "I want to hear more about penises."

"I have bragged outrageously about how perfect you are," I declared to the girls. "Sadly, I forgot to warn you to pretend that's what you were."

"Aw, Mom, really?" Camille asked. "That's so sweet."

"I am truly perfect." Fenn draped herself on a barstool in a manner James, Jess, Jace *and* Will watched very closely in one way, Celeste watched it closely in another, and I lamented for the first time how strikingly beautiful and lithe my daughter was.

She was addressing this to Bohannan, who was silently regarding all of this from his place, leaning with his ass against the sink and the apples of his palms resting on the counter behind him.

"The angels sang, and the doves cried when I was born," Fenn went on.

"Barf," Camille groaned.

"Obviously, as you can see," Fenn drawled, "the trolls grunted, and the goblins danced when Camille made her way into the world."

"Which is perfect, as a sorceress, that I'd find you," Joan purred, nuzzling Camille's neck with her chin.

"You're actually mine, I don't know where those two came from," I said to Joan.

"I wish," she replied.

Yes, Joan's parents were rather a pill.

I blew her a kiss.

She smiled at me.

"Can you show me how to curl my hair like yours?" Celeste asked Camille.

"Totally. Beauty school at Mom's tomorrow night!" Camille cried.

Celeste turned shining, happy eyes to me, and it occurred to me, in longing for a mother she never really had, she wouldn't dare to dream what it would mean to have a sister she simply couldn't have. And for obvious reasons, she'd never considered the impossibility of having several older ones.

But there it was, this cornucopia of female goodness laid out before her.

And it was something I'd had the privilege of giving to her.

As lovely as those thoughts were, they weren't the only reasons my smile was softer for her.

"Baby," Bohannan's voice rumbled low. "You need me to do anything?"

"No, Cade, I have it covered."

He gave me a look that was his neutral blended with warmth, contentedness and affection.

I tried to give that back, without the neutral.

His beard twitched up.

There you go.

I succeeded.

I turned back to the crew and noted that Jess, Jace and Celeste were paying no mind to this.

But Joan had her forehead on Camille's shoulder, hiding her

face, Camille was avoiding my eyes, but hers seemed to be shining with tears, and Fenn appeared to be deep breathing.

"You guys okay?" I asked.

Fenn's gaze found mine.

And she replied, "We're great, Mom. We're freaking *perfect.*"

I held her look.

I read her look.

I loved her look.

And then I got busy finishing dinner.

FORTY-FOUR

Confucius

The next night, I walked out of the bathroom, flipping off the light switch, while still rubbing serum in my face.

"I could have missed listening to all the Misted Pines ghost stories while sitting on my pier," I told Bohannan, who was in bed, so obviously his bare chest was also there, as was his beard, and a recent delicious discovery, his thin, gold-framed reading glasses were on his nose.

He took them off and looked at me.

I was done complaining due to the fact I was having a sexy male librarian fantasy.

He set what he'd been reading on his nightstand and ordered, "Get in bed."

I didn't get in bed, per se.

I got on him.

Straddling his hips, he put his hands to mine, and I said softly, "I think maybe one of the most beautiful things I've ever seen was watching you, Jace, Jess and James hanging all those strings of lights up and down my back clearing."

And they had. Maybe thirty sets of them. So not only my pier was hooked up with soft, romantic, safe, boogey-man-stay-away lights, the path down to it was. The deck outside the house was. They had section remotes, so I could go all in or pick parts. But house-to-pier, there was no place to hide.

They'd even started stringing some into the woods, along the path to Bohannan's house. But they stopped when they ran out.

Note to self: buy more lights so what was mine could be connected to what was Bohannan's in yet another way.

"Doesn't take much with you," he remarked.

"You did it because you wanted to make us feel safe in the light. You did it because I wanted them, and you knew they'd make me happy. You did it because it was your way to feel out James. You did it to give me some time to be with my girls without alienating the boys. That doesn't seem to me like not much."

He didn't reply to all that.

He said, "If that's the kind of guy who's defending our freedom, I'm resting easier tonight. I probably would have punched Jace or Jess in the mouth the fiftieth time they said to me, 'Talk to me, Goose.' He's good-humored and has the patience of a saint."

My lips tipped up, because James was definitely that, but I reminded him, "The kind of gal who's also doing it egged Jace and Jess on to tell more ghost stories after she'd collected some pebbles she surreptitiously started throwing into the water to freak us out."

"Got no problem with that, because she's got no fear."

"For a mom, that's terrifying."

"I'll rephrase. She's sharp as fuck, so she knows when to feel fear and use it, and she knows when it's useless, except to have a little fun."

"You've got an answer for everything."

His fingers on my hips gave me a squeeze. "I don't got an answer for how you feel about your ex wanting you back."

Quick update: I'd pulled a fast one.

We'd been busy, lots of people, lots of laughter and conversation, cooking and exploring environs, getting to know each other with everyone understanding this was happening. The families we knew for years were adjusting, expanding, and this was the family we were going to become.

But I worried Angelo might talk to one of the girls, they'd let it slip, and I didn't want that to happen when I hadn't mentioned it to Bohannan.

So, I'd told him in passing at a time when we couldn't discuss it.

I guessed now we were going to discuss it.

"I was taken aback that was where he was at," I told him, leaning forward to rest on my forearms on his chest, my face closer to his. "It's been a long time."

"I mourned her like she was dead," he shared, and I knew he was talking about Grace. "I wasn't unaware we had problems. We had a lot of words. We fought. I didn't ignore our issues, and it got under my skin she wanted me to. She was angry I couldn't get where she was coming from. But since the bottom line of it was she didn't love our daughter, I was angry she couldn't get where I was at with that. Still, when she left, even with all of that, years of it, it was a blow. I grieved. And then I realized what I was grieving. What I felt for her was dead. And I stopped grieving."

That made sense.

"What I felt for Angelo is dead too. I've considered this, and part of me actually would like to be one of those women who's forgiving. Who understands faults, and that everyone is human and they make mistakes. But my home life growing up felt precarious. My mother never truly neglected me. I was fed and clothed and went to school. She'd even ask if I finished my homework. But there was no warmth and love. I'd ride the bus home from school and think, when I got off, I could just walk in another direction and keep walking, never going home and she might not even realize I'm gone."

"Jesus, Larue," he whispered.

I nodded. "It sucked, and it still sucks and it's not okay. It never gets better. I didn't have a mom to show me the way to raise my girls. Not just know it from experiencing it growing up, but someone to talk with to get advice. To make sure I was doing things right. And I won't have someone to go to when they get married or have babies. Someone who understands, who was there before me, who'd be there *for* me when I deal with the things I'll deal with when that happens."

I ran the backs of my fingers along the fullness of his whiskers at his jaw and kept going.

"I was too young with Warren to understand what I needed and communicate it to him. That doesn't make him betraying me okay, but I was older and wiser with Angelo. I'd reflected on why I refused to work on it with Warren, and I told Angelo up front. He's lead singer and guitarist of a rock and roll band. I knew his reputation. I was even famous for 'taming' him. So, I knew I had to make it clear. That was a deal breaker. That was something I couldn't get beyond. I needed to feel absolutely safe and wholly part of our family, our marriage. And he still did it to me. But when it's gone, it's just gone, Bohannan."

"Yeah," he murmured his agreement.

"I know that's a tall order, to put that on anyone. When he was trying to talk me into working it out, he told me it put him under a lot of pressure."

"It's not a lot of pressure."

"Life happens, Bohannan."

"It's not a lot of pressure, Larue."

"I—"

He put a finger to my lips.

I shut up because that was cute and hot and annoying, all rolled into one.

"You don't forget what people say to you," he told me and removed his finger. "Not when it's important. He was not fucking a woman who was not you and then, later, brushing his teeth and thinking, 'Oh shit, I forgot. I told Delphine I wasn't gonna cheat on her.' That isn't how it works."

I felt my lips twitching because that was kind of funny.

"He knew he was doing wrong. He knew what it would mean. He did it anyway. I have no clue why he did. But he knew. That pressure bullshit was to deflect responsibility to you. The vast majority of people do not know the intricacies of the law. But they know right and wrong."

"Yes," I agreed.

"So you're over him," he deduced.

I smiled. "No. Right now, I'm over you."

His hands slid up my back.

My eyes slid to the folder on the nightstand.

"Stop worrying," he murmured. "I'm not the lead investigator on the case."

My attention returned to him. "I'm not worried about the case. I'm worried that you'll be worried about the case in taking time to string up lights and play host and be awesome and make my daughters feel safe in leaving me in your hands. You make it look effortless, but it's not."

His brows lifted. "Be awesome?"

I treated him to an eye roll. "Shut up."

This time, his beard lifted.

I stared at him.

He sighed, pushed to sitting more upright against the headboard and took me with him.

I continued to stare at him.

He laid it out.

"The boat is pretty much a dead end. We're still working it, though, even if our witness saw someone from a distance past midnight, so they didn't see much, and it's highly doubtful this guy would make that stupid of a mistake and leave that trail. My guess, definitely he wouldn't use his own boat, even if he thought he'd picked a late enough time he'd go unseen. We gotta roll on the thought that anything could be important, and if we find the boat, it might give us something. But it's a lot of legwork. Maybe every fifth house in this county, the owners got a boat."

There were three large lakes in this county, so big they crossed into two surrounding ones, so I had little doubt that was true.

"Boats are titled, and this one had an outboard, so it'd need to be registered. That said, there are folks who live up here away from the crowds, and how that could mean folks could get in their business who aren't real big on following government regulations or having them infiltrate their life. So we figure anywhere upwards to a quarter of the boats in this county, especially a small craft like the one described, the owner didn't bother to register it."

I figured that was true too.

"You can also rent fishing boats from a couple of places at the marina, but there aren't many of them. Even fewer of what there are, they're light with a dark stripe. We've isolated them, covered them, and forensics are going through them one by one to see if they can put Malorie in a boat. This is probably wasted effort. I'd put money down she was tarped before she was put in there because we know she was killed before she hit her home state. And you can't rent a boat for the night or overnight. Day rentals only and contracts all state return is by nightfall. No boats were out, unreturned. So if it was one of those, the guy helped himself so we couldn't track him. But we're eliminating that line anyway."

"Cameras at the marina?" I asked.

"Some, not comprehensive views. But the angles they had, you'd have to swim to a boat to take it without being seen, and I wouldn't put that past this guy."

I wouldn't either. He'd be determined not to be caught and go that extra mile to make that so, and being in this competition with Bohannan, doing that even more so in order to best him.

Bohannan continued sharing.

"They sent agents to Berkeley. More than one person in Malorie's dorm saw a guy hanging around that they didn't get a good feel for. A couple even reported him. They saw him before she disappeared, but they haven't seen him after. The witnesses were talked to separately, sat with artists separately, and the facial composites bear a resemblance, one that's pretty striking. So it's the same guy. No one has him in any classes or saw him around anywhere but loitering outside her dorm."

"Oh my God," I whispered.

He shook his head. "He looks a little like a guy who lives in the next town. A guy who'd have the skills to pull some of this shit off. But that guy has solid alibis for both murders. That said, I figure our guy will want to be closer to me. Never seen anyone like the man in the sketches around MP. Jace, Jess, Harry, any of the boys haven't either. We aren't releasing the composite because we can't know our guy didn't hire someone to lurk for that purpose, to throw us off on a line of inquiry that will lead nowhere, and we don't want people to find his face on someone who isn't going around killing girls. And our guy, he's not gonna make it that easy. Still, we wanna find that man in Berkeley. If he was put up to it, it's likely the bad guy did it without a face-to-face meet. But we need to rule that out. And we need to talk to him."

I nodded, then asked tentatively, "She was killed before she got to Washington?"

"Malorie was serious and studious and kept to a schedule. So her roommate knew something was up right away. When her roommate couldn't get hold of her, she reported her concerns the day before Malorie was dumped, but by that time, she hadn't been missing for even a day. She was dead at least twelve hours by the time we found her. We estimate he had her less than twenty-four hours. On this particular mission, our guy didn't have any interest in dealing with a scared, maybe fighting, likely erratic co-ed. Alice, he wanted fear and panic. Malorie, the element of surprise. This is him thinking this, baby, not me, but on that trip, he made her luggage."

Dear Lord.

I swallowed and then, "Did he…was it as bad as Alice?"

He shook his head. "Totally different MO. One hundred percent to make it so we can't get a bead on him. Or we'll get the wrong bead. He strangled Malorie with gloved hands. There was some defensive bruising, but other than that, not a mark on her."

"He didn't…?"

Bohannan didn't make me say the words.

"She was not raped or sexually assaulted in any way."

I hated the fact that I was glad about anything that befell Malorie Graham, but I was glad that she didn't bear any additional trauma before she was taken from this earth.

However.

"Alice?" I whispered.

"No, baby," he whispered back.

I let out a relieved breath.

"My job right now is not to be out there bumping into shit McGill and Robertson are doing. My job," he glanced to the file, "is to go through old cases to see if anything jogs in my mind. Brothers of victims. Boyfriends. Cousins. Acquaintances. Anyone who was keen on the crime I was investigating. Anyone who was overly helpful. Interested in what I was doing. Watchful or giving me a weird feeling."

"Wouldn't you have remembered that kind of thing without needing a jog?"

"I would hope so, but I'm still going over them."

I nodded again.

"Also, gotta read my fan mail."

This was a disgruntled mutter.

And this was a surprise.

"Fan mail?"

"The mail I get here is addressed to a PO box. We take pains to keep off the grid, including no social media. For any of us."

I was surprised. "Even Celeste?"

"Especially Celeste. She gets on, but she does it because her friend Phoebe lets her share her accounts. She doesn't post though, and she's only allowed that if I'm Phoebe's 'friend' so I can monitor it. The boys have ghost accounts, so they can use them if they need to look into something."

That was a minor miracle, keeping a teenager from having her own social media.

Though, it did go to show, regardless of what they might claim in our current society, they could survive without it.

"Wouldn't be hard to find this property, since it's been owned by a Bohannan for a hundred and fifty years and I pay taxes on it," he shared. "But records show it's overseen by a corporation that's owned by a buddy of mine. We have a contract, with me as the director of another corporation, that he administrates this property on my behalf, and I pay him. That isn't a deep trail. Still, it's a shield that might keep some out, we got it and my official address is a PO number. Same for the kids. Postman brings our mail because he knows us. Not much comes there, though. It goes to the FBI."

That didn't answer my preliminary question.

So I asked it a different way, uttering it as a surprised statement.

"You get fan mail."

"Fan mail. Hate mail. Mail telling me I got shit wrong. You write thrillers, so you can get that Percy Gibson and Al Catlin have supporters."

"Hang on," I said, and I took a moment with that.

Al Catlin was another famous case. Serial rapist. He didn't kill. But over seven years he raped nearly thirty women in nine states.

He'd been fascinating because, with method-actor-like intensity, he'd changed his appearance so completely between assaults, it took a tick in his behavior to link all of them. He gained weight, lost it, dyed his hair, changed his facial hair, wore colored contacts as well as a ski mask, Zorro-style eye mask, full-face clear plastic mask, changed the tone of his voice, assumed accents—anything to throw his victims off identifying him at all, but also in a way that would link his crimes.

Which also made it difficult to prosecute him.

But in each, he made a mistake that it was clear he didn't know he was making.

He called his victims "poodle" as he was violating them.

I'd considered writing a book based loosely on him, but I didn't get too deep into research before I gave up on it. It was far too disturbing, and I didn't want to have any hand in lionizing those behaviors. Obviously, I wouldn't have written it like that. But what many find distressing, others could find titillating, and I didn't want to play a part in that.

I made another mental note: *Get down to Googling Bohannan.*

But since I was sitting on the man himself…

"You profiled Catlin?" I asked.

"I investigated a lot of crime and profiled a lot of people when I was with the Bureau, baby. I was with them for seventeen years."

"Right," I said.

"I don't read any of that shit. The mail the FBI receives for me. They get it. They open it. They catalog it. They flag anything that needs flagged. They tell me if there's something I need to know. Now I'm reading it. All of it."

"Fabulous," I muttered.

"If it helps us find this guy, I don't give a fuck," he said.

"Of course," I replied, then asked, "Have you been able to profile him, even a little?"

Not a second passed before Bohannan launched in.

"He's intelligent. He might be ex-military, but that's doubtful. He won't like being told what to do, and he'll take pains to guard against anything he might fail at and washing out of the military because he doesn't respect authority will not be on his agenda. Also, there might be too much competition there. Too many things to excel at, someone is going to be better at something than him, and he can't have that. He doesn't work well with his attention scattered. Eye on one goal. Though it could be a lesson he learned along the way. More likely, he grew up hunting and spending a lot of time outdoors."

He took a breath.

And kept going.

"He's definitely killed, but not messing with easy targets, like a family pet. It'd be about the hunt. The quest. The test. Big game. Bears. Nice trophies. Wolves or big cats. He's fit. He's adaptable. He's accomplished. He was a star athlete. He's an excellent marksman or a prize-winning fisherman or a successful bonds trader, all of those or none of those. He's good at not just something, but a lot of somethings. He's bested people who thought they were better than him. Every challenge he's found and surpassed hasn't done it for him. So he's pursued bigger ones. More extreme ones. He has no interest in the kill, except for the response it will garner in me. He intends to play against me until he breaks me, publicly humiliates me or makes me give up, and then he'll move on to a bigger, more extreme challenge."

I was struck dumb, for a number of reasons.

That was good, because Bohannan wasn't finished.

"He has no sexual problems, though he might be into domination, but maybe not the good kind. That said, he won't cross a line. He'll find partners who get deep like he does, and he'll get explicit consent. That is not going to be the misstep he makes. Women are easy prey, so he fulfills his base instincts and gets off on games. He's young. Not in his twenties, probably mid-thirties, which intensifies his feeling of superiority, tasting so much success at his age. Even if he rigs the game by focusing solely and obsessively on only one thing at one time. Though he could be in his early forties, but not older. He's likely attractive. Probably very much so. He had a functional family who was proud of him, maybe too proud. But it isn't on them. He was born not wired right."

Holy cow.

That was a lot.

And he still wasn't done.

"The next kill won't be soon. I hope to fuck I'm right, but we got time. He's savoring this. Getting off on every second. Every reaction. He wants to prolong it. He wants the suspense. He wants the control. He's not from Misted Pines. He's not local. But he's here and he came for me. Besting me on my turf is not only part of the kick, besting unknown terrain is an added bonus. Making it even better, he's not unaware of the shit he's stirring. He was at the meeting at the city chambers. He's managed to get his hands on every one of those videos. He could have even been watching as that party in the woods turned bad. He's loving it. He's not the puppet master. He's making himself a god. And that's what he needs."

When he stopped talking and didn't start again, I noted, "So, you don't have a little profile, you have *a profile*."

The beard twitched up again.

"You left that town meeting because you didn't want to feed his ego," I surmised.

He dipped his chin. "He got off on that circus. He wanted me to watch. Wanted to watch me do it. But I'm not a puppet and he's not my god."

I decided not to dig deeper into that because it gave me the serious heebie-jeebies knowing the killer was there, with all of us, the entire town, but more specifically, anywhere near Celeste, Jess, Jace, me…and he was there to watch not only what he'd wrought, but Bohannan.

"More extreme challenge than becoming a serial killer so people will hunt him like he's a serial killer?" I asked.

"He's already figuring out what's next when he beats me, and he's assured he's gonna beat me. He'll flip that coin. He's made himself prey. His next challenge, he'll be the hunter. And he won't be after eight-year-old girls or college freshmen."

I shuddered.

Bohannan wrapped his arms around me, pulled me close and watched me closer.

"You get, he's probably watching. And I'm not talking about just the town council meeting."

Oh, I got that.

I'd been completely in denial about it.

But I got it.

Bohannan gave me a squeeze.

"If the last couple of days were days he watched, it's driving him fucking crazy I'm more interested in stringing your lights than breaking my back trying to find him. Jace and Jess too. They're bonuses for him that might even be why he picked me. I trained my boys and they're good at what they do. We're a great team. So if he beats me, he doesn't just beat me. He beats an entire team. Men, real men in his estimation. Typical alphas, who, once he takes us down, will make him leader of the pack."

"Will he…" God, I didn't want to think it, much less say it. But I had to know the answer. "…get frustrated and target you or one of the twins another way?"

"That would be a cheat. I matter to him. Jace and Jess do too. Alice didn't matter. She was a laboratory mouse. An experiment. What he did to her was gruesome, but inexpert. Malorie didn't matter. She was a pawn, important to the game, but easily expendable. Though, this isn't chess. He's not guarding his king by sacrificing his queens. This is a duel. He thrusts, I'm supposed to parry, until he forces me to thrust, and he parries."

One could say he had a definite handle on that.

But this brought us to something else I wanted to know about.

"What do, um…Jace and Jess…*do*?"

"I think you realize there's not a soul on this planet who won't open up to one of them."

I blinked.

"They're the best investigators, and interrogators, I've ever come across. And I don't take credit for that. They just had that in them. I was a decent investigator. I can get a bead, and I'm a trained profiler, so I didn't suck at interrogating, but I'm intimidating, and that never helped. Profiling was my gig. I found a home in it, for better or worse. But you got a witness who doesn't want to talk, Jace or Jess will get them comfortable. You sniffed out your last line of inquiry and are stumped, Jace or Jess will look at what you got and find three new trails to go down. I taught them what I know, and they just ran with it in ways I'd never guess. It's fuckin' uncanny."

I was careful when I asked, "Why don't they become police or follow in your footsteps and join the FBI?"

"Because they make four times as much as consultants than they would if they had a badge."

I raised my brows. "So they're twenty-seven-year-old investigative hotshots with utterly no official law enforcement training or experience?"

"You can spark a kid's curiosity in a lot of ways, Larue," he replied. "My father used to make me explain Confucius quotes to him. He'd get pissed and shout at me if I didn't understand it. '*A lion chased me up a tree, and I greatly enjoyed the view from the top.*' Great quote. Two lessons. Be calm and get in a good position to reflect on your problem. Above all, stay positive. Or think of your competition like lions, use them to drive you to the top, and take time to revel in your success. No way I'm gonna figure that out when I'm nine."

Nine?

I winced.

"'*If you're the smartest person in the room, you're in the wrong room,*'" Bohannan continued. "I did the same thing with my boys. I didn't fire Confucius at them and make them explain it to me. I taught them Confucius, and that there were other great minds out there they could learn from. And in teaching them, I made them hungry to learn. They learned. They keep learning. And they know, when they're the smartest in the room, they need to find another room."

"So you figure one day, they'll leave you," I noted quietly.

"I hope one day they will, so they can keep learning. And keep helping people."

"Outside multiple betrayals, a divorce and a decade and a half, there's another reason I'm over my ex," I told him.

Knowing what was coming (he could hardly miss it, but also, I was suspecting he was kind of a genius, so he wouldn't), he started sliding back down on the bed, again taking me with him.

"Yeah?" he asked. "What's that?"

"I'm kinda falling in love with another guy," I told him.

He rolled us so he was on top.

"I know him?"

"He's the smartest one in the room."

His nostrils flared.

His head dropped.

He kissed me.

Later, when we were both naked, and he was moving inside me, slowly, his mouth on mine, one of my hands in his hair, the other one clenching his ass, my knees high, my thighs hugging him, I understood my man, who was good with both actions *and* words, was giving me actions now.

He was making love to me because he was falling in love with me too.

This was great.

This was *marvelous*.

This gave him my June Cleaver act for at least until they caught this killer, and then we'd be figuring out if Bohannan could cook too.

And it would have remained great and marvelous if my phone hadn't started ringing.

No one got through but a select few, and none of those select few had any reason to phone me at that hour.

Unless it was important.

Or an emergency.

Shit.

Bohannan knew this, so he reached for my phone and took it from the charge pad I'd set up on what was now my nightstand.

"Fenn," he muttered.

I wasn't going to talk to my daughter with my man inside me, and he knew that.

So he slid out, rolled to his back, tucked me to his side, and I took the call.

"Hey, lovely, everything okay?" I greeted.

"Okay, Mom," she said cautiously. "I'm gonna send you a link but I wanted to phone you before instead of springing it on you in a text."

My eyes found Bohannan's.

His brows knitted ominously.

"What?" I asked.

"Well, your secret is out about your new home among the pines. And the killings are no longer a local story. And your relationship with the famous profiler handling them isn't either. And…uh…" a loaded beat, "did you know Cade is married?"

Well.

Shit.

FORTY-FIVE

Heart to Hearts

We both put our pajamas back on before I opened my texts to grab the link Fenn sent.

And I sent it to Bohannan so he could read it with me.

I was two paragraphs in when he bit off, "Fucking Dern."

And yes.

The article had Dern written all over it.

Evidence of that was that it alluded to the fact I'd picked Misted Pines to escape my stalker because I'd found it safe, due to his reputation as a stalwart law enforcement officer who ran a tight ship.

Sadly, a miracle had not happened, and Bob Welsh's activities didn't fly under media radar. Those activities were far too shocking and involved far too many famous people for that ever to happen.

Therefore, it wasn't lost on me Bob Welsh had garnered no small amount of media fascination because of what he did and why he did it.

But for the most part, Alicia and Russ weathered that storm not only because they came home and were accessible, but because both of them were far more famous than me. Though they did it by making no comment (Michael used it to get himself a few television interviews).

I was in Misted Pines, and no one knew I was there (until now), not to mention I had other things going on. Although I kept my finger on the pulse, stayed in touch with Alicia and Russ, Agent Palmer kept me informed if I needed to be, and Welsh's two victims frequently came to mind, I hoped they were doing all right and was poised to help if asked, it didn't really faze me.

And as with everything like that, once the bloom went off the rose of that story, it disappeared and would probably not reappear (because he'd pleaded guilty and would not stand trial) until (or if) one of the women came forward to tell their story or when someone got hold of it to do a documentary and/or movie for Netflix.

So even though, for all involved, one way or another, that would never be done, for all intents and purposes (for now), it was.

To be honest, the fact I was in Misted Pines wasn't very interesting.

The fact, after over a decade of being single and meticulously guarding my privacy, I'd hooked up with a lauded ex-FBI profiler who was helping with the local case of the deaths of two girls…

And that profiler looked like Bohannan.

That was going to be an issue.

But Bob Welsh wasn't the first time I'd learned the lesson that the twenty-four-hour news cycle was perhaps one of the top (if not *the* top) detrimental things to happen in society in the last few decades.

There was just not that much news.

Since there wasn't, you had to *make* that much news.

And when you couldn't make it, you had to have someone talking about it. Which spawned more interview shows than there were people who were interesting enough to be interviewed (so you had to *make* them interesting), and talking head news commentary shows, both of which existed mostly to tell people what to think.

When people should think for themselves.

Or alternately pay more attention to living their own lives.

So in the end, I knew Leland Dern's desperate ploy to save face and attempt to convince the few supporters he had left that he was who he wanted them to believe he was would be an annoyance for Bohannan and me.

But it would be brief.

Bohannan tossed his phone on his nightstand before I got to the end (so he was also a speed reader) and he had his palms to his forehead when I was done.

"Okay, honey, now I'm the expert in this, so you get to listen to me."

He dropped his hands, turned his head and studied me…no, *examined* me, like he didn't know what species I was.

Then again, he didn't get this.

Sure, he had books written about his profiling prowess.

But he didn't have TMZ sniffing around constantly.

"This will be a thing. A day. Two. That's it," I shared. "I'm not a public person anymore. Not really. No one knows I publish books. I'm known. I'm a fascination. I get it at the same time I don't. It's a nuisance. But whenever some interest in me crops up, it passes quickly. In other words, this, too, shall pass. We just live our lives like normal and in no time, it'll go away."

I scooted to him and put my hand on his chest.

"Honestly. I don't even have a PR person anymore. I never engage, and if you don't give them something to devour, it starves the insatiable beast and they can't have that happen, so they go away to find something else to make a meal of, and it never gets to be a big deal. We won't engage, and they'll go away."

"When you file for divorce, shit comes of that, Larue," was his weird reply. "You can be combative and have mediation. You can go at each other and end up in court. But you file for divorce, and you get divorced. If you don't *get* divorced, you *sue* for divorce."

"I've been divorced twice, Bohannan," I reminded him. "California law and Washington state law are probably very different, but still, I know the drill too well."

"She refused mediation. She refused to even get an attorney. I sent papers, she didn't sign them. I served her with papers, she didn't sign those either. It was going to end up in court. I called her, she said she wouldn't show. I can't divorce her *in absentia*, I know where she is. She doesn't have to agree to divorce me, but she has to agree to the legal and financial shit. I honestly didn't know if it was going to get ugly or just take time and money. In the end, I got pissed and thought, fuck it. She likes male attention, that's what our damage was all about. I wasn't looking for anybody. But she was going to find someone to give it to her, and if that got serious, she'd get serious about divorcing me. Before that happened, I didn't know Nance was gonna kick it and some hot chick with a stalker was gonna buy his house and lay claim to me."

"Hot chick with a stalker?" I teased.

I knew in an instant he wasn't feeling playful.

"Babe. I didn't keep this from you. I just lived it so long, and so much other shit was going on, I honest to fuck forgot she still had legal ties to me, and I needed to do something about that to be free for you."

"There are precisely zero people on the planet who could get away with that excuse, Bohannan, except you. No. There are five. You. Jace. Jess. And Special Agents McGill and Robertson. Maybe Harry, and not Jace and Jess. But since none of them have a teenage daughter with her first real boyfriend along with some murderer playing games, they also don't count. So it's just you."

I got even closer to him.

And finished, "I get it. I know you've had a few things on your mind, honey."

"You're safe here."

I wasn't feeling playful anymore either after I heard the steel with which those three words were spoken.

He continued, "With the kids. In my home. In our lives." A meaningful pause, "With me."

"Bohannan," I whispered.

"You belong here. It's not about you cooking. It's not about you looking after Celeste. It's not about you making me happy. It's about you being a part of us."

I put my hand over his mouth. "Stop talking."

He wrapped his fingers around my wrist and pulled it away.

"This is important."

I knew it was important.

I'd had to make my own families in order to belong somewhere, and two of those disintegrated along the way.

I'd never had the bedrock Bohannan offered in a partner.

Case in point, with my history—if he hadn't built the trust by being who he was to his kids, to the town, to his work…to me—him understanding just how huge of a blow this might be to me.

But he'd built that trust.

And he understood how deeply I needed it.

So yes.

I knew it was important.

I knew it far better than him.

I told him I was falling in love with him.

He showed me he was falling in love with me.

It was my turn to show him.

And I wasn't going to do it by making love.

I was going to fuck him.

In other words, I attacked.

Bohannan counterattacked.

In the end, we had a fuck/wrestling/making love session where he didn't fight fair, considering he wrung two orgasms out of me, and it was biologically impossible for me to compete.

He lay on his back, I lay flat out on top of him, and he pushed out, "No more heart to hearts. It's gonna kill me."

"You bitch about the craziest things."

"Babe?"

With effort, I raised my head to look down at him.

Big mistake.

He looked fabulous during sex.

After it, all sated and content and big cat got his cream, he was everything.

"I might have to pounce again," I warned him.

"It's you," he said to me. "I had her, but all along, I've been waiting for you to get to me."

Honestly?

I was fucked out.

So I shoved my face in his neck and belatedly agreed, "No more heart to hearts."

My voice was husky.

He stroked my spine and whispered, "No more heart to hearts, baby."

FORTY-SIX

Like the Wind

Megan and I pushed into Aromacobana, and I was unsurprised it was busy.

It was normally relatively busy for one.

It was the weekend for another.

And it was sunny, and the season was upon us.

The Kimmy season.

The Christmas season.

Although I was about to find out that all hell had not stopped breaking loose in Misted Pines. I could report that the town council still made certain the Christmas decorations were out and up by the weekend after Thanksgiving.

The vibe wasn't effervescent, but people were doing their best to find some cheer and live their lives.

As for me, I'd just gotten back from a long weekend in LA.

I went to see my daughter. I went to shop for Christmas. I went to shop because I didn't have a lot of clothes for colder weather. I went to shop just because I wanted new clothes. I went to pack up some things from my house and ship them to Washington. And I went to see my stylist, because Celeste *was* skilled when it came to hair, and we'd had some girlie sessions in her bathroom, and she'd tided me over.

But it was well past time.

I needed Joaquim.

He was complimentary of her, genuinely and to her face, since Bohannan had given her permission to fly down Friday after school to be with me. He'd also pulled some strings so he'd walked her to the gate, and at LAX, a TSA agent had walked her to me.

Another bonus of being with Bohannan.

We'd shopped. Joaquim did her hair too. We had facials and mani-pedis. She'd helped me pack even more things because there was stuff in my closet she wanted to wear. She'd bonded further with Camille and Joan.

And with those reinforcements, I decided to tackle the boys/consent/choice/sex talk.

She did not seem at all uncomfortable with me.

What she seemed to think was that I was crazy.

"I know that, Delly," she'd said when I got through the consent part, and the inferred at the end of that sentence was a *yeesh*. "I mean, I know there are girls who really like boys and they'll do like...*anything*. But boys who are stupid are just stupid. Everyone knows that."

Did they?

I glanced at Camille and Joan.

They appeared just as surprised as I was.

I treaded cautiously.

"When you say 'boys who are stupid,' what do you mean?"

"I mean like, if you say no, and they don't stop. Or if you're like, 'I don't wanna drink,' and they're all, 'C'mon, everyone's drinking. Let's play beer pong.' Beer pong is stupid too, by the way. But anyway, it's like, you know, beer doesn't taste good, and people act dumb when they drink too much of it. Some people think it's funny. But me and my friends just think it's, well..." Big shrug and, "Stupid."

She proved she got my drift when she went on, a might huffily.

"Will's not like that, you know. He might drink a beer, but he thinks all that being loud and crazy and obnoxious is stupid too. I never saw him do that before, but he might have done it. Still. I think it has to do with Alice. It's like, a really crappy silver lining. You know, he's learned life is too short to act like a moron. Life is serious. You don't have to act serious all the time. But there's no time to be a moron. Am I making sense?"

She was.

And this made me feel even better about Will, who was still over a lot, and I'd come to like him.

He was broody (understandable).

He was intense with Celeste (she was very into him, and he needed someone who cared, so maybe he was just soaking it up).

But mostly he was quiet and polite, serious like she said. He studied with Celeste. He went to hockey practice. He played in his games. He took Celeste out to the Double D or the Lodge. He went home to his grandmother. He avoided his parents like the plague.

And that was that.

So obviously, onward to the more difficult part: sex came in a wide variety of ways, and people should feel free to enjoy the ones that felt good to them.

She glanced at Camille and Joan that time, before she replied, "I know gay sex isn't bad."

"That wasn't gay sex," I told her.

"I wasn't finished, Delly."

"Okay," I mumbled.

"Gay sex or you know," her voice dropped, "*anal*. Or like, dress up or um…that stuff they do in those famous books."

"BDSM," I choked out and caught Joan elbowing Camille and definitely heard Camille fight snorting.

Celeste heard it too. "Yeah. Whatever. You can be gay and bi and a lot of things. A friend of mine, she, uh…finds stuff and reads it and watches it, and she thinks she's pan."

I had nothing to say to that. Though I was glad her friend was exploring so she could know herself, I still worried that "watching things" at sixteen might be a bit early.

"It's just like, you know, whatever you want, whoever you are, right?" she asked.

"Right," I answered.

"Right," Camille and Joan chimed in with me.

Then she shared she'd figured me out.

"I know I called it gross, but I didn't mean what the Pulaskis were *doing* was gross. Okay, it was. Because they're parents. And I'm sorry, Delly. That's gross."

I waved my hand in front of me because I had to give that to her.

It wasn't gross, but I'd get why a kid would think that.

"It's gross they let it out so Will could see it," she concluded. "It's gross they let their stuff mess him up. That was gross."

That was definitely gross.

Thus endeth our discussions, and I was pleased to be able to call Bohannan and report his daughter was enlightened as well as beautiful and intelligent and sweet.

And although it wasn't that he had nothing to worry about, at least she had herself together.

His reply?

"That's great, baby."

I went through all that for him (and Celeste), and that was it.

I'd take it.

I would because it wasn't the words, it was the tone.

Now I was back. It was a couple of weeks before Christmas. We had decorations up in my house and Bohannan's. My master bath was done, and a spruce up of the downstairs powder room was in full swing. My book was half written, and I might make my deadline by the skin of my teeth. I had most of my Christmas shopping complete.

And no one had been killed.

So things weren't great.

But they were all right.

And now Megan was filling me in on everything else that was breaking loose in Misted Pines.

"Apparently, even the governor can't snap his fingers and

remove a sheriff. But he did whatever he had to do, and while you were gone, Dern was removed. I've heard he huffed, and he puffed, but he'd already blown the house down. Harry is acting sheriff until the election. So far, it looks like he's running unopposed."

Another quick update: I'd been right. It was a big thing that much ado had been made over, the fact that I'd landed such a badass hot guy, but attention on me and Bohannan had been thankfully brief.

And apparently, Leland's Hail Mary play hadn't worked.

"I'm sure that's a relief," I replied to Megan.

She gave me a *You Know It* look and shared, "Harry cleaned house and he's gotta recruit a bunch of deputies, but he brought back Polly, so at least he'll know where everything is."

I shot her a smile.

She leaned into me. "Now for the juicy stuff."

I was intrigued.

"That wasn't juicy?"

It was.

But I'd find what was next was juicier.

"Audrey filed against Dale. Dale is gone. Bobby's gone. Jay and Dwayne haven't been seen in public since 'the incident,' and word is, Jay's interviewing for jobs up in Alaska. But Dale and Audrey's house is up for sale. Bobby and Lana's too. I know because I'm listing them. But I've seen hide nor hair of the men. Lana and Audrey are handling everything. Audrey told me she's moving to Spokane. Where Dale went, I do not know. *Poof*," she said. "Vanished."

Megan and her husband, Dan, owned a real estate agency in Misted Pines.

This was why Megan could stop for Aromacobana and have coffee with me whenever the mood struck us.

She was very good at what she did, so that was why she had nice handbags like me.

Probably needless to say, when media interest turned to Misted Pines because of me and Bohannan and dead girls, as I noted, I'd been right, of a sort. They were interested in us for a second.

But then something else caught their attention.

And that something else was that it took no time for them to sniff out the sex scandal. As the video clips weren't exactly kept under wraps, and they were all kinds of salacious, and the woman scorned angle was too good to pass up, those went from MP viral to globally viral.

The national media chewed on that for an entire week.

So I wasn't surprised that Dale and Bobby, who both had other things they were dealing with, took the opportunity to disappear.

"Lana is living it up with her stud muffin," Megan continued. "I honestly don't know whether to admire her or think it's crass."

I might not be at one with the extreme vindictiveness of the grand reveal, and not simply because two of the men involved had just lost children.

But I'd also seen Lana out and about with Dean, and when I did, her two sons were with them.

She wasn't exactly living it up. She didn't hide her grief.

What she was, was defiant.

She was doing exactly what countless men had done (and still do).

She was thinking first about her own happiness.

In doing that, she'd moved on to a younger, better model who did it for her.

Unlike some men, though, she loved and took care of her sons along the way, and I sensed she had genuine, and strong, feelings for Dean.

Though, as had many women, along the way she'd made sacrifices. She'd learned lessons. She'd eaten shit.

But now, she couldn't care less what Megan or anyone thought of her.

She had a man who made her dinner and did it for her in bed and rushed to her side when she needed him. A man who I knew would listen to her when she told him to calm down because he was scaring her by being upset and driving (not that Dean would do that, but the point was pertinent).

And for that, I applauded her.

Silently.

"You admire her," Megan said, and I caught her watching me.

"I think it's none of my business."

She clicked her teeth. "Oh please."

"It's true. I have an opinion about it, but my opinion doesn't matter. I'm not her. I'm not one of her boys. I hate she lost her daughter. I hope the FBI can get her answers and justice and give her and her family some peace. Other than that…" I shrugged.

"I'm finding it's no fun having a world-weary, superstar friend who's had people in her business for…" She was turning to the line when her eyes widened, and she came back to me. "Oh Lord, it's Ray."

"Ray?"

I started to assess the line ahead of us, regardless that I didn't know who Ray was, and she caught my forearm and whispered, "Don't look."

I whispered back, "I don't know who Ray is."

"Shelly's beau."

I turned and looked for cheerleader Shelly.

I saw her in the area where people waited for their coffee. She stood under an arm that was attached to a tall, muscular, dark-blond, handsome—

I swung to Megan like a timid teenager caught checking out her crush.

"Oh shit, that's *Ray*?"

"Yes," Megan hissed as we shuffled closer together at the same time we did the same forward in line. "It's Ray."

I couldn't help it, I looked back.

Right into the eyes of Ray, who was staring at me and who knew we were talking about him—and why—and he wasn't a fan.

I gave him a small, noncommittal smile and pinned my eyes to the line in front of us, talking while trying not to move my lips, "He saw me."

"Of course he did," she muttered back, and I knew she was talking the same way. "I told you not to look."

"Shelly didn't break up with him?"

"According to word on the street, Shelly doesn't know."

That made me look at her again. "That can't be."

And it couldn't, considering Ray was the man who was fucking Bobby in that video.

"Shelly isn't, you know…" She gave me big eyes and went on, "She's sweet, but not all that bright."

"I feel like I've seen that video fifteen times, and I'm *trying* to avoid it. She'd have to be on another planet to have missed it."

Megan grimaced.

We shuffled forward in line again.

"I was really shocked, you know, because he adores her. Dotes on her. They've been together, I don't know, at least two years. Her mom," she leaned in but did a furtive *glug glug* with her hand, using me as a shield from Shelly and Ray. "That whole family is a mess. Except Shelly. Her older brother is a disaster. Her dad leaves, comes back, leaves. I don't want to cast aspersions, but I swear the man deals drugs. Ray shows up and sweeps her off her feet."

"Shows up?" I asked.

She shook her head. "Oh no, I mean, he's been around, I don't know, four years. More. I mean," she gave me a look, "he's hard to miss."

He was that good-looking. I-could-see-him-in-a-Marvel-costume good-looking.

So I understood her look.

"She's a hairdresser in town. She taught Celeste a few things," she told me.

"Living at home with that mom, probably trying to find a way out. They start dating. Moved in together." She straightened a bit and said, "Obviously, marriage is sacred, but for Shelly, I could see why she'd just go."

I was feeling something strange at the same time fighting not looking at Shelly and Ray again.

"And once Malorie was found, he went off the deep end. By that I mean protective. Takes her in to work in the morning, picks her up after."

"What does he do?"

We shuffled forward again.

"He runs the rec center. Got some grants, started some after-school kids' programs. My kids are older. Too old for them. But I heard they're really neat. I hope the Bobby thing was, you know, *exploring* or something, and he marries her because he's probably not going to stay in town. Especially after that video thing. But also, Kenneth says he's super sharp. It was a real feather in the council's cap to get him to run that service. They won't keep him long at the center."

"Who's Kenneth?"

"Kenneth Warner. The president of the Town Council. The man I'm going to replace in the upcoming election."

I smiled. "So, you're running."

She returned my smile. "I talked to Dan. He's agreed. Kenneth has been on the council for thirty-five years, can you believe that?"

Yes, I could believe that. I would have guessed more like fifty. I might have even guessed he incorporated the town personally and had been on the council since Misted Pines became Misted Pines.

"I heard you were going after Gary's seat," I noted.

She shook her head, but said, "Not at first. To do it right, you should start where you're supposed to start and learn what you need." A ballsy grin and, "I'll go after Gary in the next election."

It was me returning the grin this time, though mine was happy for her, not ballsy.

"First order of business," she said as we moved to the counter to place our order, "term limits."

I was a big term limit enthusiast, which went hand in hand with being a let's-have-a-lot-fewer-old-white-guys-running-things enthusiast.

I had a feeling Megan and I didn't share a party, but I also had a feeling I'd vote for her.

I'd told her the chemistry teacher story, and she'd agreed with me, that's all I was saying.

She started ordering, and I couldn't shake the feeling I was getting, so I looked to where Ray and Shelly were standing, thinking he was still aiming his glower at me, but they weren't there.

I turned to the seating area.

And the instant I did, a man who'd been watching me averted his head.

Quickly, he pulled the hood of his blue hoodie up over his hair, got up and hustled toward the door.

My skin went cold.

He had dark hair.

And the man I'd seen out my office window skulking toward Bohannan's place had dark hair and had been wearing a hoodie.

And there was no paper cup on the table where he was sitting, and he didn't have one in his hand.

And he'd been watching me.

"What do you want?" Megan asked. "I'm buying this time."

I didn't answer.

I moved toward the door, shrugging my purse off my shoulder to get my phone.

"Delphine?" Megan called.

Hoodie man twisted slightly at the door like he was looking back at me.

He didn't quite look back at me.

He bolted out the door.

Oh my God!

I didn't think.

I bolted after him.

I didn't get a good look at him, but he was probably younger than me.

And he was a man.

He was also wearing running shoes.

I was in low-heeled booties, which were *not* running shoes.

It wouldn't matter if I was in running shoes, he would have lost me.

Still, I kept after him.

Though I realized I'd need to check out the local Pilates place, because I got a block and a half and I was struggling, and he was so far ahead of me, I'd never catch him.

In my defense, that block and a half was uphill.

However, some type of exercise was definitely on the agenda.

It was then someone raced by me so fast, he made a breeze that ruffled my hair, and I watched Ray's back as he sprinted after Hoodie Man.

Hoodie Man must have sensed he had someone in pursuit who could actually pursue, because he darted into an alley.

Ray ran like the wind and followed him.

I got my second wind and followed them both.

But by the time I got to the back alley, I didn't see them, either way.

I stopped, wheezed, pulled my bag open, and was digging for my phone when Ray came into view, coming out of a side street and back into an alley from a block down.

"I lost him!" he shouted. "You see him?"

I shook my head, gathered some oxygen, and shouted back, "No!"

He took off the other way, darting down another side street.

I pulled out my phone and dialed Bohannan.

"Larue," he greeted curtly after one ring.

"I think I…I think I just…"

I looked one way and then the other.

I was alone in the back alley.

Then I went back to Bohannan.

"I think I just saw the killer."

FORTY-SEVEN

Queen

Ray came back to me after Bohannan ordered me to "get your ass out of the goddamn alley" and I'd gotten my ass out of the alley.

Megan was at the corner of the block up from me, shouting, "Is everything okay?"

"Yeah, I'm coming right back," I shouted in return.

"You all right?" Ray asked.

He was barely breathing heavy.

I looked up into his sea blue eyes.

Seriously.

He was fabulous.

"Yes. I just need to get back to some classes. I can't even run a block."

"Was that him?" he asked.

I knew what he was asking.

Now that cooler heads might be prevailing…

Maybe?

"I don't…he was watching me, and he was being strange, and now I'm worried that I might have overreacted."

Ray's torso swung back.

"I know. I'm sorry. I…you're worried. About Shelly being safe. And I freaked you."

"You've probably had people watching you and being strange for a long time. I guess it doesn't get any easier."

Oh boy.

"When someone's killing people, though," he carried on, "it'd freak anybody."

"Yes," I agreed.

"Your friend is coming."

I looked back up the street to see Megan heading our way.

"She knows."

I turned again to Ray. "What?"

"It's nobody's business, but she knows. Shelly. She knows I'm bi."

Well then.

That was laying it out there.

"We got an agreement. That's nobody's business either, still nobody asked. I don't…" he searched for a word, "*do* anyone that means anything to me. He didn't mean anything to me. And it's not like I need that all the time. It's just something I need. And he was a good go-to because he wanted no strings. It worked. No idea some crazy women were taping us. No idea they'd blow up my life."

This poor guy, caught in someone else's web.

"I'm sorry," I repeated.

"She freaked out that day, she was so happy to meet you. She's a big fan. She loves your show. She watched it with her mom. Not a lot of happy memories with that woman, but that's one of them."

Now he was talking about Shelly.

God, I'd been what I hated people being, gossipy and in someone else's business.

I twisted quickly and Megan was almost on us.

"Can you give us just a sec?" I asked.

She halted, stepped backwards a few steps, and stopped, but didn't take her eyes from us.

And again, I returned to Ray.

I looked right at him and admitted, "Yes, we were talking about you, and I apologize for that too. However, we didn't know you and Shelly have a deal."

He started to look mad. "You of all people know, it's not your business."

I, of all people, did know that.

I nodded.

"She knows. Shelly. She knows about it. She's seen it. I showed it to her. I didn't want her seeing it somewhere else, but she already knew I'd been with him. People think she's not very smart, but she is. She's just a happy person. Desperately happy. She'd been faking that for a long time. I got her to a place she didn't have to fake it anymore. Now she has to fake it again. She's just trying to pretend it didn't happen. Let it blow over. It's not working."

"God. Again, I'm so sorry."

"Now she knows you know and she's embarrassed."

So he wasn't angry for himself we were whispering, he was angry for Shelly.

"Ray, right?"

"Like you don't know who I am," he bit.

Definitely getting angry.

"It *will* blow over," I told him.

He stared at me.

"It will," I repeated.

"Parents are taking their kids out of my programs."

"Small-minded people," I said. "That'll pass too. Kids need those programs. They need them more than the parents need to be bigots."

"I get small-minded people. Lived with that all my life. What about the kids?"

I didn't have an answer for that.

He twisted at the waist and pointed down the street. "Was that him?"

"I really don't know," I told him the truth.

I was beginning to feel foolish, so I flipped back to our previous subject, which I didn't want to talk about further, but he didn't seem to be ready to leave.

"Those women shouldn't have done that to you."

At the very least, they should have cropped his face.

"I didn't know he was a cheat," he said, clipped and hostile. "He got what he deserved. But not me. My parents could have seen that."

"I hope they don't," I said quickly.

"I hope they don't too," he replied, glanced up and rearranged his face. "Just a sec, sweetheart," he said over my shoulder.

I turned to see Shelly was approaching Megan.

"Hi, Shelly," I called.

"Was it the killer?" she called back, fear in her voice.

Now what had I done?

I shook my head. "No, I just—"

"She saw him taking a picture," Ray lied.

Shelly appeared confused, of course, for I would be used to that, wouldn't I?

"I'm having a bad day," I lied too.

One side of her face scrunched in a doubtful look, but I turned back to Ray.

"Thanks for attempting hot pursuit."

"Did you call Bohannan?"

I nodded.

"Is he coming?"

Damn, damn, and triple damn.

"Yes."

"Do you think he'll wanna talk to me?"

How did I do this?

"Did you see him?

"No."

"In Aromacobana? See his face?"

He shook his head. "I didn't notice him at all until you tore after him. I mean," he tried for levity, at the same time letting me off the hook because it was clear he was a decent guy, "this famous woman just walked in, and *she* knew *me*."

I gave him a weak smile.

"I just...well...I..." I didn't know. So I said, "He can find you at the rec center, right?"

He nodded. "And I'm a city employee, so they just gotta look me up if they need to find me."

"Okay, though, I wouldn't expect it. I think I just got jumpy."

"That's understandable," he muttered.

He started to move by, but I reached out and caught his forearm.

He looked at it, to me, and I let him go.

"Sorry for touching you," I said.

"I don't mind. Just...what do you need?"

"It *does* get better," I whispered.

He studied me.

He nodded.

Then he walked to Shelly.

Megan came right to me.

"What was that?" she asked.

"Me being an idiot," I answered.

"How?"

"Well, a young woman's body was pulled out of the lake while I made coffee and cinnamon rolls and watched, and maybe I'm realizing I've not been processing it all that well."

She flinched, grabbed my hand and tucked it under her arm as she led us back to the coffee house.

"I think we've all convinced ourselves we've seen this murderer a dozen times," she remarked to make me feel better.

"Yes."

"Though none of us raced after him like we were Cagney *and* Lacey," she teased.

"I'm totally an idiot," I mumbled, lifted my phone and walked back to Aromacobana with Megan, texting Bohannan where I'd be.

And asking if he wanted a coffee.

"RIGHT, let's go over this again."

We were in Bohannan's office.

I was getting a lecture because I'd been a naughty girl.

And I was trying to focus on that and not get mad that he was treating me like the idiot I'd been, and further not focus on how I might be able to get into acting out a "Don't Stand So Close to Me" fantasy.

"Larue," he called.

I focused on him.

"If we think we see a serial killer, we don't chase him, are you with me?"

"You're pissing me off," I shared.

His brows rose. "I'm pissing *you* off?"

"Yes. I didn't think. Yes. It was a kneejerk reaction. Yes. Pretty much anyone runs when chased. But I'm telling you, Bohannan, he was creepy. I felt it before I even looked at him."

"And you didn't see his face, but he was wearing the same hoodie he wore when he was outside by the lake."

"Not the same. I don't know if it was the same. They were just both blue and hoodies."

"You didn't tell me it was a hoodie before. You said it was a sweatshirt. You're telling me it was a hoodie now?"

"A hoodie's a sweatshirt."

"A hoodie's a hoodie."

Damn it.

He had me there.

"It was a hoodie. I should have said it was a hoodie because it was."

"Sure?"

Was I?

I nodded.

"And he just happened to be hanging at Aromacobana, waiting for you to show when it's random you hook up with Megan to get a coffee."

"You're making me feel stupid."

"I'm making you think."

"Are you going to quote Confucius to me?" I asked.

I knew instantly we were about to get in our first fight, and I was the one who shot across the bow, because that wasn't the right thing to say.

"What I'm asking," he said slowly, "is for you to tell me if he followed you in, or if he was in there waiting for you. You said he didn't have a drink. If he's following, I gotta know that. If he's waiting for you, I gotta know *that*. If he might have been waiting for someone else, I gotta know *that*. I gotta know *everything* about this guy if he's our guy, and if me asking you questions about it makes you feel dumb, suck it up."

"So you don't think I'm being an idiot?"

"No, I think you need to share what the fuck happened."

"I told you."

"What did you read on him?"

"I didn't read anything. I felt it."

"Someone watching you."

"Something *wrong*. But yes. When I turned, he was watching me."

He blew out a breath.

I crossed my arms on my chest.

He was in his office chair, turned to face me.

I was sitting on the arm of the club chair in the window.

"You know, you chasing a man down the street is going through MP like wildfire right now."

"I know," I said between my teeth.

"We've thankfully managed not to have a full-blown panic. That won't help."

"Bohannan, I already told you I feel like I screwed up, and yet I still feel right. About what, I don't know. But how many young men flee from fifty-three-year-old women?"

"Do you think he was paparazzi?"

"Could be, but they don't normally run. They chase."

"So we're back to the beginning, we don't chase serial killers."

Without a word, I stood and headed to the door.

Bohannan got there before me and put a hand to it.

Stupid, fast men.

I looked up at him.

"I'm attempting to leave," I said with forced civility.

"Don't do that again, baby."

"I already know it was foolish."

"I didn't want to say this, but I also didn't say it because I thought you knew it."

"Say what?"

"You are not a queen."

"What?"

"You are not a queen."

"Bohannan...*what do you mean*?"

"Larue...*you are not a queen*. If you're used, you're a pawn. Now, are you understanding me?"

I sucked in breath.

Because yes.

I was understanding him.

"Hawk's signal from your fob goes two places. To Hawk, and to the house up the hill. They saw you run down the street and head into an alley, where you had no reason to be, and called me before you did, but they'd already rolled out. You're covered. Celeste is covered. I just need you to be smart."

The FBI had already rolled out to rescue me.

Ah, hell.

"I didn't think. I got...I just want this to be done."

He pulled my stiff body into his arms.

"We all do, baby."

I wound my arms around him.

"I don't know who to ask," I said. "Megan might have noticed if he was there or if he followed us in, but I don't want to alarm her." I tipped my head back. "Or you could ask Ray."

"The guy who chased after him for you?"

"He didn't chase after him *for* me, he just chased after him *better* than me."

Bohannan's beard quirked.

But I nodded. "He was in Aromacobana when we got there. He and Shelly were waiting for coffees. He said he didn't notice him before I went after him, but maybe if someone talks to him, it might jog his memory."

"Rec center guy."

I nodded again.

"Harry hit him up before, since he deals with a lot of kids and their parents, as maybe a lead for someone who might know something about Alice. But I'll get Jace or Jess to stop and have another chat with Ray."

"So, we're not going to fight?"

He appeared bemused.

"What?"

"You were getting pissed."

"So were you."

"That normally ends in a fight. Is this the way we're going to fight? We get mildly annoyed and then stand holding each other?"

"It works for me."

He *was* a unicorn.

I melted into him.

"It works for me too."

FORTY-EIGHT

Awake

I lay on my side in the dark, staring at the shadow of Bohannan's back, which was turned to me.

When we'd called it a night, he'd essentially attacked me, demonstrating what "my bed is a playground" meant with a mind-boggling variety of positions, commands and locational penetrations.

It was back to basics with us, though with Bohannan taking more time—a lot more time—with primal caveman/cavewoman sex.

I was totally there for it.

When he was done with me, I was also spent, not even having it in me to get up and clean up.

For the first time in my life, I didn't care if I had to sleep in the wet spot.

Fortunately, Bohannan was not in my same state, and he cleaned up for me.

He got that done, and I wasn't proud of it, I realized cardio *was* in order, because before he even returned from the bathroom, I'd passed out.

I had no idea how long I was asleep before I woke in the dead of night, and I wasn't simply awake.

I was *awake.*

And it didn't take long for me to realize why Bohannan had put so much effort and creativity into exhausting me.

It just didn't fully take.

Earlier that day, after we made up from our non-fight, we'd again gone over what I saw and felt, and he'd shown me for the first time the composite sketches they got from the co-eds at Berkeley.

Whoever it was, he was quite attractive.

But since I hadn't gotten a good look at the guy's face, I couldn't say yay or nay.

All the witnesses in California had given a full physical description: lean, around five foot ten, wide shoulders, and chillingly that was the same not only for those who saw him in California, but who I'd chased in Misted Pines.

Bohannan had then shared that, alarming her or not, we had to pull in Megan, and Jess went off with copies of the sketches to track down Ray.

Megan told me on the phone she hadn't noticed him, but she and Dan came over so she could look at the sketches anyway.

We took that opportunity to order pizza and share a bottle of wine, more than likely so she could give me something normal to do because that was Megan. She was a good person who cared. And when you watch your friend, who was not a cop or a superhero, take off to chase a perp down the street, that would make you worry about said friend.

It was the first time I met Dan. He bore an uncanny resemblance to Ronald Reagan in his younger years. He was also funny and failed spectacularly at not showing he was worried about me, which could only come from Megan being worried about me, and he wanted us both to feel better.

Those puzzle pieces falling into place, this meant he, too, was a good person who cared.

Bohannan had left our guests to go up the hill for a brief visit with the FBI, but other than that, he stayed close to me.

The boys, however, whose normal pattern was to be in and out of what I'd come to think of as The Big House (they were in for the most part if there was food) were not around.

Bohannan was his normal self, calm and collected, but I knew what that visit up the hill was about.

I knew that if this was the same guy who'd been in Berkeley, he *could* be the guy, because him being here and *not* being the guy was a substantially more elaborate charade.

And it could have just been chance that he was in Aromacobana when I showed.

Or it could be that I was his new plaything.

So, obviously, this was not conducive to sleeping peacefully.

I rolled to my back.

Bohannan rolled all the way around, hooked me with an arm and yanked me mostly under him.

"You can't be ready for another round," I joked.

"Don't let him get in your head," he replied.

I expelled a frustrated breath.

He stroked my side with his thumb.

"Larue, he wants that. Don't play the game."

"Are you not playing the game?"

"I got no choice but to play the game."

"You can show me if things are upsetting you. Frustrating you. Pissing you off," I informed him.

"I'm not proud I had to spend seventy-five bucks replacing that cabinet door in the kitchen, but I wasn't pissed at this guy. I was pissed at Dern."

"Okay."

"You don't let them under your skin."

"That might be doable for the veteran FBI agent, but I'm struggling with that."

"You know about trash talk. During games?"

"What?"

"Football. Basketball. Whatever. Opponents say shit to each other. They do it to get into your head. They do it to break your concentration. If what happened today had to do with our guy, it was trash talking. He's trying to get into your head, which in turn will get into my head."

"So I need to stay cool for you?"

"No, you need to stay cool because we're gonna get this guy. I told you, he's leaving clues. They don't think they leave clues. They always do."

"You said you know how to commit the perfect murder."

"The perfect murder is suicide. It takes a life. It leaves no witnesses. It bears no clues. It leads to no suspects."

"Suicide isn't murder."

"That isn't a judgment. But killing is killing. And outside a killing that has the same victim and perpetrator, there is no perfect murder."

"Right."

"I also said that because you're sexy as all fuck, and I wanted to get in your pants, so I was trying to sound cool."

That almost made me laugh.

"Talk to me," he ordered.

"Are you really this calm and collected about this? About him targeting you? About him maybe targeting me?"

And about him maybe turning to Celeste, I did not say.

"No. I talked to the boys up the hill. Tomorrow, you and Celeste are going up there and you're having an in-service with them. Celeste has had this kind of training all her life, so it's a refresher for her. For you, it might be new. They're gonna teach you vigilance and self-defense. It'll help with your confidence. He sees you shaken, Larue, he's gonna get off on that."

"And we're starving him from what he needs…" I let that trail, so he'd fill in the blank.

"To get him to make a mistake."

"Could that mistake be another murder?"

"I don't think so. He plans those. He knows who his victims are going to be and he's laying them out according to that plan. It would chafe, being forced to make a kill he isn't ready to unleash yet. But he's feeding on attention. And if he's starved for it, he might do something compulsively to get it."

Holy cow.

"Like, when the media descends on Misted Pines, and his two murders take backseat to a sex scandal," I guessed.

"Like that. Like he waits for you to get back from LA and follows you to freak you, which will trigger me." He hesitated, and with care, he finished, "Bonus for him if you chase him down the street and remind the town a murderer is on the loose."

So, okay, yes.

I'd really screwed up doing that.

But my breath started coming faster, and not because of that.

"Do you think it was the guy?" I asked.

"I'm wondering now, because it's one thing to offer someone fifty bucks here and there to lurk outside a dormitory. Someone who has no idea what you're doing and could think you're just fucking with some chick who did you wrong, or playing a prank. It's something else, and it's risky, not to mention probably expensive, to keep that player on the board. Especially considering you make him come to a town where girls are getting murdered, and one of those girls stayed in the dorm where you got paid to be lurking. There are people who would do anything for cash. There are people who need it that bad, just to eat or to get a fix. But desperate people don't make good pawns."

"Okay."

"What else?" he pushed.

God, he was good.

"I don't know if it was a hoodie," I confessed.

"Baby, that happens," he said gently.

"Why do I feel like that's important?"

"Because everything is important in this. But you have to know, witnesses second guess what they see all the time. Fear is a factor. Adrenaline is spiking. The gravity of a situation plays a part. Emotional and physical reactions clash and break up shit in your brain. But think about it logically. How important is it if he's partial to wearing a hoodie?"

"I don't know," I whispered.

"It's not important, Larue. If he had some kind of fetish and wore a bright-red clown wig, I gotta know that. What he chooses to cover his body means dick to me."

"Okay."

"Okay."

I concluded it with the thing that was really haunting me.

"You think today was about him."

His pause was scary.

And what he said next was worse.

"Yeah, baby. Today was about him."

FORTY-NINE

Don't Ever

I had not yet been up to the house on the hill.

The next day, when Bohannan took Celeste and I up there, I found it wasn't a house.

It was a log cabin.

A pretty log cabin that was a little bit smaller than my place. It had a fire pit with Adirondack chairs surrounding it in the front. It had trees all around. It had no access to the lake, possibly because the pitch was very steep to get down there.

But it had impeccable views.

For instance, I could see through the trees nearly the entirety of Bohannan's compound, save for part of the boys' house, since it was tucked into the pines off to the side.

I could see my place, totally.

And I could see the somewhat bigger house up from mine on my side of the lake. It was higher up the hill, exposed to view, but it also had a switch-backed set of steps to get down to a small pier on the lake.

Taking all of this in, I swung directly into impossible, but phenomenal, fantasies of Celeste marrying some marvelous man and filling that big house up top with family. Camille and Joan moving into this cabin, expanding it, and filling it with babies. Us building a getaway cabin for Fenn (and James?) to bring their family for visits. And the boys splitting off, one of them moving into my place so they could have space for *their* families.

Yes, I was in this with Bohannan *deep*.

I was also watching David, who was doing something at the spout on the back deck. He was working on a Sunday because Robyn's pregnancy had, so far, been a display of hormonal fireworks that even her very devoted husband needed a break from on the weekends.

I knew this because it was so bad, he'd asked, falteringly, as he was so desperate to know if she was crazy, or if he was.

Unlike many mothers, Fenn, my first, had been a breeze.

Which made me completely unprepared for how Camille had done me in.

So at least I could set his mind at ease that he wasn't going crazy, and neither was Robyn, and better yet, this was temporary.

But so he could get through it, I advised him that breaks were good for the both of them.

He'd texted to say he was going to come that day for a few hours and do some work.

I stopped thinking on all this when I stepped into the comfortable, attractive, but sturdily furnished and rental-ready environs of the cabin.

They'd swept it before we got there so the guts of the case weren't spewed everywhere, but it still was clearly a command post, and a fastidious one. No fast-food debris or spent coffee mugs that needed cleaning. And the three large white boards that took up a lot of the space had been turned around.

Special Agents Everett Robertson and Ben McGill looked like who they were. Clean cut, fit, no-nonsense G-men.

The lead, Robertson, was a tall, handsome Black man wearing dark-wash jeans and a subdued dark orange turtleneck (it *was* Sunday).

His partner, McGill, was white, had thick auburn hair, a lot of freckles, and was wearing khakis and a plaid button-down under his navy sweater.

I'd met them before, briefly. They'd both been in suits then.

Nevertheless, it wasn't the first time I wondered why Bohannan had gone from the army to the FBI, and now had the appearance and wardrobe of a lumberjack biker.

I'd need to ask him about that.

It might be Sunday, but it wasn't fun day. They were in their roles and their task today was important. There were greetings and oodles of courtesy and respect, with some gentleness for Celeste due to her age.

But they had things to do that day, and talking to us was only part of them, so it didn't take long before Robertson stepped back, and McGill sat with us in the living area and launched in.

There was a brief lecture about how we were safe.

They had a tech person, who was currently not there, and I had not yet met, named Erin Reinhart who, among other duties, kept an eye on our whereabouts that pinged from our fobs. We were to continue to be sure to carry those at all times, as well as our Tasers. We were also to continue what we'd been doing, making sure more than one person knew where we were going, and when we were likely to return.

Onward from that, admirably without a smidge of blame detected in his tone, he said, "Be aware of all of your surroundings. When you enter a class. When you go down the aisle of the grocery store. As you walk to your car. Who's around you? Are they paying attention to you? What kind of attention? Try not to be alone. This doesn't mean you can't do things by yourself, but such things as finding a parking spot among cars, not parking in the vacant ones at the edge of the lot, are good habits to get into. Take a second to look in the backseat. The passenger seat. Both before you unlock your car to get back in."

He was in an armchair across from us.

Celeste and I sat next to each other on the couch across from him.

Robertson and Bohannan were on the other side of the room,

by the dining room table that fed off the kitchen behind us. I heard them, in low tones, conferring.

McGill fished in the pocket of his khakis and pulled out a set of keys. "It's good practice to walk to your car with your keys like this."

He lifted his hand, tucked his car fob in his palm, and positioned the blade of a key between his index and middle finger.

"This is assurance, it isn't your go to," he said. "If someone approaches you aggressively, you make as much racket as you can, and by that, I mean shouting and screaming, and those don't have to be words, but 'help' is a good way to go. Whatever you do, just make noise and run like hell to someplace that's populated. But if you have to use it, that key will hurt a lot worse than a scratch or a punch or even a kick."

When he got nods from us, he put the keys back in his pocket and kept speaking.

"You don't carry Mace because Mace can go wrong. If not used correctly, it can get in your eyes and incapacitate you or be taken from you and used against you..." Pause then, a subtle reminder, "Like the Taser. But if you feel like you can use it and handle yourself, we'll get you canisters that hook to your keychains, and you walk to your car with your finger on the trigger."

He waited for us to nod again, so we did.

"The more experience we have behind a wheel, the more we become conditioned to accepting our surroundings. It becomes instinct to sense things you need to know to keep you safe when you're driving, so you might not attentively check for them. I need you both to go back to basics. You get in your car, the first thing you do is lock your doors. Then check your mirrors. And keep checking them. Make note of cars behind you, but also any around you. If you see a red Jeep in the city lot by the Double D after you've had something to eat, had you seen it in the one behind the movie theater before you went in to see a movie? If you saw a blue Honda in front of you on your way to school, is it behind you on your way home? That kind of thing. If you notice patterns, or even if something spooks you, we don't care. Tell us. We'll check it out."

He paused.

We both nodded again.

"Make note of license plates, even a couple of numbers or letters and the make of a car can help us. Light is your friend. We'd really like you not to be out by yourself at night, but if that's ever the case, park under a light, keep to the lights. Don't ever be in the—"

Both Celeste and I jerked on the couch because he was interrupted by a gunshot that came from nearby.

And then another one.

"*Get down!*" McGill shouted at us as he surged from his chair.

I sought purchase of whatever I could on Celeste, which was the back of her neck, and I took her to the floor with me.

We both ran into the coffee table.

Vaguely I registered that it hurt to slam my shoulder into it, but even as heavy as it was, it lurched away at our impact, and we scrunched together on our hands and knees.

There was urgent movement around us, then I saw Bohannan's boots and looked up.

"*Down!*" he roared. "*Bellies!*" he went on.

We dropped to our stomachs, and since there wasn't a lot of room, I was half covering Celeste's body.

I still had my head up as Bohannan turned, caught a rifle Robertson tossed him, and then he motored toward the back of the house as McGill rolled out of the front, his sidearm in his hand, closely followed by Robertson, who also was holding his weapon at the ready.

I then ducked my head and pressed my face to the back of Celeste's hair.

I was panting, Celeste was doing it with me, and we coasted on terror across what felt like decades.

I came back to the room realizing I had Celeste's sweater in my grip. My knee hurt because I was pressing it into the floor, ready to use it to leap up and flee if whoever out there got to us, and equally ready to take her with me.

I heard nothing. I felt Celeste trembling against me. I then felt an intense blast of fury that subsided as quickly as it came.

And I chanced a glance up.

I was going to look back down when I saw nothing.

Except as I was thinking I'd seen nothing, I realized I saw something, and my head stayed up.

We had a direct view out the two French doors that led to a front porch that ran along the front of the cabin.

Doors that had a view to the lake.

Doors that had a view to my place.

And the view to my place showed me David was lying on my deck.

Not moving.

FIFTY

Both My Girls

It was no consolation, the changes I saw at the sheriff's department when they took us there.

Change one:

I noted a female deputy in uniform.

Change two:

I noticed two Black officers.

Change three:

When we were in what was now Harry's office, the detritus of Dern's tenure had been entirely cleared.

No standing coatrack covered in personal items like this was his home away from home.

The gunrack filled with assault rifles had been removed.

There was the desk. Two chairs in front. Both were new, attractive but utilitarian, and free of any Andy Griffith feel.

There was also a new addition of a small, round conference table with four chairs in the top corner of the room, making the statement that the man who now used that office respected his colleagues and sought their input.

A credenza behind the desk had been added. That had a framed picture of a very pretty woman who was perhaps in her twenties. She was smiling happily at the camera. Beside and just behind that, another picture of Harry with his arm slung around an older man who was likely his father, and another man his age, who was probably his brother. They were standing by a picnic table.

Where the gunrack had been, now hung a large, and rather gorgeous painting of our misty lake.

His desk was not entirely neat, but it wasn't untidy.

He worked there.

This wasn't a veritable throne room, it was a place to do business.

Important business.

Polly brought us vanilla malts from the Double D, which Pete had sent over.

We did not drink them.

Celeste cried.

Twice.

I held her when she did and silently raged.

Hours later, Jace walked in.

He was wearing his father's face.

Neutral.

"David's out of surgery. He's still with us. He's critical," he stated. "We're going home."

Celeste deflated.

He held his sister's hand, and I walked like C3PO at their sides to his Ram.

I made Celeste sit in the front with her brother.

I sat in the back.

Jace drove.

His mood was wet and stormy, and it beat through the cab like a hurricane.

Even if my mood matched it, for Celeste, I tried to cut through it.

"Harry's wife is very pretty."

"Harry's wife died a year after he married her when she broke her neck after her horse threw her," Jace replied.

The picture of the pretty girl smiling happily at the man behind the camera formed distinct in my mind.

Thus, the hard face.

I shut my mouth.

Jace took us home.

THE CURTAINS WERE PULLED, and Megan was fussing.

Dan sat at the kitchen bar with a gun holstered on his hip.

There was a lasagna staying warm in the oven, frozen garlic knots laying out on a cookie sheet, lined up to go in, and a dressed Caesar salad waiting for croutons in the fridge.

Some Mexican casserole extravaganza was cooling on the counter, ready for refrigeration or freezing, depending on our appetites and how long it took us to consume the lasagna.

I was thinking freezer.

I was sitting cross-legged on the couch, Celeste was lying on her side, her head on my thigh.

I was running my fingers through her hair.

That was when Bohannan and the boys walked in from the back deck.

Megan drifted to her man, and he curled his arm around her hips.

We all watched Jess lock the door behind him.

That was not a good sign.

Bohannan glanced at Megan and dipped his chin to Dan.

Then he looked at Celeste and me.

She'd sat up and was now plastered to my side.

And we were both looking at her father.

He switched his focus to me.

"Your guy is our guy. Robertson saw him."

Celeste took my hand.

I held tight.

"He got away, but we know who we're looking for and we know he's an excellent shot. We also know he's got resources. He got David with a long-range tactical rifle. They don't come cheap."

I refused to shift my attention to the closed drapes.

"We ran out of daylight and we're runnin' out of steam. Both lead to mistakes. We caught his trail. We followed it. But if we all keep stumbling around in the dark, we might fuck it up. What he did today, he didn't have time to cover his tracks. A fresh team has been dispatched, and they're still on it. And no, he did not vanish into thin air when he took Alice. Leland missed it, but once he got his ass out there, Harry didn't. What he had was time to plot his escape. Having that time, that was what he did. In part, literally covering his tracks. He diffused the dogs because he spent time in those woods. His scent was everywhere, except on the path to Alice. That was a straight line. One path out, then, when they picked up his scattered scent, they didn't know which path to follow. At this time, Alice had sustained a serious concussion because he'd dealt a blow to her head. He was carrying her, and my guess, she was unconscious, and he'd wrapped her in a blanket that was scented with him. She wasn't leaving a trace."

He held my gaze.

And said, "Today, he left a trace."

He seemed to want something from me, so I nodded and asked, "Is there reason people don't know this and instead think he has preternatural powers?"

"Specifics of a case are rarely released. But in this instance, that was held back for him. Yes, it scares people. No, I don't like that. And yes, that gives him what he needs. But it also can build complacency. If he thinks he's got the upper hand, if he thinks he was outsmarting Leland, and then outsmarting me, he might give that to me."

I hated that he got to further scare people.

But what Bohannan said made sense.

"Are you saying he knew Alice and her friends were going to be out there?"

"I'm saying he lured Alice and her friends out there."

Holy God.

"The girls said that?" I asked.

"It was a game, instigated by Alice."

"He got to her beforehand," I whispered.

"He got to her beforehand," Bohannan confirmed.

"Behind my boathouse, he disappeared," I reminded him.

Bohannan said nothing.

Oh God.

"Did you keep that from me too?" I demanded.

"No," he finally answered. "That time, he disappeared, and it was concerning."

Concerning?

"So he *does* have preternatural powers," I stated drily.

"No, Larue. And he never did. What he has are skills. And he proved that today by making that difficult of a shot across the fucking lake."

On that, I had nothing further.

"This is a ploy to rattle you," Bohannan shared.

I was wrong.

I did have something.

"He shot David."

"He's trying to rattle you."

I bolted off the couch, piked toward him and screamed, "*He shot David.*"

"He's feeding his need, Larue. He's got sniper skills, and that means not a soul in Misted Pines is safe. And many people who live in these mountains know guns, they know what that shot means, so they know that."

"So he meant to leave David alive?"

A hesitation.

God! This was torture!

Finally, he answered, "No, he meant to scare the shit out of you, Celeste too, and make me give chase. He meant for David to bleed out. He had no idea you'd see him and have it together enough to call 911. If David laid on your deck maybe two minutes longer, that would have happened. You saved David's life today, sweetheart."

It should, but it didn't make me feel even an iota better.

"He's the puppet master, Bohannan."

"He's rattling you."

"*Because he's god!*" I shrieked.

"And you're rattling me."

I shut up.

Because I'd never heard that tone from him.

Even when he threw the coffee mug across the kitchen.

That was when I felt it.

His tone, bearing down on the room as sure as if the ceiling had come disengaged and it was slowly falling, intent to crush us.

This was wrath, what I heard, what I was feeling.

This was end-of-days shit.

Bohannan did not like David being shot, for starters.

But it was more, and it wasn't just all the other stuff this guy was doing that he did not like.

Bohannan did not like me sad or scared or hurting.

He didn't like it at all.

And it would be the end of days if I didn't get myself together.

"I'm just worried about David," I said softly.

"I know you are. We all are," Bohannan replied, and the tone was leaking out.

"Is Robyn okay?" I asked.

He glanced at Jace.

Jace peeled off, pulling out his phone.

Bohannan looked back to me. "We'll find out."

"Don't burn down the woods just to catch this guy," I begged.

He studied me, his gaze flicking down to Celeste, then he lifted his hands, palms up in front of him and said, "Both my girls."

We flew to him, and pressed into him, and he wrapped his arms around us so tight, my ribs started aching.

He'd been so cool.

So calm.

So collected.

It dawned on me only then that she and I were on our bellies in a cabin, and he was out hunting. We were playthings, and he was embroiled in a literal death match that a madman was currently winning.

All of this just because he was good at his job of trying to help people.

His day and the last few months had been a hundred times worse than anything we were experiencing.

So, yes.

I needed to keep myself together.

I had my cheek resting on his collarbone, facing Celeste, who was doing the same.

We locked eyes.

We shared a promise.

And Bohannan held on.

FIFTY-ONE

Red Poof

"This is a disaster."

Will scowled at Kimmy (nothing to be alarmed about, Will had been scowling since he escorted Celeste home after school—another no vote to having his woman in the line of fire).

Celeste glanced at me, and her lips tipped up.

I stopped pouring chocolate fudge into a prepared pan and turned my attention from Celeste to Kimmy, who was standing in front of our Christmas tree.

"Why?" I asked.

She whirled on me. "I gave you detailed instructions."

"Kimmy—"

"You mixed and matched!" she accused.

"Bohannan and the kids have favorite ornaments," I pointed out.

And Bohannan was, indeed, a part of that. He had favorite Christmas ornaments. He had some of his mom's from when he was growing up, and even some from his grandparents.

And they were on that tree.

"This," she waved an offended hand at the tree, "obliterates *my vision*. Your house, gingerbread men and gingham ribbon. It's smaller. More rustic. It *screams* gingerbread men and gingham ribbon. The family seat *must* be about splendor and majesty." She counted them out by grabbing fingers. "Gold and cream and silver and subtle hints of glitter." She planted both hands on her hips. "You didn't even *use* the velvet ribbon I gave you."

I failed to mention, since I needed all-new holiday decorations for my house, I'd hit up Kimmy (something which, it would turn out, was mostly for David's edification, since I was never there, and now I was glad, because at least he'd had Christmas cheer around him where he worked in the days leading up to him being shot—it was a very thin silver lining, but I was clinging to it).

She'd made this her mission, and as was her Christmas wont, gone a little overboard.

Incidentally she "gave" me nothing.

I'd bought it all, and Kimmy didn't sell Christmas cheap.

And FYI, it was Monday afternoon, the day after David had been shot, and Bohannan was gone before I got up.

He left a note that told me we'd have "presence," Celeste was covered while she went to school, but she'd be coming right back home, we weren't to leave the house otherwise, and I learned it was definitely an *x* that marked the spot before he scrawled his name.

So he left me with a kiss.

Kimmy got through the deputy at the gate because she'd caused so much of a ruckus, he'd called Bohannan who had let her in.

Now Kimmy was causing another ruckus.

"They already had decorations that they like," I pointed out.

"Do I care?" she asked.

"I did the best I could to incorporate everyone's vision."

"You failed."

"I—"

I stopped talking as my attention shot to Will.

This was because Will shot to his feet.

He was staring out the window.

I turned to look out the window.

And I saw Deputy Dickerson hauling ass across the clearing.

"Delly," Celeste whispered.

Will took off toward the front door.

"Will!" she shouted.

"Come here, right now, both of you," I ordered Kimmy and Celeste. When neither of them moved, I screeched, "*Come here right now. Both of you!*"

They came.

I snatched up my Taser and hustled us into the windowless hall.

We waited there, me standing in front of both of them, facing the great room, Taser up, finger on the trigger.

"*Fuck you, where is he?*" we heard shouted from outside. Then a repeat of, "*Fuck YOU! WHERE THE FUCK IS HE?*"

"Huh," Kimmy said.

I turned to her.

She was glaring down the hall.

"I think I'll be needing to kick some ass now." She declared before she pushed forward with an, "Excuse me."

"Kimmy, don't," I snapped.

She marched into the great room and disappeared right, heading toward the front door.

"*Get your hands off me! Get your goddamned hands off me!*" Silence and, "*So busy gettin' your rocks off with a TV star, you can't catch a killer, and my boy's caught in the crossfire!*"

I looked to Celeste.

"Mr. Ashbrook," she whispered.

David's shitty dad.

We crept into the great room, and standing at the side, stacked on top of each other, like two of the Scooby Doo gang, we peered out the front window.

A man my age was stomach to the pine needles, kicking and fighting, Dickerson's knee to his back. The deputy had one of the man's arms in his grip. He and another officer were struggling to get his second hand behind his back to cuff him. Will was crouched, holding down his thighs.

"Yeah. Mr. Ashbrook," Celeste confirmed.

"*Get off me! Get the fuck OFF ME!*" he shouted.

They got him cuffed and then did that cop move where they jerked him to his feet using his arms.

No sooner was he upright than Kimmy moved in and smacked him across the face.

I gasped.

Celeste snorted.

He shook his head in surprise.

She smacked him again.

"Oh my God," I whispered.

She started wagging a finger in his face, saying something we couldn't hear.

She ended this smacking him again.

I choked back a laugh.

On a giggle, Celeste asked, "Why don't the police stop her smacking him?"

They got down to doing that, hauling him toward the cruiser in the front drive.

"*And maybe you might wanna love your son when he's NOT in intensive care, asshole!*" Kimmy shouted after them.

"*Take it to Castro!*" Ashbrook shouted back.

"*Don't think I've forgotten and DON'T YOU THINK CADE BOHANNAN CAN'T BRING JOHN KENNEDY'S KILLER TO JUSTICE. If anyone can do it, HE CAN!*"

"Oh my God, is that really a thing with her?" I whispered.

"Dad thinks she's just happy she's got an ex-FBI guy around whose ear she can bend. And I guess my grandma was really nice to her when she was growing up. Dad says she didn't have it too good, and Grandma was some good in all that bad. He says she might just want a connection with a part of Grandma. They don't have anything in common, so she's making up a connection."

This further explained Bohannan's patience with her.

And Jess's care.

"Well, he'd be able to figure that out," I replied.

Ashbrook was being folded into the cruiser and Kimmy was stomping back to the house.

We pulled away from the window and watched her walk in.

"What're you fools doin' at the window?" she demanded.

"Watching the Kimmy Show," I told her. "The crowd was surprised when a woman wearing a Rudolf face sweater complete with stitched-on red poof for a nose smacked the bad guy three times."

"He's a jackass," she said, shuffled aside for Will to get in, then looked him up and down. "Done good, kid."

"Thanks, Ms. Milford," he replied.

Next in came Deputy Dickerson, though he only swung his torso around the door.

"Sorry, folks. He jumped the gate," he explained.

"Shoulda shot him in the back, Wade," Kimmy decreed.

"I prefer handcuffs and conversations with judges," I put in my vote.

Celeste laughed softly.

Dickerson dipped his chin and disappeared behind the door.

Will locked it.

"Right then, anyone want fudge?" I asked.

And Celeste laughed softly again.

I WAS SITTING on the floor wrapping Christmas presents when Bohannan walked into the bedroom that night.

My gaze slid to the clock.

It was nearly midnight.

By the way, I'd woken up just after six.

He stopped dead and stared down at me.

"What the fuck's going on?" he asked.

I glanced around, then up at him, stating the obvious, "I'm wrapping Christmas presents."

"For the entire town of Misted Pines?"

I smiled at him.

"I'm sensing we should have talked budgets," he said to the mess, as well as the stack of wrapped boxes scattered just beyond the mess.

Which, I had to admit, was large.

(Okay, it was possibly embarrassingly massive.)

"I've never had boys to buy for," I explained.

His attention came to me.

"And it's been a few years since I've had a teenage girl to spoil."

He said nothing.

"How committed are you to the lumberjack biker look?" I queried, because I'd rolled with that on some of his presents, and I wanted to make sure he wasn't feeling a switch up.

"The lumberjack biker look?"

I flipped a hand, indicating his long body, which was full-on lumberjack biker with sturdy boots, faded jeans and a gray thermal under a thick black flannel shirt.

"I hate to shave, and I don't have time for regular haircuts, but mostly, unless I'm fucking her, I don't like anyone touching my hair. I picked two careers where I had to be on top of both. When I was done with those, that was done."

"Are you certain about the 'unless I'm fucking her' part?"

"You pull my hair, baby, anytime you want."

He was sure, I knew, because my nipples were tingling.

"Grace hated the beard," he shared. Pause, "And the hair."

"Further evidence she's insane."

His beard twitched.

"The medallion?" I asked after the irregular disk of something, I didn't know, maybe iron, which had zero designs on it but did have a hole stamped into it and a piece of leather string threaded through that Bohannan nearly unfailingly took off every night and put on every morning.

"Flattened bullet taken out of my great granddad after a man who didn't like him shot him."

One could say, if I had a million guesses, I would not have come close to that.

"Why didn't that man like him?"

"Because my great granddad was a US Marshal and there were folks still around who weren't fond of his law-abiding ways."

Righty ho.

Irrespective of how fascinating, I was done with *that* story for the time being.

"We had some excitement today, of the entertaining kind," I told him.

"I heard."

"Kimmy is life. I want to be her when I grow up."

"I'll take back the present I got for you and buy you fifty Christmas sweaters."

My heart grew light. "You got me a present?"

He gave me a look.

He didn't get me a present.

He got me a *good present.*

"I wasn't referring to her wardrobe," I clarified. "I was referring to her ability to get away with a justifiable assault in front of two officers of the law."

His beard twitched again.

I hated to do it.

But I had to do it.

"You didn't catch him," I whispered.

He shook his head. Once.

"You okay?"

He nodded his head. Once.

"Want me to pull your hair?"

He lunged, plucked me out from the mess of paper scraps and ribbons.

And took me to bed.

FIFTY-TWO

He Agreed with Me

The boys came home early the next night.

If you call 8:45 early.

Jace and Jess bolted down Megan's Mexican casserole glumly, and I watched closely, lest I need to save them from falling face first into cheesy-chili-chicken-tortilla deliciousness.

They were dead on their stools.

They dragged themselves to the basement where they were, for the time being, sleeping.

The Bohannan clan.

Circling the wagons.

Bohannan didn't linger either. He went upstairs minutes after the boys went the other direction.

I gave him some time, and then Celeste wandered up with me.

At the top landing, we hugged, said goodnight, she hit her room, and I went to ours.

I was sitting cross-legged facing the bathroom in the closed-off-from-the-outside space when he got out of the shower.

He had wet hair and was in his pajama pants that he kept on the hook behind the door.

"I know you probably want to hit it," I said softly, and I did know this because his eyes carried fatigue and his face was drawn. "But something occurred to me today, and I wanted to talk to you about it."

Without a word, he came and stretched out across the bed before me, on his side, head in hand.

"I don't know all the specifics of the case, but something you said the other night struck me," I told him.

His chin moved slightly in what I was taking as a, *Go on*, and I was also taking this not as his usual "I'm feeling like silent badass communication," but that he was too exhausted to speak.

So I hurried.

"It made me remember something I thought was weird. About Alice."

His eyes flared with interest, but he said nothing.

"She was taken the day I moved in. A weekday. A Monday."

"Yeah?"

"You don't have an eight-year-old's slumber party on a weekday."

He pushed up to his forearm.

Yes.

Interested.

"If this guy knew her, if he lured her, if he planned this with her, he had to be able to get to her. And people like this, this guy maybe especially, they insinuate themselves into investigations and…" I didn't want to do this, I was relatively certain I was wrong, because he was not the person I chased, or Robertson saw, but I had to do it, "…and Ray runs kids' programs at the rec center."

He expelled a breath and his hips listed back.

"When that guy came on the scene, and we knew he did what he did, that thought occurred to me. He'd already been interviewed by Harry after Alice was taken. So we took another look at him."

I nodded.

"I don't know why Audrey and Dale had the party on a weekday, outside it was Alice's actual birthday. The girls were not supposed to be outside. Audrey took off work early, and with another mom, picked them all up from school. They had a thing at the Double D with sundaes, came home and watched a Disney movie, had pizza and cake and presents, watched another Disney movie and then they all went to bed. That other mom was helping her take them to school the next morning. Both Audrey and Dale gave the sense that Alice was a little spoiled. She got what she wanted, and she wanted to celebrate her birthday on her birthday."

"Okay," I replied.

"And then Ray came on the scene, and he works with a lot of kids, so like I said, I had the same idea as you, and we double checked."

"Okay," I repeated when he paused.

"All those girls were friends because they were in the same dance class, which is what they did a couple afternoons after school. A few of them, including Alice, also are watched by Betty, the mom who helped Audrey out. Betty is also one of the only friends Audrey has in town. Betty lives close to school, and she's a stay-at-home mom. She picks them up, walks them to her house, or gets them to dance class. When class isn't on, she watches them after school for a couple of hours before the other parents come pick them up. They pay her to do that. In the report, notes from her interview, she referred to it as 'pin money.' Alice was one of the kids she watched. None of them were in the rec center programs, which are mostly geared toward sports and physical fitness, for boys and for girls. Just not those girls."

"The girls that don't stay with Betty?"

"Two have moms at home. One has an older sister who watches after her. No rec center."

I let out a breath, both mentally and physically.

"I'm kind of glad, because if I was wrong, I mean, Ray's been put through the wringer with that video thing."

"Yeah. He gave that to Jess. He also said he's probably going to be leaving town soon. Though he has no clue where he and Shelly would go, considering he's internet famous in a way he didn't ask for and pretty much no one is gonna hire him to work with kids anymore."

"Now that I know he's not a prideful psychopath, I feel bad for him again."

"'*To be wronged is nothing, unless you continue to remember it.*'"

"Confucius knew his shit."

A meager smile came from the depths of Bohannan's beard.

And then he asked, "You tired?"

I wasn't.

"Do you want me to be?" I asked back.

He nodded.

I bent to him, touched my mouth to his, got out of bed and went to the bathroom so I could get ready to get back in bed with Bohannan.

This, I did.

Bohannan held me in his arms in the dark and he was dead weight in seconds.

I held him back, and I had a pretty freewheeling relationship with God.

I wasn't a fan of how a lot of His supporters regarded my daughter.

I wasn't a fan of how a lot of His supporters hid behind Him to do a lot of things.

But since I figured He felt the same way, I sensed we were on the same page.

I also figured He listened to everyone's prayers, even if some of them made Him shake His head.

Though, the one I sent His way that night, I knew in my heart, He agreed with me.

FIFTY-THREE

It's Over

Bohannan's phone ringing woke us both.

He turned, grabbed it, and just like Agent Palmer, when he spoke into it, he sounded like he'd been up for a couple hours, had a run, a shower and was enjoying a smoothie when the call came.

He offered all this up with just, "Bohannan."

Then he was out of bed.

I sat up.

The light from the closet shone into the room.

I heard him say, "Pinned?"

Then I heard him say, "Yeah."

Finally, I heard him say, "Twenty."

I switched my light on.

Maybe five seconds later, he came to me dressed, bent, touched his mouth to mine and then gave me the briefest of briefs.

"They have him pinned in a cabin in Ash Peak. Shots have been exchanged, he caught Dickerson in his vest."

"Oh God."

"I gotta go."

"Do you have a vest?"

And helmet? And full body armor?

"Office. Nothing they can do, and they're gonna be pissed, but I'm leaving Jace and Jess with you."

If there was nothing to do, why was he going?

"Okay," I said.

Another touch on the lips.

And he was gone.

JACE AND JESS didn't stay left.

A couple hours later, as I sipped coffee in the kitchen and they climbed the walls of the great room (fortunately, Celeste remained sleeping through this), their phones chimed with texts at the same moment, and without a word to me (something which, later, I'd be having words with them about), they loaded up and then they blasted out in a Ram.

I did not go back to bed.

I stayed up with coffee and my laptop.

I tried writing.

That didn't work.

I tried reading.

That didn't work either.

In the end, I turned on the lights of the Christmas tree and fell into a trance that was not like what I would do when my mom wanted me to be invisible.

It was a trance that was being caught in the grip of worrying.

I pulled out of it when I heard Celeste was up and moving around, getting ready for school.

I then made a parental decision that was not mine to make, but if she was my daughter, or if I was her, it would be what I wanted, so I went up and knocked on her door.

She was just out of the shower and sitting at her vanity-cum-desk in a room that proved the tentacles of Bohannan's genius instincts went in many directions, because it was not too young or too girlie, and it was not *I'm a dad and don't know my girl needs her space like she needs her space.*

It was a room where it was space like Celeste needed her space.

Her burgeoning, self-possessed young woman was stamped all over it.

"Okay, lovely, you're staying home today because your dad got a call last night and the latest news I had, they found the guy and were in a standoff with him in Ash Peak. If you hear at school, you won't be able to concentrate. And if I didn't tell you, you'd be validly upset with me. So we're going to stay home, camp out and wait. But if you want to go to school, okay."

This brought back the pale and haunted in her that was gorgeous, but I hated it.

"I don't wanna go to school."

"Do you want breakfast?"

She shook her head. "Just coffee."

I gave her a shaky smile. "I've already got that ready."

I left her to it.

She came down dressed and got her coffee.

I left her to that and went upstairs and got dressed.

It was just over two hours later.

We'd spent that time talking.

Or, maybe because of nerves, Celeste did.

Therefore, I now knew why Bohannan was the force he was in that town.

Because the Bohannans had been the cornerstone of the community since practically its beginnings.

His father may have fallen down on the job, but we could just say that Bohannan wasn't the first overachiever in that clan.

"The town looks at us as kind of this weird, unofficial first family," Celeste shared. "It was bizarre when we first moved here because it was almost like we were celebrities. And some of them seemed like they felt some kind of…*relief* that Dad was back, and he brought all of us with him. Like, the town couldn't survive if there wasn't a Bohannan living here. I guess my great-great granddad was like a big deal. When he was a marshal, he brought down some scary outlaw gang. And Great Granddad was the sheriff, and he was a big deal too. There's even a plaque about him *and* another one for Great-Great Granddad in the county courthouse. And I guess, even though Granddad was messed up, since Dad was good at what he did, they just, I dunno, expected Dad to be that thing too. And Dad's, well…*Dad.* So really, he just was that thing."

He certainly was "that thing."

And I was looking forward to the time when I could have deeper getting-to-know-you sessions with my man that didn't involve how we were reacting mostly to current events.

Celeste also told me about how the log cabin was older than this house, because that was where the second and third generation of Bohannans lived before her grandfather built this place.

The first generation lived where my house was.

But to Bohannan's dad's fury, Fred Nance had pulled that house down to build what was there now.

And by the way, Bohannan's dad's name was Battle—Battle Bohannan—which I didn't want to think was fierce, but it kicked ass. Though I wasn't sure that was my favorite, since Celeste shared them all with me and the first to head west, fur trader Prosper, begat US marshal Obadiah, begat sheriff Lazarus who begat Battle.

And then there was Cade.

So yes, that family had a way with names because Jace, Jess and Celeste might be less unusual, but they didn't suck either.

The big house at the end, beyond my place, her grandfather built as a rental property to piss off Fred Nance, who was a privacy nut with a healthy dose of survivalist because, "When he died, they found a bunch of guns and ammunition and supplies in your closet."

So I was learning a lot of things that morning because that explained my big closet.

The Bohannan fortune had been made (and yes, it had been a fortune) in the trapping and fur trade, with some railroad investment and a local saloon and whorehouse thrown in for diversity of portfolio.

I would be curious to know how fur trading and whorehouse owning moved on to the next generation being law enforcement, but Celeste didn't know that story.

The family used to own a lot more of the land around the lake, almost all of it, but it had been sold off in parcels over the years because it was expensive to keep, and in the end, her grandfather was an alcoholic and a wastrel.

Nevertheless, Bohannan's inheritance had been significant, because Bohannan's dad might have been fonder of drinking than working, but he didn't much like banks.

Thus, he cashed in everything he could, "And when Dad opened the safe in Granddad's office, there were like, real gold bars in there, a bag of diamonds and a whole lot of money."

Onward from this, she shared the accepted local lore that her Granddad didn't come about his distrust of financial institutions on his own. Generations of Bohannan men took pains to keep the Bohannan legacy safe.

And as such, somewhere around that lake, it was widely known that there was buried treasure.

It was just that no one knew where it was.

I was digesting this latest fanciful story when a Yukon and a Ram growled into the clearing.

We ran to the window and were standing, holding hands, when all three of our boys walked in.

"Is it over?" Celeste burst out.

Bohannan looked to her and then to me.

"It's over," he replied.

FIFTY-FOUR

Profile

I made them food.

They sat all in a row and started eating it.

I positioned myself across the bar in front of Bohannan, and after he shoveled in his third forkful of scrambled eggs, and the gray of his eyes hit me, I urged, "Talk to me, Goose."

His beard quirked, his throat bobbed with his swallow, he put down his fork and picked up a piece of bacon.

And then he said, "It was Betty," and he gnawed off some bacon.

Holy cow.

"Pull some stools around this way, lovely," I ordered Celeste.

She did as asked, sat beside me, and we gave Bohannan all our attention.

He didn't make us wait.

"I was right and wrong. He was military. An army sniper. Info's still coming in, but what we know is, he's pegged a lot of kill shots. He was decorated. He got out a while ago and was making a mint taking weekend warriors from whatever city they lived in on hunting and camping trips, teaching them to shoot, the whole survival-in-a-luxury-tent thing. Lots of four-star Yelp ratings. He expanded, took corporate types and millionaires out on excursions they paid a fortune for, including hunting big game in Africa. Big man expert lording it over a lot of important men who were not real men, but they played that on vacation."

And the puzzle pieces started falling.

I nodded when he paused.

"He had that setup in Wyoming but moved it here about two years ago."

What was left unsaid was *because of me*.

"He hooked up with Betty, my guess is, because he somehow figured out that Betty's husband Ed had also had an affair with Audrey. Or maybe he targeted her because he sensed that wound, he pulled it out of her, and the rest of it came from there. She was nursing this hurt, he tapped that vein, became her lover, groomed her, and even now, under Robertson and McGill's interrogation, she was unfazed. At first, including about Alice, who according to her, was a spoiled brat."

I winced.

"Though, after she said that, McGill told her what he did to Alice. She clearly had no idea, and that shook her. But it was the only thing that shook her."

Good God.

That took "woman scorned" to a whole new level.

"Who figured out the Betty angle?" I asked.

"That'd be Robertson. Though it's Robertson because we talked shit out, I mentioned Ray, and Betty, and he got a hunch. He had her pulled in first thing. When she found out what happened, she spilled. She's beside herself, because he saw no way out, which was probably why he retreated to his own cabin. Though honest to Christ, don't know why he stayed local and didn't bolt, but I suspect something was in that cabin he didn't want us to see."

He paused to throw back a hit of coffee.

And then he went back to it.

"Even though, in the brief shootout, he also tagged one of the agents who'd been brought in for the hunt. Everyone was all geared up, and we'd been willing to run him to ground, so we were ready to wait him out, even if it meant starving him out and that took a year. So he was going to get no joy. He went to his cabin because he'd rigged that cabin. It was an inferno before anyone could spit. He died inside. She loved him, or convinced herself she did, because she convinced herself he loved her, when he didn't."

Bohannan's look on me intensified.

"He dominated her."

"Good Lord," I murmured, not missing what he was saying.

He gave her her kink, and that spilled into life.

"It's still hot, but they already found his body."

"Audrey was best friends with a woman whose husband she slept with?" I asked.

Bohannan shrugged and forked up more eggs. "I guess you take 'em as you can get 'em. Though, he set that up. What we missed was, Alice wasn't part of her afternoon kid club until this school year. Betty recruited her at the end of last year. What we also missed, but only because he wouldn't let on and she made sure she didn't, Ed's one serious dick. And that 'pin money' was all she had to play with, because he holds the purse strings, and he's not stingy with playing golf and taking scuba diving trips, but he is with her. She was tired of a lot of the other moms, especially 'the ones who work,' having Louis Vuitton when she was carrying Target. She charged twenty bucks a day per girl, five girls, she shared pretty proud that she'd earned herself a Louis Vuitton, a Valentino and a Fendi."

"Sounds like Betty had a lot to get off her chest," I noted.

"Betty lost her psychopath boyfriend and sang like a canary," Jace muttered.

I shot him a smile and looked back to Bohannan.

"And Malorie?" I asked after he swallowed his eggs. "Like you thought, just a pawn?"

"Malorie was because Betty was ticked that Lana didn't invite her into her crew. Malorie also was because Malorie drove Betty crazy. Lana was caught powerless to get out of a situation that harmed her. This meant she taught her daughter to be sure to be able to make her own way. Malorie was an overachiever, and a bossy one. She was apparently always organizing things or setting up things or making suggestions about how people could do things better, which Betty wasn't big on. Because this included Betty, who Malorie apparently told should open up her own daycare and shared she thought she was making a big mistake when Betty declined that option."

I glanced at Celeste.

She bit her lower lip even as she stretched it out.

So that was Malorie to a tee.

Poor Malorie. Probably trying to be helpful and forge her own path and someone cut that path off permanently.

"That's a part I don't get," Bohannan continued. "Because Malorie might have been a pain in her ass, but she was gone, acing all her classes, pre-law and on a trajectory she'd probably never come back to MP. And Betty never told anyone she knew Ed screwed around on her. So I don't know how she expected Lana to know to send an invitation."

I didn't know that either.

I let them all eat.

Bohannan got through most his eggs, a triangle of toast, and two rashers of bacon, before he picked it up again.

"He had a boat."

And it kept coming.

"No stripe, but it was night, and mist can play tricks."

I bet.

"And you?" I asked.

He shook his head. "They didn't mention it to her under interrogation. She didn't either. And I would say she had no clue this was all about him dicking with me. Pillow talk about how Ed done her wrong, how Audrey had to pay, which naturally, for her, formed into a plan where they worked together, without her having that first clue she was being played or it had anything to do with me. She knew about Alice. She knew about Malorie. She'd heard about David, but she swears it wasn't him. When it was because Robertson ID'd him as the guy we were chasing. She thought they were done, letting the dust settle and then she was gonna leave Ed, and they were going to ride into the sunset."

"Did he look like the sketch?"

"Not exactly. Same build. Also dark hair. But he's got Italian ancestry and looks it. I'd say attractive, but not pretty, like the guy down in Cali. Either the composites weren't quite right or whoever that guy was, was probably paid and picked for build and because they share some similarities. Betty didn't know about him, but she said our guy didn't go down to Cali except to get Malorie, so there are parts of his gig he didn't share. Though why he would choose someone who looked remotely like him, I don't get, because you couldn't miss the similarities, and if it was me, that wouldn't be what I'd be going for."

I didn't get it either.

And I guessed now we'd never know.

I was careful when I queried, "How did a decorated, ex-army sniper with a weekend warrior camp in the next town fly under radar?"

"He didn't. I mentioned him to you weeks ago. We checked him out. He had alibis. He was hunting lynx in Canada during Alice's disappearance and murder. Had passport stamps and his name on flight manifests to prove it. But this guy has the skills to cross back over the border without anyone seeing, which Betty told us he did. He also had a side piece, a woman that Betty didn't know about, who alibied him for Malorie. They're trying to find her, but my guess is, she's gone. And as we know, he did David."

"Ace athlete?"

"All-state cornerback."

"Functional family?"

"That we don't know. Though, the dad was floored and then he started sobbing when he got the call his boy went up in a ball of flame he lit himself after he was the target of a three-day manhunt because he allegedly committed two murders and attempted one. So I'd say, maybe."

"So you profiled him almost exactly," I remarked.

Bohannan held my gaze in a way I found strange.

And replied, "Yeah. Almost exactly."

I'D LET them finish eating.

It was later, in our room, after he showered, I sat on the counter between the basins as he shaved the skin of his neck.

"You don't like him for this?" I asked.

"I love him for it," Bohannan answered. "And I'm excellent at what I do. But it's like he came to life in my profile."

"Something missing?"

"I can't see it if there is. Betty copped to all of it, but David."

"But there's an issue."

"Yeah. But profilers can get twitchy. Sometimes someone just ticks all the boxes, and it gets tied up in a bow. It's just hard, when you're that close to it, when you're living and breathing it, to recognize it's done and let it go."

He put the razor down and turned fully to me.

"Sometimes, you can even miss it. You love the hunt so much, you don't want to let it go."

"Are you feeling that?"

"Maybe."

"That's not too certain," I noted.

"You were in this. Celeste was in this. The twins were in this. I don't like the idea that I was back in the game again, and now I'm feeling hinky because I got off on it."

I tipped my head. "Did you get off on it?"

"I'm good at what I do," he repeated. "I'd started casting a net, looking for a place to retire. I'll admit to feeling a little burnout. So I was thinking maybe getting out of the game and doing it early. Grace pushed that. In the end, I got out because Grace was done with me being gone all the time. She had a job. Advertising. She was a big shot. Made great money. She took three months maternity leave with the boys, only one with Celeste. We had a nanny both times. She was so serious about having me around more, she gave up her job, set up a small shop of local clients here in MP. Car dealership commercials and local store ads. Nothing like what she used to be doing, running huge campaigns for multi-national corporations. But Dad died, she saw the opportunity for a quieter life, I'd talked to her about having that in our future, she thought I'd like it. Thought it'd feel good, being home, where Mom had been. I saw that for Celeste. For me. And I thought she'd settle, and it'd make her happy. Us a family. So I did it. But that doesn't mean a part of me didn't want to."

"I see that."

"I look at a case, work up a profile, but then I send that off. I'm hardly ever in the field. I'm very rarely involved in an active investigation. And if I'm gone, it's to consult in a police station conference room or give a lecture."

"Right."

"So like I said, maybe."

"Perhaps you should be sheriff," I said quietly.

"Harry's a good man, and he's waited a long time. It's his turn."

I nodded.

He came to stand between my legs and put his hands to my thighs.

"It's not the first time I've had it, and the feeling fades, babe."

"Okay."

"We're clear for Christmas."

"Okay, Cade."

"I love you."

I blinked.

My heart rejoiced.

My mind reconjured images of family in houses all around us on the lake.

Then I wrapped my arms around his shoulders.

"Okay to that most of all, scarecrow."

Those beautiful lips in that thick, dark beard formed a smile.

And he kissed me.

FIFTY-FIVE

Balls

The day Tony Romano burned himself to death in a cabin outside Ash Peak, David was taken out of the ICU.

When I visited him the next day, he looked at me.

And then he apologized that there was going to be a delay in finishing the powder room.

AND YES, if the name Tony sounded familiar, that's because it was.

And not because it's a common name.

No, it was because, when Megan took the lectern in the chambers during the big town meeting, she'd thanked the man at the front who'd stepped aside for her.

His name was Tony.

It was *that* Tony.

He'd been first up to say something to the council and commissioners about Sheriff Dern.

Yes.

He had balls that big.

And now...

He was dead.

FIFTY-SIX

The Picture

I had a lot on my mind.

Christmas had come and gone, New Year's had come and gone, with Camille and Joan doing duty to Joan's family for the first holiday but flying up to ring in the new year with us.

Jess had been disappointed at the plethora of presents I'd laid on him, sitting among the new jeans and flannels and top-of-the-line, solar powered, tactical GPS watch, complaining, "You're loaded, you couldn't buy me a Humvee?"

(He, of course, had been kidding and that was his alpha-man way of expressing gratitude. Or, at least, that was how I decided to read it.)

Celeste, on the other hand, had not hidden in the slightest that she'd been delighted.

She now had her own Chloe.

And Givenchy padlock ankle boots.

And...*other.*

Lots of *other.*

Bohannan had grumbled, "We definitely should have talked budget."

But he didn't mean it.

I knew this because he bought me a heavy gold charm bracelet that had six identical charms on it. They were all stars. Each had a little diamond. And each had a letter.

F. C. B. J. J. C.

So I guessed I did have my own tribe, my own family, a true home where I belonged, and if I ever doubted, I just had to look at my wrist.

I loved that he made himself the B.

I also started bawling.

"Estrogen always mucks up the works," Jace complained as his father held me and stroked my back. "She carries on like this for long, we're never gonna get through the thousand presents she bought each of us."

"Like you're not taking notes for when you get your own babe," Celeste retorted.

"I am," Jace concurred. "Find myself a woman who makes good cupcakes."

At that, I pulled loose of Bohannan's embrace (not entirely, obviously), and informed him, "You're cooking for the next three months."

"Works for me," he replied. "I rock in the kitchen."

Since I had Christmas dinner all planned, it would take until the next night to find out that he didn't lie.

And since Bohannan clasped it on me Christmas morning, I hadn't taken that bracelet off.

NO, THAT WASN'T THE "A LOT" I had on my mind.

Part of that lot was what happened late that very morning when Bohannan showed in the door to my office at my house.

I didn't move back there.

In fact, I was fully moved into The Big House, clothes, books, Emmys and everything. I'd listed my home in the Hollywood Hills. And Bohannan and I were planning to take a springtime vacation to Paris.

Not to mention, just the week before, Bohannan had

approached me with the news that Jess and Jace were feeling it was time to take the next step through adulthood.

That being making their own space.

Jace wanted to move up to the log cabin. And Jess wanted to know if he could rent my house from me.

When we'd had a family meeting about this, Celeste was all in because, "The boys' house is rad. Or it will be, after an industrial cleaning. And I can move in there when I graduate!"

Even though I didn't go test out this theory, from her words I knew I was correct about the whole, that-house-smelling-like-a-used-sock thing.

Considering the fact that, during New Year's, Joan had waxed whimsical about how it would be great to get out of the LA traffic and move up to Washington (and away from her mother), and how nice that big house looked up on the hill, visions of my fantasy coming true danced in my head.

Jace was already slowly moving up to the log cabin.

Jess was giving me time to finish my book, on which I'd informed my publisher I was definitely going to miss my deadline (and again, considering the cause, my publisher was okay with that for me), while Bohannan renovated the upstairs guest room that had a view to the lake into an office for me.

I could make do with my laptop in a pinch, say, when someone was running around murdering people.

But I preferred to write in quiet solitude at my PC.

Bohannan had broken that solitude with his visit.

He was carrying a manila envelope.

He dropped it on my desk.

He launched in with minimal preamble.

"After that shit hit, I called my attorney. I also called Grace. She hadn't missed what was going down in Misted Pines and the news you and me were a thing. We had a couple of seriously fucking annoying conversations. Then she told me to tell my attorney to send her new papers. There was some back and forth as she tried to get me to intervene for her with the boys, since she's tried to be in contact with them, but they've blocked her. I told her you and me were shacked up, I didn't give a fuck if her and me were legally divorced or not, and you didn't either. Don't know if that's true, didn't matter, she didn't know it. I just wasn't gonna let her use my love for you to get her what she wants from my boys, and not only because she didn't ask to talk to Celeste. She realized she wasn't going to get what she wanted, she signed the papers."

He tapped the envelope.

And that was it.

"All that went down, and you didn't tell me?" I queried.

"It isn't all that," he refuted. "She doesn't matter. It was just a thing I wanted to do so if some reporter got interested in you again, they couldn't talk trash about it."

I said nothing, even though I felt a lot.

He did say something.

"You should know, I don't wanna get married. Not that the last one wasn't easy to get out of so I want it easy for me to get free if this doesn't work. This works. It's always gonna work. I just love who we are and how we are and how huge it is and how we don't need that. It's huge just us. And I'm seriously fuckin' down with that."

"I am too," I whispered.

"And I can keep calling you Larue. It'd get confusing if we both called each other Bohannan."

He was *so* my B.

I grinned up at him. "Yeah."

He bent to touch his mouth to mine.

And that was just who we were and how we were and how huge it was.

Because once he did that, with no further ado, he grabbed the envelope and walked out.

But there was further ado.

Because I knew, it was just me for him and him for me.

Always.

SO I WAS THINKING about that, and it was part of the "a lot."

But another part was Bohannan mentioning reporters, so I harked back to the fallout of Tony Romano and Betty Keller.

Swarthy, handsome, ex-army sniper run amuck and his sexual manipulation of a wronged housewife on the heels of a massive small-town sex scandal that involved more vengeful housewives, cheating husbands, murdered girls, a devoted father-to-be clinging to his life, a famous profiler and his more famous girlfriend, the town had been overrun with media.

And it didn't die down in a week.

I mean, the guy burned himself alive after a shootout and standoff in the woods with the FBI and local law enforcement.

It had all the hallmarks for enduring public fascination.

And all the consequences.

Kimmy was beside herself. The media and all their crew, not to mention the murder and scandal enthusiasts hitting town meant more foot traffic in her shop.

It also meant some of them were conspiracy theorists, so she had plenty of people to talk to about her thoughts on Castro.

Megan was incensed. "Misted Pines is so much more than Tony Romano and Betty Keller. He isn't even from here! He's from Maryland!"

(Megan, by the way, was the front runner to win against Kenneth Warner. She was so far ahead in the polls, rumor had it, Kenneth was going to save face by retiring. I hoped he did. She had a lot of ideas that were really good, and it'd be nice for her to hit the ground running).

It was refreshing not to be the focus of the story.

But Bohannan had had seven approaches from writers who wanted to write books about the story where *he* was the focus.

Unsurprisingly, he'd declined.

Things had just begun to settle down.

Audrey now lived in Spokane.

Since Will and Celeste were still together, and Dale continued to reach out to (unsuccessfully) make amends to his son, I knew Dale was down in Bend, Oregon.

Sarah remained in town, also unsuccessfully attempting to make amends with her son.

Bobby never returned.

Ed filed for divorce from Betty.

Betty was in jail. Having confessed to being accessory to two counts of murder, she was awaiting sentencing, but she probably wouldn't be home in a while.

Lana and Dean bought a bigger house and moved into it with her sons.

Ray apparently took my advice, and although he remained an ancillary character in this drama, his role had shifted because the town rallied around him, defending his right to his privacy and his sexuality. Now he was just the hot guy who picked the wrong playmate. So he was riding it out, and could, because his job was secure and the kids were coming back to the center.

Indeed, I'd run into Shelly a couple weeks before at the grocery store, and she was beaming because she got an engagement ring for Christmas.

But it had been a wild ride.

And it was unsettling because I understood where Bohannan was coming from.

There was a high to it, no matter how terrifying and appalling and sad it was.

The days weren't routine.

Anything could happen.

And without knowing, you could get addicted to that.

And miss it when it was gone.

BUT THAT WASN'T ALL the "a lot" I had on my mind.

The final part of that "a lot" was, instead of working on my book (I *really* had to get that done…eventually), I was driving to the place on the outskirts of Ash Peak that I'd looked up, because I thought the finalization of Bohannan's divorce needed celebrating.

And Celeste was sleeping over at Phoebe's that night.

And Bohannan's bed was most assuredly a playground.

It was time.

We needed toys.

Considering this was a spur-of-the-moment decision, I couldn't online shop.

This meant my only choice was hitting up the only sex shop in the county.

However, I was Delphine Larue.

It could be some young person was working there. One who'd never seen *Those Years* and never heard of or didn't know what the author of *We Pluck the Cord* looked like. So I could get away with hitting a sex shop and finding something fun without that news spreading near, or even far.

Or it could be I could not.

I was struggling with this, and the fact that I should not be discomfited with going to a sex shop.

It wasn't only entirely natural to seek things to enhance that connection with your partner, it was also that I should be proud. I was a vital, fifty-three-year-old woman with a very healthy sex life. My partner and I had experience and enjoyed each other and exploring and had no hang ups. And I was a romance novelist (not that anyone knew that). I should be the poster adult for doing what you liked and not apologizing to anyone for it.

I struggled with this so much, I was parked in front of the shop, which was a nice-looking wood building with a blue corrugated roof that was fitting of a rural Washington state town. It sat alone in the side of a hill without any other businesses or houses around it. It had a clean parking lot and was carefully lacking in anything crude. The windows to it were big but smoked. There was a neon sign above the door that was lit, declaring it open. It had a tasteful sign on the road proclaiming it THE JOY OF JOY. It had another sign affixed to the door that stated you had to be eighteen to enter.

And as I took all of this in, it occurred to me that people who worked in or ran sex shops understood privacy and they might not own that shop very long if they went around blabbing about their customers.

On that thought, I grabbed my purse and got out of the car.

I had my keys in hand and was walking to the front door, considering tucking them in my purse, when I saw, poking out from the corner of the building, the prow of a small fishing boat that was parked there on its trailer.

It was white with a thick blue stripe.

A slither slid down my spine as I stepped up on the wooden walk in front, moving toward the door, when it opened.

Ray came out and stopped dead.

I stopped too.

I looked into his sea blue eyes.

In that instant, all the puzzle pieces fell into place.

And showed me the picture.

FIFTY-SEVEN

The Story

He was attractive.

He was confident.

He was good at what he did.

He worked with kids, so he knew how kids' minds worked.

He couldn't *not* know Bobby was a cheater, because he'd been in that town for four or more years. Even the high school kids knew most of the story. Not to mention, his girlfriend was a hair stylist, which was the gossip mill of anywhere, and everyone knew about Bobby, and Dwayne, and Jay, Dale and Audrey.

And I'd bet dollars to donuts that Shelly did Betty's hair. So Shelly might be the one person outside Tony in Misted Pines who knew that Ed had cheated on Betty. And Tony knew because Shelly told Ray.

He ran like the wind, and yet could not catch Tony.

His girlfriend wore a T-shirt that encouraged MAKE LOVE THEN MAKE MORE LOVE, along with the bent of his job, a subtle hint to anyone who knew them that they were kind and gentle people. But in actuality, it was an overt attempt to throw people off the scent.

He'd been staring at me in Aromacobana.

He was an exceptional actor.

He'd insinuated himself as an important, but secondary part of the story.

And he was smart.

Very smart.

A mastermind.

A god.

I knew this because I also knew he knew that I'd figured it out.

He was blocking my way into the shop, and there was nowhere else to run.

So I turned and ran the short distance back to my car.

I did this screaming repeatedly and as loud as I could, "*HELP! HELP! HELP ME!*"

Ray slammed me up against my car so hard I dropped my keys.

I felt him take hold of me, and I knew I had one second to do something.

So in the dust on the door of my car, I started writing.

I got one letter written.

R.

Then he whirled me, his fist hit my face…

And I was out cold.

HE DROPPED me to the pine needles, my back to a tree.

It came as no surprise Ray was very good at tying people up.

Face to face, hip to hip, he dropped down to sit beside me.

My temple throbbed, my skin was swelling, pressing inwards from the side of my left eye.

Bohannan hadn't given me any impression he still had doubts there was more to the story.

But I knew Ray was not unknown in that sex shop, considering whoever owned it let him use their boat.

And if Bohannan went there, he'd take one look at that boat and know what I knew.

There was more to the story.

I had a feeling I came to shortly after I blacked out, and when I did, I was tied up in the back of his truck, which was moving, so he couldn't have had time to move my car.

But he did bring my purse, having no clue I still carried my GPS fob.

Though, no one was actively tracking it.

Even so, this was good.

Because all they had to do was start tracking it.

Except once he'd parked on what I would find when he pulled me out was a one-lane, dirt road in the middle of nowhere, he'd hiked into the woods a good forty-five minutes (yes, with me on his shoulder, yes, he was that fit, yes, he was that comfortable hiking through the woods, yes, he fit *the profile*).

And, due to this, I figured by the time anyone figured out he had me, by the time they tracked us into that forest (because he was not making any effort to cover his tracks), I would probably be dead, and he would have more time to get away.

I figured this because he hadn't only brought me along.

He'd brought a shotgun.

"I was gonna let it lie," he said. "I'd won."

I sat there staring at him, wondering if Camille and Fenn would stay in touch with Bohannan and the kids.

Camille, probably.

In her pain, Fenn would likely lay some mistaken blame on Bohannan before she got over it.

But they'd never have Christmas together.

Our families would never spend summers in our respective houses on the lake.

I hoped he gave Celeste my bracelet, and added a D.

Even though her mother didn't love her, her brother and father did—I did—and she needed to know she belonged.

I also hoped Bohannan found another woman to love, where the sex was not quite as great as it was with me.

And she made him just a smidge less happy.

But she made him happy.

"I'm kinda pissed I can't. Now Shelly and me are gonna have to find somewhere else to be. She probably won't mind. She hates her family, and they still drag on her all the time, even though I tell her to tell them to piss off. Though, she loves Misted Pines."

I just stared at him.

He cocked his head.

"He didn't figure it out," he noted. "I thought for sure when that video came out, he'd figure it out. He'd figure out that it's all about dick."

I said nothing.

"The first girl I fucked, man, I did not know what I was doing. We were both sophomores in high school. But that bitch *still* keeps in touch with me. Followed me around like a puppy. That's when I knew, you get good at using your dick, you can make anybody do anything for you."

Was he…?

Was he really going to James-Bond-villain-monologue tell me all his motivations?

I did not mind this.

Not that I was interested.

Just that it might be a long story.

And that would give Bohannan time.

I jumped as he lifted a long-fingered hand and tapped the side of his head.

"You were right. Small minds. That was Tony's headfuck. He's bi, like me, and swings two ways another way too, and you can't be an ace army sniper and one of the guys if you like a big dick moving up your ass. You can't be a real man and like to be tied up and have your cock whipped. For a long time, he made do with getting the other side of that, lots of pussy who'd beg him to fuck them harder and make it hurt. But a man needs what a man needs. *All* he needs."

Those sea blue eyes held mine.

"I gave him what he needed. He'd do anything for me."

Pause.

"*Anything.*"

I had a feeling Tony proved that in spades.

He shook his head, looked off into the distance, then back to me.

"I didn't like him fucking Betty, you know. That messed with my head. He was mine. But no one gave that first shit about her. She was just some guy's wife. I'm not sure anybody even knew her name until they found out she got herself addicted to Tony. She was perfect. The cops didn't pay her a lick of attention, even when she was being interviewed. She didn't matter. She was just another mom. She was nobody."

She had been treated that way.

Like nobody.

And as the ladies had a habit of doing in Misted Pines, Betty sure proved *that* was a mistake.

"He obviously wasn't supposed to get caught," he bit out. "Eventually, once I had her primed, I was gonna introduce him to Shelly, and it would be my boy, my baby and me. But for some fucked-up reason, Bohannan took you and his daughter up to where the FBI was hanging. He wasn't supposed to be there. You weren't supposed to be there. Tony saw Bohannan's SUV, but we had a plan, and Tony's good with carrying out orders and thinking on the fly if there's adjustments that need to be made. He even thought you all being there would be a bonus. He called me, told me what was up, and we agreed. He took his shots, and those three tore off out of there. He didn't expect Bohannan to come out the back, though. Tony had to veer the wrong way. His escape route impeded, he couldn't adjust quick enough and get away without being seen."

"You-you had him…do all the killing?"

He shook his head. "Not Alice. He was up in Canada. I snatched her. Funny thing, the government trains these guys to be killers. Straight-up, dead-set killers. Trains 'em, and then sends them out and orders them to kill. Put their eye to the sight, get a bead, pull the trigger. Dead. Then they come home and what? What are they good for? You kill somebody, it doesn't matter who, you could hate 'em, it'll still fuck you up."

He blew out a sigh, upset about this, though he was right in what he said, and it was upsetting.

"It fucked him up. I told him what we needed to do with Alice, he told me he couldn't do it. First time he refused me anything. Only time. But I got it. You had to draw the line somewhere. That was his line. And I gave that to him."

Which meant *he* killed Alice.

Inept, Bohannan had said.

And gruesome.

He scooched closer to me.

I fought vomiting.

"It was genius, the setup he had. Like I said, he liked it a lot of ways. So he starts that business in Wyoming, all guys all the time. These big corporate players who walk around thinking they're swinging their big dicks, snap your fingers, they'll drop to their hands and knees. He was free, making up for lost time. He was fucking so much ass and sucking so much cock, he was up to his neck in that shit. Obviously, I heard of this guy who takes you out and shows you a good time, *Brokeback Mountain* with guns and good hunting, I had to see it for myself. And he was perfect."

His voice dropped, a new expression hit his face.

"Fucking perfect."

Good God.

He loved him.

He'd loved Tony.

And if I was reading it right, he also loved Shelly.

"He was so lost," Ray told me. "She was so lost. In me, they were found."

Yes, he loved Tony and Shelly.

And yes, he thought he was god.

Because when he said that last, I could swear, he felt like light was shining from him as the savior of the fucked-up-by-life souls.

"Was gonna find a new one," he shared. "Marry Shelly and tie her to me forever, and we'd find a new one we both liked. But I need time. It's gonna take time to get over Tony."

"So, he, um…killed Malorie?"

He brightened.

I fought grimacing.

"Yeah, he liked doing that for me. Shelly, she tries to like everybody. That's the way she is. She's just a good girl." The next came through a leer. "A good girl who likes it rough, but that makes it hotter, when she's a good girl."

With ease that was chilling, he transitioned back to conversational and continued to tell his story.

"But she couldn't like Malorie because no one liked Malorie because Malorie was a know-it-all bitch. She knew what everyone should be doing and didn't mind telling you. She even came to the rec center once and told me what programs I should be offering. Like she and she alone had some lock on all the needs of a community. Swear to fuck, about a dozen times almost burned down that locker where everyone puts their used boxes. Sick of hearing how great that is. Like that locker is single-handedly gonna save us from climate change. Seriously?"

When it seemed he expected a response, I shook my head like I agreed with how moronic that was, although I thought every town could benefit from having a recycling center like that.

That said, I was getting it.

Malorie got attention. Malorie earned respect. Malorie did something people admired.

And he couldn't have that.

He was the rec center community guy who got grants for kids' programs.

She was competition.

My head shake was what he needed, because he kept talking.

"So, Tony went down and got her. And Tony killed her and brought her up. I took her out on the lake." His gaze on me intensified. "I tied her to Bohannan's pier. That was *me*."

He was proud of that.

He was proud of invading Bohannan's space like that.

That meant everything to him.

I needed this story not to be complete with that.

I needed more time.

I needed to keep him talking.

So I asked, "Did Shelly do Betty's hair?"

He smirked. "Put that together, did you?"

He knew I did. That was why I was sitting right there.

"Did you…did the people at The Joy of Joy let you borrow their boat?"

"Now," he started, like he was admonishing me. "Don't be thinking bad thoughts about Mick and Zelda. They're good people. I did *borrow* their boat. But they didn't know it."

So he took it and didn't ask them.

And if it was registered, and they were questioned about it, they could in all honesty say, *No, officer, it's been parked at our shop the entire time.*

I wondered, if he thought Mick and Zelda were good people, if he understood on some level he was bad.

I didn't ask that.

"Did he…did he, that is, I mean, did Tony stalk Malorie at Berkeley?" I went on.

He stared at me like I was crazy. "And maybe get my boy caught? Fuck no. I went down there and set that up."

"So you hired someone to throw them off?"

"Sure."

"Why did you pick someone who looked like Tony?"

He didn't like that question, so much I tensed.

"He didn't look like Tony. He didn't look shit like Tony."

"All right. I didn't see him," I placated.

"Well, he didn't fuckin' look like Tony," he muttered, and I sensed he'd slept with that guy too, which could be why that guy helped out.

But Tony didn't know he did that.

Further, Ray had a type.

"Tony's alibi for that?" I asked.

One of his shoulders went up. "I let him play. I get it. He needs pussy. But he also needed an alibi, and she was hot, but she was kind of a junkie. Give her good dick. Give her some money. Keep her in blow. Tell her what to do. She does it. Help her disappear. See ya."

Easy as that.

"So the choice of Malorie and Alice wasn't about tying them to the situation with Audrey," I noted.

"Yeah, it was," he replied. "Thought Bohannan would run around chasing his tail on that one, at least for a while. Thought that coven would get hauled in. Thought they'd look at the dads, because they're obviously all assholes. Should have known Bohannan wouldn't fall for that. Should have known they'd never suspect the women. Was counting on that with Betty. But, man, did that set off fireworks. Fuckin' hell. Those bitches went for it, and they laid those assholes *out*."

They certainly did.

"So you…didn't know you were being taped?"

He grinned. "No way, but I looked hot fuckin' that ass. I mean, Bob was old, but he was fit, and he loved it. And he had a tight ass, you know what I'm saying?"

I swallowed, and even though I didn't know, I nodded.

Now the grin was sick that spread across his face.

"Almost gonna miss that guy. He wasn't gay, not even bi, but he needed it. Would make him suck my dick to get it, and he did it. He'd gag every time, so obviously, I'd fuck his face." He laughed softly at this treasured memory. "I'd tell Tony about it, and we'd laugh our asses off. Then he'd suck my dick, 'cause Tony didn't like anyone but Shelly doing that to me. It was like he wanted to erase ol' Bob, and he was good at it, so for a while, he did."

My lips had gone so dry, they suddenly hurt, but I didn't dare wet them.

"At first, I was freaked when that tape came out, but then I saw how it'd work for me. First comes the fuckwads who think fuckwad shit about shit like that, then come the social justice warriors who'll shout 'til they're sick how it's my right to be the authentic me. In the end, I figured it'd turn my way." He tipped his head at me. "You knew it too."

I nodded again, though I didn't know that. I just knew it'd blow over because it always did.

But it had turned his way.

"So, you didn't pick Bobby because he was Malorie's dad?"

He seemed confused. "Well…yeah. How else was I gonna find out what dormitory she stayed in?" He shrugged. "Like I said, he needed it. I took my time with him. I primed him. I figure the bitches he let fuck him gave him a taste, but no one fucks like a man." He gave me another lewd look. "*You* know what I'm talkin' about. Bet Cade Bohannan fucks like a goddamn freight train."

I swallowed.

I didn't want to answer that, but as his stare started to turn into a glare, I sent him another nod.

His expression cleared, he smirked, and whispered, "Bet he hits you every night. Doesn't even give that first shit he's banging super-famous pussy. That's his due. You were put on this earth to get fucked by Bohannan."

He got his earlier nod, this time, I decided I wasn't going to respond.

He didn't mind, he had the floor and was enjoying his performance.

I knew this because, without missing a beat, his voice resumed its chatty tone and he kept talking.

"By the time I let ole Bobby have another go, he'd be gagging for it. Ready to do anything. That meant he didn't even blink when I asked about his girl, if she was coming home for Thanksgiving, where she stayed down there. Stared at my crotch the whole time he told me all about Malorie and her dorm in Berkeley. So desperate for it, I got what I needed, and the only way to shut him up was to pull my dick out and stuff it in his mouth."

My stomach twisted.

Bobby led his daughter's killer right to her.

"Why David?"

He smiled, huge, and if he wasn't so fucking crazy, it would have been beautiful.

"You were so riled up. Tearing after Tony like that." He chuckled. "That was gorgeous. Fucking amazing. I saw you show, called him in just to see if he could creep you. And yeah, he definitely creeped you." He shook his head, but there was still humor in his face. "That wasn't exactly planned. I mean, yeah, we were workin' on something. We picked you to fuck with your head, rather than the daughter. Tony had a block about her. Probably 'cause she's fucking magnificent, and he thought one day, when she was older, he might be able to get in there. 'Cause, like I said, I let him do that, you know. A man needs good pussy."

I tried not to glare at him, talking about Celeste that way.

"Though, he didn't know he'd be sharing Shelly's with me, and eventually that was all I was gonna let him have. But anyway, we picked you to start dickin' with. Then we had so much fun with you running after Tony like you thought you were Wonder Woman or something, we decided to dick with you a little bit more."

And proof positive, it *really, really, really* was *so damned stupid* I chased Tony like that.

But…

Dick with me by shooting someone who meant something to me?

"That's not what he was doing when he went to Cade's house that time?" I asked. "Trying to creep me?"

"When he what?"

"When he…he…" I trailed off because he looked genuinely confused.

"When he what?" he bit off.

"I saw him, out my window," I whispered.

For a second, he seemed thrown, tense, then he relaxed.

"Oh yeah," he said. "Right. No, he was casing the pier for later. You saw him?"

I nodded.

"Wondered why things went wired around that time," he mumbled.

And yes, he'd been paying close attention to the players.

He picked up the threads of his story.

"By the time we creeped you at the coffee shop, we were actually kinda done with the whole killing thing," he shared, like killing people had become a chore. "I mean, I was down for it again, if that was needed. But Bohannan was obviously stumped. He hadn't even looked at me. Sent his hotshot, big-man-in-town son to have a chat, dude didn't even blink. I mean, props to him. I know he saw me fuckin' some ass. He didn't give me a whiff he had a problem about it. But he didn't come close to making me."

And Jess was going to suffer for that.

I knew it.

And I hated this man.

I hated him with everything that was me.

But thinking Jess stood and talked to the man who killed Alice, and he didn't sniff anything on him…

That made me hate him so much more.

And the fact that it was me that led to Jess doing that.

That made me hate him most of all.

"And it was getting old. I mean, everyone freaks out about a murder for, like…*a week*. Then all they care about is Dale Pulaski's ex showing her skill with a strap-on. Or that the sheriff is a racist, misogynist blowhard. *They* voted that fuck in, like, *six times*, and they just figured that out? Bullshit. Half don't even fuckin' vote, so straight up, they should shut the fuck up. Half of the other half are racist, misogynist blowhards, but they'd be super pissed you called them that. Dern was just 'tough but fair' and 'the kind of man our town needs.' Yeah, he's that until you figure out what he really is, is incompetent. You just saw you in him, and you liked it. And the last half." He blew out a breath. "Well, they were just plain screwed."

Now I hated that he was right.

"I mean, seriously, if we were gonna do this, and obviously we were, we couldn't have picked a better guy to do it on his patch. It only got interesting when the FBI got involved."

God, this was such a mess, this man was so unnervingly narcissistic, I didn't know if I was trembling with fear or fury.

"So it was time to fuck with Bohannan another way. And I ask you, what's worse? Dead bodies? Or livin' for weeks, even months, maybe even years thinking another one is gonna show unless you figure shit out, and when it does, it's on you?"

He asked me, but he didn't wait for my answer.

He told me.

"Waiting. Waiting is always worse."

I wasn't sure he was right about that, but I didn't contradict him.

"So, in the meantime, we dick with you, and hype him up, make him think maybe we'll turn to his daughter, or fuck up his boys." The next came in the tone of someone rubbing their hands together with glee. "It was gonna be good."

He grew silent, reflective, looked off in the distance again.

"Then they saw Tony," he whispered.

Yes.

Then they saw Tony.

He took a breath and let it out in a nonverbal *Welp! Anyway!* and turned back to me and gave me the final thing I didn't know.

That being, instead of using his skills to cross the border unseen, why Tony stayed local.

"When he got seen, Tony knew they wouldn't let up. He knew if they found him and tied him to me, his dad would know he wasn't a 'real man.' So he called…we got phones no one knows about, not even Shelly…Shelly doesn't know anything. But he called and told me all that went down. Took it on himself to end it. The ultimate sacrifice. The ultimate show of love. He gave himself so I could be free. Then you show at Joy," meaningful pause, "and here we are."

There we were.

And I was very, very worried.

Because I had a feeling that was the end of the story.

FIFTY-EIGHT

The Hunt

Bohannan got two things wrong.

Foremost, there were two killers.

It was a team.

And secondary to that, but no less important, the ringleader had sexual issues, though probably not ones anyone would suspect.

Still, outside the fact Ray was totally unhinged, they were the crux of everything.

Putting a fine point on it, he thought his dick had superpowers.

And sadly, too many people along the way made him think he was right.

Bohannan got an added thing right.

When Ray thought he'd bested Bohannan, he found a new challenge.

I discovered this after it seemed story-time was over.

When this appeared to be the case, I wanted to know, I also didn't want to know, but mostly I wanted to keep him talking, so I asked, as if to confirm, "Was it about Bohannan?"

He touched his nose and winked at me.

That meant yes.

Even if he'd answered, he answered again.

"I told him that in my letters, didn't I? I mean, in a roundabout way. But I knew he'd figure it out. That was the most important thing. So that was the only thing meant to be easy."

I had not read the letters.

But I'd guess he did make it easy.

"Why?"

"The best in the league doesn't play the worst in the league in the Superbowl."

I faked confusion. "Are you a profiler?"

He scoffed.

"We all are. You gotta be if you're gonna get through this life," he educated me.

I didn't tell him clearly Shelly wasn't.

And I had a number more examples, considering we needed profilers at all.

For instance, seeing as I was sitting there with him…*me.*

"See, that Al Catlin, he was one sick fuck," he told me one thing I knew. "But he had it going on. I mean, seriously. How they found him…" A grin. "Bohannan was how they found him. Most those women didn't even remember he called them poodle, they were too busy with other things. Preliminarily, only three, *in all of them*, three in *thirty* mentioned that. So it took fucking years for them to realize it was one guy doing all that. And then, all they had was what Bohannan said. And Catlin, he left nothing. Still, Bohannan locked him down. *Locked that motherfucker down.*"

I thought he was going to hoot with admiration.

He didn't.

"I read that book about it, and I thought, this…now, this guy is the guy."

He said nothing more.

Not finishing with, *to beat.*

Or, *to match wits with.*

Not throwing his head back and unleashing a maniacal laugh.

Not anything.

Just *this guy is the guy.*

That was it.

It was just a game.

It was just a senseless, foul, despicable *may the best man win*.

I didn't know what to do with that.

I didn't know what to ask next.

But even if I did, he was done with me.

I knew when he looked at his watch and murmured, "I gotta go get Shelly."

Then he reached in his pocket and took out a penknife.

My mind raced, mostly with the sudden and gripping fight to stay present.

To stay there.

Not to retreat.

Not to check out.

Not to become invisible.

Which would only make me stop existing.

Literally.

But like I had before in times of extreme stress, I felt it happening.

So I focused.

I focused with everything that was in me.

My hands and ankles were tied.

We were in the middle of a forest with nothing around us.

The day was waning.

It was getting cold, the mist was…

The mist!

He opened his army knife and looked at me.

"So, this is the thing. I'm gonna be cool and give you two minutes. One hundred and twenty seconds. That's what you got."

He yanked the strap of the shotgun off his shoulder, held it by its forearm, pumped it one handed and concluded.

"Then, I come hunting."

And with that, he cut the rope at my ankles, cut the one on my wrists, I was already poised for flight, and I flew.

I had no idea, but probably at least sixty of those seconds, I just ran as fast as I could.

But then I remembered.

There was mist.

The air was cold.

The ground was also cold, it was January.

But the lake was hot.

Wherever we were, with that mist, I knew we were close to the lake.

If I could get to the edge of the lake, I could follow it.

Follow it home.

So I ran into the mist.

And I kept running.

I wished I did not slide.

I wished I did not fall.

But I slid, repeatedly.

I also did a slipping fall down an incline, slamming into my hip and descending into the fog, falling so far, I thought I'd hit lake in the end.

I slammed into some rock, my ankles buckled, and I fell to my knees.

I felt nothing.

I just surged up and kept running.

The problem with the mist was, you couldn't see anything. I had visibility maybe five, six feet in front of me, then it was obscured.

I didn't know if I was running to the lake, from the lake, beside the lake, deeper into the forest.

I didn't pause to ponder direction.

I just ran.

I hit an incline and had to climb up. It was steep. I skidded down some loose gravel and found it difficult to get a foothold to keep climbing. It seemed to take a year before I caught an outcrop with the sole of my boot, and heaved myself up, scrabbling on hands and toes.

I made it to surer footing, took my feet and kept running.

I was out of breath. A hitch was slicing through my side.

And I heard, "For an old bitch, you got a great ass!"

"Oh God," I whispered, pushing onward.

But he ran like the wind, and I was making a lot of noise and…

I slammed into a tree.

I careened off it, lost balance, threw my arms out, my body twisting in a way I didn't want it to, and I saw him through the mist, gun butt to his shoulder, taking aim.

At me.

The memory of Bohannan's voice thundered through in my head.

Down! Bellies!

I threw myself down.

The roar of a shotgun blast that seemed preternatural, like it was not one blast but two, pounded my ears.

I closed my eyes tight.

But…

Nothing.

I opened my eyes, turning to him, pushing up on a hand and arranging my feet to launch off again…

And through the mist I saw a man standing over Ray, who was down on a hand and his knees. The man had his shotgun lifted vertical in both hands above him. He brought the butt down on Ray's head.

I could swear I saw a spray of blood and Ray collapsed to the needles.

The man hit him in the head with the gun again and then immediately tucked the butt into his shoulder, took a step back and aimed it down at Ray.

"You're good, gal, you're good. Just sit tight," he called to me. "Don't run. You run, you could get lost in these woods forever."

I was gasping for air, on a hand and hip, staring through the mist at an old man aiming his shotgun at a prone Ray.

Still keeping his eye on Ray, he asked, "You got a phone?"

I pulled in another shuddering breath, then pushed out a "No."

"Bugger," he muttered.

What was…?

What was happening?

"Don't think this boy is right in the head," he remarked.

I nearly started laughing hysterically.

I would have if I wasn't shaking uncontrollably.

Moving cautiously, he bent down, grabbed Ray's gun and tossed it my way. It fell with a robust *foof* to the dirt and needles a few feet in front of me.

"You get your wits about you, little lady, you get a handle on that. You with me?"

I didn't care I couldn't coordinate my limbs.

I clambered to that gun as fast as I could.

When I had it in hand, I asked, "Who are you?"

"Yeah. Sorry," he replied. "We haven't met. I'm Paddy. Paddy Tremayne."

That meant nothing to me, even if I knew I'd love Paddy Tremayne forever.

"And I sure did like you in that TV show," he finished.

Well.

Damn.

FIFTY-NINE

Not from Where I'm Standing

Since I didn't have a phone and Paddy Tremayne didn't have a phone, and Ray was unconscious and I had absolutely no intention to get anywhere near him, nor was I going to leave him behind, because no way in fuck was I going to give him any shot at getting away, and I didn't like Paddy's chances if Ray came to and charged him since Ray had youth on his side and the body of a pro football player, and Paddy one hundred percent did not have either, we had to wait for Bohannan.

This didn't take long.

And I felt him before I saw him.

The trees closed in on us, and even Paddy grew more alert and chanced a look around.

He'd kept an eagle eye on Ray (and we'd both kept our guns aimed at him). And Ray had just woken up, groggy.

But it didn't take Ray long to realize things had gone south for him, what with being shotgun whipped, twice, bleeding profusely from the head, and half his shoulder having been blown off by Paddy's shotgun shell.

Ray did not keen in pain, whine or moan.

Ray was on his back, cradling what was left of his shoulder with his good hand and not taking his eyes off Paddy.

"Don't do nothin' dumb!" Paddy called into the mist. "Got the woman. She's all right. Got the…whatever he is. He needs an ambulance."

They formed out of the mist, first Bohannan, Jess, Jace and Harry.

Then Wade Dickerson, Dan, and—fanned out and all around—what looked like every deputy on staff and a couple of dozen other men from town, some who I'd seen around, others I hadn't, all I didn't know.

Bohannan's gaze came to me before it went down to Ray.

Same with Jess and Jace.

Also Harry, but he started talking to Paddy right away.

"You can stand down, Paddy. We got this," he said, aiming his rifle down at Ray.

Paddy stood down and seemed relieved to do it.

Bohannan tossed the strap of the rifle he was carrying over his shoulder, skirted Ray and came to me.

I noted the men were moving into position to get a lock on Jess and Jace, which I thought was smart, as Bohannan slowly took the shotgun from my hands.

I relinquished it readily.

He handed it off to someone I didn't know and asked, "You injured?"

"No," I answered.

"Can you take your feet?"

I stuck out my hand.

He used it to pull me to my feet and held it until I was steady.

When he let me go, I brushed off my jeans at my ass.

Bohannan examined me, fully, but his gaze lingered at the swelling around my eye.

"You okay?"

"I don't know how to answer that."

The trees closed in again, and before they spontaneously

combusted due to the fever pitch of Bohannan's wrath and burned us all to the ground, I said, "I'm fine."

Along with his continued visual examination, my words seemed to assuage him, until Paddy, God bless him, shared, "Swear to Christ, seen it all now. Some cuckoo-crazy young buck huntin' a famous woman through the woods. And everyone thinks *I'm* nutso for keepin' myself to myself. Now, somebody better tell me, what's this world coming to?"

And the Bohannan wrath detonated, and it didn't burn us to the ground, but it took about fifteen men to hold only three of them back.

I defused this by saying loudly, "Boys, I really want to go home!"

Bohannan pushed off from Dan and three other guys and prowled to me.

He gave every indication he was going to pick me up, so, quickly, I said low, so Jace nor Jess would hear, "He carried me in. I need to walk out."

The expression on his face scared me, but he nodded, and I didn't hesitate to let him take my hand.

He walked us wide of where Dickerson was working with a field kit to dress Ray's wound.

Even so, Ray called out, "I still won."

Bohannan didn't break stride, nor did he look at him, when he replied.

"Not from where I'm standing."

And then, holding my hand, the twins at our back, he walked me out of the mist.

SIXTY

Scorecard

Since the game was played, regardless that one side would have given anything not to play it, in order to keep score:

Ray Andrews had been an Eagle Scout.

Ray Andrews had spent the summers of his junior and senior years in high school and his freshman and sophomore years in college as a camp counselor at a remote outdoor camp in Oregon. This was because Ray's father was an avid outdoorsman, and Ray was too.

Ray Andrews was beloved by his family, as well as, until recently, his hometown.

Ray Andrews had been prom king.

Ray Andrews had been voted by his senior class as best looking, one part of the best couple, best eyes, best legs and most likely to succeed.

Ray Andrews had been salutatorian of his high school class.

Ray Andrews had been an all-state linebacker who still held the record for most interceptions in a season for any player on any team in the entire county.

Ray Andrews had earned a full ride to a Pac-12 team at a university I'd rather not name.

Ray Andrews performed so well for this team, he was eligible and encouraged to enter the NFL draft, but he was nowhere near the best linebacker not only in the draft, but he'd be far from the best in the league. The estimate of what round in which he'd be selected was very low, but it was expected he'd be selected. He chose not to enter the draft.

Ray Andrews graduated magna cum laude with a degree in non-profit administration.

Ray Andrews had an unheard-of seventy-eight percent success rate in having grants he'd written funded.

Ray Andrews had been the youngest person in history to receive a key to the city (an honor which had since been rescinded), because, in the position he held before coming to Misted Pines, his award-winning, highly funded and since-copied initiative completely revamped the school lunch program into healthier eating. Resultant surveys showed the children had significantly higher energy, better concentration and improved grades, as well as uptake in physical activities. It was widely accepted that part of the reason for the success of this program was, in doing it, he'd directly engaged the kids.

Ray Andrews had started hunting at the age of fifteen and had many kills, including bagging a black bear—he'd done that on a hunting trip he took with Tony Romano.

Ray Andrews played the stock market online in his spare time, and at the time of his incarceration, had amassed a portfolio worth seven hundred and twenty-three thousand dollars…and some change.

Ray Andrews had painstakingly, and faithfully, recorded much of his life in manifest journals.

And as such, it was learned that he had indeed, first sought out Tony Romano due to underground chatter about the depth of services he offered in his adventure business.

However, at this point, Ray Andrews had read the account of the pursuit and capture of Al Catlin, and two about the same of Percy Gibson. Therefore, he'd already moved to Misted Pines and was laying the groundwork to be a trusted part of the community so the test he intended to administer to Cade Bohannan would not result in casting suspicion on him.

Upon meeting Tony Romano, learning the fullness of his skills, and the ease in which he earned the other man's devotion, the final pieces of the plan fell into place.

Upon searching the home Ray Andrews shared with Shelly George, it was found that they'd had a highly kitted BDSM dungeon installed. And upon interrogating Shelly George, it was discovered that they had a Dominant-submissive relationship that was so much a part of their lifestyle, he selected the clothes she wore every day, and she never did anything without his permission.

In-depth study of his journals exposed that Ray Andrews was deeply in love with and totally devoted to Shelly George and Tony Romano.

In other words, with some of this, Ray Andrews could have been a really damned cool guy.

If he didn't turn his brilliant mind and abundant energy to killing people.

ON THE OTHER side of that coin:

The woman working in The Joy of Joy heard me shouting.

She was calling 911 before she looked out the window and saw Ray punch me then shove my unconscious body into his truck.

She recognized me.

She had been working at the store for only three weeks.

So, although he was a long-standing customer and friends with the owners, she, as yet, did not know Ray.

As a matter of course for Ray, his purchase that day of a new set of nipple clamps—because, as he told the clerk, his last pair had broken—had been in cash.

Upon getting the call, Harry Moran, already moving out, told Polly Pickler to phone Bohannan.

The first thing Bohannan did was contact Hawk Delgado.

Therefore, within ten minutes of my abduction, they'd called up my fob and saw where I was heading.

A deputy in the area swung by The Joy of Joy, saw the boat, remembered the report about what a boat of its description was used for, and also saw the R on my Volvo.

En route, this information was relayed to Harry Moran and Bohannan.

It was then, Bohannan knew who had me.

And why.

ONWARD FROM THAT:

Within days of the media sharing the role Ray played in the deaths of Alice Pulaski, Malorie Graham and the shooting of David Ashbrook, and with this sharing photos of Ray, Ray started receiving a trickle of fan mail.

Within weeks, it was an avalanche.

Within the month, The Joy of Joy was burned to the ground. No one was harmed in the fire.

Two days after that, Harry Moran found the arsonists and arrested them.

Also within the month, Shelly George took her own life with an overdose of sleeping pills.

Within a day of learning this, Ray was under twenty-four-hour guard because he'd gone apeshit crazy.

Two days later, Bobby Graham had been found in his car in the garage in the home he was renting outside Seattle, asphyxiated by carbon monoxide.

Not long after that, it was learned that he'd left his somewhat vast holdings to his still-wife Lana.

The day after that, a young man came forward to the police in Berkeley, California and informed them he'd been hired to play a prank on a girl in a dormitory on the campus. He admitted to getting paid five hundred dollars to do it. He also admitted to having sexual relations with Ray Andrews. That young man bore more than passing resemblance to Tony Romano.

A week and a half after that, Harry Moran arrested Leland Dern for multiple felonious abuses during his tenure as sheriff, including not following through with investigations of reports of two of his deputies' consistent sexual coercion of female suspects in custody and misappropriation of department funds. Not long after that, on the evidence presented, a grand jury indicted him.

That same day, Gary Spoonacher resigned as county commissioner.

A day later, Kenneth Warner announced his planned retirement from the town council upon the beginning of the next term.

Three days later, the woman who provided an alibi for Tony Romano in the death of Malorie Graham was arrested in a prostitution sting in Portland, Oregon. She was extradited to Misted Pines and charged with providing a false statement to the police in a murder investigation. She has since recanted her alibi.

The next week, the Misted Pines Town Council invited Paddy Tremayne to their next meeting to accept an honor for the role he played in capturing Ray Andrews and saving my life.

The next day, Paddy Tremayne, a recluse who lived in a cabin in the hills above the lake directly opposite from the Bohannan compound, a man who came to town only once a month to get supplies, called Polly Pickler to ask her to communicate his response. And that response was, "Tell them to go stuff it."

The council accepted this because it was expected, considering it came from Paddy Tremayne, but also because they had no other choice. However, they didn't know Paddy came around the lake to eat dinners Bohannan or I cooked for him regularly.

Three months after that, The Joy of Joy celebrated their grand re-opening.

Within the year, regardless that the author had not had the cooperation of any of the players, including Ray Andrews, who was reportedly furious that his and Tony's families were badgered for information, the first book about Ray Andrews and Tony Romano was published.

It was titled *Real Men.*

It was a bestseller.

And word was, they were making it into a movie.

Epilogue

THE END

But I'm getting ahead of myself…

THE END.

I typed those two words, stared at them and smiled to myself.

Finally, the next Jack Mullally was ready (after a reread) to submit to my publisher.

I was so far past deadline, the one for next year's Priscilla Lange romance was only three months away.

But…so be it.

I had a life to live.

And I was going to live it.

No more detailed planning every task and every second. I could be organized, but I didn't have the time to be obsessed with it.

I had three beautiful daughters, even if one wasn't strictly mine, two handsome sons, even though they also weren't mine, and a fabulous man, who was definitely mine.

I had a job I loved.

I had a beautiful home with a beautiful view, and a future that was blindingly bright.

And I'd also had an experience that I decided, firmly, I'd use to remind me, instead of life being a day-to-day battle, it was a gift.

You could struggle through it.

Or you could rise each day and make the most of it.

I chose the latter.

I hit save, closed the chapter, went back to the directory, opened the Prologue (and the next five chapters besides) to start reading so I could make my last-minute tweaks, when I heard it.

Concrete Blonde's "Joey."

"Oh boy," I said to my computer, sat back in my chair, my right fingers, like they did often, moving to tinker with the bracelet on my left wrist, and I looked out the windows in my fabulous new office to the mist on the lake.

This song meant I either had to get up and do something or put on my noise cancelling headphones.

There was a time when I was used to the presence of teenage girls (and their moods) when I wrote.

That time was passed.

I needed to get that mojo back.

Once the song was over, it started again.

Celeste had great taste in heartbreak songs. And that particular one was enduring. I'd listened to it myself back in the day.

During breakups.

I felt him before I turned around and saw him in the door.

Bohannan.

When I caught his eyes, he jerked his head in a backward motion, indicating Celeste's door across the hall.

Also indicating I needed to get on that.

"Joey" ended, and it started again.

Yes.

I needed to get on that.

I nodded.

Bohannan sent me a neutral look that had nuances of relieved and grateful before he disappeared from my doorway.

I knew precisely what was happening.

When spring break rolled around, Bohannan and I felt it necessary to take a break and give Celeste a fun week. Of the same mind, the twins had booked their own getaway down in Mexico.

However, Bohannan had rented two bungalows that were situated next to each other on Turks and Caicos.

We let Celeste bring her friend Phoebe and gave them their own space so they could have a modicum of being free and breezy and unincumbered in the sand and sun, but still under Bohannan's oversight.

Frolicking in the tropics with the concomitant attention a beautiful girl got from young men her age (and not her age, which was gross, and made it good Bohannan was so adept with a glower) set Celeste to understanding something.

She liked Will, very much.

But he needed her more than she needed him, and that kind of imbalance in a relationship, unless it eventually righted itself, could be smothering.

She was young, and even though much that happened in her life (and not only what had happened most recently) made it so she'd probably never be truly carefree, sometimes she had to feel that feeling.

Will was young too, but old enough to know that the behaviors of his mother and father were inexcusable. Therefore, he didn't excuse them.

This left him with a dead sister he'd adored, fatally selfish parents, and as such, he was nursing a healthy dose of growing cynicism, justified righteousness and a fierce protective streak.

Which, for a seventeen-year-old, could be a drag (yes, she'd had her birthday in February, yes, I'd spoiled her once again, and yes, this time Bohannan made clear in a way I thought he might mean it (still, I'd probably test it) we needed gift-giving budgets).

However, she had a kind and generous heart, and she knew it would destroy Will if she broke up with him.

But she wanted to break up with him.

Bohannan had been right with his head jerk.

I needed to deal with this.

I needed to, in order to let Celeste off the hook and guide her through something that anyone with a soul found hard to do: breaking a heart.

And I needed to do it because I was done with my book.

I was giving myself a short break and the next week, Bohannan and I were heading to Paris for two weeks. The second of which, Joan and Camille would meet us, and we'd stay in my apartment and enjoy each other's company and the greatest city in the world (in my opinion).

Bohannan and I were going from there to Cornwall to hole up in my cottage.

There, I was going to dig into my Lange novel, and he was going to figure out if he could work remotely from England. This along with giving a series of lectures through England, Scotland and Wales.

In total, we were set to be gone for three months with the boys in charge of Celeste.

I had doubts about this, considering they were already enjoying giving her crap about the fact they were literally going to be the boss of her.

That said, her school year would end somewhere in the middle of month two of this sojourn, and she was coming out to be with us.

But that meant a near two-month gap, and this had to be dealt with before we left.

I got up and went to her room.

I knocked softly.

Nothing.

I knocked a bit louder.

A few beats passed and then "Joey" cut off.

"Yeah?" she called.

I opened the door and poked my head around. "Hey."

She was on her belly on a diagonal across the corner of her bed, feet hanging over one side, head and arms hanging over the end.

Other than that, she was doing nothing. Not reading a book that was laid out on the floor. Her phone wasn't there. Nor were her laptop or tablet.

Indication this wasn't a mood.

It was *a mood.*

I slid fully in and closed the door.

"Can we talk?"

"I gotta get ready. Will's coming to get me in an hour."

I moved to her and then dropped to cross-legged on the floor in front of her.

"Will's what I want to talk about.

She pushed back and got up on her forearms, starting, "Delly—"

"Hear me out."

"I'm scared of what you're gonna say."

"Why?"

She didn't have an answer to that.

Which was the answer to that.

So I told her, "You know why."

"I love him."

"Are you *in* love with him?"

She turned her head away.

I pushed it.

"Can you not wait to see him? Hear from him? Get a text from him? When you connect with him, do you feel something in you shift, like you feel right? Like you have what you want? Like you were good, great, whole, but it just got better?"

She looked at me again.

"Is that how you feel with Dad?"

I nodded.

She appeared to be mulling something over, and then she said, "Okay, this is gonna sound stupid."

"Nothing sounds stupid."

"People your age don't get stuff like this."

I was wrong.

That sounded a *tad* bit stupid.

I caught the inside of my lip with my teeth in order to assist myself not to respond.

"I mean, it's not bad, but you're conditioned from your generation to want stuff like that."

I responded to that.

"Stuff like what?"

"Okay. God!" she suddenly exclaimed. "I don't know."

After she said that, she pushed up and rearranged herself so she too was sitting cross-legged, but on her bed.

"Okay, Dad is like...*a guy*," she began. "And Jace and Jess are like...*guys*. And there are girls who like guys like that."

I took a stab at a guess as to what she might be talking about.

I had noted the variety of vehicles coming and going up to the houses on either side of the lake the last few months.

I had no idea if it was the proximity or the circumstances that led Jace and Jess to keeping a lid on their dating lives.

But now that they had their own spaces, and the parking for those spaces wasn't next to where their dad and sister lived, that lid had been torn off.

I wasn't nosy.

You just couldn't miss it.

So they were now fully free to be...

Guys.

Though, I had no idea what this might have to do with Will, who was devoted to only one girl.

So was, to my great fortune, her father.

"I'm not supposed to like guys like that," she concluded.

"Because...?"

I really didn't know how to finish that, because I didn't know what she was saying, because it was totally okay for her father to have a woman in his life and her brothers to be dating.

Or was it that she thought it was unhealthy to feel attracted to men who bore characteristics of her father and brothers?

"I want to be a stylist because I'm really good at hair. And I love it when I'm finished with someone's hair, and they like it. They feel pretty."

I nodded, pretending I was following her when this new subject meant I wasn't, but then again, I hadn't really been following before.

"But it's not like being a doctor or an engineer or building bridges or something."

"You be what you want to be."

"And I want a guy who's *a guy*," she said that like it was a blurt. "And it isn't that Will isn't a guy. He totally is. But he's just so heavy. And my friends don't get it, but I see it. For a long time, Dad felt heavy. And then you were around, and he got light. You had that bad guy messing with you, and when I met you, you felt heavy. But when you're around Dad, you seem light. And you guys were like that even when everything was heavy. *That's* what I want. Not just a lot of constant *heavy*."

Now we were getting somewhere.

She kept giving it to me.

"And Jace and Jess, they aren't *heavy*. They're funny and goofs, and when they tease, it's cute, even if it can get annoying. But when it's important, they're serious and smart. But they're not *heavy*. Or if they are, it doesn't last like…*forever*."

Yes, we were getting somewhere.

"It's good to want that, lovely. That's what you should be looking for."

"But Dad and Jess and Jace are like…" clearly, she was at a loss how to describe it, and continued to be when she finished, "*guys*."

However, I had a feeling I finally understood what she was trying to say.

And thus, I explained, "There are men who have traditional masculine traits who might not seem overtly sensitive or unassuming, but that doesn't mean they aren't. There are men who have those traits who are toxic and domineering, and it's important to know the difference between having a dominant personality and a domineering one. One is assertive. The other is overbearing."

She nodded like she got that.

So I gave her more.

"There is nothing wrong *at all* with wanting to do hair and make women feel pretty. Part of being free to go forward in this world as you want and as who you genuinely are is knowing you can be whatever you want, and it doesn't matter in the slightest what anyone thinks about it. And there is nothing wrong *at all* with wanting a strong man in your life who's confident and decisive. Yes, I understand how it can get confusing. But you can't buck stereotypes by feeding into them. Not every macho man is a jerk. Some of them are very sensitive. And not every sensitive man is enlightened. Some of them are huge jerks."

I grabbed her ankle and gave it a squeeze before I continued.

"In the end, you have to learn to follow your heart *and* your gut. If something feels wrong, it's likely wrong."

I gave that a second to sink in, and I carried on.

"If Will's too needy, and that feels draining or heavy, and that isn't shifting, it could be that you can't give him what he needs. That's no reflection on you. Right now, his feelings are intense and there are grownups, me included, who have no idea what he needs. Mostly, Will needs to find it for himself, and not expect it from one person. If you want someone who feels less heavy, who makes you feel lighter, then get yourself free so you can find him."

"His life is horrible right now," she whispered. "If I break up with him, everyone is going to think I'm mean."

"Everyone isn't living your life. Everyone isn't feeling your feelings. What I say next is the most important thing I've ever said to you, so please, my lovely, listen to me."

I gave that a moment to make sure she was doing that.

When I saw she was, I presented it to her.

"You can't live your life worrying about what everyone thinks. You will never make everyone happy." I squeezed her ankle again. "The only person you need to make happy in this world is you. Your happiness will give happiness to people who love you. I'm not saying be selfish. I'm not saying you should do whatever you want without considering other people's feelings or what your actions might mean. I'm saying, learn to know when it's important. *Really* important. And make the right decision *for you*."

"Do you think," she whispered, "it'd be weak that maybe, you know, I can stay with him and then…?" Pause, before, "His parents are totally up his butt. He could ask for a Camaro, and they'd buy it for him. So he's going to that big hockey camp up in Canada this summer. He's going to be gone for six weeks. But before that, I'll be in England with you and Dad. But when I come back, when school starts, I'll be here, and he'll be at UW. And maybe, you know, when I'm gone or when he gets back…"

She let that trail.

"Will that be the right decision for you?" I asked.

She bobbed her head. "I think so."

Yes, even if she wasn't in love with him, she loved him.

"Then I'll stand by that with you."

She didn't say anything for a bit.

And then she said, "You're the best, Delly."

I pushed up to my feet, bent in and kissed the top of her head.

But when she tipped it back to look up at me, I caught her in a gentle hold under her chin.

"In the meantime, maybe find some time to talk to him. Tell him you're worried about the heavy. Tell him maybe he should talk to his grandmother about finding someone skilled who can help him alleviate some of it. For him, the bottom line is, he's not just being moody because he's feeling like being moody. He's dealing with some big things. And there are people out there who might be able to help."

"Yeah, Camille told me it was high time he found a counselor, and I think the only one he'd listen to about that is me."

I adored it that all my girls talked to each other, something they did, even Fenn all the way from Korea.

"I do believe you love him," I told her.

"But I think I get the difference now, Delly."

I smiled, let her go, walked out of the room, and felt grateful.

Because I loved that girl and I had her in my life.

Also because it had been a while.

And I hoped to God I was right.

But it appeared in this teenage-girl thing, I hadn't lost my touch.

In other words…

I still rocked it.

I MIGHT HAVE GIRLS DOWN.

But it was all-new terrain with boys.

However, regardless that I'd met them when they were grown men, I completely understood those doting mothers who had trouble not spoiling the crap out of their boys and finding it difficult to let them go.

I felt this as I stood, glaring in the direction of the log cabin, where Jason was.

Where he wasn't was there, with us, even though Bohannan had opened the Crockpot five minutes ago and was breaking up the chicken in preparation to add the spices in step two of three to the enchiladas he was making that night.

Enchiladas Celeste wouldn't be eating because she left ten minutes ago for her date with Will.

Enchiladas Jace and Jess wouldn't be eating because, after they'd moved, they started cooking for themselves and only came when I demanded their asses on stools at the bar or chairs at the dining room table in The Big House.

I turned my glare in the direction of Jesse's house.

And Bohannan's voice came at me.

"Jess isn't there. He's camping this weekend with Cynthia."

Important to note: I had recently met *Cynthia*.

More important to note: I did not like *Cynthia*.

First, she made you call her *Cynthia*.

Second, she oh-so-totally was a *Cynthia*.

And no, until I met *Cynthia*, I had never had a single problem with any Cynthias.

It was just *Cynthia*.

"And Jace is in town with the guys," Bohannan went on.

"Huh," I said.

"Huh?" he asked.

I turned to him. "Huh."

He took one look at me, turned his eyes downward and his beard twitched in the direction of the Crockpot.

"I don't like Cynthia," I shared.

He lifted his head to look at me again but said nothing.

"She's not right for him," I decreed.

"No, what she is, is a very nice girl who's into him. He likes her. He digs spending time with her. What she isn't is you, shoveling shit at him while watching over him like a hawk because you're freaked he's not dealing with the fact he didn't make Ray Andrews."

And again, but nonverbally this time, *Huh.*

Bohannan didn't need it to be verbal.

He set aside the red pepper flakes and gave me his whole attention.

"I didn't make Ray Andrews. You didn't make Ray Andrews. And we even suspected him. Jason didn't. Harry didn't. Everett didn't. Ben didn't. *No one* made Ray Andrews. His entire existence for the five years he lived in Misted Pines was *about* us not making him. That whole game was so he could prove that he wouldn't get made."

"I understand that. However, Jess isn't wise and experienced like you. Maybe he—"

"This is how you learn," Bohannan told me. "I had two murders with two entirely different MOs. One was fucked-up carnage, the other was quick and neat and not the slightest bit messy. And I didn't call there were two killers. I thought it was one trying to throw me off. That was why I was feeling hinky after we got Romano. I'd missed important things. There are times when you nail it. Every facet of it. But they're rare. It seemed I'd nailed it. My gut told me I didn't. Because I didn't. And that was because my profile was off in very important ways."

He took a breath, and although I had things I wanted to say to make him feel better about that, he kept going before I had to the chance to say them.

"Am I thrilled in the end you were running for your life through the woods? Fuck no. But no one else died. And he didn't get away with it. He confessed everything to you, so he's going down. This is one of those all's well that ends well scenarios. You gotta cling to the end being well, or just it being the end, or you shouldn't be in this business."

I loved the guy, but it had to be said he could be annoying when he demonstrated how smart, adjusted, cool, calm and collected he was.

"So, you're good with how it all turned out?" I asked, watching him closely.

"The bad guys are out of commission, so yes. But mostly, I can't go back and change anything. No one can. It played out the way it played out, and this is the end."

Yes, I totally loved the guy, but he was so adjusted, even *he* didn't need me.

"Okay then, I just miss the boys being around for dinner," I snapped.

There was a tremor of humor in his voice when he replied, "I'm getting that."

"Alice gutted him. Do you think Jess is going to be able to handle it? I asked.

"I think Jesse and Jason were born sponges. They were way above the curve in everything. And I mean that. From lifting their head on their own to crawling to walking to toilet training to reading. They were doing high school coursework in middle school and college coursework in high school. Both of them. Is Jess kicking himself in the ass he missed it? Fuck yeah. Is he gonna stew on it for a while? Definitely. Is he gonna do anything else in the end but learn from it? No."

"You sure?"

"You don't think I know my boys?"

I did.

Because it was just obvious he knew his boys.

But I had more time with this family, and this man, and since I'd had it, we'd gone beyond the getting-to-know you through current events, and we could just say, even Bohannan thought there was buried treasure somewhere out there on that land.

Among all that learning, I'd also discovered that investigative, interrogative and profiling techniques weren't the only training he'd given them.

Bohannan had been a Green Beret.

So there was also that.

In other words, they'd spent a lot of time together.

He wasn't just their father and their teacher and their badass Zen master, they were a team.

I relaxed.

"There's a new tree, up on the lookout," he noted.

Oh, and I'd learned that.

I might not be doing cardio, as such. But when Bohannan wasn't hunting criminals, he ran, and now, I hiked.

He'd run on trails through his trees on his domain, and I'd hike while he'd run.

Of course he'd run a lot farther than I'd hike, but we'd made it up to the lookout, which was an outcropping of rock, a steady uphill climb from the log cabin that had an amazing view of the lake and the town of Misted Pines.

It was his favorite spot on the land.

The sitting room was mine, but that was a close second.

"Two of them, just that one of them was planted last October," he carried on.

"What are you talking about?"

"Two red cedars," he said. "Slow growing, but if nothing happens to them, they could be there forever."

I decided to just listen to his story. He always got to the point eventually.

"Jess put his up there alone. All three of us went up there when I planted Malorie's."

At that, I caught my breath.

"Your pumpkin pieces, those are under Alice's tree. I got some bits of cardboard from the recycle locker in the city, that's under Malorie's. Now, those two girls will be up there long after we're gone. And they'll always have the best view all-around of Misted Pines."

I couldn't take my eyes off him.

"Jess is fine, baby," he said softly.

"Okay," I replied, and from what he just shared, I knew he was.

Bohannan noted I knew it, turned his attention to finishing with the spices, put the lid back on the Crockpot and then came back to me.

"I wanna show you something," he said.

He reached a hand to me.

I went to him and took it.

He led me to our bedroom.

I'd been hungry for enchiladas.

Now I wasn't.

He left me at the bed and went to the closet.

He came out with a big box.

And now I was confused.

It was a sturdy brown box, the kind you mail stuff in.

The flaps at the top were loose, though. He'd already cut through the tape.

And therefore, when he made it to the bed beside me, and upended it, all the glory that was inside tumbled in a pile on the bed.

Bohannan reached to it and started tossing things out so I could see everything.

And there as a good deal of *everything*.

When it was all laid out like a smorgasbord of deliciousness, he straightened and turned to me.

"See anything interesting?"

My gaze drifted back to the bed.

There was the gamut starting from the tame, like silk scarves and blindfolds, and the moderately naughty, like fur-lined handcuffs and feathers, to the hardcore goodness, like paddles, bondage rope, beads, rings, eggs and plugs.

Considering how sensational was The Twisted Tale of The Wives, Husbands and Madmen of Misted Pines, the small fact that my car had been found outside a sex shop had been a footnote that garnered so little attention, if it had any, I didn't notice it.

The fact Ray Andrews was five thousand shades of fucked up was picked over *ad nauseum*.

This was so huge, the fact that I, and that I was *me*, Delphine Larue, was one of his victims was a sidenote.

Jace and Jess studiously avoided any mention that my Volvo had to be driven back from The Joy of Joy that day.

Until now, Bohannan had also not mentioned it.

I honestly hadn't thought of it because I didn't need to. What we had in bed was awesome from the beginning, and that hadn't changed (though island sex was a shade more awesome, as vacation sex was wont to be).

That didn't mean it couldn't get better.

"Are you deciding?" Bohannan prompted.

I tore my eyes away from hours…nay days…nay *years* of fun and looked up at him.

"I'm spoiled for choice."

"Let me help," he said. "You do me first, and you get to pick two things."

My entire body started buzzing.

I knew exactly.

I turned to the bed, picked my two things and put them in front of him.

There was no neutral when I looked back up at him.

It was one of my favorite looks of all.

His eyes were dark and hungry.

"I really love you," I told him.

That was when he gave me *the* favorite look of all.

Showing unhidden he felt exactly the same.

ONE THING I learned after being hunted through the woods, pursued by a supremely narcissistic maniac.

It was the miracle cure for an addiction to the high of the thrill of the pursuit.

Though, upon reflection, that hadn't been my issue.

My issue was, I got together with Bohannan in the middle of

some serious crazy, and when all that was over, part of me was worried that a different thrill would be gone.

Now, lying naked on top of him after the second-best sex of my life, both of us attempting to recover enough to go down and finish the enchiladas, I realized the truth in any relationship.

The beginning was always fun.

All that getting to know each other.

Everything being new.

Day by day watching puzzle pieces fall into place.

But when the picture comes clear, and it's so beautiful, it simply doesn't get old.

I will never, ever get used to our view of that lake.

And I will never, ever get used to the beauty of Bohannan.

THAT SAID, when the next drama struck.

I'd had practice.

So I was ready.

Mostly.

The End

A MISTED PINES NOVEL

DISCUSSION AND REFLECTION QUESTIONS

Discussion/Reflection Questions

1. Did you figure out whodunit? If you did, what gave it away? If you didn't, thinking back, do you see the clues?
2. What do you feel the line is between celebrity and fan? How much of a celebrity's life is a fan/the public entitled to? Or are they entitled to any of it?
3. Have you ever lived in a place that immediately felt like home? What does home feel like? What makes a house a home?
4. Would you live in a place where someone died?
5. Were you surprised to see so many crossover characters? Kristen Ashley often pulls characters from other books and series, do you have a favorite? Which crossover you've read surprised you most?
6. Delphine's ability to "read" people and situations is not unusual. Although none of this fully defines a person, we all read cues to who people are and what their values are in everything they do: expressions, behaviors, speech, mannerisms, grooming, attire, how they decorate and care for their homes and belongings. Was Delphine's ability to read people believable to you?

7. How did you feel about Delphine's pumpkin carving ritual? Did you feel that scene was powerful? Is that something you think you might try yourself? Have you done other rituals?
8. What were your favorite tv shows growing up/when you were younger? Who is the person from your youth you'd fan over even today?
9. The wrongs done to the wives of Misted Pines impacted this community in large ways. Much of this stemmed from reducing them to singular roles (wife/mother/caregiver), rather than treating them as fully rounded individuals. How did you feel about that? If you're a woman, did you identify with it? What were your thoughts as Lana moved on with her life in ways that are stereotypical of a man in her situation (ending a relationship after finding a younger partner and without much outward emotionality, projecting a stiff upper lip when her daughter was murdered)? Did you think she was cold? Or did you cheer her on?
10. Delphine, and the narrative, ruminate quite a bit on social issues. The treatment of veterans. The stigmas around bisexuality in men, especially men who are considered "manly men." The taboos around men who enjoy anal sex. The role of the news media in the division of today's society. And the potentially hazardous legacy of long-term elected politicians when the electorate becomes complacent. How did you feel about these issues, how they fictionally played out in Misted Pines, and how they affect our society today?
11. Who do you think killed Kennedy?

Read **The 'Burg Series** for more
Kristen Ashley suspense.

For You
the story of Colt and Feb.

Try more Kristen Ashley suspense

READ THE 'BURG SERIES

For You
The 'Burg Series Book One

Lieutenant Alexander Colton and February Owens were high school sweethearts. Everyone in their small town knew from the moment they met they were meant for each other. But something happened and Feb broke Colt's heart then she turned wild and tragedy struck. Colt meted out revenge against the man who brought Feb low, but even though Colt risked it all for her, Feb turned her back on him and left town.

Fifteen years later, Feb comes back to help run the family bar. But there's so much water under the bridge separating her and Colt everyone knows they'll never get back together.

Until someone starts hacking up people in Feb's life. Colt is still Colt and Feb is still Feb so the town watches as Colt goes all out to find the murderer while trying to keep Feb safe.

As the bodies pile up, The Feds move in and a twisting, turning story unravels exposing a very sick man who has claimed numerous victims along the way, Feb and Colt battle their enduring attraction and the beautiful but lost history that weaves them together.

For You

THE 'BURG SERIES BOOK ONE

Chapter One

Angie

Until that day, I'd made an art out of avoiding Alexander Colton.

All my work would be for nothing, all because of Angie.

Poor, sweet, stupid, dead Angie.

*****

Martin Fink and Christopher Renicki were the first two uniforms who responded to my call. I'd known Marty and Chris for ages. It was good they were partners. Chris was smart; Marty, not so much.

We were out in the alley, Chris doing crime scene stuff, Marty standing by me. A couple of squad cars with their lights silently flashing had pulled in on either side of the dumpster. Other uniforms had been dispatched to hold back the growing crowd and the crime scene tape was secured by the time Alec showed up.

He'd parked elsewhere and didn't come through the bar like I expected him to. He had keys to the bar, for one. For another, he knew the bar nearly as well as I did and not only because he spent a good deal of time sitting at the end of it, my brother standing inside the bar in front of him, both of them drinking beer and talking about shit I couldn't hear because I stayed well away.

Another surprise was he also didn't have his partner Sully with him.

I watched him as he walked up to Marty and me.

The detectives in town, not that there were many of them, wore ill-fitting, inexpensive suits or nice trousers and shirts with ties.

Not Alec.

Jeans, boots, wide leather belt, sports jacket that looked tailored for him (probably a present from Susie Shepherd) and a nice shirt.

Alec was a big guy even when he was a kid, just kept growing and growing. Dad used to say if he didn't stop his head would touch the clouds. Mom thought Alec and my brother Morrie were best friends because they were both the biggest kids in the class and it just grew from that. Morrie grew out as well as up, however. Alec just grew tall and broad but stayed lean. Alec was tight end to Morrie's offensive lineman during high school, and in all things life. Morrie did the grunt work and never got the glory. Alec knew how to block and was really good at it but every once in a while he got the chance to shine.

Alec's dark hair was too long but he'd always worn it too long, even as a kid. But he'd done it then because his mother was such a shit mother. She never remembered to get it cut. My mom finally ended up taking Alec to the barber when she took Morrie. Later he kept it long just because he was Alec. It curled around his ears and neck now and, as with everything Alec, it looked a little wild.

I stood there and watched silently as he made it to me and Marty, his eyes never leaving me. He didn't even look at Angie.

"Feb," he said on a short nod.

"Alec," I replied.

His eyes were a weird color; light brown with a hint of gold. His dad had the same eyes but his dad's eyes weren't exactly like Alec's. Alec's dad's eyes were mean.

Those eyes got hard as did his mouth when I called him Alec.

They always did. Everyone called him Colt. *Everyone*. Even my mom and dad started calling him Colt after what happened years ago.

Only his folks and I called him Alec anymore, not that he talked to his folks since his dad was in prison for the second time and his mom was never sober and he never spoke to her. Not that I talked much to him either.

He hated it when I called him Alec but I didn't call him Alec to be a bitch or anything, just that he was Alec to me, he always had been.

"Colt," Chris said, calling his attention and Alec looked his way.

That was when he caught sight of Angie.

I looked at her too and wished I hadn't. I'd already seen enough, too much, so much I'd never forget.

I'd gone to high school with Angie. We'd been friends once upon a time, good friends. You could say we still were, but not good ones.

No, we weren't anything anymore because now she was dead.

Alec's midsection came into my vision and cut off sight of Angie. I lifted my eyes to Alec's face, which was still hard but now he was directing his hard look at Marty.

"Why's she out here?" he asked, sounding pissed-off.

"What?" Marty asked back, sounding as usual, confused.

"Jesus, Marty," Alec muttered, still sounding pissed and his eyes cut to me. "Go inside, Feb."

I stared at him and didn't move a muscle.

"Feb, inside," he repeated.

I still stared at him.

He took a step toward me and said low, "February."

My body jerked and I nodded. Inside would be good. Inside would be fucking awesome.

I went inside, headed directly to Morrie and my office—Mom and Dad's old office, the office Morrie and Alec and I practically grew up in—and coffee. I could still taste the vomit in the back of my mouth. I hadn't actually puked but it had threatened.

I was pouring a cup when Morrie came in.

Alec was big but my brother was enormous. He was also demonstrative.

He walked right up to me, took the coffee cup from my hand, plunked it down, yanked the coffeepot out of my other hand, slid it under the filter and then engulfed me in a hug.

I should have started crying then, I suppose. But I didn't.

"You okay, Feb?" Morrie asked, and I nodded, my cheek sliding against his big, barrel chest.

I wondered briefly why he was there. It wasn't his turn to open, it was mine.

My guess, Alec had called him.

"Sis," he whispered at my nod and I closed my eyes. He didn't call me "sis" very often anymore. Hadn't since we were kids. I missed it.

Still, no tears came.

"You want coffee?" I asked.

Morrie pulled away and gave me a look.

He didn't like what he saw, I knew it but he still said, "Yeah."

I made him a cup and we were taking sips when Alec filled the doorframe.

In the light I caught sight of the scar under his left eye. It was a little, puckered crescent moon, about the size of your thumbnail. I thought that was weird, it being that small, considering at the time it was made it bled a whole helluva lot.

As it did anytime I saw it, it made flashbacks flood my brain. Flashbacks of Alec, sixteen years old and sitting silent on the toilet seat in my mom and dad's bathroom and me, fourteen, standing there wiping the blood off his face with one of Mom's wet washcloths. Morrie coming in, giving me ice, me wrapping it up and holding it to the gaping cut under Alec's swelling eye. My dad walking in, taking in Alec, his bloodied face, his knuckles torn, bleeding and swollen, the way he held his body like if he moved it would be torture, and saying, "Police are going to your place, Colt, you're going with me. Jackie and the kids to the hospital."

That was the first time my father called him Colt. He never addressed him as anything else since.

"Jesus, what the fuck, Colt?" Morrie said upon seeing him. "Mom and Dad's bar? Seriously? Who the fuck would do that?"

Alec's gaze flicked to Morrie and he shook his head.

This was a good question, I thought. A dead body behind their bar? Crazy. My mom and dad were beloved in this town. So were their parents. So was Morrie.

Me? I wasn't sure. Maybe.

Or at least, I once had been.

"You called nine one one," Alec said, and I looked at him though I didn't quite meet his eyes.

"Yeah."

"You found her?" Alec asked.

"Yeah."

"What were you doing in the alley?"

I stared at him not seeing, then said, "Darryl."

"Fuck. Fuckin' Darryl," Morrie muttered, now he sounded pissed.

"Darryl?" Alec asked.

"He never takes out the trash at night. I tell him, every night. Guy's got nothin' between his ears," Morrie explained, telling the God's honest truth about Darryl and pulling a hand through his thick hank of blond hair. "Leaves it at the back door and forgets. First person in in the morning, usually me or Feb, take it out."

This wasn't exactly true. The first person in in the morning was usually me, not Morrie. Though, I had to admit, on occasion, namely my rare days off, it happened.

"You on last night?" Alec asked me, and I shook my head.

"Night off," I told him.

"I was on," Morrie put in.

Alec turned to Morrie. "Angie here?"

Morrie nodded. "Dude, she's always here."

This was true. Angie was a regular. She also regularly wore slut clothes and regularly got shitfaced and regularly picked up anyone who would fuck away whatever demons tortured her. Though obviously these efforts never lasted long because she was always back again, usually the next night. Angie wasn't hard on the eyes if you didn't look too close and see what her lifestyle was doing to her skin. There was no lack of choice for Angie.

"She go home with someone?" Alec asked Morrie.

Morrie moved his neck in that funny way he did when he was uncomfortable, like he was pulling at a too tight collar and tie, even though he was wearing a t-shirt with a zip-up hooded sweatshirt over it and his hand never moved.

Then he said, "Cory."

"Fuckin' hell," Alec muttered and he could say that again.

Cory's wife Bethany was pregnant with their third child. Bethany was also a screamer. And Bethany was going to have a shit fit. It wasn't the first time Cory strayed. Hell, Cory came on to me practically any time he got hammered enough to pull up the courage. It wasn't the first time he dipped his wick in Angie either. This also wasn't going to be the first time Bethany found out about Angie. Though it would be the first time Angie showed up the next morning dead in an alley and Cory would be involved in a murder investigation.

"You see anyone last night? Unfamiliar? Give you a bad feeling?" Alec asked Morrie and I knew this was brother-speak.

Alec would lay his career down on Morrie telling him he had a bad feeling about someone. Both of them could read people like books, something they could do forever. I'd never been able to lie successfully to either of them, not once, and I'd tried. It wasn't surprising Alec became a cop. It was natural-born even if on the face of it, considering his parents and, well, how he used to be, you wouldn't know it. It also wasn't surprising Morrie took over the bar. Even in our town—which wasn't huge but also wasn't small—the clientele was regular. Still, trouble could happen, especially when the races were on and anyone could wander in. You had to be able to weed the good from the bad so you could lock down the bad before shit happened.

"Nope, no one. Normal night at Jack and Jackie's," Morrie answered.

Alec looked at me. "Where's the trash?"

I again stared and repeated, "The trash?"

"You said you went out to the alley to take out the trash. Crime scene, far's I can see, is unaltered. Where's—?"

Alec stopped talking because I started moving. I wasn't thinking much of anything. I didn't even know why I was moving.

I plunked my coffee cup down, walked past Alec and went to the bar. The heavy panel was already up and over on its hinges where I guessed I'd put it when I went in to make the 911 call. I walked behind the bar and stared at the two huge bags of garbage that were sitting on the floor by the phone.

I hadn't even noticed I'd carried them back in and dropped them to make the call.

I turned around and saw Alec was standing close, his eyes on the trash.

"I just went to the door," I told his throat, seeing his neck twist, his chin dipping down to look at me but my eyes didn't move. "I just went to the door," I repeated then my head jerked, my ear going toward my shoulder and I felt a weird pain in the back of my neck at the sudden movement. "I just went to the door," I said again, for some stupid reason now whispering, "opened the door and saw her."

That's when I cried.

I didn't feel anything, didn't see anything, didn't hear anything, didn't taste the coffee in my mouth, just cried hard while my brain filled.

I saw her. I saw Angie and all her blood and all her exposed *parts*. Parts I should never see. Parts with skin, parts without, all of it, all of her, lying lifeless in the alley by the dumpster.

Then I heard Alec say, "I got her," and I realized his arms were around me.

I pulled away and stepped away. Distance with Alec, hell with *anyone*, but *especially* with Alec, was good.

I swiped at my eyes, controlling the tears, not looking at him. "I'm okay."

There was silence for a while but Morrie moved in close to me. I could feel his bulk filling the long space behind the bar.

"You gotta walk me through your morning," Alec said and I didn't want to but I lifted my eyes to his.

"What?"

"Walk me through your morning, Feb," Alec repeated.

"I came in to get ready to open—" I started.

"Your full morning," Alec interrupted.

I felt my mouth open, my lips parting. I could feel the sensation of skin separating from skin like it was the first time I'd ever done it when I knew I'd done it before. It just didn't feel like it then. It felt like the first time and it felt like my lips parted in slow motion.

I wished I'd brought my coffee with me.

"I woke up—"

"What time?"

I shook my head. "Normal time. Seven o'clock, seven thirty."

"You get up at seven thirty?" Morrie asked, like I had a screw loose.

"Yeah."

"Shit, Feb, we own a bar," Morrie stated. "How do you get up at seven thirty?"

"I don't know, I just do." And I did. Even if I lay my head down at three thirty in the morning, I woke up between seven and seven thirty. It was a curse.

"You woke up. What next?" Alec cut in giving Morrie a *shut up* look. I'd seen him do that a lot over the years. Usually Morrie didn't shut up. This time he did.

"I fed the cat—"

"Did you do it alone?" Alec asked.

I stared at him then said, "Feed the cat?"

He shook his head but it was a rough motion, jerky. "Wake up."

I sucked in breath, not wanting to answer the question, not wanting Alec to have that information, either answer I could give. But knowing I had to, I nodded.

He nodded his head, that motion was rough and jerky too. "What'd you do after you fed your cat?"

"I did yoga."

Alec's brows snapped together and now he was looking at me like I had a screw loose. "You do yoga?"

"Well…yeah."

He looked away muttering, "Christ."

I didn't know what was wrong with yoga but I didn't ask. I wanted this to be done. In fact, I wanted the day to be done, the year, I wanted it to be a year from now when all this would be faded and a whole lot less real.

"Like I was saying, I did yoga, took a shower and then walked to Meems'."

"Anyone see you walk to Meems'?" Alec asked.

"What's this about?" Morrie sounded like he was getting pissed.

"Just let me ask the questions. It'll be over and we can move on," Alec answered.

"Jessie," I cut in, still on a mission to get my story out so this could be over and we could move on. "I walked to her place and then Jessie walked with me to Meems'."

Jessie Rourke and Mimi VanderWal were my best friends, had been since high school.

"You and Jessie went to Meems', what next?" Alec asked.

"We hung out at Meems', had coffee, a muffin, shot the shit, the same as every day," I answered. And it was the same as every day, although sometimes Jessie didn't come with and it was just me and my journals, or a book or the paper, and my cup of coffee and muffin at Meems'.

I preferred when Jessie was there. Meems owned the joint and by the time I got there it was a crush so she didn't have time to gab. She had a plaque that said "reserved" that she put on my table, though everyone knew it was my table and no one ever sat there in the mornings but me. She didn't need the plaque, one of her kids carved into the table, "Feb's Spot, sit here and die." Meems' kids were a bit wild but they were funny.

"When'd you leave Meems'?" Alec asked.

I shrugged. "Ten o'clock, probably around there. Came straight here." Coming straight to J&J's wasn't far. It was two doors down from Mimi's Coffee House. "I opened up, started the coffee going and went to the back hall to take out the trash I knew was probably there. It was there. I opened the door, grabbed the bags and—"

I stopped and looked down at the garbage bags beside me. The rest didn't need to be said.

Alec's voice came at me. "You see anything else, Feb?"

I took in a breath because I needed it and I thought it was a big one but it felt shallow. My chest felt empty like I could breathe and breathe but there was not enough breath to fill it, never would be again and I looked at him.

"Anything else? Anyone in the alley when you went out?"

Morrie got closer to me, his arm sliding around my shoulders. "Jesus, Colt. What the fuck you sayin'?"

"She's warm," Alec answered, his words were clipped, short, bitten off like he didn't want to say them but he had to and he wanted them out of his mouth as fast as he could do it.

"Warm?" I asked.

I watched his teeth sink into his bottom lip. I knew why he did this. I'd seen him do it a lot in my life. He did it when he was seriously, *seriously* hacked off.

"The body," he said. "Angie."

"What?" Morrie asked.

"She's still warm," Alec answered. "She's not been dead long."

"Oh my God," I whispered. That empty feeling in my chest started burning. The vomit rolled back up my throat and I had to swallow it down.

"Are you fucking *shitting* me?" Morrie exploded.

"You see anything, Feb? Hear anything? Any movement? Anything?" Alec pushed. He wanted answers but he was going about it quiet, gentle.

"Jesus fucking Christ," Morrie cursed.

"Morrie, you aren't helping," Alec told him.

"Fuck that, Colt. My sister opened the door to a fresh murder scene!" Morrie bellowed. "You're sayin' the guy coulda been out there?"

I felt my muscles seize.

Alec either saw it or sensed it and his voice went scary when he said, "Morrie, for fuck's sake, you aren't fucking helping."

Morrie and Alec may have been best friends since kindergarten but they fought, a lot. It was never pretty and it could get physical. It hadn't happened in a while but, then again, nothing this big had happened in a while.

"I didn't see anything," I said quickly and I didn't. And, at that moment, I was glad I didn't.

I didn't want whoever did that to Angie to get away with it and, if I saw something, I wouldn't lie even though it would scare the shit out of me. But I didn't see anything and this was a relief.

I wasn't a bad person. But I wasn't a good person either. I didn't do good things like Alec did. I was just a normal person, I kept myself to myself. I also had been a bartender my whole adult life and grew up in a bar, not to mention I now part-ran one. So I kept other things to myself too. It was a job hazard. Everyone told you everything when they were hammered. Shit you did *not* want to know.

But I'd have done the right thing for Angie.

I just hoped Alec knew that.

He looked me direct in the eye and I let him. This went on awhile and was very uncomfortable. Not that I had anything to hide, just that these days anytime Alec stared me direct in the eye, it made me very uncomfortable. I'd been able to avoid it mostly for years, but now there it was.

"You're stayin' with me until Colt finds this fucker," Morrie told me and I broke eye contact with Alec to stare at my brother.

"I am not."

"You stay with him or you stay with me."

This came from Alec.

I transferred my stare to him, thrown for a moment because while I was perfecting the art of avoiding Alec, I pretty much figured he was returning the gesture.

"I'm not doing that either."

"Two choices, Feb," Morrie stated, his arm getting tight around my shoulders.

"I didn't *see* anything!" My voice was getting higher.

"Not takin' chances." Morrie didn't sound like he'd be easily swayed.

"This is ridiculous," I muttered, getting pissed.

I was a normal person and kept myself to myself, meaning I *liked* to keep myself to myself. Not have myself living with my brother and *definitely* not Alec.

"Ridiculous?" Alec said, his voice weirdly soft and compelling, drawing my attention to him and his face was hard again. He was angry, at *me*.

And I knew why.

I'd seen it, all the gruesome, bloody evidence of it in the alley.

"I'll stay with Morrie."

Morrie's arm gave my shoulders a squeeze.

Alec bit his lip again, still hacked off about something, what at that point I didn't know, but he kept staring at me, making me think it was me. Then he let go of his lip and clenched his teeth, making both of his jaws flex and I wondered if he was biting back words.

He succeeded if that was what he was doing since without saying anything, he nodded to me then to Morrie and he walked away.

***For You* is available now.**

About the Author

Kristen Ashley is the *New York Times* bestselling author of over eighty romance novels including the *Rock Chick, Colorado Mountain, Dream Man, Chaos, Unfinished Heroes, The 'Burg, Magdalene, Fantasyland, The Three, Ghost and Reincarnation, The Rising, Dream Team* and *Honey* series along with several standalone novels. She's a hybrid author, publishing titles both independently and traditionally, her books have been translated in fourteen languages and she's sold over five million books.

Kristen's novel, *Law Man*, won the *RT Book Reviews* Reviewer's Choice Award for best Romantic Suspense, her independently published title *Hold On* was nominated for *RT Book Reviews* best Independent Contemporary Romance and her traditionally published title *Breathe* was nominated for best Contemporary Romance. Kristen's titles *Motorcycle Man*, *The Will*, and *Ride Steady* (which won the Reader's Choice award from *Romance Reviews*) all made the final rounds for Goodreads Choice Awards in the Romance category.

Kristen, born in Gary and raised in Brownsburg, Indiana, was a fourth-generation graduate of Purdue University. Since, she has lived in Denver, the West Country of England, and she now resides in Phoenix. She worked as a charity executive for eighteen years prior to beginning her independent publishing career. She now writes full-time.

Although romance is her genre, the prevailing themes running through all of Kristen's novels are friendship, family and a strong sisterhood. To this end, and as a way to thank her readers for their support, Kristen has created the Rock Chick Nation, a series of programs that are designed to give back to her readers and promote a strong female community.

The mission of the Rock Chick Nation is to live your best life, be true to your true self, recognize your beauty, and last but definitely not least, take your sister's back whether they're at your side as friends and family or if they're thousands of miles away and you don't know who they are.

The programs of the RC Nation include Rock Chick Rendezvous, weekends Kristen organizes full of parties and get-togethers to bring the sisterhood together, Rock Chick Recharges, evenings Kristen arranges for women who have been nominated to receive a special night, and Rock Chick Rewards, an ongoing program that raises funds for nonprofit women's organizations Kristen's readers nominate. Kristen's Rock Chick Rewards have donated hundreds of thousands of dollars to charity and this number continues to rise.

You can read more about Kristen, her titles and the Rock Chick Nation at KristenAshley.net.

facebook.com/kristenashleybooks
twitter.com/KristenAshley68
instagram.com/kristenashleybooks
pinterest.com/KristenAshleyBooks
goodreads.com/kristenashleybooks
bookbub.com/authors/kristen-ashley

Also by Kristen Ashley

Rock Chick Series:

Rock Chick

Rock Chick Rescue

Rock Chick Redemption

Rock Chick Renegade

Rock Chick Revenge

Rock Chick Reckoning

Rock Chick Regret

Rock Chick Revolution

Rock Chick Reawakening

Rock Chick Reborn

The 'Burg Series:

For You

At Peace

Golden Trail

Games of the Heart

The Promise

Hold On

The Chaos Series:

Own the Wind

Fire Inside

Ride Steady

Walk Through Fire

A Christmas to Remember

Rough Ride

Wild Like the Wind

Free

Wild Fire

Wild Wind

The Colorado Mountain Series:

The Gamble

Sweet Dreams

Lady Luck

Breathe

Jagged

Kaleidoscope

Bounty

Dream Man Series:

Mystery Man

Wild Man

Law Man

Motorcycle Man

Quiet Man

Dream Team Series:

Dream Maker

Dream Chaser

Dream Bites Cookbook

Dream Spinner

Dream Keeper

The Fantasyland Series:

Wildest Dreams

The Golden Dynasty

Fantastical

Broken Dove

Midnight Soul

Gossamer in the Darkness

Ghosts and Reincarnation Series:

Sommersgate House

Lacybourne Manor

Penmort Castle

Fairytale Come Alive

Lucky Stars

The Honey Series:

The Deep End

The Farthest Edge

The Greatest Risk

The Magdalene Series:

The Will

Soaring

The Time in Between

Mathilda, SuperWitch:

Mathilda's Book of Shadows

Mathilda The Rise of the Dark Lord

Moonlight and Motor Oil Series:

The Hookup

The Slow Burn

The Rising Series:

The Beginning of Everything

The Plan Commences

The Dawn of the End

The Rising

The River Rain Series:

After the Climb

After the Climb Special Edition

Chasing Serenity

Taking the Leap

The Three Series:

Until the Sun Falls from the Sky

With Everything I Am

Wild and Free

The Unfinished Hero Series:

Knight

Creed

Raid

Deacon

Sebring

Wild West MC Series:

Still Standing

Other Titles by Kristen Ashley:

Heaven and Hell

Play It Safe

Three Wishes

Complicated

Loose Ends

Fast Lane

CPSIA information can be obtained
at www.ICGtesting.com
Printed in the USA
BVHW071754060122
625611BV00001B/1

9 781954 680067